~ the ~
Love and Danger
Box Set

Amy Gamet

Love and Danger Box Set
Copyright © 2014 Amy Gamet
ISBN: 9781497424401
Printed in the United States of America

Meant for Her
Copyright © 2012 Amy Gamet
ISBN: 978-0-9882182-0-8
Printed in the United States of America

The One Who Got Away
Copyright © 2013 Amy Gamet
ISBN: 978-0-9882182-2-2
Printed in the United States of America

Artful Deception
Copyright © 2013 Amy Gamet
ISBN: 978-1496067586
Printed in the United States of America

Meghan's Wish
Copyright © 2012 Amy Gamet
ISBN: 9781482503371
Printed in the United States of America

ALL RIGHTS RESERVED.
This book contains material protected under International and Federal Copyright Laws and Treaties. Any unauthorized reprint or use of this material is prohibited. No part of this book may be reproduced or transmitted in any form or by any means, electronic or mechanical, including photocopying, recording, or by any information storage and retrieval system without express written permission from the author / publisher.

Contents

Meant for Her ~ 1

The One Who Got Away ~ 149

Artful Deception ~ 291

Meghan's Wish ~ 435

Meant for Her

For Brian,
who always believed I could do it.

Special thanks to Laura Davis, Deyôn Waller, Pam Kaptein,
Melissa Sharp, Dale Richards, and Paul Richards.

Meant for Her

Chapter 1

Hank Jared was running.

Four miles in, he hit his stride. Heavy metal music poured from his headphones, drowning out all but the rhythmic beating of his shoes on the pavement. The neighborhood around him was upscale and well-manicured, with stately rolling lawns and automatic sprinkler systems that wet his dark hair and tan, bronzed skin.

His physical conditioning was evident in the controlled swish of air in and out of his lungs, the defined muscles of his calves and thighs flexing in synch with the pumping of his arms. He checked his watch. Plenty of time to get back and pack before his flight.

Five days before Christmas, and it feels like the middle of May.

He had been in Florida nearly a month, working on a case for Admiral Barstow. While Hank enjoyed the sunshine and novelty of swimming in December, his amusement turned to irritation when he saw his first palm tree covered in Christmas lights.

He needed a blue spruce, and he needed it quickly.

By nightfall he'd be in the Adirondacks. His mouth formed an unconscious smile at the thought of his destination. His little sister was getting married on Christmas Eve, and the whole family was gathering at his mother's house for the event.

I'll be walking her down the aisle.

The thought brought with it the faintest grief, a wave by now so familiar Hank simply accepted its crest. It had been more than five years since their father passed away.

Ray Jared had been a strong, kind man with a boisterous sense of humor, a love of the outdoors and a deep dedication to family. Kelly's wedding made their father's absence as tangible as a shadow where sunlight once shined, and Hank was both honored and saddened to stand in the spot his father should have occupied.

The residential neighborhood ended in a cul-de-sac, lined on one side with evergreens. The hedges obscured a ten-foot high chain link fence, a small opening in the foliage marking an entrance to another space beyond.

Hank slowed to a walk, retrieving a plastic card from his running pack. He slid it through a small card reader on a steel post, the gate unlocking with a metallic click.

Acres of turf surrounded what looked like a business complex. The newest field office of the U.S. Navy was nothing if not discreet. Hank enrolled right after college, having always dreamed of a career in the armed forces.

The military was his life.

His breathing slowly returning to normal, he dug in his pack for his cell phone and dialed the familiar numbers.

"Don't be mad, mom," he said when she answered. "But I'm not going to be able to make it." He sounded devastated to his own ears.

"Hank William Jared, that wasn't funny when you were ten, and it sure as hell isn't funny now."

He chuckled. "It's a little funny."

"It might be a little funny if the caterer hadn't double booked."

"You're kidding."

"Nope. And it would have been downright hilarious if the wedding bands had arrived at the jewelers."

Maybe he picked the wrong day to joke with his mother.

"I can fix this, Mom."

"How are you going to fix it?"

"I'll treat for pizza."

"That's very helpful, dear."

"I am a helper, you know."

"Yes, you are. What time does your flight get in? I have a to-do list here with your name on it."

Hank was sure she had an actual piece of paper that said HANK across the top. With three children and a family business to run, his mother had a great deal of experience delegating responsibility. "Three-thirty. Who's picking me up?"

Meant for Her

"Ron. He and Kelly have been playing chauffer all week." Kelly's fiancé had seemed like a nice enough guy the few times Hank had met him, but he was happy to hear that Ron was playing taxi driver so they'd have a chance to talk. Without his father, it seemed like his responsibility to give Ron the third degree.

Kelly met him on an airplane when she was on her way home from college for Christmas break two years ago. Hank got the feeling there was more to that story, and he intended to get the whole truth from Ron before the wedding.

"No worries, Mom, I'm on my way..." Hank was interrupted by a call waiting beep. He checked the caller ID and frowned.

"Mom, I have to take this."

"Work?"

"Yes."

"Don't answer it, Hank. Bad things come in threes and we only have two."

"I have to."

"I know you do," she sighed. "Call me later."

Hank clicked over to the incoming call.

"What can I do for you, Admiral?"

"I've got a nasty virus. Almost a third of the company is infected." Julie Trueblood rested her forehead on her fingers as she leaned over her desk.

"Are you going to be able to make it for Christmas?"

Julie never planned on making it to her aunt's house, though she had plenty of time to fit it in before her trip with Greg. She spun her chair around and watched fat snow flakes falling at an alarming rate over the city of Boston.

"Even if I clean up all the computers, I'm afraid I'd need a fleet of tiny reindeer to pull my sleigh and get me out of the city. What's your weather like?"

"A little snow, I think. We have a few inches already."

Julie knew that 'a little snow' to her aunt might well be enough to put the entire northeast into a state of emergency. Aunt Gwen was pushing hard for Julie to make it out to Vermont this

Meant for Her

year, and had extended an open invitation for the long weekend. It was a solid three-hour drive in good weather, and this was anything but.

"I don't know. Let me run and see what progress I can make on this virus. I'll give you a call in a couple of hours," she said, instantly regretting that she hadn't simply said no.

"Alright, Jules. Best of luck. I can't wait to see you."

Julie cringed into the receiver. "Bye, Gwen."

She turned her attention to the computer in front of her and sighed at the work ahead. Firewalls and anti-virus software could only do so much. Someone was always out to make a better virus that could slip in under the radar and wreak havoc on a stranger's computer. Or in this case, more than eighty of Systex Corporation's desktops.

Her morning had been spent identifying the virus and downloading the fix. Now she needed to spend ten minutes on each machine to get it working again. Picking up the phone, she dialed Becky's extension.

"Becky's House of Beauty."

"I need help cleaning up a virus. It's going to kill the rest of the day."

"Yee haw! I'll be right in."

Julie shook her head and smiled as she replaced the receiver. Becky had been her roommate at MIT, where they both majored in computer science—Julie with a double major in math, Becky with a minor in social work. Becky was good enough at what she did to have Julie's job, but she lacked the finesse necessary to climb the corporate ladder.

If it bothered Becky that she worked for Julie, she didn't let on.

"Okay, what are we up against?" asked Becky, walking into Julie's office without knocking.

"Eighty-one machines, ten minutes to fix each one."

Becky's eyes lit and she smiled widely. "I'd say the company should buy us lunch."

"Deal." Julie checked her watch. "Let's get through two-thirds of them before we break, though."

The crime scene was easy to find.

The Orange Palm Motel had a turquoise pool, white lounge chairs, and a string of tangerine doors—the overly bright pattern now violently interrupted by a swath of blackened siding. The fire had buckled the roof shingles, blown out the window, and left gray swirling murals of soot and ash on neighboring units.

Hotel guests stood in the parking lot or sat on cars, watching the drama being played out before them like theatergoers staring at a stage. Police milled about behind yellow tape as firemen and EMTs packed up their gear.

There was no one to rescue here.

Hank ducked under the tape and strode toward the charred motel room, flipping open his badge as he was approached by a uniformed officer. Hank shook his head when the other man raised his hand and walked away, knowing the cop hadn't gotten a good look at Hank's badge.

That was too easy.

He replaced it in his pocket and withdrew a pair of vinyl gloves, pulling them on before confidently slipping into the room.

The darkness was near complete, the smells of burned wood and plastic clinging to the wet air. There was another odor as well, and Hank knew at once the room had been occupied. He withdrew a slim flashlight from his pocket and began searching for the body.

A beam of light shined on him.

"Detective Johnson, Jacksonville P.D."

He turned. "U.S. Navy Lieutenant Hank Jared."

"Navy?"

"Navy."

Johnson lowered his beam to Hank's chest. "Is our victim military?"

"The Navy has an interest in this case."

"An interest in this case," Johnson repeated. "Is that a no?"

"I didn't say that."

"The victim's in the bathtub," said Johnson. "Unidentified male, unless you're going to tell me who he is." He shined the light back at Hank. "You going to tell me?"

"What makes you think I know?"

"You're here. There must be a reason for that. I wouldn't even know who to call, but the U.S. Navy is here, and I'm trying to figure out why."

"Let me know if you come up with anything."

Hank headed for the bathroom, carefully making his way through the debris and pooled water on the floor.

The body was terribly burned. "He die in the fire?"

"Coroner's on his way."

Hank shined his beam in Johnson's eyes, and the other man sighed heavily.

"He was shot."

"Accelerant?"

"The arson dog caught a whiff of something."

"Anything else interesting?"

Johnson nodded. "A key to a safe deposit box near the body. A ring. No other personal items or identification, though they might have been fuel for the fire. Every car in the lot is accounted for. The room was rented to one Mark Smith. Clerk doesn't remember him—checked in three days ago."

"You wouldn't mind if I came with you to check out that safe deposit box."

"Of course not, officer."

"I swear, he had to be six foot eight. Just massive," Becky stood up and mimed what looked like King Kong tromping over tiny buildings. "His shoulders barely fit through the door. Biceps like that guy on the Energy Pump commercial." She flexed her own shapely arms and flung her red hair backwards as she admired her small muscles.

"And so he walks up to me and says, 'Have dinner with me.' Just like that. Can you believe the arrogance?"

"I'm guessing you said yes."

"Heck yeah, I said yes! I practically threw myself at his feet and begged for him to be the father of my children right there in the bar! Then I decided I should wait until after our date just in case he was psychotic."

"Just in case."

Meant for Her

"Right." The waiter appeared to refill their drinks.

"And?"

"And, what?"

"Did you go to dinner with him?"

"Gino's Via Abruzzi." She smacked her lips.

"And the man?"

She wrinkled her nose. "Too much baggage."

Julie turned to her Cobb salad, arranging one forkful with a tiny piece of chicken, a leaf of lettuce, bacon, and avocado.

"You're eating that salad like it's the last thing on earth you can control."

"Very insightful, Dr. Phil," said Julie as she dipped the tip of her concoction in blue cheese dressing. "Anything else you'd like to analyze today?"

"How about your love life?"

Julie gave her a warning look.

"How is Greg?" Becky asked in an overly bright tone.

"He's good. Fine."

"Good. Fine."

Julie glared at her. "He asked me to go on a trip with him for Christmas." She knew better than to tell Becky that Gwen had invited her for the holiday, too.

"Really? Where to?"

"He didn't tell me." Julie hesitated before adding, "He bought the tickets as a surprise."

Becky slammed down the iced tea she'd been drinking. "Without asking you first?"

"Yes."

"You hate surprises! Doesn't he know how much you hate surprises?"

"I don't hate surprises!" Julie began making another perfect Cobb salad forkful as she spoke. "It's romantic. It's thoughtful."

"It's fan-tastic!"

Julie put down her fork with a loud clink on the table. "Say it."

"Nope. Everything's good. Fine."

"Just say it."

"Say what? That you're pretending to like the idea of a

Meant for Her

mystery trip when we both know you'd rather have all the hair on your body pulled out by the root? Or that you're dating the most unappealing bachelor this side of the Mississippi because you don't want to be alone for Christmas?"

"Christmas doesn't have anything to do with it."

"Ah, but you concede my other point. The guy's a waste of plasma."

Julie could feel a headache beginning to throb in her left temple. Why was she having this conversation? "Why do you have such a problem with Greg?"

Becky took a long sip of her drink before answering. "He gives me the creeps." She bit down on a piece of ice. "And honestly, Jules? I don't think you like him any more than I do. Pretend it's January, sweetie. Let it go."

Julie knew she should defend her boyfriend, but nothing came to mind. How come nothing came to mind?

Because a waste of plasma is an apt description.

She used her fork to redistribute the chicken evenly over the surface of her salad. When had she decided that it was better to date someone she had no interest in than to be alone? It wasn't just Greg, he was just the latest in a continuous stream of guys she didn't even like. The kind of men who had always been attracted to her.

"You're right," said Julie.

Becky was halfway through a bite of her Philly steak sandwich and talked with her mouth full. "I am?"

"He's an ass."

Becky slammed the table with her open hand, getting the attention of several other diners. "That's what I'm talking about!"

"He annoys the absolute crap out of me."

"Amen, sister!"

"He talks about random, bizarre things. Invasive bamboo and the growth cycle of hair. I can tell you more about asphalt than you would ever want to know."

"Let it all out."

"When he touches me I want to pat his head and tell him to sit."

Becky snorted. "Please tell me you haven't slept with him."

"Ugh," Julie visibly shuddered. "His hands are wet. Not just damp, Becky. Wet. Always."

"Feel better?"

Julie turned sad eyes to her best friend in the world. "I wanted to like him," she said quietly.

"I know, sweetheart."

"I wanted to love him."

"Let's not get carried away."

Julie pulled out her cell phone and dialed before she could reconsider. "Greg, it's Julie. I'm not going to make the trip this weekend. We need to talk. Call me when you get this."

"I wonder where he was going to take you."

"Don't you dare."

"Oh, relax. You did the right thing." Becky took another bite, a string of cheese running from her mouth to the bun. "I'm just saying, someplace warm might be nice at Christmastime. Maybe a few palm trees."

Marianne Jared was standing in her large country kitchen making Christmas cookies en masse, holiday music playing in the background. With her daughter's wedding just days away, she was calming her nerves and preparing to feed the hungry crowd that would be descending.

She had the gingerbread men stacked up on cooling racks, and had just started blending butter and sugar for the next round when the phone rang.

"Hello."

"Hi, Ma."

She felt her stomach clench at his tone, and walked away from the stand mixer, leaving it running. "What's wrong?"

"I'm not going to be able to make it to the wedding, for real."

She brought her hand to her face and pinched the skin between her eyes, counting to five before trusting herself to speak. "Why not?"

"There's a case here in Jacksonville. Barstow insisted I handle it." He sighed heavily. "I'm so sorry, Ma. I can't get out of this one."

"Did you tell him you're scheduled for vacation? That's it's been on the books for months?"

"Of course I did. I even told him about the wedding." Hank cursed under his breath. "He was adamant. I'm so angry I could put my fist through a wall. Any of the investigators could handle this. There's no reason I have to do it."

She could hear the pain in his voice, knew it was genuine.

"Ma, if there's any way in hell I can make the ceremony, I will."

She nodded, staring at her feet. "We miss you."

"I miss you, too."

"Hank Jared is here to see you."

Julie didn't recognize the name. It was probably a vendor, though it struck her as odd that a sales rep would be doing cold calls the day before a holiday weekend. "I'll be right out."

As the Vice President of Technology for Systex Corporation, Julie was frequently the target of cold calls from salespeople working for computer companies.

She rounded the corner to the reception area and got her first look him. *Yes, Virginia, there is a Santa Claus.* He was considerably taller than her own five foot ten, with wavy dark brown hair, wide shoulders, and a presence that was totally masculine.

Julie felt butterflies stirring in her stomach and hoped she didn't make a fool out of herself. She was always uncomfortable talking to men who were more beautiful than she was. This guy was so far out of her league, she might trip over her own shoes.

"Mr. Jared. I'm Julie Trueblood. What can I do for you today?" The sweet smile on her face belied the pounding of her heart in her chest. He was even more attractive up close, with honeyed brown eyes and the lightest shadow of a beard on skin that looked tan from the sun.

"I'd like a few words with you, Ms. Trueblood."

"About what, exactly?"

Hank eyed the receptionist, who stared right back. "It's a personal matter."

She was hoping to skip out a little early today and had no intention of getting stuck with a sales rep for an hour. "What company do you represent?"

"The U.S. Navy."

The world around Julie froze for an instant, with the words hanging between them like the first gunshot of a battle. She remembered to breathe in, then out. She blinked her eyes.

"Come with me, Mr. Jared." She led the way from the lobby through a short hallway that connected to a longer corridor, feeling his presence behind her like a shadowy figure stalking her through a maze. Memories of other Navy officers assaulted her, panic rising in her chest with every step.

Julie motioned for him to enter the room before her, then locked the door and stepped behind her desk. "What can I do for you today?" she asked, her voice flat.

"I'm not sure." Hank leaned back in his chair and watched her. "Someone set fire to a motel room in Jacksonville, Florida yesterday morning."

Her brows drew together.

"The room was occupied at the time."

She flinched and looked away. "That's horrible."

"I flew up here this morning because I thought you might have some information about the case."

"Why would you think that? I don't even know anyone in Jacksonville."

"But you know someone in the Navy."

Her eyes slammed into his, and she knew she gave herself away. She raised an eyebrow and smiled at him without humor. "A friend from college is a Navy pilot."

"Is he."

"Yep. And there's always Richard Gere."

"Zack Mayo."

Julie rolled her eyes. "Whatever."

"The actor's name is Richard Gere, the character he played was Zack Mayo."

"You know what I meant."

"What I know is that you're messing with me, and I don't appreciate it."

Julie leaned forward on her desk. "I'm not messing with you. I don't know anyone in Jacksonville, and I haven't known anyone in the Navy in almost ten years."

"Who *did* you know in the Navy?"

Julie crossed her arms over her chest.

"I'll find out eventually, Ms. Trueblood."

"But you'll have to work for it, Mr. Jared. And that will please me immensely."

He held up a man's ring with a flush black stone. "Have you seen this before?"

Yes. Oh, God, yes. "No."

"You're lying to me."

"I'd like you to leave," she said, standing and crossing to the door.

"I'm not done yet." Hank reached for his briefcase. "There was a key to a safe deposit box inside that motel room. Inside, I found this."

He held up a single sheet of white paper, "JULIE X. TRUEBLOOD" scrawled in heavy black ink.

"Funny thing to include your middle initial. There are hundreds of Julie Truebloods in this country, did you know that?" He put the paper back into his briefcase. "Someone wanted to make sure we found you."

"How do I know you didn't make that yourself?"

"You don't. But that wasn't the only thing in the safe deposit box."

Hank handed her a yellow lined page torn from a legal pad. Four lines of scrambled text rushed along, without a nod toward spaces or punctuation. They defied interpretation, which hadn't stopped Hank from staring at them for the past twenty-four hours.

Julie lifted the paper between shaking hands.

"The safe deposit box was registered to John McDowell." Her eyes finally met his, her face contorting into a horrified frown.

"Do you know him, Julie?"

Her eyes filled as silent sobs racked her body. "Go. Please go."

Meant for Her

Hank stepped forward, opening his arms to her, and she was drawn to the comfort he offered. She leaned against him, too distraught to care that he was a stranger, a Navy officer. She wept, inhaling the heady smell of him, his body heat palpable through the fine cotton of his dress shirt.

"Who is John McDowell?" he asked quietly. "Is that his ring?"

The pointed question turned the man from comforter to interrogator. She flew out of his arms, ashamed that she had let herself seek solace there.

"Get out of my office."

"Ms. Trueblood…"

"Get out of here right now or I'll call security and have you removed!"

He nodded and raised his hands in surrender, reaching into the pocket of his coat.

"Call me if you want to talk, or if you need help. Whoever hurt this man is still out there." He pulled out a business card and pointedly placed it on her desk. "I just want to help you, Julie."

Then he was gone.

Chapter 2

The evening landscape glowed blue in the moonlight, as a silent rush of flurries fell in a continuous swirl onto the blanket of white below.

Inside, a freshly cut pine tree glowed with a single strand of white Christmas lights, its illuminated branches bare of ornamentation. Two dogs slept in front of a crackling fire, one small and gray, the other big and yellow and loudly snoring. Neither was disturbed by the low howling of the wind nor the clink of tools from the kitchen table.

Gwen Trueblood's art studio was pristine, with neatly kept wooden drawers and rows of labeled plastic containers. But it was a glorified closet, a staging area where she stored her supplies and prepared her materials. The kitchen was where she engaged her art, whether it be a bold pair of fused glass earrings or a loaf of fresh, crusty artisan bread.

Granite countertops mixed rich hues of gold with rusty reds and oranges in bold waves and specks. The cupboards were handcrafted of warm cherry with strong lines and careful moldings, their hardware a unique mixture of colored glass and sparkling metal that coordinated with the sunset colors of the granite around them.

A hefty island was surrounded on three sides by generous work areas, industrial appliances, and two oversized sinks. Pendant lights hung like jewelry, glittering in their display of brightly colored glass and dazzling metal. In the daytime the room would sparkle from the sunshine pouring in from the tall south-facing windows.

An impressive coffee maker and a craft kiln were displayed with equal prominence on the counters, along with a hand-woven basket filled with fresh fruit, an irregular loaf of golden-crusted bread, and a half-full bottle of red wine. Gwen was expecting company despite the weather, so she worked on a glass mobile and a rich pot roast at the same time. Both were for her niece.

She selected a deep purple from the stack of glass sheets before her, and worked to score it carefully before snapping the

Meant for Her

sheet into perfectly formed pieces. Beneath her hands, the glass became a series of graceful triangles that longed to twirl on metal strings.

In her mind's eye, Gwen could see Julie driving through the snow, though the treacherous travel was not what concerned Gwen. Far more worrisome was the heavy heart she sensed in the woman at the wheel, and the simple reality of her destination. She knew that Julie would not come to Vermont unless something was terribly wrong.

She had invited Julie here, as she did every Christmas, hoping that her sister's daughter would come for a visit. But she understood more than anyone that Julie had her demons, and her reasons for staying away were not likely to change.

Pulling the pile of glass sheets onto her lap, Gwen sifted through them as she thought about Julie. Purple was the dominant color, but she could also feel red and sharp bits of yellow. She took the colors out of the pile and began to score the sheets into small shapes and skinny lines. Relying on her natural sense of balance and proportion, Gwen worked to create shapes that represented the emotions clamoring around her niece, then set them on top of the purple triangles in pleasing asymmetry.

As she completed each piece, she added a metal hook between the layers of glass and arranged them on the rack for firing. The pieces would fuse together in the kiln, creating one smooth surface that retained the separate colors. Then Gwen would combine the fused glass pieces with hammered brass and mirrors to create a mobile for her niece.

Gwen set the rack into the kiln and fired it up. The pieces of glass would slowly be transformed into their new shapes—reminiscent of the old, but stunning in their combinations. The high temperatures required for the metamorphosis meant that the pieces would not be cool enough to touch until morning. Gwen reflected that the process of change was often an arduous one, both in art and in life.

Turning her attention to the large copper pot simmering on the stove, she removed the lid and bent her head close to the soup to inhale its rich scent. It was not a fatted calf, but the intent was the same. Gwen was celebrating the arrival of her long lost niece,

Meant for Her

and she wanted everything to be special for her. Mentally she imagined that Julie was getting close, so she began to chop up the parsley and basil on a thick bamboo board. They would be added to the pot just before serving.

The ringing of the doorbell woke the dogs and set them to barking. Gwen smiled and rushed to answer the door, her joy at Julie's arrival somewhat tempered by her concern. She opened the door and a dense gust of icy wind entered the cozy house.

Upon seeing her aunt, Julie's half smile collapsed into a grimace. Gwen pulled her into the house as she shut the heavy door against the arctic air, bringing Julie straight into her arms for a tight squeeze. A stranger might have thought they were sisters rather than aunt and niece, separated by only ten years or so and equal in height and build.

"What's wrong, Julie?"

She choked on the words as they came out of her mouth. "My dad died."

There are a lot of freakin' Julie Truebloods.

This time, the X wasn't helping, either. Hank was sitting in a dark hotel room in downtown Boston, a laptop and a beer on the desk in front of him, trying to find the connection between the dead guy in the motel fire and his Julie Trueblood.

Well, not *his* exactly.

"She wanted me to work for it," he said to himself, trying various combinations of her name and the few facts he had in this case. It wasn't until he typed "Julie Trueblood Navy" that he was rewarded for his efforts.

NAVY COMMANDER JOHN MCDOWELL ACCUSED OF ESPIONAGE, VANISHES.

"Holy shit."

Hank's brow creased as he frantically scrolled down the screen, searching for Julie's name. What did she have to do with an infamous traitor?

"Gwen Trueblood, McDowell's sister-in-law, has been granted temporary guardianship of McDowell's minor daughter, Julie. The commander's wife, Mary McDowell, died of cancer

ten months ago."

Julie Trueblood was Julie McDowell.

Hank had seen a 60 Minutes piece on the case years ago, though he never would have recognized the woman she had become. John McDowell was a cryptographer for the Navy, who passed the contents of secret messages on to Uzkapostan. He was single-handedly responsible for the sinking of the U.S.S. Dermody that killed eighty-eight soldiers.

If Systex knew about her background, she'd be fired faster than an arsonist at a fire station. Systex was a major manufacturer of information systems, with several substantial government contracts. No wonder she went by Trueblood.

He searched for "Julie McDowell Navy" and was rewarded with thousands of hits. Clicking on images, Hank's screen was transformed into a collage of photos taken around the time of the scandal. One black and white in particular caught his eye, a young Julie trying to get through a mob of reporters, her eyes wet, a backpack strap on her shoulder.

Hank wanted to throttle that photographer.

His cell phone rang and he checked the caller ID.

"Merry Christmas, man."

Chip Vandermead had been Hank's roommate in college. Hank called him occasionally when the Islanders played the Penguins, but Chip's position as an analyst with the NSA is what kept him on Hank's speed dial.

"How's Melody?"

"Pregnant."

"So you said. That's great."

"Twins."

"Oh, crap."

"We're going more with the, 'Isn't it wonderful?' approach, but 'Oh, crap' has crossed my mind."

"Sorry, man. That's awesome. Congratulations."

"She's due on Valentine's Day, but she's never going to make it. She's as big as a house." Hank heard a woman yelling in the background. "What? I'm not talking about you." He chuckled. "So, what's up? I know you didn't call just to wish me a Merry Christmas."

Meant for Her

"I need a favor."

"Of course you do."

"I have an encrypted message, and I need to know what it says."

"Tell me about it."

"Four lines of text, Seventy-nine characters all together."

"Can't help you."

"What?"

"It's too short. Unless someone wanted you to be able to read it, and used a known cipher that's able to be read with a computer algorithm or something. Who wrote it?"

"Commander John McDowell."

"You're kidding."

"Not kidding."

"The man's a legend. Personally, I thought he was dead."

"He is now."

"What happened?"

"Somebody shot him, then set a fire to cover it up."

Chip whistled. "Where'd the message come from?"

"A safe deposit box. The key was at the scene." Hank looked at the hundreds of pictures of Julie on his computer screen as he talked. "I need to know what that message says, Chip."

"I can run it through the computer, but don't get your hopes up."

"Thanks. I owe you one."

"You owe me a hell of a lot more than one, Jared. Do you know anything else about this message? Sometimes it's the littlest thing that helps break a code."

Hank thought for a minute, wondering what might be relevant. "The only other thing in the safe deposit box was a sheet of paper that said Julie X. Trueblood. I already tracked her down. Looks like she's his daughter, going by her mother's maiden name."

"Okay. I'll see what I can find out."

Julie wrapped the sky blue terry bathrobe around her warm, damp body and walked out of the bathroom, a cloud of steam

Meant for Her

following her into the much cooler bedroom. Her wet hair was piled on her head and wrapped in a pale yellow towel, just like the one she used to dry herself off out of the shower. Gwen had a masterful understanding of creature comforts, and Julie smelled of mint and rosemary from the decadent shampoo, soap and lotions her aunt provided.

Warm hardwood floors gave way to plush carpeting beneath her feet as Julie made her way to the window seat and sat down on its edge. She took in the familiar view below, the landscape's pristine blanket of snow shining bright in the late morning sunshine. A gently sloping yard bowed before rolling hills in the distance, and the horizon spoke of mountains tinted purple by the tilt of the earth itself.

Julie leaned forward and pressed her forehead to the cold glass, allowing her eyes to close in recognition of the peace she felt in this place.

This room had been hers when she lived with Gwen, and she acknowledged it for the haven that it was both then and now. It was ironic to be comforted by these walls after years of avoiding the solace they so freely afforded. Julie had not been here once in the time since college.

Vermont reminded Julie of the darkest time in her life—her own despair over her father's disappearance. Here lay the ashes from which she had risen like a phoenix, and only another fire could have brought her back again. In this place she was the daughter of a traitor, stalked by the media and villainized by the Navy officers who continued to interrogate Julie long after her father escaped their influence.

Her return to Vermont had been determined the moment Hark Jared set foot in her office. Last night, Gwen listened intently as Julie told her about the fire that killed her father. She thought of it now, picturing the scene as if she witnessed its deadly fingers reaching to destroy her ultimate hope—that her father would some day return to her and to his rightful place in her life.

Opening her eyes, Julie was surprised to realize that there were no tears on her face, as if the well of grief had simply gone dry from her great gulps at its waters in the last two days. She

Meant for Her

touched her cheeks with her hands and marveled at their normal texture, dry and soft.

The reality that life continues despite tragedy was both an odd comfort and a bad joke that rubbed at her and made her chafe on a spot that was already raw.

Julie had stumbled into bed last night after talking to Gwen until the wee hours of the morning. Now she looked around the familiar room and saw it had been transformed. The antique furniture that had been painted a bold coral when Julie lived here now matched the pale yellow of the fluffy towel on her head. Bed linens of turquoise and bright yellow toile seemed to hum in their bold contrast to the muted blue of the walls. A bulky duvet was wrapped in a lemony fabric that felt like the softest bunny, and the pineapples atop the four posts of the bed had been gloriously decorated in hammered gold and blue glass.

Walking to the bed, she again sank into its inviting depths. She pulled the duvet over her robed body and closed her eyes, wishing for the sleep that she suspected would not come.

She willed her mind to think of something else. An image of the sexy Navy officer filled her head. Hank Jared. Even his name was sexy. She remembered what he smelled like—pungent soap and something exquisitely male. Her knees almost buckled when her eyes had first locked with his.

A knock at the door disrupted her reverie. "Come in."

Gwen handed her the phone. "It's Becky."

"Hey, what's up?" said Julie.

"I'm at your place. I came to feed Sammy like you asked, and Jules, someone's been here."

"What do you mean?"

"I mean, someone broke into your condo. It's pretty bad. Your dresser drawers have all been dumped out onto the floor, and the kitchen cabinets are open and everything's messed up."

"Someone broke into my condo?" She sat upright in bed. A cat meowed on the other end of the phone. "Is Sammy okay?"

"Yeah, he's fine. He was locked in a closet and none too happy about it. He's okay now."

"Did they steal anything?" In her mind, Julie ran through a list of her valuables, most of them electronics, and most of them with her on this trip.

"I don't see your laptop or your iPod."

"They're with me. Becky, do you think Greg..." Julie let her voice trail off, not wanting to say the words out loud.

"I know, he was my first thought, too. Was he upset when you dumped him?"

"He never called me back. I just figured he got the message and wanted to avoid the whole conversation."

"It looks like he was upset."

"Yeah. Looks like." Julie realized Gwen was watching her, her eyes questioning. "Someone broke into my condo and trashed the place." She choked on an unexpected sob as she said the words, covering her mouth with her hand.

Gwen sat and touched her shoulder. "That officer said you might be in danger."

"It's just some loser boyfriend I dumped last week, Gwen. Either that, or some neighborhood kids up to no good..."

"I don't think so, Julie." Julie looked into Gwen's eyes, and what she saw there sent a chill down her spine. Gwen had a sixth sense about some things, and Julie had learned long ago to listen when her aunt spoke with this quiet authority.

"Uh, oh," said Becky into Julie's ear.

"I feel a darkness. I don't want to scare you, but there's evil here." She held Julie's eyes as tightly as she held her hand, wishing to impart strength to her niece at this time. "Did the ex-boyfriend have a darkness about him?"

"I wouldn't say that," said Julie.

"Well, I would," chimed Becky. "Tell Gwen that I would, Jules. Tell her."

"He gave Becky the creeps."

"So maybe it is the boyfriend, then. Or it might have something to do with your father's murder."

That possibility was feeling very real to Julie.

"Perhaps it's time to call the Navy officer who came to see you in Boston. It will give you a chance to get a look at that encrypted message from the safe deposit box, too," said Gwen.

"I don't want to see the message."

Gwen turned exasperated eyes to her niece. "Your father

Meant for Her

finally wrote you a letter after all these years, and you're not even going to read it?"

Jingle Bell Rock played on the car radio, but Hank wasn't listening. A knot had settled in the valley between his shoulder blades, and he tried to stretch his arm across the steering wheel to release the tension. The lines on the pavement slid by in hypnotic straights and curves as his mind tried to make sense of the last several days.

Johnson had hit it out of the park before Hank even realized something was wrong. *Given what I know about this scene, I wouldn't even know who to call, but the U.S. Navy is here, and I'm trying to figure out why.*

Hank didn't like playing catch-up. Someone knew the body in the motel room was Commander McDowell before he was called to the scene like a puppet. Admiral Barstow had been the one to send Hank there, but that didn't necessarily mean he was the one pulling the strings.

Hank dialed his commanding officer.

Formidable and unconcerned with niceties, the admiral exerted his influence skillfully over those under his command. Hank was one of the few who remained unaffected by the other man's demeanor, and suspected he had earned the admiral's begrudging respect.

"What do you have for me?" said Barstow.

"The motel fire was deliberately set to cover up a murder, sir," said Hank.

"Whose murder?"

"It seems the body is that of Commander John McDowell."

The line was silent, and Hank resisted the urge to speak to fill the void. If his suspicions were correct, the admiral was already well aware of who had died in that fire.

"What makes you believe the body is McDowell?"

Hank told him about the ring, the safe deposit box, Julie Trueblood and the cipher. "Dental x-rays were sent in for positive identification."

"A lot of good that will do."

Meant for Her

"Sir?"

"All of McDowell's service records are gone, from his basic personnel file to the data from his last assignment," said the admiral. "Including his dental records."

Hank was stunned. It was no small feat to make someone's entire military existence disappear. "What happened to them?"

"They were deleted from our computer system, either by someone in the Navy with the clearance to do so, or by someone who hacked into that computer system."

"People can actually hack into the Navy's computers?"

"Computer gurus with exceptional code breaking knowledge and expertise," said the admiral. He pronounced guru like it had quotation marks around it. "Someone like McDowell's daughter."

"Is she that good?"

"McDowell was one of the best cryptologists the Navy has ever seen, but the daughter was rumored to be some kind of prodigy. McDowell bragged she was better than he would ever be. Then she grew up and got herself a degree in mathematics and computer science."

"That's why the Navy kept interrogating her when her father disappeared. If she sympathized with him, she was a threat to national security just like he was."

"Yes. And it's why the Navy has kept tabs on her all these years, no matter what she wants to call herself."

Hank didn't allow himself to consider his next words. "You knew it was McDowell in that motel."

"We got an anonymous tip."

"An anonymous tip," Hank repeated. The sheer convenience of such a tip made it suspect.

"A voicemail left on my line. It said we'd find McDowell and his last secret."

"The message from the safe deposit box."

"Yes. Send me a copy of it."

"Yes, sir."

"And you get Julie Trueblood to decipher it, Jared. If anyone can, it's her."

"I'll see what I can do." As Hank hung up the phone, he

Meant for Her

steered his SUV onto the exit ramp. According to his GPS, he was less than half an hour from Gwen Trueblood's house in Vermont. He had been about to head to the airport for his flight back to Jacksonville when Julie phoned and told him about the break-in. He had offered to come out, and she had quickly accepted.

It wasn't like Hank to keep things from his commanding officer.

"Sometimes, you've got to trust your gut," he said to himself.

Chapter 3

As Hank stepped up to the front door of the unlit house, he had an uncomfortable feeling, like he had shown up for a party on the wrong day. He found it hard to believe no one was home after a personal invitation and a five hour drive.

Hank heard nothing when he rang the bell, so he knocked loudly on the door for good measure. He was rewarded with the barking of dogs who quickly came to the other side of the door.

Turning around, Hank surveyed his surroundings by the day's last light as he waited. The white farm house had a wide front porch with turned railings and a painted wood floor. A two-story barn loomed to the side of the garage, and distant snow-covered fields were studded with split-rail fences.

The land reminded him of his mother's property, and Hank was acutely aware that he was just a few hours' drive from his family's home in the Adirondacks. He imagined his mom and siblings sitting around the big dining table with glasses of wine, and promised himself he would do everything in his power to make the ceremony tomorrow.

Everything except walk away from a case.

The door opened behind him and Hank turned to see the face he hadn't even realized he'd been missing. It was there in the hitch of his breath as he looked at her.

"Thanks for coming, Mr. Jared."

Her blonde hair was tied up and away from her face, her eyes calm and clearly grateful.

"Of course."

Was this the face of a traitor?

If Julie Trueblood had hacked into the Navy computers to protect her father, she no doubt believed that what she had done was right. As she held the door wide for him to enter, he realized that the moment might come when he would need to arrest her. Hank crossed the threshold and hoped he wouldn't have to do that.

"The power's been out since this morning," she said. "There's a generator in the barn, but we haven't been able to get it working."

"Maybe I can fix it."

"I'll pretend I wasn't hoping you would say that."

"Why?"

"So I can seem like a tough, independent woman who doesn't need a man to do anything mechanical."

"And fry it up in a pan?"

"Exactly." She had a beautiful smile, he noted, just as it fell. "Of course, I'm already hamming up the damsel in distress routine pretty well."

"I'm glad you called. Someone breaking into your home is unsettling for anyone. Given the circumstances, you were right to call me."

She accepted his words with a nod. "Come on in," she said, stepping aside and motioning for Hank to follow her down the dim hallway. "Watch yourself, it got dark all of a sudden." She trailed her hand along the wall to navigate in the dim light as she called out, "I think it's about time to pull out the candles, Gwen."

They stepped into the kitchen, where a tall woman with flowing blonde curls was busy unpacking boxes of candles and candle holders. "One step ahead of you," she said. She smiled warmly at Hank, and he knew they must often be mistaken for sisters.

"Gwen Trueblood, this is Hank Jared," said Julie.

Hank extended his hand. "That's a lot of firepower, Ms. Trueblood."

"Call me Gwen," she said, lighting candles as she spoke. "I heard you may be able to fix our generator."

"I can give it a try."

"Wonderful," she said, taking a flashlight off the counter and handing it to Hank. "Any tools you might need are out in the barn with the generator. Julie, will you show him where it is?"

"Sure thing." Julie grabbed a down jacket off the back of a kitchen chair and pulled on tall winter boots before leading the way out the back door. When they were alone, she turned and waited for Hank to walk beside her.

"Mr. Jared, I owe you an apology."

He could smell her scent, clean and light, floating on the

crisp winter air as he stepped closer. *In a different time and place…*

"It's Hank," he said. "An apology for what?"

"For losing it when you were in my office," she said, her embarrassment plain. "For throwing you out on your ear when you tried to be compassionate."

At her words, Hank remembered the way she had fit in his arms, warm and solid. He knew that he wanted her back there again, and the knowledge made him uneasy. "It must have been quite a shock," he said with sincere sympathy.

Julie frowned. "You know, then."

He nodded. "I did have to work for it, if it makes you feel any better."

She turned back toward the barn and began walking slowly through the snow as she spoke. "I hadn't seen my father in ten years."

Hank knew the admiral wouldn't believe her. "That must have been hard for you."

"I understood it. My father came to see me the day he disappeared."

He raised his eyebrows. "I read the official report. It says the last time you saw him was the night before the disappearance."

"I lied. I got home from school and he was waiting for me at the kitchen table."

The sound of their footsteps through the snow and a blowing wind were the only noises between them. They crossed the last of the field between the house and the barn. Julie lifted the cold metal latch and opened the door, lighting her flashlight for the darkness within.

She led the way as Hank followed closely behind her. At the far end of the barn, she opened a small door and revealed an organized workshop. A red generator had been pulled into the middle of the floor.

"Here it is."

Hank crouched down in front of the machine and extended his hand for the flashlight. She gave it to him and watched as he oriented himself to the older generator.

"The fuel lines are intact. Electrical looks good so far."

Meant for Her

"Yeah. I couldn't get a response from the starter."

She did say she had already tried to fix it. He would do well not to underestimate this one. He moved on to examine the starter. "What did you and your dad talk about that day?" he asked.

Julie leaned back against the wall. "He told me what was coming," she said quietly. "The accusations. The charges of treason." Julie took a trembling breath. "He told me he was leaving."

The picture of Julie surrounded by reporters flashed in his mind and Hank felt a surge of adrenaline, as if her father were here and he could beat some sense into the man who was willing to abandon his daughter to save his own skin. *Didn't he know what that would do to her?*

"He told me who set him up."

Hank looked at her in surprise. Nowhere in the file was there mention of any kind of conspiracy.

A part of him clutched at the idea, wishing there was a way for this woman to be clean of her father's sins, but the experienced investigator knew better. McDowell was a father who didn't want his daughter to believe he'd done something terrible.

"His commanding officer gave him messages to decode, just like always. He told him they were from Uzkapostan, but in reality they were coded messages from our own Navy. The content of the messages were things like coordinates and location names, dates, that sort of thing. Nothing that let my father know they were really our own intel."

Julie stared into the distance. "Until the Dermody went down. My father realized that the coordinates of the ship when it was sunk were identical to the coordinates he had decoded the day before."

"What did he do?"

"He escaped." Her features were oddly blank as she continued. "He went to the bank and emptied his accounts, then he came home to talk to me. He told me he would call Barstow and confront him once he was safe…"

"Barstow?"

"Yes, Captain Thomas Barstow. Do you know him? He was my father's commanding officer."

If Hank had been standing, he might have fallen over. He heard himself answer in a monotone voice that sounded like a stranger's. "He's an admiral now."

"An *admiral*?" Her hands were clenched at her sides. "That man should be the one laying in the morgue right now. Not my father. Barstow is the traitor."

Hank watched her fury, saw her chest rise and fall. Hank was a man who trusted his own gut, and his instincts were telling him that Julie Trueblood was telling him the God's honest truth.

"Why did he run?" he asked. "Why not defend himself?"

"My father was born in Uzkapostan. He still has family there."

People had been convicted of espionage on less.

If Julie was correct and the admiral was responsible, it would have been damn near impossible to prove it. Hank turned back to the generator. He needed to think.

"Do you believe me?" she asked.

Hank's hands stilled, but he didn't answer, unsure of what to say. He would have been a lot more comfortable if she hadn't asked the question. His hand fiddled with the starter, and he saw her turn and walk out of the workshop from the corner of his eye. He looked up, staring after her and rubbing his lip with the back of his hand.

Then he was there, grabbing her hand and turning her around to face him, his body too close to hers. He had only meant to stop her. "I believe you," he said.

He could see the desire in her eyes, feel it in the air between them as her scent met his nostrils and he fought for control. He forced his hands to unclench, and released her.

As he stepped back, Julie made the smallest noise deep in her throat, a hum of disappointment. It was enough. He grabbed her, pinning her between his body and the barn as he kissed her forbidden lips with his own.

Lust was there, swift and hot, surprising him with its intensity. She returned his bruising kisses, her passion matching his as they climbed higher, each short of breath, pulses racing.

A loud banging noise startled them apart.

"What was that?" asked Hank.

"It sounded like the barn door slamming in the wind," she said. "But I thought I latched it behind us."

"You did. I saw you."

Hank quickly grabbed the flashlight and pulled out his weapon. "Stay behind me." Halfway back to the door they had come in, they heard the same slamming sound in the opposite direction.

"It's the back door," said Julie. "Not the one we came in." The pair doubled back and walked around a stack of hay, suddenly greeted by an unexpected expanse of white. The open barn door moved slowly in the icy breeze, the snow-covered field beyond glittering in the moonlight as the wind howled ominously.

Clearly visible in the radiant snow was a trail of footprints, leading from the back door of the barn through the field for as far as the eye could see. Julie sank into a squat and bent her head between her knees.

Hank moved closer to the tracks and examined them in the light of his flashlight. "They're recent, but they have about two inches of snow cover," he said, considering. "What time did it stop snowing?"

Julie's gaze dropped lower. "It had already stopped when I got the mail. Noon. Lunchtime."

"So these were made this morning."

"The snow cover might be from blowing snow. It's windy."

"The snow's too wet. Feel it."

Julie didn't move from her crouch.

Hank knelt down next to her. "You okay?"

"Yeah."

"You don't know who made them?"

Julie licked her lips, swallowed. She shook her head. "Gwen and I are the only ones here."

Hank's mind raced, trying to make sense of the tracks. He stared off in the distance and saw another farmhouse, its windows lighted a warm gold in the evening darkness.

And he knew what the intruder had done.

"What time did your power go out?" he asked.

"Ten thirty." Julie's eyes followed his. "They got the generator, too. Didn't they?"

"I think so." Hank extended his hand. "Probably put something in the fuel. I could check but that would take time. We need to get out of here, Julie."

She took the help he offered as she nodded. "I know," she said, rising. "We're taking Gwen with us."

"I know."

"And she'll bring the damn dogs."

"That's okay."

They retraced their steps back to the farmhouse, the wind biting at their hands and faces as they went. Her hand was nestled in the solid warmth of Hank's, something he didn't examine too closely.

"Hank?"

"Yeah?"

"I want to decode that message."

"I know. It's in my car. You can do it on the way."

"Where are we going?"

"To a wedding."

It took Julie and Gwen less than twenty minutes to gather what they needed and climb into Hank's SUV. The dogs sat in the backseat with Gwen while Julie took the front, buckling her seat belt with a measure of relief. The irony that she should find comfort in the presence of a Navy officer was not lost on her, and she made a mental note not to trust this man completely.

The car smelled like Hank, and Julie inhaled his scent deep into her lungs. She might not trust him, but he smelled like a million bucks. If someone bottled that smell, they could control the entire female population.

"I had a feeling I wasn't going to need those candles," said Gwen.

The gate of the SUV slammed shut and Hank walked around to the driver's side. Opening the door, he slid across the leather seat and handed Julie a yellow lined paper. "The message from the safe deposit box," he said, reaching to buckle his seat belt.

Julie swallowed against a lump that suddenly formed in her throat. Gingerly she unfolded the single crease and gazed upon her father's handwriting. She had gotten a glimpse of the cipher in her office, but now she had time to really look at what she held in her hands.

Recognition hit her like a blow as she touched the familiar letter shapes with her fingers. Her memory of her father had grown diluted in his absence, misshapen by the accusations that had led to his departure. Sometimes she didn't know who he was anymore, or who he had ever been. The simple paper in her hand was like a snapshot of her real dad, sweet and strong.

Gone forever.

Her eyes burned.

"You recognize the handwriting," said Hank.

Julie reached into the bag between her feet. "Yes," she said quietly. She pulled out a spiral notebook and a pencil, never looking in Hank's direction.

"It was like that with my David," said Gwen thoughtfully. "The littlest thing, out of the blue, like a light in the darkness. Then I'd feel the pain all over again when I realized he was gone."

Hank's eyes in the rearview mirror were sympathetic. "Who was David?" he asked.

"My husband," she said, smiling fondly. "It will be eleven years ago in January that he was killed in a skiing accident."

"I'm sorry."

"Me, too." Gwen sat up a little straighter. "Julie, Julie. Do you still remember how to crack those codes?"

"It's been a long time," she said. "I don't know if it will come back to me."

"That message is meant for you, Julie. Your daddy didn't write that for anyone else. I'm sure you'll know just what to do."

Julie wished she had Gwen's confidence in her abilities. Opening to a clean page in the notebook, she began writing.

"Can I ask what you're doing?" said Hank.

"Counting letter frequencies."

Hank cursed softly under his breath. "I forgot about Chip." He pulled out his cell phone.

"Who's Chip?" asked Julie.

"My buddy at the NSA. I asked him to run that through the computer."

Julie's wasn't happy he had brought in a professional cryptographer. She was reminded once again that she and Hank had different objectives. "It won't do any good."

"So he told me." Hank opened his cell phone and dialed. He left a message on Chip's voicemail to call him back ASAP. "His wife is eight months pregnant with twins. Maybe she went into labor."

Julie worked quietly as they drove, completing the frequency chart and looking for letter patterns. It was very basic work, but she had to start somewhere.

"Julie, I'm sorry to interrupt you," said Hank.

"What is it?"

"I need to call my mother and tell her we're on our way. I will tell her and my sister the truth, but I think it would be an easier visit if we have a cover story for everyone else."

That sounded reasonable. "Okay."

"So, I was thinking you could be my date for the wedding, and Gwen could be your aunt from Vermont who just happens to know my sister. Maybe that's how we met—through your aunt and my sister."

"I do some jewelry design," piped Gwen from the backseat., "including wedding bands."

"Perfect," said Hank. "Actually, last I heard the wedding bands were MIA, so that might actually be true before we're done here."

"What a coincidence!" said Gwen, smiling from ear to ear. "It's like serendipity. Don't you just love when the universe aligns to make things happen?"

Julie turned around in her seat to glare at her aunt like she was insane. Gwen rewarded her effort with a wide grin, and Julie shook her head. To Hank, she asked, "You want me to be your date for your sister's wedding?"

"It seems like the easiest way to explain a stranger's presence at a wedding, don't you think?"

"Yes, I guess it is." She turned back to her notebook. "Just don't expect me to do the chicken dance at the reception."

"We're more of an electric slide kind of family."

Julie stared at him blankly. "I really need to do this," she said, holding up the notebook.

"Of course. Sorry." A moment later, he slid his shoulders to the left in a wave-like motion.

"Boogie woogie woogie," came Gwen's high-pitched voice, earning her an appreciative chuckle from Hank.

"Really, Gwen?" said Julie.

"Oh, pooh, Julie. Fine, I'll be quiet."

The three of them cruised the rest of the way into the Adirondacks and New York State without another word.

It was just after nine o'clock, but it felt much later to Hank as he drove along the winding roads that snaked up the side of Moon Lake Mountain. He kept careful watch for deer and other wild animals, everyday hazards for those driving through the heavily wooded area. Tall pines flanked the road on either side, with the occasional mailbox denoting a home nestled somewhere behind the dense trees.

His mother had been so happy when he phoned to tell her he was coming after all, and he was just as excited as she was.

Beside him, Julie worked diligently in the dim light of the overhead reading lamp. Gwen had fallen asleep shortly after they stopped for coffee at a diner called the Truck Stop Inn, and Hank could hear faint snoring, though he wasn't sure if it came from the woman or one of the dogs.

"I can't stare at this anymore," said Julie, closing the notebook and returning it to her bag on the floor. She took a long sip of cold coffee.

Hank shook his shoulders and grimaced. "I don't know how you do that."

"The code breaking?"

"Cold coffee. Gives me the heebie-jeebies."

"Tough guy like you, bothered by a little cold coffee?" She smiled at him, her voice playful.

"It's like kryptonite to Superman."

"Did you really just call yourself Superman?"

Hank gave her his best offended look. "Not exactly. But I could be Superman."

"Really."

"Absolutely."

"I don't think so, hot shot Navy man."

"Whoa, wait a minute. The similarities are downright eerie if you give me a chance."

Julie laughed dismissively. "Well, there's the cold coffee thing. I'd love to hear the other similarities."

"Superman's tall. I'm tall."

"One."

"Superman has dark hair."

"This car ride just got a lot longer."

"Superman loved his family, fought for right over wrong, and would do anything for Lois Lane." He held up his fingers as he counted off his reasons.

"Ah, Lois. I was wondering about her. Why isn't she your date for the wedding? Important assignment from the paper?"

"You were wondering if I had a girlfriend?" he asked, looking at her intensely, the slightest smile playing on the corners of his lips.

She looked like she swallowed a bug. "Not really. I was just playing along."

"Playing along," he agreed, nodding. "I see." She was full of it, and the knowledge pleased him immensely. "There is no Lois. But someday when I find her, I will do anything for that woman."

The smallest voice in the back of his head suggested he already had, which was ridiculous.

"How much farther to your mom's house?"

"We're almost there now."

A wide right turn ended in one final hill as the SUV crested the highest point of the mountain. A wide vista opened before them, the light of the full moon clearly visible without the cover of the forest, Moon Lake glistening in the rays of its namesake.

"Beautiful," she said softly.

Hank had been watching her, and silently agreed, but he was

Meant for Her

thinking nothing of the landscape and everything about the woman beside him.

"The house is up here another mile or two."

"Great," she said, rubbing her hands on her thighs. "Who's going to be there?"

"My mom, Marianne. Tough as nails, with a soft side. You'll like her." *If she likes you,* he added to himself. His mother was not one to suffer fools gladly, but Hank wasn't overly concerned. If anything, his mother would probably like Julie too much. That's why he made sure to tell her that Julie was only pretending to be his girlfriend. "She took over the family business when my dad passed away a few years ago."

"I'm sorry."

"Thank you."

"What's the family business?"

"Our first product was organic fruit soap. We've expanded over the years to include natural gardening products."

"Wait, as in Uncle Billy's Rockin' Organic Fruit Soap?"

"That's the one."

Julie laughed. "Who came up with that name?"

"Kelly. My father thought it would be a fun family project to market it at the local Agway one summer. I designed the packaging, Norah wrote the copy. We never expected it to take off."

"Who's Norah?"

"My older sister. She'll be there tonight, along with her husband Steve. She's a professional cellist with the Boston Philharmonic; he teaches linguistics at Northeastern."

"Any more brothers or sisters?"

"Nope. That's the whole family."

Julie rubbed her hands together. "Your mom is Marianne, Kelly's marrying Ron, and Norah's married to Steve."

"Relax. You'll be fine."

"I'm not good with names. I make associations to remember them."

"What do you mean?"

"I get pictures in my head that help me remember. Like your sister, Kelly. Kelly Ogden was my best friend in the fourth grade.

So I picture her standing at the altar with Ronald McDonald."

Hank knew that the polished and athletic Ron wouldn't appreciate this game at all. "Go on."

"For your sister, I picture Nora Roberts playing the cello on the back of one of her books."

"Who's Nora Roberts?"

Julie looked at him like he had blasphemed. "Just one of the best romance novel authors of all time, thank you very much."

Hank raised his hands in mock surrender. "What about Steve?"

"The book with the cello is about a linguistics professor at Northeastern who falls for an older student. A music major. It's very touching."

"Is that a real book?"

"Of course not. Didn't you hear me? I'm just trying to remember their names."

He laughed at her absurd thought process. "Whatever works for you." He slowed down as they drove alongside several hundred feet of stacked stone fence, then turned onto a driveway that meandered away from the road and back toward the lake. "This is it."

Julie turned around and woke up Gwen, then watched as the tree-lined driveway opened to a wide, snow-covered lawn. The big house was a mixture of Tudor and log cabin styles, clearly one-of-a-kind in its design. There was a three-car detached garage and what looked to be a large screened porch off the side of the residence.

Hank pulled to a stop in the circular driveway. "Leave the bags. I'll come out for them in a bit." Julie opened her door and stepped out into the chilly night air.

The front door opened and a slender woman with long gray and black hair appeared under the porch light, some fifteen feet from the car.

Hank helped Julie with her bag as Gwen stepped out and stretched her legs. Raising his voice, he said, "Mom, I'd like you to meet Julie and Gwen Trueblood. Ladies, this is my mom."

Julie swore quietly.

Hank realized her problem at once. He sang quietly, "Sit

Meant for Her

right back and you'll hear a tale, a tale of a mighty ship…"

Chapter 4

"And this is where you and Julie will be staying," said Marianne, opening the door to a single bedroom with a queen size bed and its own bathroom. Julie's cheeks heated as she thought about sharing that bed with Hank.

Hank spoke in a low voice. "Ma, I told you it's not like that."

"I understand that, dear. But this is Kelly's wedding weekend and we have a full house. I had to do some rearranging to get you a room at all. Gwen has to sleep in the office with cousin Josie on the last air mattress. This," she said, gesturing to the red and gold guest room, "is the best I can do. There are clean towels in the bathroom closet and an extra blanket in the chest," she said firmly, walking away.

"I'm sorry," Hank said to Julie. "I'll sleep on the floor."

"Damn straight, you will."

"Come on. I'll introduce you around."

Julie looked around the room, wishing she could barricade herself within it. "Do you have to?"

He looked at her quizzically. "What's wrong?"

"What if someone asks how we met, or something else I don't have an answer for?"

"Lie."

"I'm a terrible liar."

"Well, then, this should be good practice for you." He steered her toward the stairs, almost running into his sister.

"There you are. Ron and I would like to say a few words before everyone heads out," she said, gesturing downstairs. The rehearsal dinner ended shortly before Hank and Julie arrived, and close members of the family were still congregated at the house.

Julie begrudgingly followed Hank down the stairs, and took her place next to him in the entranceway between the foyer and living room.

Kelly and Ron made a striking couple. She was petite, with the same honeyed skin as her brother and dark hair that fell in lustrous waves down her back. Ron was much taller and quite

Meant for Her

muscular, like a model or fitness trainer. His head was completely bald and shiny, his kind and handsome face suggesting he might have been a blonde or a redhead at one time.

"We want each of you to know what it means to us that you're here to share in our wedding. I wasn't sure this day would ever come," she said, garnering a laugh from those who knew the couple well, "and well, we just wanted to say thank you."

"Mom," she continued, "we owe you a special thanks." To the room, she said, "When the caterer double-booked and cancelled on us last week, my mother stepped up and offered to do the cooking herself." Gasps could be heard around the room. "We couldn't do this without you, Mom." Claps and a few cheers followed.

"And to my brother, Hank, who will be walking me down the aisle tomorrow," she paused and bit her lip to keep the tears that threatened in check, "I am so very glad you were able to make it. There's only one person I'd rather have at my side, and I'm sure he is smiling down from heaven at the thought that you will stand in his place."

Ron put his arm around his fiancé and raised his glass in Hank's direction. Julie felt a knot in her throat at the sense of loss these people so obviously shared, on the eve of such celebration. It occurred to her that Hank had missed the rehearsal dinner because he was helping her at the farmhouse. Would he have missed the entire wedding if she had still needed him in Vermont?

Lois Lane was one lucky woman.

Hank looked up at that moment. Their gazes met and locked, sharing a moment of intimate appraisal. Everything about this man attracted her, and she felt a tingling sensation in her abdomen. Hank's eyes dropped to her lips, and she knew he wanted to kiss her.

She flashed back to the barn, and their brief, fiery kisses, her cheeks heating at the memory. The realization that she wanted him even more now set her into a small panic.

Forget about Superman. He isn't even trustworthy.

She broke eye contact and took a step away.

Kelly and Ron finished their remarks, and Julie turned on

her heel and walked away from Hank. She'd rather face a hundred and one people who thought she was in love with him than face the man himself.

She spent forty-five minutes in the kitchen, listening to his great aunt Phoebe describe her trip to Paris, then ten more talking to Ron, who got her a beer. Feeling pleasantly relaxed from the drink, she slipped up the stairs to turn in for the night.

Hank caught up to her just outside the bedroom door, turning her around by touching her shoulder.

"Do you know that everyone in that room thinks we're fighting?"

Julie bristled at his tone.

"I may be sleeping on the floor," he continued, "but there's no need for the whole world to know it."

"Don't be ridiculous. I was only kidding. You can sleep with me."

"What?" His pupils dilated and he leaned toward her.

"In fact," she said, looking up at him through her lashes, "I'm kind of tired."

"Hey, Hank," said a voice just behind him. He turned and saw Kelly's fiancé. "I'm going to get heading home. I'm glad you were able to make it," said Ron as he shook Hank's hand. "It means a lot to Kelly, and to me."

"Couldn't have kept me away if you'd tried," he said, smiling at the other man. "Ron, did you meet my girlfriend, Julie?"

"Yes, downstairs," said Ron.

Julie smirked, leaning on the door jam. "Ron was telling me how he and Kelly met."

"Now, don't go telling on me before the ceremony. I've almost made it without being discovered." Ron chuckled, a goofy grin on his face. "I'm going to head home. I'll see you both at the church tomorrow. Sorry if I interrupted anything," he said with a wink, then walked away.

Hank rounded on Julie. "He did interrupt something, didn't he?"

Julie's eyes went wide. She made certain Ron was out of earshot before she whispered, "I was just pretending."

He moved into her personal space, his eyes smoldering and purposeful.

She took a step backward into the bedroom and watched as he advanced on her by equal measure, closing the door quietly behind him.

"Were you pretending in the barn?"

"The barn?" she asked, continuing her backward retreat. She stopped when the back of her legs hit the bed.

The bed!

Her lungs sucked in air as her pulse hammered away.

"You do remember the barn. I can see it all over your face." he bent his head purposefully, his hand reaching for the back of her neck.

Julie wanted it so badly. She wanted this strong, sexy man to kiss her like mad, to take possession of her body and make her forget everything else, but a nagging voice wailed in her head. Her life was a complete disaster. She just lost her father. She was being hunted by a crazy ex-boyfriend or her father's killer, maybe both. You don't find love in the middle of all that.

You find men who prey on women who don't have their shit together.

The thought had her pushing him away. "Whoa, hold on a minute. I was just putting on a show for your new brother-in-law," she said, standing taller and squaring her shoulders.

"He's not my brother-in-law until tomorrow," He corrected her, staring at her full breasts, then back to her lips.

"I'm going to take a shower," she said, sidestepping to get past Hank's wide shoulders. Walking to the dresser, she began digging in her overnight bag for her pajamas, flustered when she couldn't find what she wanted. Feeling like an idiot, she picked up the whole bag, went in the bathroom, and locked the door.

She sank down onto the toilet seat, clutching her bag, and breathed deeply as she closed her eyes. Sadness and fatigue surrounded her in a drenching wave. She was enjoying the sexual banter with Hank, then suddenly she saw herself as he must see her—a grieving, messed up woman with nowhere to go and just a handful of people who loved her.

Hank wasn't interested in her awesome personality. He was

a Navy officer who just happened to be sharing her bedroom tonight, and figured he may as well get lucky. Kill two birds with one stone. She knew his type well and had little respect for them. The familiar uniform just added insult to injury, pointing out what she should never have forgotten.

Hank Jared was not someone she could trust.

Julie stood and turned the hot water on full force as she began to undress. She resented the fact that she was stuck here, pretending to be someone she wasn't just to stay one step ahead of a nameless, faceless enemy. As the water sluiced over her skin, she shivered in spite of the heat. Her mind was full of images—a burned out hotel room, the window seat at Gwen's house, a rusty red generator and footprints in the snow.

She thought of the message from the safe deposit box as she let the water run down her bent head and shoulders. Her quick cryptanalysis in the car had begun to awaken memories of processes long since forgotten. She knew and understood every class of cipher ever popularized, from simple substitution and Masonics to the latest in computer generated random keys and transport layer security. Her mind played the options like notes on a score, trying different combinations and looking for patterns that would confirm or deny their collusion.

Grabbing a bar of sweet-smelling soap, she began to wash away the experience of the day while her mind raced through secret codes and memories. Something was bothering her about the message, interfering with her thoughts like a car parked in the middle of a freeway. There was a familiarity about the cipher that eluded her, ringing the faintest of bells in her jangled memory.

Frustrated with herself, she tried to stop focusing on it, hoping it would gather itself together in her subconscious and emerge as a coherent whole if she left it alone.

Julie turned off the water and opened the shower curtain, gazing through the steam at the bathroom door with annoyance. It was going to be a long night with Hank sleeping on the floor just feet from her bed. The thought of him in such close proximity made her pulse pick up, and she cursed her own attraction to the man.

Meant for Her

She dried her hair with the towel before wrapping it around her torso. The pajamas she'd frantically been searching for earlier were now clearly visible at the top of her duffle bag.
That figures.
An old favorite, they were knit of soft green cotton, with a boxy tee and wide pants that were about as alluring as a potato sack.
"Thank God for ugly pajamas," she said to herself.
The bedroom was dark when she emerged, with just a small nightlight in the bathroom behind her to light the way. Maybe he was already asleep. She stood still, waiting for her eyes to adjust to the inky blackness.
"I'm on the floor, between the bathroom and the bed. Don't step on me."
She could just make out the bed posts and began walking toward them in the darkness. Three steps in, she kicked something solid.
"Ouch!"
"Sorry!"
"Seriously? Because I didn't tell you exactly where I was?"
"I said I'm sorry."
"Well then, I guess it didn't hurt."
"Oh please, you're fine."
"You just kicked me."
"What are you, a baby? Because you're carrying on like one."
She heard him stand up in front of her. "You're calling me names, now?"
"If the shoe fits..." she was startled when he pulled her against him.
"Shut up, Julie," he said, kissing her roughly. She pushed against him half-heartedly, even as her mouth responded to his and kissed him back passionately. His hand slipped beneath her top to caress the bare skin of her back.

He hadn't meant to kiss her.
She had been playing games with him, flirting and retreating, and Hank didn't like games. While she was in the

Meant for Her

bathroom, he made the decision to keep their relationship professional. He had no intention of jeopardizing his career for Julie Trueblood.

That was, until she opened the bathroom door and he saw her body silhouetted in the light of the doorway, the thin fabric of her pajamas teasing him like the sexiest lingerie.

His body's response had been instantaneous.

This woman made him feel like he was in high school, all hormones and raging lust. He might die if he couldn't get close to her, couldn't rub her smooth skin and feel her body pressed against him.

Her breasts pushed at his bare chest, separated from him only by the light material, and his hand reach up in an intimate caress, making her moan. Her head fell back and he grabbed the hem of her shirt, lifting it upward.

Julie jumped back, recoiling from his hands. "I don't want to do this."

Hank's stare bored into her own in the dark room. "Liar," he said thickly. "You want to as much as I do."

Her chin lifted in denial and she opened her mouth to speak.

He didn't want to hear it. He was tired, he was aggravated, and he was bordering on crazy. He sank down on his makeshift bed before she could pretend she wasn't on fire, just like he was. "Goodnight, Julie."

She stood shock still for a moment before finishing her walk to the high poster bed, and scurried under the covers. "Goodnight."

The carpeted floor was rigid beneath Hank's frustrated form, and he punched the pillow in an attempt to get comfortable. He imagined resting his head on Julie's soft breasts instead, and knew that sleep would be hard to come by this evening.

"Just so you know, tomorrow's a big deal to me and my family. I'd appreciate it if you try to be a convincing girlfriend."

"What does that mean, exactly?"

"Pretend you like me, Julie. Don't cross your arms over your chest or walk away when I speak to you. Smile at me once in a while. Dance with me at the reception and hold my hand if you can stand the thought."

He was about to ask if she'd heard him, when she finally replied, "Okay."

"Okay, what?"

"I'll pretend to like you."

"Great. Thank you. I hope the experience isn't too painful for you."

"Goodnight, Hank."

"Goodnight, Julie."

The pungent smell of wood smoke burned Julie's nostrils and woke her from a sound sleep. She sat up in bed to a room she didn't recognize, completely alone and terrified. Reaching for the bedside lamp, she turned the switch and heard a click, but no light came on.

In the distance, someone laughed maniacally, and an old red generator appeared next to the bed, lit as if by a spotlight. Her father stood before her, his lifeless eyes staring at a fixed point on the wall. In his hands, he held a severed electrical cord. "Did you check the starter?" he asked.

Julie heard a piercing scream, but did not realize it was her own.

The bedroom door opened, and she could see leaping flames of orange and red violently consuming the hallway beyond. Gwen appeared through the wall of fire completely unscathed, and entered the room wearing an old-fashioned nurse's uniform.

"Telegram," said Gwen. "I have a telegram here for Julie McDowell."

"That's me," Julie said, but her aunt didn't seem to hear her. "That's me," she said again, but to no avail.

Next to the bed, the generator roared to life with a great shudder, and Julie pressed her hand to her frantically beating heart. She felt rich beading beneath her fingers and looked down at the bodice of a white wedding gown.

Hank!

She had to save Hank! She knew he was in this house, burning in the fire that had been meant for her alone. Desperate to find him, she threw back the covers on the bed and got up,

Meant for Her

standing face-to-face with a burned-out skeleton in a Navy officer's uniform.

The screaming wouldn't stop this time. Flames broke through the door to the bedroom. Nurse Gwen stood next to an eye chart emblazoned with the beginning of the cipher from the safe deposit box. "Cover your left eye, please. What does this say?" she asked Julie.

"I don't know! I don't know!" she wailed. The dead body in the Navy uniform grabbed at her arms, shaking her. "Get off of me! Let me go!" she wailed in horror.

"Julie!" Shouted the corpse. "Julie! Wake up! It's just a dream!"

"Get off of me! I have to find Hank!" she screamed, yanking her arms free of her captor and connecting with the solid bones of his face.

"Julie! It's me! It's Hank! Wake up!"

Hank was here? Confusion had her fiery dream evaporating into nothingness. Slowly the weight of her eyelids lifted and she saw Hank's face just inches from her own in the darkness.

Her hysterical screaming stopped, and a relief-stricken wail began. He was okay. He was safe from the fire. "You're all right," she said between great gasps of air.

He wrapped her into his arms, pulling her tightly against his chest as he spoke in a calming voice. "I'm fine. You were having a bad dream. Everything's okay now." He cuddled her against his warm body, gently stroking her hair.

"Everything was on fire. My father was there, and he was…" she tried to find the words to describe her gruesome vision, "burned. It was horrible."

Julie wiped her eyes, her hands shaking.

"How awful for you."

She realized that Hank had actually seen her father after the fire, and cringed at the thought. She didn't want to imagine what he had seen, didn't want to know he had seen it.

"There was a generator with a severed cord. And Gwen was there in a nurse's uniform, trying to give me a telegram."

"It sounds like your mind has had a lot to take in over the last couple of days."

"Yes." She snuggled closer to his chest, burying her face in his T-shirt.

"Was I in your dream?" he asked, his fingers tentatively stroking her shoulder. "You called my name."

"Yes," she said, suddenly shy. "I couldn't see you, but I knew you were in the building and the fire was going to get you. I was trying to save you." She left out the part about the wedding gown.

Hank gently rubbed her back and she felt her body slowly relax into the mattress. "Hank?"

"Mmm hmm?"

"Are we safe here?"

"Of course."

"Are you sure they don't know where we are?"

"I'm positive. No one followed us here, and I didn't tell anyone where we went." He hadn't even told Barstow, a fact which might come back to haunt him. "How else would someone know where we are?"

"I don't know."

Hank's brow furrowed as Julie settled back into the crook of his arm and fell back asleep.

If Julie was correct, then not only were she and Gwen in danger, but his entire family. Hank gave himself a mental shake. Her bad feeling could not be based in fact.

They hadn't been followed, of that he was certain. He had deliberately set the GPS to avoid expressways so he could better watch the cars around them. Still, his gut didn't like this. The people who Hank loved most were gathered in this house. Was it possible he had put them all in danger by bringing Julie and Gwen here?

He laid awake in the night, Julie curled by his side, for some hours after that. His eyes finally succumbed to sleep as the first light of Christmas Eve beckoned on the horizon.

Julie was gone when Hank woke up to rays of bright sunshine on his face. He'd have to remember to close the blinds

Meant for Her

tonight.

He caught a whiff of coffee on the air, his mind turning to the day ahead. There must be a million things to do, and they had let him sleep late. He pulled a green polo over his head and went to see what he could do to help.

Voices flowed up the stairway, the sound reminiscent of a million other family get-togethers. For a moment, he imagined his father downstairs with the others, talking and laughing over morning coffee. Hank's feet stilled on the top step, his eyes landing on the familiar photograph of him with his dad, fishing poles in their hands.

For just a moment, he was sure he could feel his father's comforting presence, smell the scent that belonged to him alone.

I love you, Dad.

Hank walked down the steps, smiling, suddenly certain his father would not miss Kelly's wedding after all.

"Well, look who finally decided to get out of bed," said Marianne. She was standing at the sink filling a large coffee urn with water, her warm smile contrasting her reproachful tone. "We were going to sneak in and take turns poking you with a stick in another half an hour."

"You should have woken me."

Gwen, Kelly and Julie sat at the table, working on something small with their hands. Julie stood up, flashing Hank a bright smile. "Merry Christmas Eve, sweetie," she said, leaning in for a quick peck on the lips. Hank's jaw dropped open. "Want some coffee?"

"That'd be great."

She walked to the counter and poured coffee from a Thermos. Hank watched as she put in one scoop of sugar and a small splash of milk. Someone had been paying attention when they stopped for coffee yesterday.

"Thanks," he said, taking the cup from her. He could get used to this.

"Gwen's making wedding bands for the ceremony today," said Julie.

"Just temporaries," said Gwen. "I don't think the bride and groom want to wear jewelry made out of paperclips forever."

"They're so beautiful, we just might," said Kelly. "Look, Hank."

She walked to him, holding something out for him to see. It was an intricate weaving of silver metal, strung with what appeared to be shining blue gemstones and glittering diamonds.

"That's incredible. You made that out of paperclips? What did you use for stones?"

"The colored ones are beads from Gwen's necklace, and the diamond-like ones are tiny crystals."

Hank eyed Gwen incredulously. "You just happened to have those things with you?"

"It was the strangest thing," said Gwen. "I was packing for our adventure and I stopped short as I was about to head downstairs. I forgot my beaded blue topaz necklace, I thought to myself. I hadn't intended to bring it, mind you. But after years of these kinds of thoughts you know when to listen."

She threaded a tiny blue bead onto a thick wire. "So I grabbed the necklace out of my jewelry box and asked the universe," she said dramatically, raising her head up high, "Is there anything else I need to bring? Then I thought about those crystals in my studio. So I grabbed those, too."

A chill ran up Hank's spine.

"Does that happen to you a lot?" asked Kelly, sitting back down.

Gwen touched the younger woman's hand on the table. "It does."

Next to Hank, Julie stepped on her tip toes and whispered in his ear. "Can opener." At his quizzical look, she nodded in Gwen's direction.

"The first time it ever happened, I was in college," said Gwen. "I was leaving my dorm room to go to class when I thought, 'Oh, I've forgotten my can opener.' I didn't need a can opener for class, of course." She took a sip of her coffee. "That day at lunch, a friend pulled out a can of soup, but had forgotten to bring a can opener. I said, 'That would explain why I brought this.'"

"That's amazing," said Kelly.

"It is. Very helpful, too," she said with a wink.

Meant for Her

Hank turned thoughtful eyes to Julie, remembering her concerns for their safety here at the house. "Does that ever happen to you?"

"Never."

"I'm afraid the universe lacks a large enough sledge hammer with which to hit my niece over the head," said Gwen.

"What's that supposed to mean?" asked Julie.

"It means you know more than you are willing to admit, even to yourself."

She cocked her head to the side. "Maybe. Maybe not."

Turning to Hank, she smiled and slipped her arm around his waist. "Can I help with anything today?"

He nearly spit coffee all over himself. "I have no idea." Just to see what she would do, he put his arm around her shoulders and pulled her close, dumbfounded when she settled pleasantly at his side. He shook his head. "What needs to be done, Ma?"

"More than you can possibly imagine. I have a list for you," she said, reaching to the bulletin board on the side of the refrigerator and handing him a piece of paper. He was oddly pleased to see his name scrawled across the top of it, just as he imagined it would be. "You're in charge of setting up the big things at the church hall. The tables and chairs, the buffet and the bar. Steve will go with you."

"I can handle that. Are the tables and chairs being delivered or do I need to pick them up?"

"Delivered. They should be there already. You need to go to the liquor store and stock the bar. Mid-shelf, Hank. No cheap stuff, nothing too expensive either." Marianne stirred an enormous pot with a spoon nearly three feet long.

"Julie, how would you feel about doing the decorations? I would head over there myself, but I need to stay here and work on the food."

"I'm almost done with these rings, Marianne. I'd be happy to give you a hand with the cooking," said Gwen.

"That would be wonderful," said Marianne, her shoulders dropping and a sigh escaping as she worked.

"And I," said Julie, "will decorate. What do you have in mind, Kelly?"

"A winter wonderland," she said excitedly. "The centerpieces are done, but not much else. The church hall was supposed to be vacant yesterday so I could get in there take care of it myself, but there was a funeral reception so nothing is finished. I have a lot of materials, but no real plans. There must be hundreds of yards of red ribbon alone."

"What else do you have?"

"Gold spray paint, white snow paint, oodles of fake snow, a few artificial Christmas trees, gold glitter, a whole mess of evergreen garland…"

"Julie," Hank interrupted. "I'm going to wash up so we can head over to the church. About fifteen minutes?" asked Hank.

"Sure. I'll be ready." She flashed him a radiant smile. "What do you have in mind for the head table?"

Julie pulled the door to the SUV closed behind her and reached for her notebook on the middle console. "Isn't Steve coming with us?" she asked.

"He's meeting us there."

She opened to a clean page, intending to work on the cipher, and found her thoughts drifting to her father. An unconscious frown came over her face.

"You okay?"

"This message is beginning to drive me crazy," she said, then decided to tell him the truth. "And I miss my dad. I miss my dad a lot."

He took the key out of the ignition and turned to face her. "I'm missing my dad a lot today, too."

She nodded, feeling tears begin to build up in her eyes. She didn't want to have this conversation with him, but she was wise enough to see that she needed it.

"It's been so busy, coming here. Everything that's going on. I haven't had a chance…"

"To mourn."

She nodded vigorously, an embarrassing sob escaping as she did.

"I just want to crawl under a rock and be alone for a while."

He bowed his head. "I know. I wish I could give you that

Meant for Her

chance." His lips pressed together in a thin line. "We could pretend you're sick, but I really would feel better if you were with me."

"I'd feel better, too. I'm just babbling."

He reached for her hand and held it. "You're not babbling. And you're entitled to feel however you feel."

She took a deep breath and took her hand back from Hank's, again reaching for the notebook in her lap.

"Chip," he said, digging in his pocket for his cell phone.

"He never called you back?"

"No."

This is Chip Vandermead. I can't take your call right now…

Hank sighed. "Chip, it's Hank. I'm getting worried. Call me when you get this." He hung up the phone and started the engine.

"Do you think she had the babies?"

"I don't know."

"What's the alternative?"

Hank's eyes met hers as he pulled out of the driveway. "I don't know that either. That's what worries me." He turned his windshield wipers on as snow began to collect on the glass. "Tell me something. If Chip can't crack that code, why are you so confident you'll be able to?"

"Gwen says it was meant for me. That my father wrote it, intending for me to be able to read it."

"Chip said that short codes are harder to break."

"As a rule, they are. Often it's impossible. But Gwen's right—if my father wanted me to be able to read this, he would have made sure to use a cipher or symbol I would recognize."

The moment she said the words, Julie froze. In the space of an instant, she understood what her subconscious had been trying to tell her since she first saw the secret message.

"Oh my God. Oh my God! A cipher I would recognize!" she yelled, clutching Hank's arm. "Let me use your phone, please!"

"What is it? What do you recognize?"

Grabbing Hank's phone, she opened the web browser and typed in the first six characters of the cipher from memory. Clever bastard, she thought, smiling at his ingenuity as she used the internet to quickly confirm what she already knew.

Meant for Her

"The first line of the cipher isn't part of his message at all. It's the beginning of a message that got King Leopold the Fourth executed for espionage in the Fourteenth Century!" she smacked his upper arm, a big grin lighting her face.

"Your father knew you would realize *that*?"

"He taught me the Leopold cipher when I was little. It was fun for a kid, because you make this decoder out of rings on a dowel. I brought it to show and tell."

"Sounds like a secret decoder ring."

"It is sort of, yes."

"So now you can decode the message."

Julie scoffed. "Not even close. Knowing the type of cipher is half the battle. I still need to break the code."

"Don't you just have to build the rings?"

"It's not that simple. They have to be aligned on an axle in the right order. There are thirteen factorial possible positions, which means millions of possibilities. That's the strength of the cipher."

"What do you do now?"

"I need to find the keyword. It will tell me what order to put the rings onto the axle. It could be a number, or a word or phrase." She was missing the vast capabilities of the computers that surrounded her when she was at work. "If I had access to my computers, I would write a simple program which tries out all possible combinations, then just wait until it hits on one that makes sense."

"How long does that take?"

"Hard to say. It depends on how lucky you are, and how many machines you have searching for the right combination simultaneously. Days, weeks, maybe months. It certainly would be a lot easier if I could figure out the combination on my own, in whatever way my father expected me to discover it." Julie bit down on her lip and looked out the window, unseeing.

Hank pulled into the parking lot of a small white church with a tall four-sided steeple. "This is it." Steve's sedan was already in the parking lot.

"Can I use your phone one more time? I'm going to have Becky use my work computers to search for the key."

"Sure."

When Hank waited for her to make her call, she looked at him uncomfortably. "I'll be right in."

She doesn't want me to hear her conversation.

Clearly she didn't trust him, which reminded him of Admiral Barstow and his own deception. If Julie knew who he worked for, he'd be guilty by association.

And what about her? Hank still wasn't sure if Julie sympathized with her father. She may even have helped him commit espionage, or deleted his Navy records. Was she working to hide important facts right now?

The unpleasant thought stuck with him as he walked to the door of the church and let himself in. The building appeared to be empty, its long wooden pews glistening in the light from the stained glass windows. Hank looked at the simple altar and the cross behind it, and found himself saying a silent prayer.

Please let her be innocent. Please let her trust me.

Chapter 5

Julie put her hands on her hips and surveyed her handiwork. The church basement had been greatly improved, but it was a far cry from "transformed".

"These lights have to go," she said.

Raising his head, Hank looked up at the fluorescent fixtures that ran the entire space. "The fluorescents?" he asked, raising his eyebrows high.

"They're horrible, aren't they? I feel like I'm shopping in a discount clothing store, not enjoying a winter wonderland with my one true love."

"Maybe Kelly and Ron are a couple of tree huggers. Maybe they *love* fluorescent lights. Maybe," he said, raising his index finger, "they'd be angry if you changed them."

"Just the other day," said Steve, taking a break from arranging tables, "I heard Kelly talking about how she hoped to be married under LEDs. But if that's not possible, I'm sure fluorescents are the next best thing."

"Marriage is all about compromise," agreed Hank.

Julie rounded on the men. Clearly, they were thick as thieves. "Do you two lunkheads think this is Kelly's dream? To celebrate her marriage to Ron under lights that give everything the horrible glow of energy efficiency?" she shift her weight onto one hip and crossed her arms. "I think not."

Hank rubbed the back of his neck. "What do you suggest?"

"How about candles?"

"Candles to light the whole space?" He spun around, holding his arms out to his sides. "Do you know how many candles that would take?"

"Is there a DJ coming? He might have some lights for the dance floor," said Julie.

"I don't know if there's a DJ, or a band, or the Boys Choir of Harlem."

"Who are you calling?"

"My mother," he said, walking to the far end of the room.

Julie busied herself by decorating the last Christmas tree

with red ribbon while she waited.

"There's a DJ, and he comes with his own light display. Including," his eyes lit up, "his very own spinning disco ball."

"Oh, well, you have to have a disco ball to do the Electric Slide."

"Bingo."

"All right. The DJ's lights should illuminate that half of the room fairly well, and the centerpieces each have one candle. We can bump that up to five or six..." her voice trailed off as she surveyed the large basement.

"That's still a hell of a lot of candles," said Hank.

"Sounds like a fire hazard," said Steve.

"Got a better idea?"

Hank snapped his fingers. "As a matter of fact, I do."

Two hours later, Julie finished hanging her last strand of white Christmas lights and stepped back to admire the room. Gone was the drab and depressing basement, and in its place glittered a gorgeous, romantic setting for the beginning of Kelly and Ron's life together. She also added four more candles to each centerpiece, not wanting to give up her idea completely.

Steve had been summoned back to the house to help deliver food to neighbors' ovens and refrigerators, and Julie was feeling his absence. He had acted as a buffer, and she wasn't sure what to do with Hank now that it was just the two of them.

He stood on a step ladder, connecting several strands of the twinkling lights to the center of the ceiling in a spoke-like pattern. Julie watched his beautiful body in silent appreciation, the muscles of his arms and shoulders clearly visible beneath his t-shirt. The gentle light that filled the room flattered him, glorifying his amber skin, and Julie savored the chance to observe him unnoticed.

In a different time and place, she could have cared for this man. She knew it like she knew her own face in the mirror. Julie had been looking for Hank Jared in every man she had ever met, and now she understood why each of them had left her cold and unaffected.

I never knew a man this good could care about me—know every skeleton in my closet and want me anyway.

Meant for Her

Hank stepped off the ladder to grab the last string of lights from the floor, climbing again to add it to the bundle. Raising his head, he caught her eye and smiled.

Julie felt her breath hitch in her chest as she stared at him from across the room. Her gaze spoke volumes that she herself would never give voice to, and she was waiting for his answer as they stared at each other. She knew she should look away, do something else. But that would break the spell, and it was a lovely, intoxicating magic to behold.

Moments slipped by before Hank picked up his tools and completed hanging the last of the lights. Julie didn't move, knowing he would come to her. They each felt it, and both were powerless to stop it.

Hank stepped down and strode toward her purposefully. He surprised her when he reached out with the gentlest of touches and stroked her face.

Closing her eyes, she leaned into his caress. Hank's hand went around to the back of her neck, his touch tingling on her skin like the lightest of raindrops. Julie opened her eyes, and seeing the desire she felt mirrored in his eyes, leaned toward him to enjoy the kiss that his talented fingers promised.

He drew her inside the circle of his arms. Their mouths met hungrily as hands skated over each other, exploring.

His beard raked over her smooth skin, leaving a trail of sensation in its wake. She could feel the evidence of how much he wanted her, and reveled in her own power to excite this man.

Someone coughed near the stairway, and the couple sprang apart. Julie turned her back in embarrassment when she saw the man standing there.

"Hank William Jared, I thought I told you not to go kissing girls in my church basement," he said with a thick Irish brogue. Tall and thin, he had white hair and an athletic build that contrasted with his heavily lined face.

"I must have forgotten," said Hank, shaking the older man's hand with a boyish grin. "Father McHale, I'd like you to meet Julie Trueblood. He reached for her arm, spinning her around. Julie, this is Father McHale. He's the priest who'll be marrying Kelly and Ron today."

A priest!

Julie wanted to melt into the concrete floor beneath her and die an invisible death. She heard herself say politely, "It's nice to meet you, Father."

To his credit, he didn't seem at all uncomfortable at having caught them in such a compromising position. "I'm also the priest who heard Hank William's first confession, when he was just a wee lad. I'm there in the confessional every Saturday, by the way." He rocked forward and back, with his hands behind him. "Or if you two are serious, perhaps we can have us a double ceremony." He winked conspiratorially at Julie.

I wish I was dead.

Father McHale looked around at the fully decorated church basement. "I must say, this looks wonderful."

"Thank you," they said in unison.

"Oh, and Hank, your mother called. She'd like you to call her back. Seems your cell phone must not get a signal down here."

"Son of a..." he pulled out his cell phone. "Sorry, Father. I've been waiting for an important call."

"I must be on my way. I have to see about building a roulette wheel for Monte Carlo night," said the priest. "I'll see you both at the ceremony." He walked back up the steps.

"Can I meet you in the parking lot, Julie? I need to see if Chip called."

"Sure. I'll be right there."

By the time she made it to the car, Hank was behind the wheel with the engine running.

"Is everything okay?" she asked.

"I missed his call."

"Did he leave a message?"

When he didn't answer, she thought she was being presumptuous. "It's none of my business."

"It is your business." He backed out of the parking spot. "His wife had the twins. They're fine, but she hemorrhaged after the birth."

"Oh, my God. Is she going to be okay?"

"They're not sure yet."

Meant for Her

That wasn't all Chip had said on his message, but it was all Hank was prepared to share. The rest, he was going to pretend he never heard.

Julie gazed at her reflection in the mirror and bit her lip. The dress was a deep blue silk that clung to her body in the most flattering of places, grazing her hips and cinching in tight under her accentuated breasts. The skirt billowed out around her legs with a feminine flourish, stopping just above her shapely ankles.

While the neckline and hem were modest, the dress was racier that Julie would have liked for a wedding. She vaguely remembered Hank telling her to pack something appropriate, but she was crazy out of her mind after seeing the footprints leading from the barn. She had reached into the closet and grabbed several dresses, figuring one of them would be fine.

She glanced wistfully at the other two outfits that hung in the closet. The first was a safe and boring pink sundress, which would have been perfect if it were June instead of December. The second was a blazer and skirt combination that was far better suited to a funeral or job interview—perhaps a job interview at a funeral parlor—than a celebration of love.

Which left the dress she was wearing. Flaunting might be a better word.

No one will be looking at me anyway, except Hank.

At the thought, she relaxed her shoulders and tried to see herself as Hank would see her. Twirling slightly and smiling at her reflection, Julie's fears were confirmed. This dress had no business at a wedding. Unless maybe it was worn by the bitter ex-girlfriend of the groom.

There was a soft rap on the door. "May I come in?" asked Gwen.

"Yep."

Gwen's mouth dropped open. "You look incredible!"

"I look like a French whore."

"You most certainly do not." She grabbed Julie's arms and held them out to her sides. "You look like a fine and cultured woman, who just happens to have a glorious body."

Julie felt the first stirrings of pride at Gwen's assessment.

She turned toward the mirror and twisted to see the back of the dress in the mirror. "You don't think it's too much?"

"Well, it is breathtaking. But Kelly's a fine-looking young woman and I don't expect you'll be stealing the bride's thunder, so to speak."

"It wasn't the bride I was worried about."

"Ah. Hank." Gwen gave Julie a conspiratorial smirk. "It might be a bit too much for Hank."

"I'll wear the pink one," Julie said, reaching for the mundane sundress. "Maybe Kelly or Marianne has a sweater I can put over..."

"I said it may be too much for Hank. I didn't say you should change."

"I'm not comfortable."

"On second thought, you're right. You should change. You wouldn't want that tall, dark and incredibly sexy man to lust after you."

Julie slowly turned from the closet, one hand on the pink sundress. "You think he'd lust after me if I wore this?" she asked, looking down at the blue silk number and brushing an imagined piece of lint off its fine surface.

"Definitely."

"Well," she said, peeking at herself in the mirror, "he is my boyfriend."

"You want him to be happy, of course. I just love weddings," she said wistfully. "Don't you?"

Julie nodded as she walked to the dresser and began brushing her hair. "I remember your wedding, Gwen. It was beautiful."

"It was."

If ever two people complimented each other, it was David and Gwen. They had made a striking couple—she with her curling blonde hair, smooth complexion and soulful blue eyes, he like a sandy-haired Greek god, all muscle and sinew.

"Did I ever tell you how we met?" asked Gwen.

Julie squinted her eyes. "No, I don't think so."

Gwen sat down on the bed. "I was living in New York City. The first time I saw him, he was sitting on an upside-down milk

Meant for Her

crate in Hell's Kitchen, holding a cello and a bow. I figured he was a street musician."

She had a far-away look in her eyes as she continued. "A red-headed girl was coming toward him from the opposite direction, and she asked him if he was going to play. 'Not right now,' he said, and she says, 'No one will give you money if you just sit there." Gwen laughed.

"He told her he didn't want anyone to give him money, he was just listening to the music of the street. I remember I loved how he said that."

"Wasn't he a composer?"

She nodded. "For movies, mostly. I was getting close to them now, and he turned to me with this beautiful smile and said, 'Would you like to hear a song?' Before I could answer, the red-head says, 'I thought you weren't going to play.' And I'll always remember," she said, putting her hand to her heart, "he said, 'That was before the most beautiful woman in the world tried to walk right by me, and all I had to stop her was a cello.'"

Julie sat next to her aunt, placing her arm around Gwen's shoulders. "That sounds just like him."

Gwen nodded, reaching up to hold Julie's hand. "We were inseparable after that. We never spent a single night apart, not from that very first day."

"Do you think you'll ever get married again?"

She shook her head. "No."

"Why not?"

"It's like that old saying. Lightning doesn't strike the same place twice. It was unbelievable that it happened the first time. I'm certainly not expecting it to happen again."

Chapter 6

"Son of a bitch!" Hank swore, shaking his injured index finger. "I have an idea," he said sarcastically, "let's use a giant, three-inch needle to hold a little tiny flower onto our jackets."

"Let me help," said Marianne. She took the pin and expertly attached the boutonnière to the lapel of his tuxedo on the first try.

Feeling like an awkward teenager, Hank gave her a pained grin. "Thanks, Ma."

"You're welcome," she said, brushing at the fabric of his tuxedo. "Now where's Kelly? We have to get this show on the road or the groom is going to beat us to the church!"

"If he shows up," Hank said under his breath.

"That is not funny."

"Of course it's funny." He looked at his mother as if she were crazy, earning him a playful slap on the back of his head.

Marianne walked to the stairway. "Kelly, we have to go!"

A pair of white pumps emerged onto the landing of the staircase. Kelly's dress was pure white, its length held up in her hands as she descended the stairs, exposing a layer of tulle. The fabric glistened with fine beading and just a touch of shimmering iridescent sequins, spread in clusters throughout the skirt. The bodice was strapless, its fabric wound in an elaborate knot that fell in a sweetheart neckline, complimenting her figure. As her glowing face came into view, Hank could see she wore her hair up in a fancy and delicate style, her only jewelry a shimmering purple stone on a fine gold chain.

"Oh, Kelly." His mother was crying. He could hear it in the tone of her voice. "You look wonderful." She held her youngest daughter. "My baby's getting married."

"I love you, Mom."

"I love you, too."

Kelly made a strangled little sound. "I miss Dad."

"Me, too." Marianne released her and squeezed her upper arms.

Kelly nodded and wiped at her eye makeup. Hank swallowed the knot that was forming in his throat and opened the last remaining box from the florist. Inside was a large teardrop bouquet of bright yellow roses and purple poppies.

His father had tended a yellow rose bush in the backyard for twenty years, just so he could share the blooms with his wife. The flowers reminded all the Jared children of their dad.

Hank handed the bouquet to his sister and kissed her gently on the cheek. "You look beautiful, Kelly."

"Thanks."

"Last chance," he said, determined to lighten the mood. "You want me to get you the hell out of here?" he smiled at his kid sister, so grown up and gorgeous. "No questions asked. I'll take you to Disneyland, Tahiti, wherever you want to go."

Kelly grinned despite her tears. "Nope."

"You sure?"

"Yep."

"Okay then." Hank gave his sister a tight squeeze. He lifted his head and saw Julie standing in the doorway, her hair falling in soft curls around her slender shoulders, the blue dress flowing along her body, and his heart stopped beating. "Wow."

Julie blushed. "Do you like it?" She raised her arms and spun in a circle.

"You look amazing."

She walked over to him and planted a kiss right on his lips. "Thank you."

Hank's eyes went dark as he snaked an arm around her waist and held her against him. "You're welcome," he said softly.

"All right, you two. Get in the car. We are going to be on time," Marianne said with purposeful optimism. Despite her firm tone, a secretive smile graced her lips as she ushered Hank and Julie out the door.

The way Julie saw it, she had one single day to be Hank Jared's girlfriend, and she was damn sure going to make the most of it.

"Can I get you anything?" he asked.

It was the second time Hank had come by the table where Julie and Gwen's sat. Julie was disappointed when she realized they weren't sitting together, but soon discovered the separation

Meant for Her

gave them a chance to stare at each other across the crowded room like they were in the high school cafeteria.

Each time she caught his eye, she felt brazen and bold; each time she caught him watching her, she was excited and unnerved.

"I think we're good. Your mother is an incredible cook," said Julie.

"This gravy is positively scrumptious," agreed Gwen.

"I'm going to move to this table after I dance with Kelly."

"You don't need to, Hank," said Julie. She didn't want to disrupt the wedding in any way.

"I want to." He looked at her, his face clearly showing her he spoke the truth, and she got a funny feeling in her stomach. "Kelly doesn't mind," he added, correctly guessing the reason for her refusal.

"Okay then."

"Sure I can't get you a drink?"

"Kamikaze, on the rocks," said Gwen, reaching between them and handing Hank her empty glass.

"You got it, lady."

"On second thought, I will take a drink. Something fruity and tropical."

"Coming right up." Hank walked to the bar and Julie's eyes followed him all the way there.

"My boyfriend has a great butt."

"Indeed."

The dinner music was an eclectic mix of 70s and 80s pop, and Julie's brow furrowed when Tommy Tutone's 867-5309 began to play.

"What's the matter?" asked Gwen.

"Every time I hear a number, I think I should try it in the cipher. Not because I think it will work, but because I have absolutely no idea what will."

"You'll know when it's the right one." Gwen took a sip of her water. "Doesn't it have to be thirteen digits or something?"

Julie shrugged. "Not really. If a key isn't long enough, you just put the leftovers in order at the end. Like for 867-5309, it doesn't have a one, two, four, ten, eleven, twelve or thirteen in it. So those numbers would go at the end."

Meant for Her

"Isn't that clever."

"It works the same way for word keys. Take the letters of the alphabet that aren't in the keyword and tack them on at the end of the word, in alphabetical order."

"Ladies and gentlemen," said the DJ, "may I call your attention to the front of the room, where Mr. and Mrs. Sorenson are about to cut the cake." James Taylor's "How Sweet It Is" came on in the background as Kelly and Ron fed each other wedding cake with guarded movements, laughing.

"I imagine a cultural anthropologist would be an interesting date to have at a wedding," said Gwen.

"Why is that?"

"Look at these crazy rituals we engage in. Feeding each other cake. The throwing of the garter and the bouquet. Makes me wonder where it all came from."

"I don't think they do the garter and the bouquet anymore."

"Aw, really?" Gwen's disappointment was obvious. "Why not?"

"Sexist maybe."

"Oh, pooh. Some people take themselves far too seriously."

Hank returned with the drinks.

"Thank you, dear." She whispered in Julie's ear, "I was hoping to catch the bouquet, you know," then she winked.

In the end it was Ron who played dirty first, dabbing cake on the end of Kelly's nose. That move earned him an ear full of yellow fondant, and buttercream frosting on the better part of his tuxedo vest.

"I have to go get ready for my dance with Kelly. I'll see you ladies in a little bit."

"Break a leg," said Julie, leaning in to kiss him on the cheek.

"You two make a very handsome couple," said Gwen as he walked away.

"If only."

"If only? Why if only?

Julie looked at her like she had amnesia. "We're not really together, remember? I was just thinking…" she let her voice trail off.

"That you wouldn't mind if he really were your boyfriend."

Meant for Her

"Dangerous thought, right?"

"I think it's a splendid thought. Hank Jared is a good man. He's handsome, comes from a good family. What's so dangerous about that?"

"He's a Navy investigator."

"Oh, yes. And in your book, that's akin to being an errand boy for Satan."

Julie rolled her eyes. "I didn't say that. It's just that I don't know where his loyalties lie."

Gwen took a sip of her Kamikaze. "Do you think his interest in you extends beyond your ability to decode the cipher?"

"That's what I'm worried about. I don't know for sure."

"You don't trust him."

"No."

"Are you basing that on reality, today? Or are you basing it on your past experiences with officers in the Navy?"

Julie watched several guests posing for pictures at the next table. "Probably past experiences."

"It would be a shame to convict that man of crimes he hasn't committed, even if the only punishment is the impossibility of a real relationship between the two of you. You have the spark. I can see it. The chemistry between you is popping."

Julie fingered the spruce centerpiece. "You might be right." She dropped the foliage and stood, grabbing her purse. "I'm going to the ladies room. I'll be back."

"I'll be here."

Gwen took a sip of her drink, enjoying the tang of triple sec and lime. She usually chose to drink wine, but special occasions merited special pleasures, and there was nothing she enjoyed more than a wedding. True love—particularly between young people like Kelly and Ron—was a sheer joy to witness.

She could see the love between Hank and Julie, too, glowing like the tiniest ember. If it was carefully fanned, its flames could roar to life and keep them toasty warm for years to come, but at this stage it was just as easily extinguished.

Gwen planned to do what she could to send careful breezes their way.

Her love for her niece was fierce and strong, and she had

Meant for Her

long hoped for Julie to find true love like she herself experienced with David.

She watched Ron and Kelly dance their first dance together, as her memory flashed back to a picnic in the mountains, off a trail she and David frequently hiked together not far from the house. They had eaten mangos, rice salad and stuffed radicchio, drinking ice cold sake from Japanese cups. They made love in the woods, their picnic blanket spread on the ground, their clothes littering the forest floor.

David Beaumont was beautiful a way that only young men can ever be, his sculpted runner's body lithe and agile, his skin at once both supple and rough. Gwen wondered now what her husband would have looked like at forty-five, the age he would be now had he lived. If he aged like his father, he would only have grown more handsome, with smile lines instead of wrinkles and streaks of light gray hair to accentuate his chiseled features.

"I'm back," said Julie.

Across the dance floor, the DJ stood with Hank and Kelly. "Ladies and gentlemen, as most of you know, Kelly's father passed away several years ago, so he isn't here today to dance with his little girl. Hank Jared, brother of the bride, will be standing in his father's place." The crowd clapped quietly, as Luther Vandross' "Dance With My Father" began to play.

Julie tried not to cry as she watched Kelly struggle to do the same. Hank spoke to his sister, making her smile as he pulled her into his arms. Julie was spellbound by the lyrics of the song, grief for her own father rising up, choking her.

How lucky Kelly was to have Hank to lean on, to make her smile in the middle of such a difficult moment. Watching him talk to his sister as he gracefully moved her around the dance floor, Julie wished for that man with all the concentration and might of a child wishing on a star.

The song ended and Hank wrapped Kelly in a tender embrace before kissing her on the forehead and walking her back to her new husband. Julie watched him take his drink off the head table and make a bee-line back to where she sat with Gwen. As he come closer, she stood to embrace him.

Hank held her, letting her be the first to let go.

"The song," he said.

Julie nodded.

"I'm sorry."

"No. Don't be. It was beautiful." She wanted to tell him that Kelly was lucky to have him as a brother, but she was too choked up to get the words out. Hank's eyes met hers, then he kissed her on the forehead as he had done his sister, and she clung to him again, reveling in the comfort of his arms.

Lifting her head, she said simply, "Thank you." Then kissed him on the mouth, as if it was the most natural thing in the world. When they separated, their hands remained together.

"Would you like to dance?" asked Hank.

"No, not yet. I'm waiting for the Electric Slide."

"A girl after my own heart."

It wasn't long before the DJ played the wedding classic. Marianne stood and raised both hands to the sky, giving a loud holler as she headed for the dance floor. She pulled family and friends with her as she went, grabbing Hank by the arm and pointing in Julie's direction. He did as he was told, heading over to collect her, and she graciously met him halfway to the dance floor.

As they stepped and clapped in unison, Julie couldn't remember ever having so much fun at a wedding reception. Gwen's loud, "Boogie woogie woogie," could be heard over the music, making Julie laugh and smile so wide her face hurt.

None of this is real, she reminded herself. Like Cinderella at the ball, her greatest fantasy was doomed to disappear when the clock struck midnight, leaving this dream in tatters.

Enjoy the ball while you can. Especially that prince.

As if he could hear her thoughts, Hank caught her eye and smiled a wolf's grin. There was a promise therein, that he would come to her if she allowed it. Julie felt her heart leap, pulse pounding, breath coming fast. The music ended and Julie stared back at him meaningfully, then looked pointedly at the door that led out of the basement.

She went first, knowing he would follow.

The air outside was cool. It was warm for December, but she could still see her breath hanging in little puffs. Footsteps behind her and she turned around, almost lunging into Hank's waiting arms. Their mouths met hungrily, Julie struggling to get closer, pressing her body to his and angling her head to return his passionate kisses.

"I can't keep my hands off you." He kissed her neck and shoulder.

Julie was lost in him, the flavor of his mouth and the smell of his skin. Were they really standing in a church parking lot, making out like teenagers? She felt naughty and daring, the emotions only increasing her excitement. She lifted her head and ran her hands in his thick dark hair.

"I think I like being a convincing girlfriend," she said between kisses.

His mouth stilled against hers, his hands stopped their exploration of her body, and he pulled back.

"Whoa." He reached behind his neck to remove her arms. "You sure had me fooled."

The tone of his voice set off warning bells in Julie's head, yet she didn't understand just what she had done. "What's the matter?"

"I'm not a toy, Julie."

"What?"

He rubbed his hand roughly along his lips. "I'm not here for your amusement."

She felt as if she'd been slapped. Hank knew they were just pretending. So why was he so angry? It wasn't like he was really hurt, because he didn't care about her one way or the other. This was all a façade.

"I'm sorry if I offended you," she said, bewildered. "I thought you wanted me to be convincing." Julie stood rigidly still, suddenly chilled by the cold night air.

"We should get back," said Hank, his jaw set.

Julie looked at him beseechingly, already missing their earlier closeness. She wanted to understand why he was upset, her scrambled thoughts not making any sense. She opened her mouth to speak, but couldn't decide exactly what to say.

The door behind her opened and Ron appeared. "There you are. Kelly's about to throw the bouquet. Marianne insisted I find

Meant for Her

you two."

"We'll be right there." The door closed behind Ron. Hank smiled widely and offered his arm. "Ready, honey?"

The sarcasm wasn't lost on Julie, and she pouted, narrowing her eyes at him. She could play this any way he liked. Unless he tried to kiss her again. *That would definitely not be happening.*

She mirrored his confident grin and took his arm. "Of course, sweetheart. I wouldn't miss it for the world."

He walked her inside and deposited her back at her table before walking off. Gwen smiled widely and handed Julie one of two full Kamikazes.

"Welcome back!" shouted Gwen over the increasingly loud music.

"Thanks," she said, taking a long swig of the potent cocktail.

"Lover's quarrel?"

"Something like that."

"You look like you've been making out in the backseat of a Chevy." Gwen laughed at her own joke, and Julie used her hands to try to straighten her hair.

It was no use. "I'm going to the ladies room." She stood up to leave just as Marianne came up behind them.

"All the single ladies! That means you two!" said Marianne.

Gwen hopped out of her chair with a flourish. "I'm ready."

"I was just going to the ladies room," said Julie.

"Nonsense, you look fine," said Gwen, steering her toward the dance floor as she winked at Marianne. "I just love the tossing of the bouquet. Such tradition! I'm so glad they don't mind being sexist."

"I think I'm going to be sick," said Julie, then she downed the rest of her drink in one long gulp. Shaking her head, she worked to change her attitude. Hank Jared was not going to ruin her evening. She did some boxing moves, bobbing and weaving. "Let me at 'em. Lookout, all you eligible bachelors!" She put her arm around Gwen as they made their way to the dance floor. "The Trueblood women are on the prowl!"

They took their place on the dance floor with several teenage girls, a beautiful brunette, three bridesmaids and a matronly woman with black frizzy hair. One of the bridesmaids turned and rolled her shoulder away from the onlookers as she covered her face.

Julie felt her pain.

The DJ played a drum roll, and Kelly turned her back to the dance floor.

Please, don't let me catch that damn thing.

Then it was airborne, ribbons trailing behind it like a missile's tail. The bouquet bounced off the clawing fingers of a bridesmaid and headed for the frizzy-haired woman, ricocheting off her bust and landing squarely in Julie's begrudging arms. She looked at the roses and pansies like they were a pipe bomb waiting to explode.

"Woo hooo!" screamed Gwen, laughing. "Way to go, Julie!"

Across the room, Hank leaned on the bar and ordered a scotch on the rocks. Damn if she didn't look beautiful, clutching those flowers like she wished the ground would open up and swallow her whole. So sweet and innocent.

Too bad it's all an act.

"Looks like you have some garter-catching to do," said his mother, sitting down on a barstool beside him. "A glass of your best Chardonnay, please," she said to the bartender.

"I hear it's all mid-shelf. No cheap stuff, but nothing great," said Hank.

"Bastards," she answered, smiling. She squeezed Hank's hand. "Thanks for everything you've done for the wedding. Your father would be proud."

"Thanks, Ma."

"Trouble in paradise?"

He took a sip of his drink and chewed on an ice cube. "Didn't you hear? That was just a reasonable facsimile of paradise. Not the real thing."

"Looked pretty real to me."

Hank motioned to the bartender. "Julie is a fabulous actress."

"I see." Marianne squared her shoulders to face her son, her head tipped to the side. "It must be confusing for her, pretending to be your girlfriend."

Meant for Her

"Why is that?"

"Because she has very real feelings for you."

Hank scowled at his mother. "I think you're mistaken."

"Hank," she said softly, "a woman can tell these things. And that young lady," she gestured to Julie across the room, "is completely taken with you."

When his mother walked away, Hank turned back to scan the room and saw her. She was standing with Gwen next to the dance floor, watching anxiously as the single men assembled for the throwing of the garter.

Ron made his way to the front of the dance floor, Kelly's garter in-hand, and some possessive instinct had Hank up and on his feet before he could think better of it. Julie caught his eye as he assumed his place in the group of men on the dance floor, bending his knees like a baseball player in the outfield.

"Don't worry, baby," he yelled to Julie. "I used to play shortstop."

Ron turned his back to the men and threw the garter over his shoulder, which bounced off the low ceiling and landed on the opposite side of the floor. A young blonde man snatched it up and held it in the air victoriously with a loud cheer.

Without missing a beat, Hank walked over and opened his wallet, handing him a hundred dollar bill and taking the garter as the crowd laughed and cheered.

Hank swung his prize around on one outstretched finger, eyeing Julie like a cat eyes a mouse. A warm flush spread from her face to her chest, and he realized he was excited to put the garter on her leg, even if a hundred people were watching.

Anything just to touch her.

A chair appeared in the middle of the dance floor, and the DJ ushered Julie to the seat. For a moment she hid her face behind the bouquet, then bit her lip and forced her hands down into her lap. The theme from Mission Impossible began to play and laughter erupted again.

Hank paced in front of her, planning his attack. Stealthily he walked toward her and kneeled, then he lightly stroked his finger along the blue silk up her knee, exposing her calf.

He uncrossed her legs and took off her shoe, feeling her

anxiety in the way she held herself. When he surprised her by tickling her foot, she shrieked, the crowd laughing along with her. He slipped the garter onto her ankle and began inching it upward.

Julie shot him a warning look as he passed her knee, prompting him to look at the crowd for guidance. The hoots and hollers egged him on, as he knew they would. He pushed the lace and ribbon up onto her thigh, his eyes connecting with hers once again. As she looked at him, he felt her legs relax and open to him the slightest bit, the look on her face offering him the world.

Hank had never wanted a woman as much as he wanted Julie in that moment. He felt his fingers tremble. He gave the garter one last pull high on Julie's thigh, snapping it against her skin and watching her flinch. Then he retreated, pulling her dress back down as he went. He stood and helped Julie to her feet before he kissed her, his lips on hers clearly saying, *to be continued.*

Chapter 7

Snowflakes began to fall as Kelly and Ron waved goodbye from the window of the white stretch limousine, a large "Just Married" banner hanging from its trunk.

Hank stood in the cold and watched the tail lights disappear into the night. Norah and Steve had headed home an hour earlier, anxious to get back to their lives in Boston.

That meant there was another bedroom available at the house, if he chose to use it. Hank suspected Julie would share his bed tonight if he asked her.

He knew it was wrong to sleep with someone he was protecting as an officer of the Navy, someone who might be involved in this case more than he would like. Hell, who was he kidding? She was definitely involved. It was just a matter of degree. Hank shivered in the cold and cursed the situation.

The church doors behind him opened and closed.

"Hi," said Julie.

And he knew.

Julie Trueblood had gotten under his skin, maybe even into his heart. How the hell had that happened? Why did it have to be this woman who affected him so strongly?

He turned to see her standing on the steps of the church, her blue dress swirling in a light breeze, snowflakes twirling in the air between them.

"Merry Christmas, Hank," she said, smiling lightly. "It's just after midnight."

He would remember this moment always—how she looked—how it tore him up inside. "Merry Christmas, Julie."

"Are you ready?"

"Yeah."

"Your mom needs some help loading up the car." Julie opened the church door and waited for him to come inside. "Kelly and Ron get off okay?"

Hank nodded. "They said goodbye."

"It was a good day," she said, smiling at Hank and resting her hand on his back as they headed downstairs together. "You did good, Hank."

"We all did." They reached the bottom of the stairwell and Hank held the door for her.

An hour later, the group walked into Marianne's kitchen. Julie slipped off her high heels and covered a yawn. "I'm exhausted."

"Me too. Let's go to bed," said Hank.

Julie's head snapped up at his suggestion. "I need a few minutes to unwind."

Marianne opened a cupboard and withdrew a round bottle. "Nightcap, anyone?"

"Chambord," said Gwen appreciatively as she pulled back a chair. "Absolutely."

"Yes, please," said Julie.

"Why not," said Hank, closing his eyes.

"If you're tired, you can go ahead," said Julie.

"I got my second wind."

Marianne stifled a laugh as she poured the drinks into cordial glasses. They were a heavy cut crystal in pale pink, each one shaped like a tiny vase.

"Marianne, these are precious," said Gwen.

"They were my mother's."

"Just lovely. Really."

Hank thought of the china cabinet in the dining room, chock full of crystal, and wondered how long the women were going to stay up.

Julie rubbed her neck with her hand, and Hank saw his opening, walking behind her to rub her shoulders. She made little sounds of pleasure as he worked her tired muscles, her skin warm and smooth beneath his strong hands.

"Sure you don't want to go to bed?" he whispered in her ear.

Julie straightened her shoulders abruptly and lightly shook off his hands. He stepped away, his ego stinging from her response.

"It has been a long day. I think I am going to go to bed," he said.

"Goodnight, Hank," said Julie sweetly.

Once upstairs, he undressed in a huff. Hank had wrestled with his conscience and fully committed himself to breaking the rules, only to realize that Julie had no intention of coming to bed with him.

What kind of game was she playing? It seemed her affection was directly related to the size of their audience. He shouldn't have listened to his mother. He had been right all along. Julie was playing the role he had asked her to play, and was not interested in a real relationship with him.

"Stupid, stupid, stupid," he said to himself as he stepped into the shower. He let the hot water run over his head and flow down his face before he grabbed a bar of soap and worked up a heavy lather on his arms and chest. His mind replayed their kisses outside the reception hall and his body responded to the memory.

Was she really just pretending? Hadn't she felt even a portion of what he felt?

The rest of his body got the same punishing treatment with the soap before he turned off the water and hastily dried his body. He was a grown man, damn it, and these games were making him crazy. Hank pulled on a clean pair of black briefs and considered grabbing a T-shirt and shorts out of deference to Julie.

She can close her damn eyes if she doesn't like it.

Throwing back the covers on the bed, he dropped onto the cold sheets and waited for her to come in. It was nearly an hour before she did—time that did nothing to improve Hank's mood. He watched as she closed the door as quietly as possible and tiptoed into the room.

"I was starting to think you were sleeping on the couch."

In the darkness he saw her straighten to her full height. "I was talking with your mom and Gwen."

"You were avoiding coming to bed with me."

She didn't answer him.

"Why, Julie?" His eyes were adjusted to the dim light of the room, and he saw her cross her arms over her chest as he waited for a response. When none came, he asked again, "Why are you avoiding me?"

She snapped at him. "Because you don't really like me

Meant for Her

anyway, and I don't want to sleep with someone who…"

"Whoa, wait a minute. I don't really like you anyway? What are you talking about?" Hank swung his legs out of bed and walked toward her.

She stepped backwards and bumped into a dresser. "This whole charade. You pretending to like me."

"I do like you, Julie."

"No, not like that. Like a man likes a woman."

"I do like you like a man likes a woman."

"No," she said, shaking her head. "I'm not being very clear."

Hank reached out and stroked his hand down her arm.

"Please don't touch me," she said, recoiling. "I'm trying to make you understand."

"I understand. You think I don't like you like a man likes a woman, but you're wrong."

"I know you're attracted to me, Hank, and I'm attracted to you, too. That's not what I'm talking about."

Now he was confused. He furrowed his brow. "Go ahead."

"You want to have sex with me, but you don't really care about me."

Silence filled the room.

Julie let out a huff and moved to step around him.

His hand on her arm stopped her. "Wait." His fingers trailed slowly down her arm. "I do care about you." He stepped closer, his scent invading her senses. "Enough to get involved when every rule the Navy has, and every rule I have for myself, tells me not to."

His words lulled her closer, tempting her with their promise. Her shaking fingers skimmed his chest, reaching higher until her hand curved around his broad shoulder. With the lightest pressure she pulled him to her, his mouth finding hers with unerring accuracy in the darkness.

She tasted like berries and spicy mint, and Hank leaned into her. He thought he could remain unaffected, aloof, enjoying her body and the pleasure she offered without involving his heart. She brought him to a place he had never been before, where bodies melded and feelings entwined, inseparable from one another. They met on a battlefield, a firestorm of emotional

Meant for Her

victory and defeat, where he fought for self preservation and was beaten down, rising stronger, more powerful, having opened his heart to love.

Julie hummed to herself as she poured a cup of coffee. She had woken up in Hank's arms, the sunlight streaming in from the window, feeling content and happy. Carefully lifting his arm, she slipped out of bed and lowered the blinds so Hank could continue to sleep, then dressed and headed downstairs to see what the day held in store.

She had always been a morning person, enjoying the feeling of the entire day laid out before her. On the rare occasion she slept in, she usually felt sluggish and off her game. This morning, the house was deserted, and Julie didn't know if Gwen and Marianne were still sleeping or if they were doing other things. Gwen had little respect for time in general, and could be found sleeping or awake when least expected, so Julie had learned not to assume anything.

An unopened box of chocolate-covered doughnuts beckoned her, and she thought about helping herself to one or two. She was starving, and wondered if a night of passionate lovemaking was to blame for her terrific appetite. Her manners wouldn't allow her to open the doughnuts, so she rummaged through the cupboards until she found an already opened box of Lucky Charms.

She had loved that cereal since she was a little girl, though she only ever ate the marshmallows. Reaching for the box, a memory flashed through her mind.

Her mother was leaning over, a golden locket dangling from her neck to Julie's young face. "It's my good luck charm," she said.

"Why is it good luck?"

"When I was fourteen, I fell in love with your father. He was eighteen, and my mother wouldn't let me see him because he was so much older."

"He enlisted in the Navy, and he asked my parents if he could send me letters. He didn't want my mother to know what

Meant for Her

he was saying, so he wrote in code. Your father always loved codes," she laughed, fingering the locket.

"He used numbers to stand for letters in the alphabet, then he made pictures around the outside of the paper with dots. The number of dots in each line stood for that letter of the alphabet."

"That's so cool."

"Yes. My mother thought he was quite an artist, all those decorative lines around the page. Only I knew the truth. He hid his love for me in the designs on the page."

Julie fingered the locket, for the first time noticing the dimpled dots that comprised its decoration. "Is this a code?" she asked, mesmerized.

"It is."

"What does it say?"

"It says, 'Beautiful'." Her mother smiled and Julie thought she was indeed the most beautiful woman in the world.

Frantic now, Julie put down the box of cereal and searched the room for a piece of paper. She saw a magnetic notepad on the refrigerator and hastily reached for it.

Down the left-hand side she wrote out the letters of the alphabet; next to them she numbered one through twenty-six. Across the bottom she wrote BEAUTIFUL, then she wrote the corresponding number below each letter. Some of them were two digits. In the end, she was staring at thirteen individual numbers.

"Oh, my God, Oh, my God, Oh, my God," she whispered to herself, staring at what she knew was the key to deciphering the code from the safe deposit box. She needed to tell Hank. She turned to head for the bedroom when a cell phone on the counter in front of her began to vibrate. She glanced at the screen.

ADMIRAL BARSTOW

Time stood still. Julie was paralyzed, betrayal surrounding her like a thick smoke. The phone continued to vibrate as panic rose up like bile. Barstow was calling Hank, and there could only be one reason for that.

He really was an errand boy for the devil.

Chapter 8

The women stopped at a Wal-Mart for supplies and cash, taking out as much money as the ATM would allow and gathering the materials Julie needed to create the cipher wheel. Then they headed south in Hank's SUV.

Julie was sitting in the passenger seat, which was now parked an hour and a half away from Marianne's at the Albany airport. In her lap were twelve slices of a paper towel roll, each neatly marked into twenty-seven equal sections. The thirteenth was in her hand, along with the ruler and a pen. It was careful work, but she was nearly done.

A light green minivan pulled into the next parking spot over, and Gwen hopped out of its driver's side door. Julie finished the last of her measuring and climbed out to join her.

"I thought a minivan was more practical, in case we needed somewhere to sleep."

"Good call."

The women worked to move their belongings and supplies to the new vehicle, Gwen once again taking her place at the wheel. She turned around in her seat to back out cautiously, then headed toward the interstate.

"Julie, I had to give them a credit card and a driver's license," she said.

"Crap."

"I know. But they wouldn't give me the van without it, and they wouldn't take the prepaid credit card. My license says Trueblood, but I had a MasterCard in the name of Gwen Beaumont, and she let me use that one when I pretended I had just gotten married and it was all I had."

"Wait, you took David's name?"

"I tried it on for size. I went back to Trueblood after a month or two." Gwen took a last sip of her soda, the straw taking in air with a loud slurp.

"Maybe the different name will be enough to throw them off." Julie said hopefully, though her voice sounded false to her own ears.

Meant for Her

No use crying over spilled milk.

Julie inserted the battery into the disposable cell phone she picked up at Wal-Mart and held the power key, its display coming to life. She hit the internet browser button and immediately looked up the Leopold Cipher.

"Are you almost done?"

"Close."

Each of the thirteen numbered rings would be labeled with all the letters of the alphabet on it and one blank, each in a different order. This is what she needed to look up, and she meticulously copied them from the internet site to the rings she had created. The key—the thirteen numbers she gleaned from "beautiful"—would tell her the order of the rings themselves.

"Nothing to it, but to do it," she said to herself. With shaking hands, she grabbed another roll of paper towels and slid the towels off it, then used the scissors to slice the cardboard open with one long cut.

"What's that for?" asked Gwen.

"I need a dowel to put the rings on. It has to be a little smaller in diameter than they are." She cut a long piece of duct tape and put the roll back together, with a sliver of itself tucked inside the roll.

"This is so exciting!"

Julie smiled at her aunt's enjoyment, her own stomach in knots. Digging in her pocket, she found the paper where she had written the cipher key and began to place the rings onto the long roll in the correct order.

"Now what?" asked Gwen.

"Now I turn the wheels to spell out the first thirteen letters of the coded message." Julie skipped over the first line, knowing that had only been a reference for her to know to use the Leopold cipher.

"You put the gibberish in?"

"Yes."

"How do you get the message out?"

Julie finished lining up the first thirteen letters of text, using a piece of tape to hold them in position. "You roll it around until you find the line that makes sense." As she spoke, she opened

Meant for Her

her palm and let the cipher wheel roll slowly down her fingers. Her eyes scanned line after line of gibberish before the words suddenly jumped out at her.

I AM NOT DEAD

She jerked her hand back as if she'd been burned, and the cipher roll fell to the floor of the van.

"Holy shit!" Julie snapped.

"What?"

"'I am not dead'! It says, 'I am not dead'!"

"Holy shit," said Gwen.

"My father is alive!"

Hank didn't know she was gone until lunchtime.

Since Julie put the blinds down, he slept until almost eleven. When he couldn't find her, he looked for the dogs and figured the women had taken them for a walk.

He sat alone at the kitchen table, sunlight streaming in the windows and a hot cup of coffee in front of him, planning his future with Julie Trueblood. It would be touchy, given her involvement in this case, but he had no intention of letting her go. Hank knew a good thing when it stared him in the face, and that woman was as good as it got.

He was in up to his knees emotionally. It wasn't just physical. Hell, they had rocked the physical world off its axis last night, but that alone wouldn't have him sitting here thinking about their future. His mind was telling him this might be the one he had waited his whole life for, and Hank was wise enough to embrace that possibility and not let it get away from him, no matter who their relationship might upset.

Barstow's going to shit his pants.

Hank smiled at the thought as he lifted his cereal bowl to drain the remaining milk. Still, he wanted to minimize the negative consequences that dating Julie could have on his career, and that was going to take some doing.

Marianne walked in, carrying several grocery bags. "Morning."

"Hey, Ma. Merry Christmas."

"Merry Christmas. I thought you were out."

"Why?"

"Because your truck's not here."

Hank's brows snapped together, then he stood up and peered out the window.

"I do know what your truck looks like," said his mother sarcastically.

"Yeah. I know." He sat back down at the table and shrugged. "Julie must have taken it."

"Where is she?"

"I don't know. I just got up a few minutes ago. I thought she and Gwen took the dogs for a walk."

"In the truck?"

That was odd. There must be a good explanation for why the two of them, the dogs and the truck were all missing. "Did they leave a note?" He hadn't really looked for one. A sick feeling settled in the hollow of his stomach as Marianne scanned the counter tops, shaking her head.

"The pad is out, but no note."

She wouldn't just leave.

As if to prove it to himself, Hank walked to the pantry and looked inside, his eyes resting where the dogs' food had been since the women arrived.

It was gone.

Hank stared at the spot longer than necessary.

Julie was gone.

But why? It didn't make sense. He was working to keep them safe. What had changed to make them want to leave?

The only thing that had changed was a night of incredible sex. Was she running away from a relationship with him? Julie had not seemed upset by them taking things to the next level. On the contrary, she seemed as moved by what they had shared as he was.

Then what? What could possibly make them take off in his SUV like that?

An image of Julie flashed in his mind. *"Are you sure we're safe here?"*

Panic slammed into Hank and set him reeling, his eyes darting to doors and windows, locks and unbroken panes.

"Was anything out of the ordinary this morning?" he asked his mother.

"No, not that I noticed. Why?"

Hank's cell phone rang and he glanced at the caller ID. ADMIRAL BARSTOW was displayed across the screen in big blue letters. He could see Julie standing where he stood, seeing what he was seeing.

"Son of a bitch!" Hank smacked his hand down violently on the counter. "She saw my phone. Son of a bitch!" he screamed, pounding his fists as the phone continued to ring.

Marianne turned from her groceries and stared at her son.

"Jared," he nearly shouted into the receiver.

"Where the hell have you been? I've been calling all morning," said Barstow.

Any doubts about Julie's departure vanished in an instant. Julie and Gwen were running for their lives.

Running for their lives, from me.

"It's Christmas Day, sir," Hank bit off the words, barely restraining his frustration with the older man.

"What goddamn difference does that make?" he barked. "You work for me, Jared. Not forty hours. All the fucking time. Do I make myself clear?"

Hank fought against the desperate need to verbally rip apart his superior officer. He concentrated on breathing in and out, feeling the air fill his lungs, and heard himself say, "Of course, sir."

"Where are you on the McDowell case?"

"Julie's still working on the cipher."

"You're sure she would tell you if she solved it?"

Not anymore.

"Yes, sir."

"Do what you have to in order to earn her trust."

"What do you mean, sir?"

"I mean," Barstow chuckled, a dirty throaty noise that disgusted Hank, "she's a beautiful woman, Jared. She just lost her father and she's vulnerable. Do what you need to do to ingratiate yourself with her."

Hank felt nauseous and angry, self-loathing warring with

Meant for Her

indignation in his blood.

That's what Julie thinks I did. She thinks I betrayed her.

Barely trusting himself to speak, Hank didn't respond at all. In his mind, his fist connected with Barstow's face. It was all he could do to remain silent.

"One more thing."

"What?"

"What the hell are you doing at the Albany airport?"

"Sir?"

"Don't play with me, son. Now, I'd like to know," he drawled out, "why you're touring the goddamned Northeast without updating me on this fucking case. I shouldn't have to call you to find out your fucking flight itinerary. Do you understand me, Jared?"

Realization dawned clear. "You have a GPS on my car."

"Of course I do." The admiral snickered. "And you'd better start explaining."

"I remember her," said the young man at the rental car counter. He had a swatch of dyed blonde hair amidst masses of brunette curls. "Did she do something wrong?" He held his hand to his chest, wide-eyed.

Hank had been showing Julie and Gwen's pictures around to ticket agents and car rental employees for nearly an hour. It had taken thirty-five minutes to have their pictures sent from DMV in the first place.

"When was she here?"

"Just before lunch. Let me pull up the transaction." He typed efficiently into his computer. "Eleven twenty-two. She rented a light green Honda Odyssey. What did she do?"

"I'll need the license plate number."

"Of course." He leaned over the counter and whispered, "Was it a robbery? There was a bank robbery right down the street last week."

"No." Hank looked at his watch, which read 3:34. They had more than a four hour jump on him. At least they were driving, not halfway to Mexico on an airplane.

"It has Illinois plates, number F73 8M1. I'll write that down

Meant for Her

for you." He grabbed a purple sticky note and looked at Hank from under his lashes. "Did she skip bail? I won't tell anyone."

"I can't discuss the details. Thanks for your help."

He straightened and handed Hank the paper. "Is there anything else I can do for you today, sir?"

"No, that's all."

He pulled back the note before Hank could grab it. "Airport security has surveillance footage, if that would be helpful."

"Really?"

The clerk nodded, allowing him to take the paper, then leaned over again and whispered dramatically, "Was it a *murder?*"

The airport security office was small and outfitted with a limited supply of dated equipment. Hank sat in the darkened room as a white-haired man in a blue uniform shirt held down a fast forward button on what looked like an old VCR.

"There's one more feed from the south parking lot," he said.

Julie must have parked in the quadrant of the parking garage not covered by the first three tapes Hank watched. He rubbed his forehead against the throb that was beginning to take over.

Just when he was convinced that this tape was yet another dead end, he saw his SUV pull right in front of the camera. "That's it," he told the security officer. "That's the truck."

The officer rewound the tape and began again, when the truck first entered the camera's field of view. Hank could clearly see Gwen driving, and as she pulled in, Julie sitting in the passenger seat. What were those things in her lap?

He watched as Gwen got out of the truck, presumably to go rent the minivan. Julie remained behind, working on something.

"Can we zoom in and see what she's doing?"

The other man pressed buttons on the archaic machine, and the image on the screen became cropped and grainy. "Is that better?"

"No."

The security officer laughed. "It's not like you see in the movies, is it?"

Hank thought of all the high tech security equipment he was

88

Meant for Her

used to dealing with, but kept that to himself. "No, it's not." He watched on screen as Julie wrote something, unable to see exactly what she was doing. Ten minutes later, Gwen returned with the van.

It wasn't until Julie threaded the rings onto the new paper towel roll that he realized what she was making.

The cipher wheel. She must have broken the code!

But when? She had trusted him up until this morning. If she had discovered the key before then, she would have told him. It must have been right around the same time as Barstow's call, maybe even at Marianne's house.

Hank dialed as he continued to watch the screen. "Ma. The notepad on the counter. Use a crayon or a pencil or something to see if you can read what was written on it last."

"Hang on, let me find a pencil." There was a long pause. "There are all these letters and numbers down the side... then the word 'beautiful' at the bottom with some numbers written under it."

Hank bent his head in a moment of gratitude to the universe. "Read them to me," he said to his mother.

His next call was to Chip Vandermead, though he hated to call him when Melody wasn't doing well. He answered on the first ring. Hank told him it was the Leopold Cipher and that the keyword was beautiful. It took Chip only moments to plug the information into his computer.

I AM NOT DEAD
I CAN PROVE MY INNOCENCE
BUT NEED YOUR HELP
MEET ME AT UNCLE LEOS

Chip was even able to cross-reference McDowell with Leo, pulling up several hits in the case file of one Leo Basinski, an immigrant from Uzkapostan whose last known address was just outside of Washington, D.C.

The highway was virtually deserted, given the lateness of the hour and the holiday. Hank made his eyes wide and blinked several times to say focused on the road. His mind kept going back to the hotel room in Jacksonville, with a body in the bathtub that someone now wanted him to believe *was not* Commander John McDowell.

Why had been so quick to assume it was his body in the motel room in the first place? Without positive identification, it was a bad judgment call on his part to have jumped to that conclusion, no matter how obvious it seemed at the time.

Sloppy. That's what it was.

One fact remained. Commander McDowell was involved in this case somehow. He might even have been the one to shoot the John Doe in the bathroom, or set the fire. Maybe both. And who was the dead man, if not the commander himself?

Hank thought of Julie, no doubt elated by her father's miraculous rise from his assumed grave. For her sake, he hoped McDowell was innocent of any wrongdoing and would find a way back into her life.

He doubted it, but he hoped.

A black and white checkered flag on the GPS screen showed he was getting close to his destination.

Protocol said he should have called Barstow about Leo, but now that the admiral was flying blind without that GPS, Hank wanted to keep him in the dark. No way in hell was he tipping his hand until he knew for sure Barstow wasn't a threat to Julie.

Leo wasn't really her uncle. Julie vaguely remembered him from her childhood as a short, dark-haired man with glasses, who wore too much cologne. Their family would have brunch at Leo's restaurant every month or so, with the occasional dinner at his home.

Her eyes scanned the row of brownstones, many decorated with Christmas lights for the holiday. The women walked in the road until they reached a shoveled driveway, allowing them access to the sidewalk without stepping through snow. Several doors down, a particularly frightening iron gargoyle sat atop a stone pillar, just as it had in Julie's childhood.

"I always hated that thing," she said, reaching it and pausing to consider its gruesome mouth and fangs.

"It really isn't befitting the architecture, is it?" asked Gwen.

The women climbed the steps to the door and Julie knocked, exchanging a nervous glance with Gwen as she did.

"Maybe no one's home," said Gwen.

Julie shook her head. "I can hear the TV."

"Knock louder."

At Julie's uncomfortable look, Gwen stepped forward and pounded on the door. A moment later, a bald man with thick glasses and a hunched gait opened it. He stood before them, staring at Julie for too long without speaking.

"I don't know if you remember me. I'm Julie, John McDowell's daughter."

"I know." Said the old man, coughing loudly. It was a thick sound, and it made Gwen grimace.

"Is my father here, Leo?"

He glared at Gwen.

"This is my aunt, Gwen Trueblood."

Leo shook his head.

"Why not?" asked Julie.

He opened his mouth to speak and coughed several times instead. When he could manage, he said, "Just you."

"It's okay," said Gwen, turning to face Julie. "You can do this without me."

Julie nodded, taking strength from her aunt's words.

"I'll be in the car."

Leo waited until Gwen was back inside the vehicle before he stepped back for Julie to enter.

The small room was stale with the smell of boiled vegetables and cigar smoke, its blinds closed to the outside. An overly loud, outdated television played *Wheel of Fortune*.

"In the basement," he said, leading the way through a tiny dining room with a bowl of fake fruit and a built-in corner hutch.

Leo opened a narrow door, gesturing for her to go ahead.

The stairway was poorly lit, and Julie held on to the low handrail as she navigated the steep steps. Leo closed the door behind her, cutting the meager light in half and making her start. Her feet stopped moving as she gave her eyes time to adjust to the darkness. There was a smell of damp earth and something foul that Julie couldn't place. She began to descend again, the temperature dropping with each step down.

As she slowly made her way to the basement, she couldn't help but feel she was headed underground like the damned. This was not a place of resurrection, fresh and new, but a place of desperation and despair. She realized with fear that her father might not be here at all, and resisted the urge to turn back.

In her mind she saw a picture of her father, dead in a motel room. She hadn't been able to really believe he was dead until this very moment, when she was just steps away from the promise of him alive.

What the hell's the matter with me?

Ahead of her, the staircase ended on a square wooden landing. A wall of packed earth faced her, a thick invasive root visible in the densely packed clay. Julie neared the bottom step and her head lowered enough to see the basement. Time itself stopped moving, the air around her fixed and still.

A slick smile spread across his lips. "I knew you'd come," he said.

Chapter 9

Gwen sat in the green minivan staring at the light over Leo's door. The bulb was yellow, making his doorway standout from every other on the street in an odd display of color. Another person would have thought nothing of that light, but it bothered Gwen like an ice cube that doesn't float to the top of the glass.

Something isn't right inside that house.

She considered knocking back on that door and attempting to talk her way past Leo, but her gut told her to stay put—at least for now. She tapped her foot with uncharacteristic nervous energy and waited, whether for Julie to return or for the decision to go in after her, she didn't know.

Her mind wandered over her beloved niece. Gwen was fiercely protective of the woman she had become, and knew Julie's heart was fragile where her father was concerned. John McDowell had never worked especially hard to spare his daughter pain, and it was with great effort that Gwen had kept her dislike of the man a secret from Julie.

She remembered with lucidity the teenager she had taken in when John abandoned his daughter. Gwen had been on her own emotional journey after David's death, unsure at the time if she could provide the girl with what she would need to heal.

Julie had been devastated, grief for her mother still oozing and raw, before her father left her as well. In his wake, a formal investigation followed that soon focused exclusively on her as a potential colluder, or at the very least, a threat to national security.

Gwen stood steadfast by her side, fending off Navy investigators and media reporters like wolves at the door, working to help Julie keep from shutting down emotionally. Teaching her to trust her own instincts, rely on herself again. Together they spent hours just talking, often walking through the Vermont hills that surrounded the farmhouse.

On one of their walks, a year after Julie's arrival, they came across a mother deer and her fawns grazing in an open meadow. Gwen's big yellow dog was grazing in the grass alongside them.

Meant for Her

"Well, would you look at that," said Gwen. "It looks like Zeke has made some new friends."

The women watched the scene in silence for some moments.

"It's like us," said Julie. "You're the deer, and I'm the dog."

Gwen tilted her head. "What do you mean?"

Julie looked at the ground and frowned. "You took me in like I belonged with you."

Gwen had thought she might weep for this brave girl who felt so alone. "You do belong with me, sweetheart." She put her arm around Julie's shoulders. "We're family."

The memory brought a tight smile to her lips as she stared at Leo's brownstone. John McDowell was also Julie's family.

He hadn't always been so selfish. Gwen remembered when he first married her sister, he had been charming and strong. He loved Mary. It was her death that had changed him, made him angry and bitter.

Why did you bring us here, John?

Gwen bowed her head before the divine, praying for guidance and the safety of those she loved. When she raised it again, the yellow light over Leo's door had begun to flicker irregularly. She drew her lips into a pucker and curled her fingers around the steering wheel. Slowly and deliberately, she filled her lungs completely with air and focused all her energy on her niece.

The gun was the first thing Julie saw, her eyes drawn to its shiny metal butt sticking out of the holster.

John McDowell stood before his daughter in a dirty T-shirt and green sweatpants, the weapon held by leather straps that were meant to be concealed beneath a jacket.

"Dad?" Her voice was ragged, her throat constricted.

"Julie-girl," he said, his arms open wide to receive her.

It was a scene she had imagined so many times before, it felt surreal when she finally ran the few steps into his arms. "I thought you were dead," she choked on a sob.

"I know. I'm sorry."

Julie released him, stepping back and wiping away the tears that wet her face. "I can't believe you're really here," she said.

"It's so good to see you."

"It's good to see you, too." His tone was placating, as if he had simply left the room for a few minutes, rather than disappearing for ten years.

Julie took a good look at her father. His hair, once a salt-and-pepper black and gray, was now completely black, like it was when she was little. The youthful color contrasted with the deeply set lines around his mouth and the sagging of the skin under his dark-colored eyes.

She took in his clothing, her brow furrowing at his bare feet.

Where are his shoes? He's always so meticulous about his shoes.

He was at once both comfortingly familiar and unsettlingly strange. Julie ran a trembling hand through her hair as she looked at the room around them. It was set up like a small studio apartment, its dirt floor covered with a braided rug. A sagging couch was draped in tired pink fabric, next to a bed with striped yellow and brown sheets.

A power strip hung in mid-air, suspended from an orange electrical cord reaching down from the ceiling above. Julie's eyes followed the lines to a small refrigerator and a computer on a makeshift desk.

The overall feel was one of a bomb shelter or tomb, the earthen walls enhancing the sense of being buried alive. Julie shivered and wished for a window or door.

"How long have you been living here?"

"I don't know. A few months."

She tried to imagine anyone choosing to stay in this place a single moment longer than necessary. "Where did you live before that?"

"What?" He squinted at her.

"Where did you live before that?"

He began to pace between the desk and the couch. "What difference does that make?"

"It's okay, Dad. Never mind." Julie rubbed her eyebrow. "Your message said you could prove your innocence, but you needed my help."

A smile graced his face, brightening his features as he

brought his chin up. "I do need your help, Julie-girl."

"Anything, Dad."

He blinked repeatedly. Julie saw little dots of sweat collecting on his forehead.

"You have to believe me."

The urge to run out of the basement and away from her father appeared suddenly, frightening in its intensity. She could see herself darting around him to make it to the stairs, clay walls under her fingertips as she raced up the steps, reaching the front door before Leo could even stand up from the couch and *Wheel of Fortune*.

Can opener.

"What is it?" she asked instead.

"Do you remember when your mother told you she had cancer?"

"Yes." She took a step backwards, increasing the distance between them. Her father stepped forward.

"You asked me that day, 'Why did she get sick?' Do you remember that?"

"I remember being upset," Julie swallowed against the dryness in her throat, an image of her beautiful mother forming in her mind.

"You asked me why she got sick. And I didn't tell you the truth." He was standing so close to her, she could smell his sweat.

"It was a rare form of cancer." Julie said, mechanically repeating the words she'd been told.

"Yes. A rare form of cancer that you only contract if you're exposed to ionizing radiation."

"Ionizing radiation?"

"Yes."

"Where would she be exposed to that?"

"At Camp Harold." He stepped away from her, cool air rushing in to fill the space he had occupied.

Julie's mother had been a Navy structural engineer, working at the same base as her father. The two had married on the base. Her mother had died on the base.

"When she was diagnosed, that goddamned Navy doctor

Meant for Her

said it was just one of those things that happens. Bullshit. I looked into it. It's caused by ionizing radiation from TENORM in the concrete on the worksite. They knew it was there." His body contorted in rage. His nostrils flared with each breath and his clenched arms shook. "They knew all along."

He turned to the fridge and grabbed a beer, opening it and drinking it down in one long gulp before pitching it into a tall white garbage can. The sound of it hitting other empties punctuated the silence before he opened the fridge and found a replacement.

"You want to know why your mother's body is rotting in the ground? The U.S. Navy killed her, sure as I'm standing in front of you."

Julie recoiled from the image he painted. "One or two people made a bad decision…"

"Not *one or two*," he said derisively. "It ran all the way up the chain of fucking command, right to the Pentagon. Nobody said diddly! That's what killed your mother. The U.S. Navy, and the absolute authority it holds over the people enslaved by it."

He stood shock-still, staring at one of the electrical cords hanging from the ceiling. "They killed the only person I have ever loved."

I love you, Daddy.

The words rang out in her head, unbidden.

"But I got those fucking bastards."

She watched him suckle at the can of beer as a light humming began to sing in her ears. Then it clicked.

He really is a traitor.

"The Dermody." She wasn't asking for confirmation. She knew it now. For ten long years she had suffered for him, believing this man was an innocent victim. Eighty-eight men had perished when that ship went down.

John McDowell had killed them all.

A cold sensation trickled down from the top of her head to her abdomen. Julie stole a peek at the stairway, now seeming so much farther away. It was too late to make excuses and leave unquestioned; the opportunity for safety had passed untaken.

Her father was waiting. Julie said a silent prayer. *Please get me out of here. Help me get back to Hank. I think I love him. I shouldn't have doubted him.*

Julie heard the drip of water nearby. She listened as she counted the drops, one, two, three. Her lungs filled with air, calming her, and she knew what she had to do.

"Thank you, Dad."

"For what?"

She reached out to him. "For taking good care of mom," she said, squeezing his arm. "For getting the people that did this to her."

A proud smirk appeared on his face. He lifted the beer can and finished the rest of the brew. Tilting it toward Julie, he asked, "Oh, I missed you, Julie-girl. Do you want one?"

"Absolutely." Her palms were soaked with perspiration. "You said you needed my help. What can I do, Dad?"

"I'm still working covert ops for Uzkapostan." He puffed his chest as he spoke. "Been living there since I left the states. Once the Navy fucked me, I figured there's no place like home, right?"

Julie tried to keep up with his quick change of mood.

"So anyways, they've been getting weapons from the Navy for years. They had a backstage all-access pass to the U.S. Navy supply arsenal, via their own invisible account on the network."

The technology maven in Julie was horrified. "That's awesome."

"It was, it truly was, until somebody shut it down six months ago. I need you to get us back into that database."

Only a handful of people in the world could do that, and Julie knew she wasn't one of them. "Anything for you, Dad."

"I would do anything for you, too. Do you know that?"

I'd sink a whole ship full of sailors for you, baby.

"Yes, Dad."

He smiled like a child who couldn't keep a secret. "That boyfriend of yours, Greg?"

The hair on the back of Julie's neck went up. "Yes?"

"He was sent to bring you back to do this."

"What?"

He waved off her excitement. "I have always been so proud of you. I told everyone who would listen how my girl was a natural-born code breaker. They thought it would be too dangerous if I came back here myself, so they sent Greg to come get you."

Dizziness crept into the back of Julie's brain, her father's words beginning to ring like church bells in her mind. "They sent Greg?"

"Yeah." His expression turned dark and ominous. "Fucking hotshot thought he could do this without me. Bring you back himself and take me out of the loop." His laugh was too loud, his happiness pronounced. "I took care of that dumb ass son of a bitch."

"The motel," she whispered.

The body in the bathtub was Greg.

"You know about that?"

Julie battled the sick fear that made her want to double over. "Of course. The code in the safe deposit box. That's how they found me."

"Oh, right. Yeah, right. He wasn't good enough for you, Julie. We'll find you somebody real good when we get home. A nice Uzkapostan boy like your old man."

"We're going to Uzkapostan?"

"Tomorrow morning. The same flight Greg was going to take you on."

"I don't have my passport."

He flashed her a cocky smile. "Oh, yes, you do. I got it from your apartment."

With an eerie sense of déjà vu, Hank ducked under the yellow police tape and approached the smoldering building. A guttural scream rose in his chest and begged to be freed as he walked closer to the brownstone and the familiar smell of waterlogged timber.

No. No. No.

"Sir, you need to step behind the barrier."

He flashed his badge. "Who's in charge?"

The fireman nodded to a woman standing beside a large red SUV. He identified himself, his hands shaking as he flashed his badge and asked, "What do we have here?"

Meant for Her

"Explosion. Appears to have been deliberately set, probably natural gas. One confirmed dead."

He could feel his chin trembling. "Male or female?"

"Male. From the neighbor's description, it appears to be the owner, Leo Basinski."

Hank pressed his palms to his eyes and nearly wept with gratitude.

"You okay, mister?"

"Yes. I thought it was a friend." He took a big breath. "Was there anyone else in the building?"

"Negative. Neighbor says he lived alone."

Hank's cell phone vibrated in his pocket. He fished it out and saw an unfamiliar number with an 802 area code.

Vermont.

He stepped away from the SUV. "Hank Jared."

"It's Gwen."

"Thank God. Where are you guys?"

"Julie's not with me."

"Where is she? I'm sitting outside Leo Basinski's house, watching them carry him out in a plastic bag, Gwen. What the hell's going on?"

"Oh, my God. We were just there!"

"Where's Julie?"

"She's with her father. I'm following them, Hank. Ninety-five north. I think Julie wanted me to call you."

"You think?"

"Yes."

"I'm getting in the car now. You can fill me in while I drive."

It hadn't been easy to convince him to come to Boston.

She told her father the computers at Systex Corporation had superior processors to the ones in Uzkapostan, which would enable her to hack into the Navy procurement database in half the time. That was a lie, but in Boston she had a fighting chance to save her own ass.

She was driving Leo's late model sedan down the interstate,

Meant for Her

the smell of old cigar smoke thick in her nostrils. Her father was in the passenger seat, a beer and a gun in his lap. The gun was for protection, he said, but Julie didn't believe him.

She'd watched that gun kill Leo, and it had probably killed Greg, too.

"Slow down. We don't want to get pulled over," he said.

That's what she was hoping for, which is why she was speeding. Easing her foot off the accelerator, she glanced in her rear view mirror to check for the minivan that had been following them since they left the house. Her father hadn't known Gwen was waiting outside for Julie, having shot Leo before the other man had a chance to tell him.

Call Hank. Tell him to come to Boston.

Julie was concentrating hard, and her head was beginning to pulsate in tempo with her own heartbeat. She was trying to send telepathic messages to her aunt for the last hour, feeling like an idiot trying to bend a spoon with her mind at a slumber party.

She didn't even believe in this stuff.

His business card's in my purse under the seat. Gwen, call Hank. We're going to my office in Boston.

Her father belched in the seat beside her. "I need to take a piss."

"I'll get off at the next rest stop."

"I gotta piss now. Pull over."

Julie knew she'd lose Gwen if she did that, and her grip tightened on the wheel. "It's the interstate, Dad. A cop might stop if we pull off the road."

He leaned in close to her, the stink of beer and unbrushed teeth permeating the air. "Just. Fucking. Pull. Over."

Julie put on her turn signal and felt Gwen's question as soon as she touched the brake.

Keep going, Gwen. Keep going.

As if in answer, the minivan swung around them, continuing down the road. Julie watched it disappear in the distance, leaving her completely alone with her drunken crazed murderer of a father, and a gun.

Chapter 10

The Prudential Tower stood sentry in the distance as Hank turned down Boylston and headed once again for the offices of Systex Corporation. The city streets were empty, the parallel lines of concrete sidewalks and asphalt streets dominating the landscape.

He couldn't help but feel he was going in circles, both literally and figuratively. Two visits to Boston. Two arson scenes. Chasing Julie south then north again. Chasing Julie even when she was standing right in front of him.

She was something else.

Hank rounded the corner and found the coffee shop Gwen had described, unlit except for its sign. The minivan idled at the curb and he pulled up behind it. Her willowy figure headed toward the passenger door.

"That was fast," she said, reaching for her seatbelt.

"I made up some time."

"Lucky you didn't get pulled over."

Hank pulled away from the curb and made a sharp left into the Systex parking garage. "Who said I didn't get pulled over?"

Gwen rubbed her hands on her thighs. "What's our plan?"

"Damned if I know."

He steered the car around the concrete pillars of the hulking structure, empty of cars at this time of night. "I'm hoping Julie left a way for us to get in."

"She might have."

"She better have." He pulled into the first spot after a series of handicapped spaces. Turning his body toward Gwen, he asked, "Do you know how to shoot a gun?"

"Yes."

He raised his eyebrows.

"I'm a country girl, Hank. I know how to shoot."

He nodded, handing her his backup. "We have to assume McDowell is armed."

"I think Julie's trying to tell me as much. I keep picturing a gun."

Meant for Her

A fierce protectiveness surged through Hank at her words. The simple reality that she could be hurt released a torrent of energy. "Let's go."

An elevator next to the Systex Corporation sign marked the entrance to the offices. Hank stepped up and pressed the button, which lit beneath his hand. The doors opened and the pair stepped inside, neither knowing who or what they would be facing when the doors opened again.

"I need to write some code to have my computer analyze the database encryption type."

"What does that mean?"

"I have to see what type of security they're using. I'm going to write a computer program to help me find out."

Julie sat down behind her desk and opened several windows on her computer. The first would make it look like she was writing the program for her father. The second would allow her to send text messages from her desktop to Gwen's cell phone. She set up her programs so she could quickly toggle between the two if her father came to look over her shoulder.

She typed, "IN MY OFFICE IN BOSTON. R U HERE?" Then she switched windows and began writing the computer program.

"This is where you work?"

"Yes."

"What do you do?"

"I'm the Director of Technology. I handle all the computer issues for Systex." Julie forced her eyes to stay fixed on the screen in front of her, though they wanted to seek out her father's face.

The man's a murderer and a traitor, and you're wondering if he's proud of you?

She swallowed her juvenile thoughts. "There's soda in the kitchen, just through there, if you're thirsty." Julie was certain he would have preferred something alcoholic, but she had neither the means nor the inclination to provide it.

He scratched his forehead with his thumb. "Coffee?"

Meant for Her

"You can make some."

His brows snapped together, but he went in search of the machine. Julie flipped back to her texting program and saw that Gwen had answered.

"OUTSIDE MAIN DOOR. KEYPAD CODE?"

Julie felt the breath she'd been holding in her lungs release in a grateful huff. "568*14. STAY IN LOBBY. HAS GUN. KILLED LEO. SUNK DERMODY."

"R U OK?"

"4 NOW."

"HANK IS HERE."

Hank is here.

Julie made a little sob as she read the words.

"What are you doing?" said her father from the doorway.

How long had he been standing there? "Writing the program." She deftly toggled back to the other screen and hid the message from Gwen, though she could feel her cheeks burning a telltale red.

Her back stiffened as he walked behind her to see for himself, staring at the pitiful few lines of code that patterned the screen. It must have been enough to satisfy him.

"Where are the coffee filters?"

"In the cupboard to the right of the sink."

She counted to ten before walking to the door to make sure he was gone. Again she messaged her aunt. "CALL POLICE. GIVE THEM CODE TO GET IN."

It took several minutes for the reply.

"WILL DO."

Julie's shoulders caved in and her head fell to her chest. She had been in her father's company for nearly twelve hours. Her body and mind were fried from the constant state of high alert.

With a deep cleansing breath, she lifted her head and refocused her attention. She needed to get the gun away from her father so no one got hurt. She tried to predict how he would react, but her father was not acting like himself. Julie feared he would lash out at her as he had done to Leo and Greg.

For the moment, she busied herself writing what she hoped looked like a legitimate program, buying herself some time for

Meant for Her

Hank and the police to arrive. She managed to complete several screens full of computer code before the smell of burning coffee pulled her attention away.

Pushing her chair back from the desk, Julie prayed that everyone would be safe when this showdown was ended, then headed for the office kitchen.

"She wants us to call the police," said Gwen. They were standing in the lobby of Systex Corporation, the light from the EXIT sign highlighting the gloss on the tall black reception desk.

"The Navy should handle this, not local law enforcement." Hank rubbed the side of his index finger along his lip.

"I trust your judgment."

His eyes met hers. "I wish I knew who to trust."

"Barstow?"

"That's the question. The call should go to him."

"Hank, Julie says her father really was working for Uzkapostan. He was the traitor."

Hank's poised his thumb over his cell phone. "I believe her best chance of getting out of here lies with Barstow."

"That's all that matters now."

It was that simple, wasn't it? He loved her, and he would do whatever he could to get her out of here unharmed. For the first time, his decision had nothing to do with loyalty to the Navy or his own sense of right and wrong. He didn't care about anything except Julie.

"Barstow," answered the voice on the line, sounding no different at two in the morning than at two in the afternoon.

"We've got him, sir. I need backup at the offices of Systex Corporation in Boston, Massachusetts, ASAP. We have a potential hostage situation."

The gun was on the counter next to the coffeemaker, surrounded by a fine sprinkling of sugar that contrasted with the reflective black granite. She considered grabbing it, and imagined herself in control of the weapon. Could she turn it against her father to save her own life?

Meant for Her

John McDowell was an imposing presence in the tiny kitchen. He stood at the sink, his back to her as he sipped his coffee and considered a piece of abstract artwork that hung between the two sets of wall cupboards. At fifty, his wide shoulders were still heavily muscled, his back graceful and catlike in its proportion and curvature.

"You'll never get there first," he said.

She swallowed against the tightness in her throat. "What?"

"The gun," he said, turning to face her. "You'll never make it to the gun before I do."

Julie stood up straighter and met her father's eyes fully. It was then, in the office kitchenette, that she was able to see him as he really was for the very first time. The last mask had been removed, the final act performed.

John McDowell stood before his daughter, a man broken by hatred and his own willingness to allow evil into his soul. They squared off, each taking measure of the other, and Julie knew he would kill her as easily as he had killed the others. As soon as he realized she couldn't hack into the Navy's computers, she would be dead.

An unexpected freedom washed over her. She was not afraid. Suddenly able to distance herself from her father, she saw that her own achievements as a human being had surpassed the father she once adored. She was not beholden to him, but the victor in a battle that had been raging inside her since he left her alone in the world.

She needed only to placate him until the others arrived.

"I'm trying to help you, Dad."

"Of course you are."

The ring of the elevator arriving on the floor punctuated the silence, setting their tableau in motion. Her father reached for the gun with one hand even as his other came around her midsection, pulling her to him and placing the barrel of the pistol at her temple.

Julie fought him, writhing against the steel bands that were his arms. He ignored her attempts to free herself, dragging her toward the lobby where the elevator had surfaced and taking cover behind a tall potted plant.

Meant for Her

The lobby was lit only by security lights, leaving areas of shadow throughout the waiting room and offices beyond. Julie's eyes raked through the familiar room, looking for any sign of Hank or Gwen. Had they been so foolish as to alert her father to their presence, or had the ringing of the bell been a deliberate distraction?

"Who knows you are here?" he hissed, the damp heat of his breath collecting in her ear. When she didn't answer, he snaked his arm across her neck and pressed painfully on her throat. "You double crossed me. This is how you treat your father?"

Julie fought for breath against the pressure of his arm, panicky in her search for air. A glass shattered on the wall next to them, and his arm yanked back in surprise. He pushed the barrel of the gun harder into her head and used her as a human shield, twisting and turning in an attempt to see the person who had thrown the glass.

From the corner of her eye, Julie glimpsed the doorway of the kitchen, dark against the lighter hallway. They had left the light on, she was sure of it. Someone was in there, the faintest silhouette of a human form hovering knee-high in the door frame.

So long as her father held a gun to her head, anyone who came to help her would be held as hostage as she. An odd calmness allowed Julie to consider her choices with a distant reserve. She could stay captive in his arms, or she could fight back.

Thrusting her weight to the right, her father's legs were forced apart as he tried to counterbalance her move. Her heel shot up quickly into the open space, connecting with his groin. His yelp of pain coincided with a loosening of his grip, and she pounded her elbow into his vulnerable solar plexus.

Her attention was focused on the kitchen doorway. She began to run, Gwen's silhouette now visible as her aunt got to her feet. Time slowed and the distance to the kitchen grew longer, moments held suspended as she waited for her father's inevitable reaction.

The walls pivoted around her and she knew she was going down, confused and panicked as her body began to fail her. Julie never heard the shots that entered her back and slipped into her chest cavity. The last thing she saw was Gwen's face, stricken in horror as her beloved niece fell to the ground, thick red blood seeping from the holes in her body.

Chapter 11

"The layout is a square within a square," Hank said, recalling details from his initial meeting with Julie. "Offices on the perimeter, lobby in the middle, surrounded by an inner square of offices. Walkways from the lobby connect to the perimeter hallway."

Backup arrived fifteen minutes after he called Barstow, which felt like a fucking eternity. His muscles flexed as adrenaline flowed and he worked to keep himself in check.

"You're with me," Hank said to the tallest of the men. "You two take the other stairwell."

"I want to come, too."

He turned to Gwen. Anyone else, and he would have said no unequivocally. "Why?"

"I'll be needed."

He nodded. "Keep your gun ready. You are my shadow. Stay a foot behind me, one hand on my back so I know exactly where you are."

She nodded.

Then they were moving, four flights dimly lit by security lamps and emergency exit signs, each of them on high alert.

Hank knew Julie was in danger. He could feel it in the marrow of his bones, as if the love he felt for her tethered them together on some cosmic level. Would she be alive by the time he got to her? The idea that he could lose what he had waited so long to find was incomprehensible. Would he be able to save her or was he already too late?

Pushing the thoughts away, he brought his focus back to the steady rhythm of his shoes on the stairs beneath him. The last flight came into view, ending at a single black steel door with the Systex logo in royal blue.

The team emerged silently onto a long corridor with brown industrial carpeting. Hank recognized it as the outer perimeter hallway. At the other end, two doorways spilled light into the darkness. Just then, a sliver of someone's head popped out and peeked in the opposite direction.

Was that Julie or McDowell?

The team inched forward, the men checking the offices along the way before giving the all-clear. It was a necessary step, but Hank itched to race toward the lit doorways, protocol be damned.

They were twenty feet from the same doorway when she emerged from it, walking away without ever turning in their direction.

Hank hesitated, unsure if McDowell would enter the hallway as well, when Julie turned into the second room. She was gone in a heartbeat, and so was his chance to alert her to his presence.

The smell of burned coffee reached his nostrils as he hovered close to the wall and inched toward the door. He heard McDowell's voice trailing out of what must be the kitchen.

"You'll never get there first."

"What?" It was Julie, so close. Right in the next room. His palms were hot and clammy, his eyes fixed on the doorway as he forced himself to take deep, slow breaths.

"The gun. You'll never make it to the gun before I do."

He's going to shoot her.

Hank's grip tightened on his weapon and he gestured to the men, holding three fingers up in the air, a countdown to action. He gave Gwen a shake of his head, telling her to stay put.

"I'm trying to help you, Dad."

He heard the stress in her voice, and knew that McDowell could hear it, too. Julie was running out of time. Two fingers.

"Of course you are."

One finger.

The ring of the elevator interrupted his countdown, unexpected and loud.

Hank froze and the men looked to him for direction. Sounds of a scuffle came from the kitchen, and Hank rounded the corner, weapon drawn, just in time to see McDowell exit the room from a door at the opposite end of the galley.

Julie was held securely against his chest in the classic hostage position.

"Gwen, stay here," he barked in a harsh whisper. "You two, take the perimeter hallway left. I'm going right." He jogged back the way the way he came, passing the stairwell and continuing on to the lobby.

Who the fuck was in that elevator?

The thought mocked him as he ran, heading toward a back entrance to the same lobby McDowell just dragged Julie into. He would have the advantage of surprise, though he had no idea what he would see.

Ten feet from the final turn to the lobby, gunfire exploded, one bullet for each of the three steps he took too late. He rounded the corner and watched Julie's legs bend and buckle under her lifeless form, collapsing at Gwen's feet.

A tortured howl ripped from his gut as he charged into the lobby, sweeping his gun from side to side in the shadowy space. The slightest reflection off the metal elevator doors caught his eye as they slipped silently together.

He fired his gun and the bullets embedded themselves into steel, never coming near their intended target.

The other men charged into the lobby from the opposite direction, weapons drawn. "He's in the elevator," barked Hank. "Split up and take the stairwells, now! I'll call for backup." They took off running at Hank's instructions. He dialed 911 as he rushed to Julie's side.

She lay on her stomach in a thick pool of black blood. He heard a rhythmic wet sucking noise, which he realized with horror must be her breathing. Gwen worked Julie's shirt up to see the damage the bullets had caused.

"I need an ambulance, quickly," he said to the emergency operator, giving him the address. "And police assistance. A fugitive has escaped from the same scene."

"I'm looking for Julie Trueblood," Becky said, hearing her voice waver. "She was brought in by ambulance about an hour ago."

She had been in hysterics since Gwen phoned, and knew her eyes must be bloodshot as all hell. The woman behind the information desk gave her a sympathetic look, clearly used to seeing visitors skirt the border between life and death.

"She's in the ICU. Follow the signs to the blue elevators. It's on the fourth floor."

Becky swerved around people like pylons as she followed the blue ceiling tags to the elevator bank, only to find a crowd waiting for the next available car. She opened the door to the stairwell and bounded up four flights instead.

Not bothering to look for a reception desk, she grabbed the arm of a young man in scrubs. "I'm looking for Julie Trueblood."

A voice called out behind her, "Becky?"

She turned to see a man who looked weary with fatigue and stress, his clothing covered with stains that might be blood.

Too much blood to come from someone who was still alive.

"Are you Hank?" Her nostrils flared, eyes squinting as she approached.

"Yes. She's asleep, but you can..."

Her hand connected solidly with his face, a crisp clapping sound in the quiet of the hospital corridor.

"You were supposed to protect her!"

Hank cocked his jaw back into alignment. "I know."

"She trusted you to keep her safe, and now she's fighting for her life because you *did a shitty job of it*!" Becky glared at him, accusing eyes boring into his.

Hank met her gaze, seeming to accept her rage as just punishment. Then Gwen was there, holding her, telling her it was all right, which of course it wasn't.

"Come see her. She has lots of tubes sticking out, but she's still our Julie." Gwen put her arm around the younger woman and ushered her toward another tiled hallway.

"Is she going to be okay, Gwen?"

"It's too soon to say for sure."

"What do you think?"

Gwen squeezed Becky's shoulder and frowned a small smile. "I think we should hope for the best."

Hank stood staring out the window, unseeing. The waiting room was angular and blue, full of squared-off metal chairs and rectangular couches, the people on them subdued.

He was giving the women time alone with Julie, but every

Meant for Her

moment he was away from her was its own special torment. McDowell was out there somewhere. Who's to say he wouldn't come here looking for the daughter he had failed to kill?

His cell phone rang in his pocket and he pulled it out to look at the screen.

He turned back to stare at nothing as he answered. "Jared."

"You are the biggest fuckup I've ever had the misfortune to command."

"Sir."

"Not only did you manage to let a notorious fugitive escape in the middle of downtown Boston, you allowed him to seriously injure a civilian."

"What do you want?"

The silence lasted so long, Hank was about to hang up.

"I want you to get back on track, Jared. This McDowell business is a goddamn train wreck, and you're the conductor. I'm shipping you out to Seattle. There's a case there…"

He interrupted. "I'm not going."

"Pardon me, son? *What did you just say?*"

"I said, I'm not going."

"I was under the impression you're an enlisted officer of the U.S. Navy."

Hank took the phone away from his ear while Barstow continued to speak. Snowflakes began to fall from the gray December sky and an image of Julie came to mind, standing on the church steps in her blue silk dress. Flurries swirled around her in the crisp night air.

Turning the phone over in his hand, he stared at the red button for several seconds before he pressed it, firmly. He was never one to do something without considering the ramifications of his actions.

Becky stared at the thin layer of orange grease on the pepperoni pizza as the elevator stopped on each floor between the basement and the ICU. This time the wait didn't bother her, having seen enough of Julie's eerily still form tucked into a hospital bed to last her for a while.

The tray was laden with food, from Cobb salad and rice

pudding to the pizza and a small turkey sub with American cheese. She sipped at a chocolate milkshake as the doors opened onto the fourth floor, and she went in search of Hank.

She found him at Julie's bedside, bent over in a chair, his forehead resting on the white sheet next to her hip. His hand held Julie's tightly, and Becky felt even worse for having attacked him.

He's in love with her.

He had changed into scrubs, the green color highlighting his bronze skin as it contrasted with Julie's pallor. But it was the way he sat, as close to her as he could be, that struck Becky most.

She considered herself to be an excellent judge of character, and she knew instantly that Hank Jared was a good man.

Crossing to the window, she curled up in a blue vinyl recliner and placed the tray on the table beside her. She was wrong to have said what she did, wrong to have slapped him. Her temper was fiery and explosive, often getting the better of her, but it was nothing compared to the remorse that typically followed.

Becky was a pro at apologizing.

The room was overly warm, hot and stuffy, a view of twilit Boston visible from the tall window next to her chair. She reached into her jeans pocket and retrieved a ponytail holder, quickly snapping her wild red locks into a loose bunch on top of her head to help her cool down.

She stared at the John Hancock building, her mind quiet. In the reflection of the hospital room, she saw Hank sit up and gently stroke Julie's arm from shoulder to wrist.

"I'm sorry if I woke you," said Becky, turning to face him.

"I was awake."

She noted the dark circles under his eyes. "When's the last time you slept?"

"Night before last."

"Gwen, too?"

He nodded.

"You can sleep at my house."

He looked at Julie, and Becky suspected he would not leave.

Meant for Her

"Hank, I'm sorry."

He held up his hand. "Don't be. You were right."

"I'm sure you did the best you could." She reached for the tray. "I brought you something to eat."

His eyes took in the veritable buffet. "Just a little something?"

"I wasn't sure what you'd like."

"I could really go for a milkshake."

Becky's eyes went wide.

"I told you I wasn't sleeping."

Her eyes narrowed. "How'd you know it was a milkshake?"

"I can smell ice cream from forty paces."

"Harrumph."

Gwen walked in, her normally graceful posture now rounded and lax. "I spoke with the doctor."

"And?" said Becky.

"He says the next twelve hours are critical, but she seems to be holding her own."

"Thank God," said Hank.

"I need some sleep," said Gwen.

"You can sleep at my place. I was just telling Hank."

"I'll take the first watch," he said. "Go get some rest."

"Thank you, Hank. Ever since I lost David..." her voice trailed off and she grimaced, looking at the floor. "Hospitals are difficult. But I'll be back."

Julie felt like she was swimming in thick water, unable to surface. She drifted in and out of consciousness as she paddled, her haze interrupted by vivid dreams and less tangible oddities from the world around her hospital bed.

She saw her mother standing in a field of tall grass, at once laughing and beckoning for her to come and play. At one point she could feel the hospital bed beneath her own still body and smell Gwen's favorite chicken soup, as if the woman were sitting beside her.

And there was Hank.

He wasn't with her in the water, but she could feel him somewhere near the water's edge. He wanted her to come out, but she didn't know how.

As she let herself drift in the current, she could smell his special scent and wished she could follow it. She could hear his voice.

"Please come back to me."

The love she felt for him swelled in her heart, making her buoyant in the water. She tried to move closer to him, deliberately pushing at the thickness around her with limbs that were tired and heavy. The water began to thin, becoming less fluid and feather-light, like a cool breeze.

She became conscious of her body, her closed eyelids. She worked to open them. The room was bright, sunlight streaming through the window onto the white sheets around her.

Hank held her hand, his unfocused gaze not realizing she was awake. She wanted to tell him, but speech was too hard.

This was a hospital room. Was she in an accident? She tried to remember what happened. An image of Gwen's stricken face emerged in her mind, and she saw herself fall to the ground.

Gunshots. There had been gunshots.

My father tried to kill me.

Panic had her suddenly jerking her arms up, her head moving from side to side.

Hank was there, touching her face. "It's okay, Julie. You're all right."

"My father?" she asked, her voice a dry rasp.

"Do you remember what happened?"

"Shot me."

"Yes. He shot you. The bullets punctured your lung, severed an artery. You're going to be okay."

"Where is he?"

Hank grimaced. "He got away." The terrified look on her face bored straight to his heart. "You're safe now, Julie. I promise. I won't let him get close to you again."

She nodded, tears welling in her eyes. Her own father had shot her with a gun, hoping she would stop living. The enormity of the thought defied comprehension. Looking back into Hank's eyes, she saw they were glistening and full of emotion.

"I let you down. I'm so sorry, Julie."

Meant for Her

Julie shook her head as she reached up to stroke his cheek. "Not your fault."

"Yes, it is."

"No, Hank." Forgiveness filled her eyes. "*His* fault."

He brought her hand to his lips for a kiss. "I love you, Julie." He looked into her eyes. "I knew it before, but I didn't say anything and I almost lost you. I'm not going to lose you again, and I'm not going to go another day without telling you how I feel."

"I love you, too," she whispered.

Thomas Barstow stepped off the elevator onto the fourth floor and entered the ICU. He was dressed in khakis and a white polo shirt, an unremarkable choice. He met the eyes of no one as he strolled comfortably through the corridor and slipped into Julie Trueblood's room.

Two hours earlier, he called the front desk from a hospital courtesy phone and got her room number, then he waited in the lobby until he saw Hank leave the building.

He was virtually invisible.

It was always unfortunate when a situation required him to act directly. Whenever possible, he preferred to have others take care of the messier parts of his job. Still, the young soldier in him thrilled at the squeeze of adrenaline, the covert performance he was enacting on a live stage.

She was sleeping, and he took a moment to admire her simple beauty, so much like her mother's. It was ironic that her end would be at his hands, just as Mary's had been. Mrs. McDowell had been mere months away from death when he killed her, the cancer's havoc near complete when he learned she intended to name him in a lawsuit about the ionizing radiation at the worksite.

He couldn't allow that to happen.

Barstow walked to the head of the bed and examined the IV lines that entered the back of her hand, reaching into his pocket for the small glass vial and syringe.

"Hi."

The voice behind him made him drop the drug back against

the lining of his pants. He turned to see a lanky redhead holding a cafeteria tray laden with desserts. He donned his warmest smile, the grandfatherly tone. "Hello there."

Becky stepped forward and put the tray down, eyeing him warily. "Who are you?"

He had only a moment to consider the question. "Tom Barstow," he said, offering his hand.

"Becky O'Connor." She scowled at him. "How do you know Julie?"

"I don't, actually. I'm Hank Jared's commanding officer." He carefully smoothed his features into an expression that exuded authority and trustworthiness, watching as she visibly relaxed in response.

They always do.

She picked up a macaroon. "What are you doing here?"

"I need to speak with Ms. Trueblood about what happened. I heard she's regained consciousness."

"Yes, but she's very tired."

"Of course. I wish it could wait, but with her father out there somewhere it's important that I speak with her as soon as possible."

Becky nodded. "Do you want me to wake her for you?"

"That would be good. Thank you."

Becky leaned in and touched Julie's arm. "Wake up, Jules. Someone's here to speak to you."

Barstow watched as she slowly opened her eyes.

"Hank?"

"Hank went back to my place to sleep for a while. This man needs to talk to you about what happened."

He forced the breath in and out of his lungs despite his desire to hold it. Julie turned her eyes to his. As soon as they connected with his own, he knew he had made the wrong decision.

Julie Trueblood recognized him, and the last time he'd introduced himself, it was as someone else entirely.

Meant for Her

Chapter 12

The taxi let Hank off in front of a Craftsman bungalow with green siding and red trim. He stepped out into the street under gray, stormy skies, careful to avoid the piles of slush and brown, melting snow. Digging in his pocket, he took out the key that Becky gave him and walked up the chunky front steps to the covered porch.

He unlocked the big wooden door and stepped inside, where he was greeted by a barking Pug. *Lucy? Lainey?* He couldn't remember what Becky said. The dog's scrunched black face and beady eyes contrasted with its sand-colored body and the mirth of its curled tail.

Stepping around the animal, he walked through the living room to the kitchen and helped himself to a glass of water. He leaned his tired body on the counter as he drained the glass.

"Ever since I lost David..."

Hank moved to the table as he pulled out his cell phone.

"Hank," answered Chip. "Did you find McDowell?"

"Yeah. Then I lost him again."

"Shit."

"Yeah." Hank rubbed his free hand down his face. "How're Melody and the babies?"

"They're great."

"She all right?"

"Uh huh. She's stable. Doctor says she's out of the woods."

Hank's head fell back. "That's awesome."

"What do you need?"

"Julie Trueblood was shot by her father last night."

"Oh my God. Is she okay?"

"I think so." He closed his eyes. "Chip, the message you left the other day. David Beaumont."

There was a pause on the line. "I thought you didn't want to pursue it."

"I don't. But I can't stop thinking about it." Hank opened his eyes and sat back in his chair. "I mean, the guy was a music composer. What the hell does he have to do with *anything*?"

"I don't know. Do you want me to see what I can find out?"

"Yeah. Yeah, I do. But be safe. If it comes down to it, it isn't that important. Got it?"

"Got it."

"Thanks, man. Give my love to Melody."

"Will do."

He hung up the phone and stared at the kitchen wall, unseeing.

Gwen was a special lady. If there was something to this, she deserved to know the truth.

Becky stood outside the nursery and watched a father cry over his newborn son. A nurse was checking the baby over and chatting with the dad as she moved her stethoscope over the baby's chest.

Becky had wandered off when Barstow wanted to talk to Julie, and found the hospital had little to offer in the way of entertainment. A quick spin through the gift shop yielded a coffee mug with "I love my Pug" drawn out in symbols and pictures, before a sign for the maternity ward caught her eye.

There were three other infants in the room, two girls and a boy, each wearing hand-knitted caps of pink or blue and swaddled in white blankets with pink and green stripes. As she watched, a woman in a bathrobe walked gingerly in, showed the nurse her wristband, and wheeled one of the girls out of the nursery.

Someday, that will be me.

Despite the pang of her biological clock, Becky was in no rush to settle down. On the contrary, she enjoyed dating different men and not getting too attached to any of them. How could one man be as interesting as three or four?

At the moment, she was seeing a professional weightlifter, an architect, and a veterinarian, each of whom had qualities she liked. The vet was getting clingy, though, and she suspected she would need to let him go soon.

She looked at it like fishing for the perfect man. Catch and release, before they died in the bucket, or proposed marriage or something equally ridiculous. In the last three years, two men

Meant for Her

had proposed, and Becky was quite sure there was a distinct odor in the air at the time.

A little girl and an old woman entered the nursery hand-in-hand. The girl wore a pink T-shirt that said, "Big Sister" and the woman picked her up as they joined the man and the newborn boy.

Becky's heart constricted as she watched the father take the girl from the woman and introduce her to her new baby brother.

Oh, Meghan. I miss you so much.

A very young woman with raven hair, ivory skin and bright green eyes appeared in her memory. Older by nearly five years, Meghan O'Connor acted like a second mother to little Becky. She braided her long red hair, dressed her in pretty outfits, and took her for walks around the yard in the stroller.

As the girls grew up, they only grew closer, spending hours playing basketball, doing each others nails and telling secrets. At sixteen, Meghan was in love with Liam Wheaton, a strikingly handsome boy with strong features and dark brown hair. He was from the wrong part of town, with the wrong kind of family, and the girls' parents had forbidden Meghan to see him.

Young Becky had begun lying for her sister, so the couple could spend time together.

The last day Becky saw her sister, Becky was eleven. Meghan and Liam had taken her on a picnic in the country. There was a big field of golden grass and a small, shallow river where they spent the day wading and looking for crayfish.

"Always remember how much I love you, Monkey." Meghan was staring at her sister, the sunlight streaming through the trees behind her, making her look like an angel.

The next day, she and Liam were gone.

That was a very long time ago.

"Can I help you with anything?"

She turned to find a blonde-haired young man with piercing blue eyes and matching scrubs checking her out. Residents weren't usually assigned as hall monitors, and she suspected her veterinarian might be replaced by someone else with medical training.

"Hi." She put her hands in her back pockets. "I'm Becky."

Meant for Her

He tilted his head back and smirked. "Jim Hanguerer."

"Nice to meet you, Jim. Would you like to buy me a drink after your shift?"

He grinned widely. "I would love to."

"You're Barstow?"

This man looked like he had swung by for a visit between church services and a round of golf. The very idea of him being a threat to her was laughable, yet her stomach churned with anxiety at his mere presence.

"Would you excuse us please, young lady?" he asked Becky. When she was gone, he pulled a chair up beside Julie's bed and sat down. "I am. But you remember me as someone else, don't you?"

Her mother's last day on this earth, in a hospital room not unlike this one, a younger Julie returned from the chapel to find a stranger at her mother's bedside. He had introduced himself as Henry Goldstein. She wondered who he was to her mother, why he came to see her just hours before her death.

"Why did you lie to me?"

His lips pressed together in a firm line. "I didn't want you to tell your father I came to see your mom."

"Why not?"

"Mary and I were friends. She was the head engineer at a project I was overseeing at Camp Harold. Your father got the wrong idea."

A memory flashed in her mind, the family at a truck stop off the interstate, her father screaming at her mother in the parking lot, onlookers staring in shock.

"You were flirting with him. I saw you, damn it!"

So many times, so many accusations. Her father's rages were legendary, her mother's acceptance of his jealousy baffling to her daughter.

"I'm sorry he did that to you."

He nodded. "I got to say goodbye to Mary. That's all I cared about." He looked down at his hands, absently rubbing his fingers. "I still miss her, your mother."

"So do I."

Meant for Her

"Taken from this world far too soon." He cleared his throat. "Anyway. I didn't come to talk about the past, I came to talk about what happened yesterday at Systex."

Julie walked him through the events of the last five days, though he already knew about many of them from Hank. He sat forward in his chair, never interrupting as she went through the details of her ordeal.

When she was finished, he bowed his head. "I'm sorry for all that you've been through, and I'm sorry I have to ask you this, Julie, but I do." He met her eyes with his own. "Are you sleeping with Hank Jared?"

She felt her cheeks heat at the intimate question, feeling much as she had when the priest had caught her and Hank kissing in the basement. She looked at her hands in her lap.

"I see." He sat back in his chair, weaving his fingers together as he frowned. "I'd like you to break it off."

"What? Why?"

"You are the daughter of the most famous American traitor since Benedict Arnold. A lot of people—not me, mind you, but a lot of people—believe you were involved. It will destroy his career, Julie. Everything that young man has worked so hard to achieve."

"I haven't done anything wrong."

"I know that, but it doesn't matter. It's all perception. You are perceived to be the enemy, and Jared is perceived to be one who's sleeping with the enemy. He was going to be promoted to commander, Julie. Do you know how hard he's worked for that?" His eyes implored her. "That won't happen now."

Julie could feel her lower lip beginning to tremble and she bit down on it, hard. "But I love him," she whispered.

"If you really love him, you'll do what's best for him." Barstow leaned forward in his chair, his eyes beseeching. "I've worked with him for eight years, watching him persevere day in and day out for his career. He's a Navy man, through and through. It will break his spirit if that's taken away from him."

Was he right? Would Hank lose something that was so important to him, for her? "I'll talk to him about it."

"You know what he'll say, Julie."

123

Meant for Her

Yes, she did. He could be on fire, and he'd deny it if it would make her happy. Just a few hours ago, he told her he loved her and the world was at her feet. Now just as quickly, it was hanging by a thread.

"Maybe you can two can make it work after everything falls apart. I don't know. But I suggest you think long and hard before you make that choice, because you're making it for both of you."

Tears welled in her eyes and began to spill out over her lashes. "Where will I go? My father broke into my apartment once. I'm not safe there. Hank was taking care of me."

"I can protect you, Julie."

She stared at him, a dignified man with kindness in his eyes and an olive branch in his hand. He was her mother's friend, her lover's commanding officer. He would keep her safe.

Her head nodded in agreement, feeling the tears fall as she did. A gasping sob brought her hand to her mouth.

If you love something, set it free...

She cried until she fell asleep, a dreamless relief from the most difficult of days.

Hank didn't know what kind of flowers she liked, so he bought one of each.

A few hours of sleep had done him a world of good, and as he walked into Julie's hospital room he had a bounce in his step and a smile on his face.

She was sitting in the blue recliner, watching the rare winter thunderstorm rattle the city of Boston. The blanket of white had been ripped off the landscape by rain, leaving only shredded bits of snow smeared and diminishing in its wake.

"You're up," he said as he crossed to her, kissing her cheek. "That's terrific. How are you feeling?"

"Good. I'm good." She sat oddly still, her hands clenching the arms of the chair.

"What did the doctor say? Has he been in to see you?"

She nodded. "He says I'm going to be fine."

Hank offered her the flowers. "I brought you these. I wasn't sure what you liked."

"Thank you."

Meant for Her

"Is everything okay? You seem preoccupied."

She looked back to the storm out the window. "I guess I am."

"What's going on?"

Lightning flashed and Hank found himself counting, waiting for the thunder. He got to five before she answered him.

"This isn't going to work."

Thunder crashed outside the window as shock glanced off Hank like a blow. He must have misunderstood. "What do you mean?"

"You and me. It's not going to work."

"Why the hell not?"

"I don't want to be with you, Hank. I'm sorry."

He stared at her unmoving body, her eyes never leaving his. The stillness that captivated her contrasted with mother nature's violent outburst outside. A different kind of storm took hold in his heart.

I'm not going to lose you again.

"You said you love me."

"I was upset. I confused gratitude with love."

"What, and the last six hours have cleared it all up for you?"

She looked away from him, another flash of lightning capturing her lifeless features.

"What happened between now and then, Julie?" He knelt before her on the tile floor. "Because I love you. I want to make a life with you."

She turned back to him quickly, her eyes angry and harsh. "I don't love you, Hank. I never did. You almost got me killed, you let my father escape. I'm lucky to even be alive. Now for God's sake, get the hell out of here."

Hank traipsed through the hallways, down flights of stairs and got lost. A trash can beckoned and he threw away the flowers he had bought for the woman he loved. He was angry, he was confused. He was emotionally devastated.

Somehow he got back to his car in the parking garage, rammed the key in the ignition and started to drive. Where he was going, he had no idea.

Meant for Her

The city streets were congested with traffic and he felt the world closing in on him. He picked up the ninety-three expressway and headed out of the city, quickly accelerating beyond the speed limit on the slick roads. He pulled his cell phone out of his pocket and dialed Barstow.

"You need to get a uniform on Julie Trueblood's hospital room."

"I thought you were taking care of that."

"Not anymore." He looked down and disconnected the call. He lifted his gaze and saw a family driving beside him on the road, reminding him that he was not the only one who might be hurt if he drove recklessly.

"Fuck." He said to himself, easing off the accelerator.

He ran his hand through his hair. What would he do now that Julie was gone? He had let her down, failed to protect her, and she couldn't forgive him. He understood that. He couldn't forgive himself, either. The knowledge burned at his gut like a physical pain. Julie Trueblood had every right to want him out of her life for good.

He just didn't have any idea what the future would look like without her in it. She had made him happier in a few days than anyone had made him in his whole life.

Gwen found Julie an hour later, propped in the same blue recliner like a lifeless doll. Outside the window, rain fell in a constant pour from the heavens.

"Julie, are you all right?"

Slowly her head pivoted to face Gwen. "Yes."

"Where's Hank? I thought he would be here?"

"I sent him away."

Gwen cocked her head to the side. "Why?"

"I didn't want him here anymore."

The healer in Gwen instantly wondered if Julie was suffering an infection. She walked over and put her hand on Julie's forehead.

"I'm not sick."

"Then what's going on?"

"What do you mean?"

"Why did you send Hank away?"

Julie frowned and shrugged her shoulder as if she had no idea of the answer. "I just don't think we should be together anymore."

Gwen sat down on the edge of the bed, close to her niece. "You broke up with him? What the hell is going on, Julie?"

Julie raised her eyes to Gwen's. "I'm not good for him, Gwen."

"Of course you are."

She looked at her hands in her lap. "I'm John McDowell's daughter. How do you think that's going to play at the office?"

Gwen pursed her lips. "I imagine it will be difficult for Hank at first."

"I imagine it will ruin his entire career."

"That's for Hank to consider, Julie. Not for you to decide for him."

Julie looked frankly at Gwen. "And what do you think he would say?"

"He would choose you, of course."

"Exactly."

"So that's it, then. You just sent him away." Gwen stood and walked to the sink, washing her hands and grabbing a paper towel. "I think you're being very selfish, Julie."

Julie turned wide eyes to her aunt. "No, I'm being very unselfish. I'm setting him free."

"You," she said, pointing at her, "are conveniently escaping a real relationship with a good man by bowing out gracefully at the eleventh hour. Shame on you, Julie. You're not even going to give him a chance, are you?"

"I'm doing this for Hank."

"Oh, bullshit, Julie." Gwen's chest heaved and her nostrils flared as she grabbed her purse off the bed. "You have a chance at happiness, my dear, that many people never get. Now, I'm going for a walk. I'll return when I am no longer angry enough to throttle you."

Hank got out of the cab, pulling his red and black carry-on behind him. The airport loomed wide before him, its curbside

Meant for Her

crowded with vacationers and businesspeople jockeying for position at makeshift check-in counters.

His uniform glittered in the midday sun, every badge and pin in perfect place, his shoes polished to a flawless shine.

The military was his life.

Barstow had called back, and this time Hank didn't hang up. He gave Hank orders to travel to Seattle for an investigation into the disappearance of two ensigns during a training exercise. It was a high profile case, and the admiral hinted that Hank would finally be promoted to commander if the investigation was resolved satisfactorily.

A family walked in front of him, husband and wife similar in height and build to him and Julie. Three small children followed behind, the oldest a girl, maybe five. She turned to Hank and waved, her other arm pulling a pink monster suitcase behind her.

He turned to walk into the airport, but his feet refused to move beneath him. A month ago, a year—he knew exactly what he wanted. Today all of those dreams were within reach. All he had to do was get on a plane and do his job.

But he didn't want those things anymore. He wanted Julie Trueblood.

Any other lieutenant could be standing where he stood, wearing the same uniform he wore, headed toward the same destination to perform the same job.

He turned in the opposite direction and gazed into the bright afternoon sun, shielding his eyes so he could make out the skyline of downtown Boston.

Julie.

Gwen had called this morning to let him know Julie had been discharged. She also asked him for a gun to give her niece, unable to obtain one herself on short notice. He proposed a trade—the weapon for Julie's address.

"I'm sorry, Hank. She wouldn't want me to tell you."

"And it's illegal for me to give a firearm to an unlicensed civilian."

The address was tucked in his lapel pocket. He pulled it out and knocked on the window of a cab as it began to pull away. "I

Meant for Her

need a ride," he said, climbing in as he loosened the collar on his uniform.

Chapter 13

Julie sat on the floor of the expansive room, the last bands of the setting sun streaming in through the floor-to-ceiling windows. Wood floors were stained a modern black, the walls covered in warm gold paint. An equally modern kitchen ran along the short wall adjacent to the windows, a hefty island and barstools rounding out the space.

Barstow had called her at the hospital this morning. "It was a textile manufacturing plant in the seventies. Being converted to loft apartments. This is the first unit that's come up for sale."

"Really, you don't have to…"

He cut her off. "It's an investment. You'll rent it from me, once you get on your feet. I'll have someone drop off the keys."

She had packed an overnight bag with the essentials, including a pillow and blanket. These she set up on the floor next to containers of Chinese take-out and a bottle of cheap Chianti from a liquor store down the street.

The only thing she put in the kitchen was the pistol Gwen had given her. It was in the drawer to the left of the sink, and in her mind it seemed to take up all the cupboard space and every square inch of countertop.

Isn't it just like Gwen to give me firepower?

Julie sipped her wine from a plastic cup as she let her eyes glide from one side of the space to the other, bumping up and over the square surfaces of the kitchen until they came to rest on the heap of her own belongings.

They didn't fit in here any more than she did.

Barstow's offer of protection seemed like a godsend at the time, but sitting in the emptiness made it clear that more had changed than her address. Hank was gone, and she was completely alone.

She had sent them away, of course. Becky and Gwen would never abandon her. A part of her needed this solitude, like an injured animal wandering away from the pack to lick its wounds.

The bottle in her hand was heavy with wine, and she rubbed her fingers against the woven basket that covered its smooth glass bottom. She loved these bottles as a child, their dark glass artfully drizzled with a rainbow of candle wax.

Tomorrow, she knew, she would move on without even unpacking.

The gun from Gwen was a sign. She was in charge of her own protection now. Barstow was as unnecessary to her as the boxes of detritus Becky had so carefully hauled here from Julie's condo this afternoon.

None of it mattered without Hank.

Maybe she'd go south, just until it got warm, then rent an old house and plant a garden. Watch it grow. That would beat the hell out of the damn snow and ice and writing computer programs she didn't even care about.

The sun slipped below the skyline as Julie reached for the Chinese food bag. Two fortune cookies rattled in the bottom and she pulled them out, slicing open their wrappers with her teeth and slipping the papers from their crunchy folds.

Believe in love and it surrounds you.

She scoffed out loud—a bitter, desperate sound—and flipped to the second fortune.

Enemies and friends have similar features.

She thought of Barstow. He had been an enemy in her mind for so very long, only to be an ally in the end.

A loud clang of metal on metal came from the entryway and she started, adrenaline quickly shooting into her bloodstream. She slowly rose to her feet and strained her ears to hear, unable to see past an eight-foot high divider that separated her from the foyer space.

The silence that followed mocked the original clamor, and she fixed her gaze on the kitchen drawer some ten paces from where she stood. The path to the kitchen was visible from the doorway, and she hesitated, unsure of what to do next.

"Julie? Are you here?"

She exhaled the breath in her lungs, recognizing the admiral's voice. "Tom, you scared the shit out of me."

He walked into the space wearing a black leather jacket and aviator glasses, carrying a pizza box. "Sorry. I didn't think."

Julie watched as he put the box on the granite counter top

Meant for Her

and pulled out a cell phone, checking his messages. Crisp jeans landed on black leather boots, adorned with simple silver chains. She wouldn't have recognized him, were it not for his voice.

"You hungry?" he asked.

"I already ate. Chinese."

He shrugged out of his coat, revealing a gray T-shirt underneath. Julie was surprised by how muscular his upper body appeared in this outfit, compared to the polo shirt he had worn to the hospital. He turned back to the kitchen and began opening cupboards. Her gut clenched, thinking of the gun.

"Got any plates?"

"No, there's nothing."

"Oh, well." He picked up a piece of pizza and took a large bite.

Julie tugged at the hem of her sweater. She thought he brought her pizza to be kind, but it looked like he was making himself comfortable on a barstool at the kitchen island.

Oh, please, go away.

She debated whether or not to offer him a glass of wine, neither wanting to be rude nor encouraging him to stay. Rubbing at the back of her neck, she decided rude was preferable. At least he might take the hint and leave.

An image flashed in Julie's mind, a picture of her firing the gun at Barstow. It was so real, more like a memory than anything, and it scared her. She looked beseechingly at the admiral. Was she losing her mind?

He met her eyes as he masticated, the muscles of his jaw working as he stared with eyes void of compassion. Gone was the affable and empathetic man who had visited her in the hospital, the stark contrast unsettling and dark.

Fear began to hum in her belly as the image returned. This time she could see the bullet entering his body, his head jerking back and to the side, blood splattering the taupe wall behind him. Her eyes traveled to look around the loft—failing to find any such wall.

"Would you like some wine?" she asked.

"Sure."

From her camp on the floor she retrieved her overnight bag,

digging a bit before finding another plastic cup. She poured him Chianti and delivered it to his side. In one quick twirl, she caught the cup with her elbow and sent it to the floor, spilling its contents on his pant leg as it fell.

"Damn it to hell," he said, standing quickly.

"Oh, no. I'm so sorry," she said, hands splayed in mid-air. "There's a towel in the bathroom. You can rinse it out."

He stormed away, his body hulking from side to side like a much younger man. She positioned herself in front of the silverware drawer and waited until he was out of sight before grabbing the gun and tucking it in the waistband of her jeans.

Grateful for her bulky sweater, Julie pulled the yellow and green yarn down over the weapon and began to pour Barstow more wine. He reappeared the instant she picked up the bottle, making tiny beads of sweat pop out on her forehead.

"I am sorry, Tom. Did it come out?"

He walked up to her and grabbed her by the elbow. "How about we cut the bullshit, shall we?"

"What do you mean?"

In one move he reached his other hand under her sweater and pulled out the gun, then held the side of it against her nose. "Bullshit, Julie."

He pushed her away, making her lose her footing and stumble onto the floor.

"You want to play games? Let's play a little truth or dare, shall we?" He worked to dislodge a piece of food from his teeth.

Julie got her feet beneath her, crouching on the floor beneath his imposing form. "Why are you here?" she said.

"Waiting for your father. I sent him a text message with this address an hour ago."

Her skin prickled hot and cold. "Why?"

"Oh, sorry. My turn." He was smiling like the Cheshire cat, clearly enjoying himself. "I dare you to stand right here in front of me," he gestured to the floor, "and tell me you haven't been in contact with your father in all these years."

It was ridiculous, but she felt her own desire to challenge him as she rose before him and raised her chin, speaking the truth. "I haven't been in contact with my father in ten years."

The slap met her face with such force, her head whipped around.

"Liar! The game is *truth* or dare. Nothing but a cunning little opportunist, just like your mother."

Hatred dripped from his voice, coating the words in ugliness. If he hated her mother, w*hy had he gone to see her in the hospital?*

Something clicked in her memory, a doctor in a white lab coat saying her mother would be going home tomorrow. Julie had gone to the chapel to give thanks for prayers answered, and found Henry Goldstein in her mother's room upon her return.

Thomas Barstow.

"You killed her!"

"She left me no choice." He raised arms at his sides. "She was going to name me in the lawsuit about the radiation. It would have destroyed my career, just like you are trying to destroy Jared's. The apple doesn't fall far from the tree, now does it?"

There was no statute of limitations on murder. Barstow had no intention of letting her walk out of here alive.

Too bad it's not his decision to make.

The courage roared up insider her, the will to fight for herself and win. She deliberately focused on the scene in her mind, Barstow's blood splattering on the wall. Confidence swarmed through her as she watched him fall, knowing that her premonition would become reality.

Her fingers itched to hold the cold metal of the gun, which rested on the granite next to his half-eaten pizza. Déjà vu wafted over her like a cloud shadowing the sun. She had already lived this moment in the kitchen of Systex, her father standing before her, her opportunity fading as she hesitated.

I will not hesitate again.

"This is so much fun. I've often dreamed of what it would be like to talk to you. You're the only person who can really *appreciate* all that I've done."

Cold sweat lingered on her back, her underarms. "What else is there?"

He puffed his chest. "Pour me a glass of wine. And don't

spill this one, you clumsy bitch."

She retrieved his cup from the floor and filled it, bringing the bottle back with her to the island. She took a seat at a barstool across from Barstow and her gun.

"Ah, these horrible little Chianti bottles with the baskets on them. Leo used to have them on every table."

"You knew Leo?"

"Of course. I introduced him to your father when I recruited McDowell to work for Uzkapostan." He swallowed half his wine in one sip. "We were quite a team, your father and I. I had access to information, he had the ability to decode it. It was un-fucking-believable what we were able to accomplish."

"Until the Dermody went down."

He nodded. "Our greatest triumph, but we were discovered when they traced the leak to my office. Fortunately for me, everything pointed to your father." He winked at her.

"But you were both guilty."

"No," he said, his eyes widening. "*We were both heroes.*"

He picked up the gun and twirled it around by the trigger guard. "Your father went back to Uzkapostan and everything was fine, until he started blackmailing me. At first I figured I was helping a comrade survive on the lamb. I knew your father wouldn't turn on me. But over the years he has gotten greedy. It is affecting my bottom line.

So I plugged the security hole in the Navy's procurement database, knowing he'd come out of hiding to get you to fix it."

"You've been trying to track him down ever since."

He nodded. "I almost had him that night at Systex. I threw the glass against the wall to try to separate you two."

"It was you in the elevator!"

He raised his glass. "Indeed."

"But he got away. So you gave him my address, hoping he would come after me, and you could get to him."

He pointed at her, a teacher to a star pupil. "Very good. Except he's not coming to get you," he began to laugh. "He's coming to protect you!"

Julie didn't understand. "He shot me."

"Your father didn't shoot you, Julie McDowell." His evil

eyes glittered as he spoke. "*I shot you.*"

She saw him reach for the gun, but she snatched it off the granite first. Her hand clutched at the metal but failed to get a grip, the weapon dropping to the floor with a heavy rattle. Julie pivoted to retrieve it and Barstow kicked her away, picking up the gun himself.

She ran, her feet hectic as they worked to push her to safety, Barstow's footsteps thunderous behind her. She darted around one side of the barrier separating the loft from the front door and entered the darkened foyer.

Gunshots exploded just as she reached for the door handle.

A hundred and eighty pounds of weight slammed into her, propelling her into the steel entry door. Julie screamed. The body that crushed her fell to the floor, and she turned to see her father, blood streaming from his neck.

He had been hiding behind the wall, and deliberately placed himself between his daughter and her attacker.

"Daddy!"

His voice was a rasp, barely a sound. "Run!"

"Oh, that's so precious. A father rushing to save his daughter." The admiral clucked his tongue. "But it was all for naught, McDowell." He laughed hysterically. "Because you're blocking the door!"

Julie saw that he was right. Her father's body blocked her only escape. In that moment it didn't matter that she was trapped. All that mattered was that he had not tried to kill her, but had saved her instead.

"I love you, Daddy," she whispered. McDowell took a final racking breath, then he was gone.

Barstow's cell phone rang and he checked the caller ID before answering it, the gun pointed at Julie. "What is it?" his smile turned to a scowl. "When?" He listened, then hung up the phone. "It seems your boyfriend's missed his flight to Seattle. I wonder where he could be headed?"

Hank stood on the street outside the apartments, pacing. The door to the building was locked, with no way to ring the individual units. Alarm bells jangled in his brain as he phoned

Gwen.

"No, it was definitely open this afternoon," she said. "Do you think she's all right?"

"No."

"I'm on my way."

"Call 911 first."

"I will."

He put the phone back in his pocket and strode to a bank of windows. He took off one shoe and used the heel like a hammer to break the glass, then clear away the shards. The opening was nearly three feet square, and he hoisted himself up and over the wall.

He was in a large empty room with a steel door at the far end. He jogged to it, threw back the lock, and entered a darkened hallway in search of the stairs.

A red exit sign led him to a stairwell, and he took the steps two at a time as fast as his feet would propel him.

Becky's words tormented him as he climbed. *"It was your job to protect her, and you did a shitty job of it!"* Flight after flight he flew, breath coming in great gasping whooshes of air as he pushed his body to go faster, get there sooner, prevent what had happened from happening again.

Three deafening gunshots rang out on the other side of the fire door, half a flight from the seventh floor landing.

"Hank doesn't know where I am."

Barstow touched his finger to his chin and pursed his lips. "Now, why don't I believe that?"

"I broke it off, just like you told me to."

"That was excellent advice on my part. I had to extricate you from your bodyguard. Plus, I don't think he's ready to settle down, that one."

Julie's attention was drawn to the wall behind Barstow, which wasn't visible from the rest of the apartment. Unlike the honeyed gold that graced the other walls, this one was taupe.

There would be no Calvary, no knight in shining armor come to rescue her. Gwen had given her firepower, and though that gun was in Barstow's hands, the gift had little to do with the

Meant for Her

weapon. The universe raised its mighty sledgehammer and hit Julie Trueblood over the head with it.

Like a movie flashing in the darkness, she saw herself kneel before her father's body in grief, surreptitiously removing the concealed pistol from the ankle holster she knew he always wore. A warm feeling surged through her belly, and she knew her father would be happy it was his gun that would save the life he had died trying to protect.

She nodded her head slightly and allowed her lungs to fill with air. With more faith than she knew she possessed, Julie began to mimic the moves she envisioned in her mind. The emotions came of their own volition, first her face crumpling in grief. Her shoulders caved in around herself as racking sobs took her breath away, true feelings overtaking her as she allowed them to come freely to the surface.

Leaning over the body, *the last time she would touch this man*, she reached around his legs in an awkward embrace. She stealthily slipped the gun from its hiding spot beneath his trouser leg.

Barstow ordered her to stand up, as she knew he would. She bent at the waist, hiding the gun, until she nearly reached her full height and turned on him.

His face fell when he saw what she had found, his eyes hardening as he began to raise his own weapon.

Julie fired three bullets, each of them seeming to hang in midair. Barstow's head twisted at a horrible angle, blood splattering onto the wall behind him in a predetermined design.

He fell to the ground, dead.

The sound of his body hitting the floor was grotesque. For some moments she stared at his form, unable to comprehend what had happened. She looked up, gazing at the pattern of blood on the wall, realizing she stood in the presence of God. She fell to her knees.

Thank you for saving me.

Someone pushed the door behind her furiously into her father's body, and for a while Julie just watched. She heard Hank call her name, finally moving from her stupor to pull at her father's weight and allow Hank entry. He rushed in, his hands

Meant for Her

running up and down her body. Julie could hear sirens. She could see his lips moving, but she wasn't focused on the words.

For now, there was just the blood on the wall, the floor under her knees, and the awe in her exhausted spirit.

Chapter 14

"I think you're a complete asshole."

Julie walked by her, carrying an armful of folded towels, and put them in the trunk of her car. It was already loaded with several turquoise duffel bags, a pillow and a worn lavender comforter. "You're entitled to your opinion, Becky."

She never did unpack the things she brought to the loft apartment, quietly nodding when the officer explained they would be tagged as evidence and held for at least thirty days.

Shopping seemed like a better idea.

Reaching into her jacket pocket, she took out her keys before letting the warm down parka slip from her shoulders.

"This is for you." She handed the coat to Becky.

"Don't go."

Tears threatened, fast and hot against her lashes. "I'm leaving," she insisted, her voice a desperate rasp.

"Hank loves you. Hell, I love you."

Julie opened her arms and hugged her tight. "I love you, too." Slowly, she let her arms fall away from her friend. She climbed behind the wheel, numbly starting the engine. "I'll call you when I get where I'm going."

Red blotches mottled Becky's ivory skin. "I'll miss you."

"Enjoy that promotion. You deserve it."

She nodded, tears running freely down her face. "Drive safe, you stupid crazy bitch."

"I will."

Julie closed the door against the cold winter air and turned the key in the ignition. With a sad smile and a wave at her best friend, she pulled away from the curb and headed toward the interstate. Relief percolated through her mind, bringing with it the first real peace she'd experienced in what seemed like weeks.

After the incident, as she had come to refer to it, Hank had driven her to the police station in his SUV. He seemed to understand that she needed to be left alone. Julie was interviewed, and when she emerged she was grateful to find only Gwen waiting to take her home, a book of Sudoku puzzles in her lap.

"Hank said to tell you he loves you. He had some work to take care of in D.C."

And she knew.

The military was Hank's life, and it was the antithesis of hers. It was crazy to believe they could make it work.

She would be gone before he ever returned.

Moon Lake glistened silver in the morning sunshine, the Adirondack Mountains frozen in waves of purple and blue on the horizon. Hank pushed the lawn mower over his mother's rolling property, the noise from its engine drowning out all other sounds. The muscles of his arms and back reveled in the exercise, while his mind enjoyed the simple monotony.

Anything to keep from thinking about Julie.

He'd gone looking for her when he got back from D.C., only to find a For Sale sign in front of her condo. The dread in his belly clawed at his insides as he drove toward Becky's house, fearing he knew what she was going to say.

"She's gone, Hank."

"Where?"

Becky stood in the doorway of her bungalow, gazing at the horizon. "South. Someplace warm." She looked at her feet, then back at him. "I told her not to go. Actually, I told her she was an asshole, but she went anyway."

"Do you have a number for her? An address?"

"I do," she bit her lip, "but I can't give it to you, Hank. I'm sorry."

He stepped backwards away from the door, down the walk, reeling from the events of the last hour. When did she leave? Why hadn't he been here for her when she was making that decision? In his heart he believed he could have stopped her, convinced her to stay.

"Tell her I love her, Becky," he said, his throat knotted with emotion.

"She knows."

"Just tell her." He pivoted on his heel and headed back to his car, not knowing where he would go or what he would do. He only knew he would go out of his mind if he couldn't get to her, couldn't talk to her, couldn't touch her.

He finished mowing and released the safety bar, shutting off the engine. He pushed the mower back to the garden shed behind the house, finding his mother inside, potting up plants.

"Hey, Ma."

"Hey, yourself."

"Lawn's done."

"Thanks." She scooped a handful of potting soil around the bare roots of a hosta.

Hank rolled the machine into its spot next to the wall. "I'm going to Vermont."

"What for?"

He put his hands on his hips. "I'm going to ask Gwen for Julie's address. What's the worst that can happen? She won't tell me?"

Marianne put the pot aside and picked up an empty one. "It's about time, Hank. Give Gwen my love."

The ringing of the doorbell set the dogs to barking as Gwen rolled the damp mass of spongy dough in cracked wheat berries. She set it in a wicker basket to proof, the final rise before baking on the stone she had heating in the oven.

She washed the flour from her hands and dried them on a fluffy red towel as she walked to the door. A warm spring breeze blew in through the windows, carrying with it the sound of wind chimes from the front porch. Gwen opened the heavy door to find Hank Jared standing with his hands in the front pockets of his jeans.

"Hi, Gwen."

A warm smile lit her face as she opened the screen for him. "Hank! Come inside." She opened her arms to him for an embrace of genuine affection. "It's good to see you."

"You too."

She walked into the kitchen, beckoning him to follow. "I was just finishing up some baking. Can I get you something to drink? I have some fresh iced tea."

"That would be great." It smelled like cookies as he walked

Meant for Her

into the kitchen and sat down at the island. "You can probably guess why I'm here."

"Becky managed to hold out and not give you Julie's address." She reached into the refrigerator to grab the pitcher of tea. "She wasn't sure she'd be able to do it."

"I need to see her, Gwen."

"Yes, I know you do." She grabbed a couple of chocolate chip cookies from the cooling rack and put them on a plate in front of him. "To be honest, I expected you to contact me sooner."

Hank put both hands around his iced tea, looking into the glass. "When I found out she was gone, I thought there must be some misunderstanding. She wouldn't just leave without telling me where she was going. So I went to Becky's." He looked her in the eye. "That's when I realized she hadn't just left town, she'd left me."

Gwen looked into his deeply troubled eyes, her heart going out to him. He'd lost weight, but more than that he lost the warm glow that used to shine from his spirit.

"She's in South Carolina." Reaching into a tall cherry cupboard, she got herself a glass and filled it with the brew. "After she got out of the hospital, she spent one night at Becky's, then just packed up and drove away. I don't think she even set foot in her old condo, except to get her cat. She called a woman who does estate sales and a Realtor and that was that."

"Can I have the address?"

She nodded, taking out a fabric address book from a drawer and copying it onto a small sheet of paper. She held it out to him.

"Be patient with her, Hank. I love her more than anyone, but running away is the only way she knows how to deal with her problems. Julie has never learned how to stay."

"Well then, I guess I'll have to teach her."

"I wish you luck, my friend," she said, smiling warmly.

Hank reached out and pulled her close for another hug. "Thank you, Gwen."

"Take some cookies. It's a very long drive."

Julie stood in the sunny yellow kitchen cutting slices of

avocado, an orange tiger cat purring at her feet. A vibrant plate painted with red and blue daisies was laden with salad greens, its edges chipped from age. She added chunks of blue cheese and crumbled bits of bacon strips, haphazardly covering the pile with pieces of hard boiled egg and cold grilled chicken.

Grabbing a pitcher of freshly squeezed lemonade, she headed out the kitchen door and onto the screened porch, the humid air instantly covering the smooth glass with a fog of condensation.

This house had been a haven for Julie, a small painted lady with a pinky-red exterior and yellow shutters. The porch overlooked a lush garden bursting with plump vegetables, and a glorious weeping willow she imagined had been planted by the original owners.

She filled her days walking in the sun, weeding her garden, or reading on the porch. It was only at night that the dreams of him came, sure as the moon rose into the sky. She lay in his arms, desire a living, breathing animal with a will of its own. Steeped in his scent, she surrendered to her lover once more, every touch marking her his, every emotion connecting their spirits.

With the sunrise and consciousness came a rededication to live without him, to keep her tears inside, to plan a future without Hank Jared. Some days, she even thought it was possible.

She sat eating her salad, swaying in a white wooden rocker, unaware that some bites had more chicken, others too much egg. She didn't move when the doorbell rang, assuming it must be a delivery man or solicitor, and not caring to engage either one.

"Julie."

He was standing at the corner of the house, next to the white rosebush. She stopped rocking and stared at him, shockingly handsome in khaki shorts and a fitted polo shirt. She hastily finished chewing the salad in her mouth and set the bowl aside, slowing rising.

"I couldn't stay away." He took a step toward her. "I tried to, but I missed you so damn much."

Emotions came raging to the surface, choking her. She covered her mouth with her hands. He moved more swiftly now,

Meant for Her

covering the distance that separated them, coming onto the porch, his eyes never leaving hers. Then he was there, his arms around her, her face pressed into his neck, his scent surrounding her.

"Oh, Hank."

He stepped back, holding her face in his hands and watching the emotions play over her features. "Don't leave me again, okay?" She nodded as he covered her face with kisses. "Don't do that to me. We belong together."

He bent his head to hers as she reached for him, their lips meeting and melding, becoming one. Her arms clutched at him, pulling him tighter against her body as heat surged through her belly, fluid and warm.

She led him into the house, up the stairs to her bedroom.

Everything she had run from reared to life inside her, the fervent hopes and dreams of this love, of this man, coursing through her body. She opened herself to him, her mind and soul, allowing the love she felt to flow freely, uninhibited and proud.

There was a truth between them that was remarkable and strong despite their separation, and she reveled in their passion, seeing for the first time that their love for each other was honest and good, and could see them through the darkness.

Hank Jared was meant for her, like a flower was meant for the sun.

And she knew. She was going to hold on to this man forever.

Julie cuddled up to Hank's back and threw her leg over his. They had been making love and sleeping, on and off for the past twelve hours.

"I don't even know where you live," she said, giggling.

He cleared his throat. "With my mom."

"You do not."

He turned his head into the pillow. "Actually, at the moment I do."

"Why?"

He rolled onto his back, lifting his arm for her to snuggle closer. "I used to keep an apartment in D.C., but I wasn't there enough to say so. I gave it up when I resigned my commission. Then I couldn't bring myself to get another place without…"

She interrupted. "When you *what*?"

"Resigned my commission. I left the Navy, Julie."

"What? When?"

"When I went to D.C. for my debriefing after Barstow died."

She sat up, pulling the sheet up to cover herself. "Because of me? They made you resign because of me?"

"They didn't make me resign. I quit."

"But why?" She waved her hand at him. "You love the Navy. The military's everything to you!"

"No, Julie. *You are everything to me.*" He caressed her cheek. "The Navy was just a job."

She threw the blankets back and strode to the bathroom.

"I did it to make you happy," he yelled after her.

She stomped back into the room, tying a light blue robe around her waist. "Well, why the hell didn't you ask me first? You just go and quit the Navy like it's freakin' Burger Hut and expect me to be grateful?"

He put his hands up. "Wait. What's happening here? You hate the Navy. You couldn't stand that I was an officer. Does any of this ring a bell? You didn't want to be involved with me because of the Navy."

"I didn't want you to quit, Hank."

"I got that. But I don't understand why."

"Forget it. Just forget it." She paced the room. "I don't want to talk about this right now."

She turned and headed for the porch, the cool night air smelling of rain. She sat in her rocker, mentally daring him to follow her. When he did not, she let her shoulders drop and took a deep breath, the pungent smell of honeysuckle only now permeating her awareness.

The buzzing of cicadas mixed with the chirp of frogs and the steady rhythm of her rocking chair. Her body cooled along with her temper, and she began to feel sorry for fighting with Hank.

How could he think that leaving the Navy would make her happy? She didn't want him to give up what he cared about. Her father was the traitor, the murderer and the psychopath. It was her problem, and she should be the one to pay the price for it. Not Hank.

An hour passed before she saw him standing in the doorway, and she stopped moving.

"May I join you?"

She nodded.

He sat in the wooden porch swing across the way, his muscular arm draped across the back in artful silhouette.

"I'm sorry I got so upset," she said.

"Can you explain it to me?"

She set her chair to rocking. "I don't want you to sacrifice something you love for me."

He was quiet for a moment, and she waited to see what he would say. "Why not?"

"It makes me uncomfortable."

"Julie, that's what people who love each other do."

"No, it isn't."

"Sure, it is. They sacrifice and they compromise, they bend over backwards to make each other happy. That's what it means to be in a committed relationship."

He made it sound so rational, so reasonable. She had never been in love before. Her parents had never gone to such lengths to make each other happy.

Okay, bad example.

Her eyes began to burn as the truth made its way to her lips. "I don't deserve it."

He was up in an instant, kneeling before her chair, grabbing her hands and holding them in his own. "You do," he said, kissing each palm. "And if you'll let me, I'll spend the rest of my life trying to prove it to you."

She leaned over, her forehead resting against his as she cried. Was it possible that this incredible man knew everything about her past, and loved her anyway?

"Will you let me, Julie? Let me show you how much you deserve it, how much we both do?" He reached up and gently put his hand on her neck. "Will you be my wife?"

"I'm not good at this, Hank. I don't know what a healthy marriage looks like."

"We'll learn together, Julie. We'll figure it out as we go."
All the women in the world, and he wants to marry me.

A sob escaped as she nodded. "Yes, Hank. Yes, I'll be your wife."

The One Who Got Away

For Mom and Dad,
Thanks for being my greatest cheerleaders.

~~~

Special thanks to Laura Davis.

The One Who Got Away

Chapter 1

Gwen Trueblood slid the glass door open and stepped into the cool night air, sniffing greedily at the pungent scent of damp earth that greeted her. She felt the dew on the deck boards beneath her bare feet and smiled, her thin top lip sliding over its too-full counterpart.

Mornings were her favorite time of day, the hours before sunrise a seemingly magical gift reserved for those who appreciated their wonder. It was in this time that she did her best work, her mind free from the hazards of daily living and at once completely her own.

Already her fingers longed to drag a brush, heavy with paint, along the textured surface of a canvas. She would work on the last of an acrylic series she was doing for a show in New York. It was an abstract grouping, and she had yet to decide what she wanted to do for the last installment, having spent the better part of yesterday layering it with a background of the deepest purples and blues.

Images flipped through her mind as she sipped her hot coffee. A tree, its green leaves silhouetted against a darkened sky. A pond, at the edge of a forest. A storm.

A storm.

Dancing wind and the smell of coming electricity, the sky just beginning to mist. An image of her niece's new husband came to mind. Hank Jared's spirit was strong and good, a force to be reckoned with. She would include his energy in the painting, fighting the storm that surrounded him.

Decided now, she headed inside the old farmhouse, turning on lights as she went.

Sitting in front of her largest easel, she reached for her palette and paints. Her steady hand layered black and white onto the purple surface, instantly transforming it from a simple solid color to a turbulent scene. With broad strokes she worked a mass of red acrylic into the canvas with a thick butter knife. She spread it in large swirls, its texture like buttercream frosting piled high atop a cake.

The One Who Got Away

The picture before her was now a swirling purple background with a red structure near the top. Turning her head to the side, Gwen considered with her eyes before reaching to blend a blue and a sea green into a vibrant, singing turquoise. She began to apply the paint to the canvas in a similar shape, this time in the bottom right corner. The energy of the color against the stormy background reminded her of David, and she smiled contentedly as she worked to make the shape more soothing in appearance, with rounded edges and a thick substance of acrylic.

When Gwen looked at the canvas, she didn't see the blocks of color that made up the composition. She saw Hank Jared and David Beaumont, riding out a storm. The energy of the piece felt right, but something was missing. Perusing the metal tubes of paint, her eyes landed on a peacock green and she froze, the image of Colin Mitchell invading her memory.

He'd been wearing a polo shirt exactly that color the day everything changed. She picked the tube up and held it, the warmth of her hands quickly heating the metal. It wasn't the first time she'd thought of him, though she usually pushed the memories aside as quickly as they surfaced. Instead, she twisted off the cap and squeezed a small amount onto her fingers, spreading it between her thumb and forefinger.

It was a beautiful color, at once intense and lovely, and she stared at it, remembering Colin's handsome face. The younger brother of David's best friend Rowan, Colin was a college student when he lived at their grandmother's house just north of New York City. Rowan had parties there the summer Gwen and David were dating, the short train ride along the Hudson River seeming to take them away to a magical land.

Another memory threatened, and Gwen wiped the color onto her apron before it could breathe new life into its lungs, but she was not willing to forsake the color. Using a tapered brush she worked it into the hairs and began to paint. With every stroke, the door she had firmly closed on Colin memory eased apart another crack, exposing something raw and base beneath.

Her cheeks heated as she remembered the warm golden brown of his eyes, staring into hers, the light summer's breeze picking up his dark hair and ruffling his shirt. But it was the way he looked at her, and the sheer attraction she felt pulling her to him that she remembered now.

They were standing on the patio overlooking the Hudson River on the evening of a glorious summers day. Where the others had gone, she did not know.

Are you with David? he asked.

She could hear the baritone of his voice, not a child at all, but a grown man. There was an understanding between them already that if she was alone, she would be his, and she thrilled at the flirtation. A wind gusted, holding her caftan firmly against her body, and she reached up to tuck her hair behind her ear. This man was appealing, but she was very much in love with someone else.

I am, she answered, a smile on her face and pride in her voice. His intense eyes never left hers as he raised his glass and nodded once, making her belly tingle.

There had been other parties after that one, and Colin was always there in the background, keeping his distance from Gwen. On her way to the final party of the summer with David, Gwen stared out the train window at the miles of passing river, its expanse glimmering in the late afternoon sun, and her pulse raced a little faster, knowing they would soon see Colin.

The admission was difficult for Gwen, though she recognized lust for what it was, and not some deeper betrayal of the man she loved. As the train rocked down the track, bringing her closer to him, she allowed herself to do what she had never done before. She fantasized about Colin Mitchell.

Gwen molded the paint into a textured construction as she allowed herself to remember her dreams of touching that young sexy boy with her hands like she now touched his energy with her brush.

She was flushed, goose bumps rising up on her arms and legs as she worked. This was dangerous territory, an area of her memory that should be cordoned off with hazard tape and left well enough alone. But Gwen delved deeper, her eyes briefly closing as she imagined Colin's lips at the side of her neck, much as she had on that train ride fifteen years before.

She heard herself breathing deeply, felt her lips fall apart. It

The One Who Got Away

had been a dream, a daydream, a mistake. The past and the present mingled and danced, finally free from the confines of her mind and forever emblazoned on the canvas. Gwen rested her brush on her palette and stared at her creation.

By the time she and David got to the party, Gwen had nearly forgotten about the dream. She got herself a glass of wine while David went off with Rowan to play cards, then stepped onto the veranda to enjoy the stunning views and the cool summer breeze.

She could feel Colin's presence the moment he joined her on the patio, though she did not turn around. Her body remembered her dreams of this man, every nerve in her body tingling in anticipation like a schoolgirl with an overwhelming crush. She was being silly, playing with fire, never considering she might be burned.

His voice was deep and vibrated in her belly. "I had a dream about you."

She heard his footfalls approach, could hear him breathing behind her. "You did?"

It was little more than a whisper when he spoke. "A daydream."

Shame swept up the back of her neck. She'd been caught, like a child. She had poked the lion with a stick and now he stood so close to her, poised to attack.

"It was so real..." he said.

Gwen raised her hand. "Don't." She hadn't meant to betray David, would never have done it if she'd known Colin was aware.

His voice was throaty and snaked up her arms. "And so damn good."

She was horrified at what she had done, but at the same time she wanted Colin to touch her. She could feel the need coming off him in waves, the answering echo in her own body begging him to do it.

"Colin!" Rowan's voice behind them was sharp, startling her.

Colin's voice dripped with annoyance. "Yes?"

"I need your help inside."

They all knew he was lying. She was so embarrassed. When

she was able, she turned and faced Rowan, avoiding Colin's stare. "Is it something I can help with?" she asked, crossing the patio and heading into the house.

What have I done?

Gwen cursed herself and her damn libido, her attraction to this boy and her stupid response when he called her on it. She should have slapped him across the face. Isn't that what an innocent woman would do?

That's probably why it never occurred to you.

She found David in the basement, telling him she wasn't feeling well and wanted to go home, neither of which was a lie. That night, she lay in bed beside David and stared at the ceiling, explaining to the universe in general and to Colin Mitchell in particular that what had happened between them would never, ever, happen again.

Her eyes dropped from the easel to her bright green fingertips. Until she painted a peacock green glob on a stormy purple canvas, it had not.

~~~

Hank Jared pulled into the driveway of the old white farmhouse, the dread that had been brewing for days settling in his stomach like an anchor. In his mind's eye, David sat beside him in the passenger seat, leaning forward in eager anticipation. Which was weird, considering Gwen's husband David was dead, and Hank had never even met the man.

Hank forced his eyes open wide and blinked several times. He was losing it. It was a long drive from South Carolina to Vermont, and his legs ached to stand. He picked up a manila envelope, tracing his fingers down its creased edge. The papers inside had occupied his conscience for too long, their delivery now far overdue. They brought news of events unimaginable, and he deeply regretted that he would be the one to share their secrets with his friend.

He bided his time, surveying the landscape. Two more homes were visible in the distance, the rolling hills that separated them lined with long rail fences and old oak trees. Gwen's house stood tall and narrow, with a wide front porch and gingerbread trim. A green porch swing swayed invitingly in the warm

The One Who Got Away

summer breeze, and Hank imagined Gwen and David cuddled upon it, gently rocking as couples do.

Opening the door, Hank was hit with the scent of a recent rain shower and the heavy sweetness of summer flowers. It seemed only right that Gwen's house should smell like Mother Nature's very own. He often thought of his wife's aunt as a flower child stuck in the wrong generation.

The windows of the farmhouse were open, their curtains blowing in the warm morning breeze. He sighed heavily. At least she was home, and this would be the end of it. A fat yellow dog stood from where it had been laying on the wet grass, its tail wagging happily at Hank.

"Hey, Zeke." He bent to pet the animal. "Where's your mama?"

Chapter 2

"What if they find me?" asked the man, his shoulders hunched and his eyes wide. The tracks of recent tears were visible on his cheeks.

Colin felt sorry for him. It was one thing to sit across the table from a mobster or a drug runner. Javier Martinez was an academic who had been in the wrong place at the wrong time. Colin leaned back in his chair and gave his most confident look. "They won't. But if you are ever threatened, you call us and we move you immediately."

"My family..."

"Your wife and kids can come, too."

Martinez looked into his lap.

Picking up his coffee, Colin took a sip and waited. It was a difficult decision to wrap your head around. He had often wondered if he himself could do it—walk away from everyone he knew, leave behind all that he had worked for and start completely over.

Martinez raised his head and fixed Colin with a penetrating stare. "Has anyone in the program ever been killed?"

"No one who followed the rules has ever been killed."

"The rules."

"Yes. No contact with anyone from your former life. Not friends, not family outside of those who are moved with you, not colleagues from work. No one."

"I'm a scientific researcher. I publish several times a year..."

"That will have to stop."

Martinez's face contorted.

Colin had sat here before, watched other men wrestle with the decision to give up everything in exchange for their safety. He didn't envy Martinez, and he didn't judge him his grief.

"I need to talk to my wife."

"Of course. Would you like me to get her now?"

He nodded.

Colin pushed back his heavy metal chair and stood up, grabbing his coffee as he went. At the door, he stopped and

The One Who Got Away

turned back to the other man. "I'm sorry you have to make this decision, Mr. Martinez."

Colin walked down a corridor, crumpling his coffee cup as he went. His stomach burned from the brew and his morning's work. Cases like this were his undoing. Everything the Martinez family had worked to build was about to be abandoned, leaving only the people themselves to carry on. It was unfair. It was horrific. It was just another day at the office.

He had become a U.S. Marshal to make a difference, to be a champion for the innocent. The simple reality was far less heroic. Colin stepped into a waiting room and closed the door behind him. "Mrs. Martinez, your husband would like to see you."

She raised bloodshot eyes to his. "What happens if Javier doesn't testify?"

He had been expecting the question. They always asked. He perched a hip on the table. "He'll be free to go back to his life."

"They'll leave us alone if he doesn't testify."

"They might." She was young, maybe late twenties. Too young to walk away from her mother and father, to have her children grow up without grandparents. "But the man who took a picture of your little girls getting off the school bus still knows where you live, still knows their names and what they look like. Are you comfortable with that?"

Her bottom lip quivered as she spoke. "I haven't been comfortable with anything since my husband watched that man on the subway get shot to death."

"Mrs. Martinez, I wish I could undo what's been done already, but I can't. All I can do is offer you and your family a way through this."

"We'll lose everything."

"You'll have a fresh start."

She put the back of her hand to her lips. "Officer..."

"Deputy Mitchell."

"Deputy Mitchell," she said, looking very serious, "what would you do if you were Javier?"

How he wished in that moment that he could wipe this away, make it as though it had never happened. What he was offering was the next best thing. "I would enter the program,

Mrs. Martinez. I wouldn't be here if I didn't believe in it. WITSEC can give you a new life."

"I don't want a new life, I want my old one."

It pained him to say the words that needed to be said. "That's already gone."

~~~

Gwen walked into the sunroom carrying a painted wooden tray laden with two glasses of iced tea, a loaf of crusty herb bread, and butter. "I made the bread this morning with fresh thyme and rosemary from the garden."

"It looks fantastic."

"It does." She smiled at him, genuine affection lighting her face as she ripped a chunk off the loaf with her hands. She began to cover the steaming bread with butter, flashing Hank a conspiratorial wink. "One of my favorite vices. And how is your beautiful wife?"

"She's good." His flat mouth quirked with humor. "She's remodeling." Julie and Hank had just bought a new home in South Carolina.

"Oh, what fun! I adore home improvement projects. There's nothing like sculpting your environment, bringing your own sense of beauty into a space. It's art on a grand scale, don't you think?"

He looked around the room they were sitting in. It was narrow and tall, running the length of the farmhouse, with windows on three sides and old-fashioned pine wainscoting. The hardwood floor was wide-planked and scarred, with a time-honed honeyed finish.

A wicker cage chair hung from the ceiling in one corner, its bright yellow cushions coordinating with the rich paisley sofa on which he sat. A blue yoga mat lay unfurled in the middle of the floor, next to a wicker basket with a brass bell and a small book.

"I'm beginning to think so. Before we got married, I had a bunch of old furniture left from college that was all banged up. Julie gave it to Goodwill and bought brand new stuff that started out all banged up."

"Shabby chic."

He nodded. "That's what she said."

They smiled at each other.

"Why didn't Julie come with you?"

The bread in Hank's mouth turned suddenly thick. He worked to chew it as he reached for his drink. "She doesn't know I'm here."

Gwen leaned forward in her chair.

"I knew she'd want to come, and I needed to talk to you alone."

"What is it, Hank?"

He, Gwen, and Julie had been through a lot together in the last year, difficult times they might like to forget. Hank had been sent to investigate a murder and found a cryptic message with Julie's name. It turned out the message was meant for her to decode, and its secrets led them on an incredible journey.

Sweat broke out on his palms. "Do you remember, when Julie was trying to solve the cipher, I had my friend Chip run it through the computers at the NSA?"

"The man whose wife had the twins?"

"Yes."

She nodded. "I remember."

"Well, he didn't just run the cipher. He went looking for any references to the case at all. And he got a hit when he put in Julie's name and cross referenced it with McDowell."

"What did he find?"

"David Beaumont."

"David?" She sat upright. "My David?"

Hank nodded. "I didn't know why at first. And Julie was hurt, I was such a mess. I had to think about her."

"Of course you did."

"But afterward, I asked Chip to see what else he could find out. Why David Beaumont was listed in the NSA records at all."

"That doesn't make any sense. He was a composer."

"I know."

"But this is almost a year ago."

He nodded. "It took a long time to find the answer."

"And?"

"David Beaumont was in witness protection. He was listed in the NSA Database because by marrying you, he was now

The One Who Got Away

associated with one of America's most wanted criminals, McDowell."

~~~

Colin was sitting at his desk doing paperwork when the thought of Gwen went through him in with a rush of heat. He lifted his pen and raised his head, exhaling like a man who'd been kicked in the stomach. Her remembered her scent, the breeze in her hair. Could feel her eyes on his, uneasy.

Sometimes he went weeks, or even months, without thinking of her this way. Then suddenly she'd be there, her presence as tangible to him as if she had been leaning over the desk.

Naked.

Not that Colin had ever seen Gwen naked, but he had pictured it more times than he could count. That woman excited him like no other ever had, and he'd never even touched her.

He had come close once, though.

Colin shook his head as if to clear it and turned to the clock. An hour past quitting time. He cleaned off his desk, then stood and pulled his suit coat over his dress shirt, flipping the collar down in one practiced motion.

There was no point in going home now. Already, his mind was shutting down all rational thought so he could wallow in memories of his dead friend's wife. Gwen's blue-gray eyes laughed at him in his mind, like a bride waiting to be taken to bed.

Bride. What the hell are you thinking?

He was saved from his own thoughts by the ringing of his cell phone. Glancing at the caller ID, he saw it was his brother, Rowan.

"How does he know?" Colin said to himself. He would swear, all he had to do was think of Gwen and his brother would come to her virtual rescue, more than fifteen years after the fact. The thought put him back in time, on the patio overlooking the river as he teetered on the edge of sanity itself. His body so close to Gwen's back, he could feel the heat of her along his entire torso like an intimate caress.

He reached up tentatively toward her arm, inching closer. Colin had wanted this for so long, had wanted this woman since

The One Who Got Away

the moment he saw her. The fabric of her dress grazed his sensitive palm and his eyes closed in anticipation of the touch.

Rowan's voice behind him was fierce. "Colin!"

Colin had been so frustrated. Angry. He spent the rest of the evening drinking heavily and trying to catch Gwen's eye, until Rowan pulled him into a bedroom.

"What the hell are you doing?" asked Rowan, hands on his hips.

"None of your goddamn business," said Colin, aware of the slight slur in his speech.

"David's our friend, Gwen is his fiancé, and you are so far out of line it's not funny. That makes it my business."

Colin's ears started to ring. "They're engaged?"

Rowan nodded. "And you'd better not screw this up for David. Do you hear me?"

Indignation rose up inside him. "I wasn't the only one out on that veranda."

Rowan stepped closer. "You were the one whose hands were in the wrong place, brother."

"She wanted me to touch her."

"Bullshit."

"She did."

Rowan shook his head and ran his hand through his thick dark hair. "Did she say that?"

"Not exactly."

"Not exactly. What are you, a freakin' mind reader?"

Colin didn't answer, just stared at him.

"Fuck this." Rowan pulled his wallet out and shoved money at his brother. "I'm calling you a cab. Go to Dante's, or Michelle's, or whatever. But you can't stay here."

"I'm not going anywhere."

Rowan pointed his finger at Colin's chest. "You are, if I have to throw your ass in the cab myself."

Colin got in Rowan's face. Colin was bigger across the shoulders, stronger any day of the week. "You and what army?"

David stepped into the open doorway. "This army," he said quietly.

Colin stared at David, as much a brother to him as Rowan

ever was. Colin had known him for as long as he could remember, had lived with him for more than ten years after David's father went away, loved him like family. Colin swallowed against the knot in his throat.

Gwen was a fantasy, the woman he wanted and could never have. David was so much more. Colin looked at the floor, raising his hands in surrender as the room pitched violently to one side. "Okay. I'll go."

It was the last time he ever saw David.

Colin's phone continued to ring, pulling him out of reverie. "Hey, Rowan," he answered. "What's up?"

~~~

Gwen's lower lip hung open. "Witness protection? Are you sure?"

"Yes."

"But why? What for?"

"I don't know. Chip tried to find out, but all the records are erased, every track covered."

"Well, someone must know for sure."

"The U.S. Marshal's office is responsible for changing the identity of witnesses."

Gwen's stomach took a dive, making her instantly nauseated.

Colin is a U.S. Marshal.

Hank was unaware of her distress. "The only way to find out would be to go through them. Maybe as David's widow you can get them to reopen the case."

Gwen was hot, dizzy with the implications of his words. Hadn't she known this day would come? A reckoning of sorts, an obligatory meeting with the man who had caused her eye to stray so long ago? Gwen believed in fate, and had suspected for some time that her path would cross Colin's again, forcing her to face her feelings for the man.

"Reopen the case?" she repeated, not understanding.

"The investigation into David's death."

She blinked her eyes, waiting for the words to make sense. "You think he was murdered?" It was hard to say the words, no less believe them. "The coroner did an autopsy. It was an

The One Who Got Away

accident."

"How can you be sure?"

"I was there, Hank," she said, holding her arms to her chest. "I went down with him the first few runs, then I went to the lodge to wait for him. It was only fifteen minutes or so before the paramedics came blazing by, and I knew something was wrong." She remembered the scene in great detail, the pitch of the sirens, the frantic energy that followed them up the mountain.

"Did you see anything unusual?"

"No," she said quickly, bowing her head. Just as fast it snapped back up again. "Wait, there was a man, a man in a big red parka. Someone David recognized. I didn't think anything of it at the time, but now…David said it was someone he knew a long time ago. Oh, my God, Hank," she whispered, her eyes wide with terror. "Do you think he killed David?"

～～～

Bright winter sunshine reflected off the snow, the landscape dotted with skiers in bold colored jackets and hats. It was a beautiful day for skiing, warmer than usual with only the slightest breeze.

Gwen stood to the side of the ski lift, waiting for David to finish his run. She enjoyed skiing, spending time outdoors and the sway of her body over the earth, but her husband was the real skier, slicing down trails with well-practiced accuracy and speed. He had taken a more challenging trail, while Gwen chose to stick with something simpler.

She saw his neon blue parka coming down the hill, watching as he sank into a crouch to gain speed, then turning into a wide arc, his skis throwing snow high into the air.

He caught up to her, his smile radiant. "Did you have a good run?" he asked.

"I hit some ice up on top, but the rest was powder."

"Mine was a little dicey, too." He put his arm around her and squeezed. "I'll ski with you this time."

Gwen smiled at her husband, so grateful she had this man to love above all others. David was her lover and her confidant, the one she looked for when she wanted to share her view of the world. "I'd like that," she said.

The One Who Got Away

They took the ski lift back to the top of the mountain, the view a spectacular treat in itself. The rugged Vermont terrain was a mixture of tall mountains and deep valleys, everything covered in white and tinted varying shades of blue in the distance.

David was quiet on the way up the mountain, a far-away look in his eye. He'd been more reserved than normal for the last week or so, and Gwen was beginning to get concerned. "Is everything okay? It seems like something's bothering you."

He leaned back and lifted his arm for her to sit by his side. "The chase scene from that new film is driving me crazy. I can't seem to get the drum section right." He sighed. "And I've been thinking about my mother lately."

His mom had been killed when David was only six, the victim of a burglary gone wrong at the beauty shop where she worked. The family had been rocked to their core, David's dad packing up his young son and promptly moving to a new town that didn't hold such horrific memories.

"When I was in New York last week," said David, "I took the train up to Connecticut to visit her grave."

"Why didn't you tell me? I would have gone with you."

He shook his head. "I didn't have anything new to say, and I needed to go alone. It's a part of me that's always going to be a little raw."

"I'm sorry, David." She hugged him tightly. "Sorry you have to go through this."

The ski lift crested the mountain and they approached the exit ramp. The pair slid off the chair with practiced ease, and they turned toward the trail Gwen just completed, nearly bumping into a big man in a red parka. David stopped moving, staring into the goggles of the other man.

"Michael?" asked David.

"No," said the man, sidestepping the pair and skiing away. David continued to look after him as if he had seen a ghost.

"He looks just like someone I went to school with."

"From Vassar?"

"No. Not from Vassar." He shook he head. "Before that."

"They say everyone has a twin."

The One Who Got Away

    David stared after the man for several seconds before turned to his wife. "That must be it. Are you ready?"
    "I am."
    "Good. Let's rock this bunny slope, beautiful."

Chapter 3

    The screen door slammed behind her as Gwen walked outside, noting the rain clouds that threatened on the horizon. The warmth of the day was still evident, though the sunshine had been replaced by overcast skies and an eerie pink glow over the landscape. Hank had left an hour earlier, the remaining loaf of herb bread tucked in a brown bag for the trip.

    Needing to get a handle on her own emotions, Gwen had tried to meditate, sitting on the yoga mat in the sunroom and ringing the brass bell in an attempt to focus her thoughts. But the news of the day was her undoing, disrupting her natural rhythms, forcing her to leave her house to find the solace she craved.

    The graveyard had been on the land since the seventeen hundreds, its early occupants unknown to Gwen except by their names, now barely visible on the weathered stones that marked them. It had seemed only right that her husband be buried here, closest to the person who had loved him best. Gwen rarely visited the cemetery, believing that her husband was neither there nor gone, but a part of the greater universe that surrounded her every day.

    She unlatched a wrought iron gate and walked into the cemetery, nodding to the two tallest grave markers as she did. "Hello, Lucy, Caleb." A small wooden bench sat beneath a tall maple tree, and Gwen sat on it, resting her arm along the back and turning to where she knew a small metal plaque was tucked deep in the overgrown grass. "David."

    Had he been brought to his eternal rest prematurely, by someone who meant to do him harm? Gwen pictured what she could remember of the man in red from the ski resort, which was very little. Had a childhood acquaintance killed her husband? After her initial memory, Gwen quickly realized she couldn't be sure of anything. She needed to know more about David and the witness protection program, information available only to the U.S. Marshal's Office.

    Rowan had been so proud when Colin was accepted into the prestigious program. Even David had been excited. Her

The One Who Got Away

husband's reaction made more sense now that she knew his own family had been relocated.

"What should I do?" she asked into the air, which had begun to pick up speed in anticipation of the coming storm. The answering silence was pronounced, and she felt tears wet her eyes, fresh grief for the man she could no longer talk to. Mourning her husband's death twelve years earlier had been the most difficult thing Gwen had ever done, and she didn't want to go back there, didn't want to feel what it was like to lose him all over again.

She had been a young bride, a seemingly younger widow. David had been seven years her senior. At thirty-six, Gwen had already experienced more of love and loss than some people see in seventy years.

Murdered. Was it possible? Could it be that she had been so close to evil, that it had reached into her life and taken her greatest love?

She wept harder, grief spilling out onto her cheeks as the wind carried away her cries.

When she was able, she wiped her face with the back of her hand, lifting her head to the swirling gray sky. "David, you deserve to have your murderer put away and punished for what he did." Her voice grew quiet. "But I don't want to do this. Forgive me, but I don't want to do this. Please..." she begged, her voice trailing off as the first drops of rain began to fall on her bare arms.

Her head dropped to her chest as the rain picked up speed, falling in fat drops, cooling her heated skin. She allowed it to overtake her, soaking her shirt and shorts, small rivers trailing down her legs and onto her sandaled feet before disappearing into the earth.

She breathed in the tangy air and allowed her mind to empty of the fear, the wishing for something different. The sound of the rainfall filled her head as she lifted her face to the sky. Poised before the universe, Gwen asked for the guidance she would need to complete this journey.

The kind eyes of Colin Mitchell appeared in her mind, clear as a photograph, making her wince. She could see David's reaction when Rowan had shared the news, his eyes wide with wonder. *A Deputy with the U.S. Marshal's Office. Can you believe that, Gwen?*

Everything was clear.

Gwen sat in the rain, letting the droplets water her spirit like they were watering the earth around her. Time passed and the tempo of the rain began to slow. Gwen opened her eyes, noting the sun already peaking through a hole in the clouds.

A robin landed on the bench next to her, its feathers lit by sunshine. "Looks like I'm going to Cold Spring," she said to the animal, which cocked its head to the side and looked at her. "The Hudson Valley in summer." She had always loved that area, had missed it like she'd been born there, though she never expected to be going back.

Standing, she walked several steps to David's marker, kneeling in the wet grass and kissing her palm before pressing it to the raised metal letters. "Anything for you, my love." She stood, mentally calculating the time it would take her to drive to the train station in Albany. "Anything at all."

~~~

When Colin left the office, he'd gone to the gym and picked up two games of racquetball in an attempt to exorcise the Ghost of Gwen. When that didn't work, he bought a six-pack of Stella Artois and had himself a private party out on the veranda, watching the Friday night boat traffic glide across the river and wondering what might have happened if he'd confronted that woman all those years ago.

It was a pastime he rarely allowed himself, thinking about Gwen. He preferred to live his life in the here and now, with real live women who existed right in front of him and didn't make him feel like half of some mystic puzzle they had no intention of putting together.

Colin stood at the kitchen sink, washing out the tall pilsner glass that had been his weapon of choice last night. Only in the last few hours was he starting to feel better, the emotions that had come to a boil now cool and relenting.

It was time to get over Gwen Trueblood.

Maybe he should think about settling down, finding a

The One Who Got Away

woman to love and get married. Since Rowan married Tamra and had the baby, he was feeling decidedly envious. There was something nice about being part of a couple, having a family of your own. He turned around and took in the kitchen of his grandmother's house where he had lived alone for the better part of a decade.

He wasn't lonely, exactly. He just wanted something better, even if he couldn't imagine having those things with anyone other than Gwen. He cursed out loud at the direction his thoughts were taking again.

Colin stepped into the garage and reached for his bike helmet. A ride would clear his head, exhaust his body, give him some focus. God knows he could use some focus right now.

He clipped his bike shoes onto the pedals and fastened his helmet. His old Miyata had thousands of miles on it, its sleek steel frame as solid as the day it was built. How many of those miles had been spent thinking about Gwen?

A train whistled in the distance, but Colin paid no mind. He was already absorbed in his riding, the feel of the pavement beneath the narrow wheels, the breeze on his face. He imagined a life without Gwen in it, without heartache and disappointment, without a standard for all other women to be held to, and fall short of. And for a short while as he rode, Colin was happy.

~~~

Gwen stepped off the train, her cork wedge sandal landing squarely on the concrete platform. The sun shone in her eyes and she pulled her sunglasses down from their perch atop her head, unsticking one long blond curl as she walked. Her long sundress had three wide bands in the colors of frozen sherbet, its light fabric revealing her graceful neck before it draped snugly across her breasts.

Colin's home was a short walk from the station, nestled in a small clearing of trees across the tracks, but Gwen headed in the opposite direction. She sought out the waters of the Hudson River with a thirst in her soul that needing quenching.

A path emerged from the parking lot and she took it, a smile on her lips as she followed a curving route of stepping-stones over a rise, and the view before her opened to expose the deep

The One Who Got Away

greens of the dramatic river valley. Sharply rolling hills rose along the opposite bank, their tree-covered surface lush and inviting.

Gwen's feet stilled and she closed her eyes, taking a great breath into her lungs as she soaked up the heady scents of water and earth that surrounded her.

It was just as she remembered.

She exhaled in a trailing breath, opening her eyes to a ghost, standing before her in her memory. An impossibly young David stood in green shorts and a sun-kissed tan, beckoning her to follow. His image faded as quickly as it had appeared, and Gwen began to move, her footfalls on the familiar path seeming to erase the time since her last visit to this enchanted place.

The Chapel Restoration came into view and she giggled in anticipation.

How many times had she been here? The first was for Verdi, of that she was sure. A new Italian tenor, whose name escaped her now, who went on to become quite famous. He had sung the lush aria with the muscular skill of a well-trained voice, bringing Gwen to joyful tears.

She had wandered off from Rowan's party, leaving David playing cards with his friends as she explored. She'd been drawn first to the water, then to the music floating on the humid night air, calling her to sit and listen on the porch of the Chapel, its great round pillars framing doors left generously open to the summer night beyond. Gwen climbed the stone steps now, flanked on either side by the Chapel's cobblestone foundation, remembering that first evening that had drawn her to this perfect sanctuary.

The Chapel had once been a Catholic Church, though its Greek Revival architecture looked more like a tiny Parthenon than any cathedral Gwen had ever seen. Rowan had explained how it had been abandoned and brought back to life, now serving as an ecumenical chapel and performance center during the summer months.

She had always been able to feel God here, as if the universe had focused its energy on the small rectangular structure like a child collecting the sun's rays with a magnifying glass.

The One Who Got Away

    Gwen pulled at the door of the chapel, sharply disappointed to find it locked. Reaching up with her hand, she ran her fingers along the white painted surface, feeling the layers of paint and the texture of the wood beneath. How many layers since she'd been here last?
    A guitarist playing Chopin.
    A poetry reading, snuggled on a wooden pew with David.
    "May I help you?"
    Gwen jumped, turning to find a young pregnant woman in jeans and a t-shirt eying her strangely. "Oh, you gave me a start!" Gwen said, resting her hand on her chest as she began to laugh. "I was just thinking, 'If these walls could talk,' and then they did!"
    The woman dropped her shoulders and took out a large key ring. "Sorry about that, I didn't mean to scare you."
    "It's okay. Are you going inside?"
    "I am. I work here." A mop and broom were tucked under her arm. "But the Chapel's closed to the public, except for scheduled events. There's a listing of programs online."
    Gwen nodded, stepping back. "I understand, of course. You can't let every crazy ninny who shows up on the porch inside for a look-see." She smiled wide, staring at the girl, looking every bit the crazy and at least somewhat the ninny.
    The girl tilted her head. "It used to be open all the time, but with the vandalism..."
    "It's been vandalized?"
    She nodded. "I have to do a graffiti check of the outside of the Chapel every week, along with the boulders on the bluff."
    The building was situated some twenty feet from the water, which dropped down fifteen feet in a small cliff. Gwen had been down there numerous times, and knew the spot the woman was referring to. "Oh my, in your condition those rocks could be treacherous. Let me help you."
    The woman's eyes lit momentarily before she shrugged off the suggestion. "That's all right, I can do it."
    "Please, I insist," said Gwen, giving the girl's upper arm a light squeeze before turning on her heel. "I'll go check now, you just get started inside and I'll be right back to let you know if I

found anything." Gwen strode to the shore and made her way down the cliff to the beach. Covered in small rocks and gravel, the area was clean except for a small collection of beer bottles, which she took with her back to the lawn and deposited next to the steps. Vandals were one thing, but Gwen could understand the desire to congregate at such a glorious spot and share a beer with friends. Hadn't she done as much with David and Rowan?

She walked back to the door of the Chapel, peeking in and seeing the girl tuck a strand of wayward hair behind her ear as she worked to polish the pews. What must it be like to be pregnant, to feel a life growing inside your womb? At one time in her life, Gwen thought motherhood would be a given for her, but she was no longer quite so certain.

"All I found were some empty beverage containers. I put them on the steps."

"Thank you." She put one hand on her hip and bit her lip. "Do you want to come in?"

"I do," said Gwen dramatically, "but I don't want to get you in trouble." She winked.

"It's all right, you can come in. I'm Crystal," she said, extending her hand.

Gwen shook it, taking in the tired look on the beautiful young woman's face. She couldn't be more than twenty and clearly becoming uncomfortable in her pregnancy. "I'm Gwen. Congratulations on the little one."

"Thanks," Crystal said, her face brightening as she raised a hand to her protruding belly. "Can you believe I'm got another month left? I don't think I'm going to make it."

"How exciting!" Gwen walked around the edge of the space, her hand trailing along the pews as memories from her youth came flooding through her mind.

"Me and Danny," said Crystal, "are getting married in the Chapel this fall."

"Oh, how lovely!" Gwen sighed, imaging the young Crystal as a bride. "I've always loved it here. You're a very lucky lady to be beginning a marriage within such hallowed walls."

"You've been here before?"

"Many times, years ago," she said, waving her hands.

The One Who Got Away

"Before my husband and I were married, we used to come up from the city to visit a friend right across the tracks."

Crystal's brow furrowed. "Who?"

"Rowan Mitchell."

"I know Rowan. His grandmother was the school librarian at the high school when I was there. She was a nice lady. Do you know her, too?"

Gwen shook her head. "She was never home when I was here. I understand she was quite the world traveler."

Crystal nodded. "She used to bring souvenirs into school, to show students from her trips."

"Indeed, the house was filled with them."

"Are you going to see Rowan today?"

"No, his brother Colin."

"Colin doesn't live here anymore. He married an Italian woman a few years ago and moved over there. They have a son, I think."

Gwen's face fell, her eyes wide. A stinging sensation splashed into her abdomen. *A son. Colin is married with a son.*

She chastised herself for feeling betrayed. What business was it of hers if Colin Mitchell got married? She had never given the man any reason to believe she was interested in him. She wasn't interested in him. Heavens, she hadn't even seen him in more than ten years. A picture of Colin with his young bride and baby appeared in her mind, and she bristled at the thought.

"I'm sorry you didn't know," Crystal said quietly, "but Rowan must know where Colin is. Maybe he could put you in touch. Was it important?"

Honest to a fault, Gwen considered telling Crystal the truth, but she could imagine the young woman's response. *Murder. Witness protection.*

"I just wanted to catch up with an old friend." She stood up, decided. "I'm going to stop by and pay Rowan a visit while I'm in town. He was a good friend to my husband, and I've let too many years go by without stopping to say hello. It was very nice speaking with you, Crystal. I appreciate you letting me inside."

"You're very welcome. The Chapel was meant for everyone, don't you think?"

The One Who Got Away

"I do, Crystal. I do."

Chapter 4

She made her way back through to the train station parking lot, carefully crossing the tracks and disappearing into the woods like a child. Despite the time that had passed since her last foray through these trees, Gwen knew she could find the house with her eyes closed.

Set back some two hundred feet from the river on a small hill, the Mitchell home stood separate from the more modern developments that had sprung up since it was built at the turn of the century by Colin's great grandfather, a retired shipping captain. It was a unique home with a four-story round turret that was part of the lower two floors, and extended beyond them like a lighthouse. The front of the house faced the water, a wide veranda reaching toward the lustrous river below.

A winding driveway connected the house to the street, but this direct route through the forest was the path she had always taken with David. Ducking under the branch of an oak tree, Gwen enjoyed the intimacy of her backwoods approach, feeling like a child crossing the backyards of her neighbors to visit an old friend.

Rowan Mitchell. She smiled at the name. Her husband's best friend, Rowan and David had been inseparable until life took them in different directions. David became a musician, primarily working in New York City, then a composer of soundtracks for theater and film, while Rowan took over the business world. The last Gwen knew, Rowan was the Chief Financial Officer for one of the largest publishing houses in the world, living and working somewhere in California. He'd been David's best man at their wedding.

The house came into view, its pale green exterior shining in pleasant contrast to its darker green surroundings. A large weeping willow graced the west side of the property, its branches waiting to shade the veranda between the house and its million-dollar view. Stone steps extended from a lower lawn up to the house proper, edged with a grand scale garden of rhododendrons and small round azaleas.

The One Who Got Away

The flowers were new and lovely, showing an awareness of form that Gwen's artist's eye could appreciate. She struggled to reconcile the obvious talent of the gardener with the businesslike image she held of Rowan, and decided he must have hired someone to care for the property.

Gwen's feather-light touch graced the bold magenta of the rhododendron as she swayed up the steps, their fruity scent reaching her nostrils in abundance. She inhaled deeply into her lungs, releasing the disappointment of the day, and worked to open her mind to new possibilities.

~~~

A movement in the distant yard caught his eye and he squinted, trying to make out whomever had wandered onto his property. It wasn't unheard of for an interloper to appear, with the house so close to the train station and the Chapel Restoration. Rowan had several times suggested their grandmother fence in the land, but she had refused, saying she would miss the deer and other wildlife making their way to the river.

It was a woman, blond with a bright orange dress. She moved with a casual grace that was vaguely familiar, heading directly for the stairs that rose to the lawn and veranda.

Colin turned off the tap and leaned toward the window.

Gwen.

The word was a breathless wish, an aching curse. His heart lurched, even as reason slammed down on his thoughts with a heavy foot. He turned away from the window and spun in a circle.

He lifted his head to the window again, expecting not to see whatever had reminded him of Gwen and froze, his mouth falling open. She stopped to smell a bright purple blossom next to the stone staircase, her eyes closing and a smile spreading across her lips.

His body clenched, blood pumping. He knew her like he knew his own reflection. Had seen her countless times in dreams, in waking awareness so keen he would swear she must be feeling it right then, too.

Sweat broke out on his hands as he clenched and opened them. He walked to the door and stepped outside just as she stepped onto the veranda, their eyes meeting across the small space.

"Gwen," he said, his voice husky and bare. He lifted his arms ever so slightly, opening to her in invitation, watching her face as she wavered before closing the distance and settling against his chest.

He was on fire, her unique scent encompassing him as he held her. A long curly lock of her hair stuck to the stubble on his cheek.

"I've missed you," she whispered, and his heart swelled. She had come to him. After so much time, so many rebuffs, Gwen Trueblood was finally back where she belonged.

Gwen reveled in the feel of his muscled torso against her softness, the strength of his solid arm holding her to him. Lust came quickly, and she daringly welcomed it like a hand trailing behind a boat in the ocean. Deliberately she leaned into him, her hand trailing up his bicep to rest at the base of his neck, grazing the bare skin there with the lightest of touches.

She knew she stood at the threshold of something she could not rescind. Colin had always been her downfall, her temptation, her weakness. His spirit was as familiar to her as the scent of her own home, and she rejoiced in seeing him again, even knowing as she did so that it was like playing with a deadly snake. You could only do so for so long before it would strike you.

They stood in the summer sunshine in this place of her youth, their bodies gently swaying. Gwen heard the low moan of attraction deep in his throat, and battled the urge to return it. It would be so easy to turn in his arms and bring her mouth to his. With more strength than she knew she possessed, she lifted her head and smiled at him casually.

"Hello, Colin."

His voice was intimate and deep. "Hey there."

She lowered her arms and stepped back. "You weren't supposed to be here."

"What do you mean?"

"I heard you were living in Italy, married with a young son."

"Rowan's living in Italy, married with a young son."

The One Who Got Away

She smiled wide, showing her teeth. "Ah. But not you."

"Nope. I'm right here. Same place I've been since the last time you saw me."

The words strummed through her head like a chord, and she caught herself. She wasn't interested in Colin. It was just exciting to feel something—anything—for a man.

He reached down and took her hand in his, leading her to a seating area. "I wondered if I would see you again."

"Yes," she said, sitting down on a wrought iron loveseat with a plush yellow cushion. "I wondered that, too."

"How've you been?"

"Good. Still in Vermont. Still in the same house." Of course, Colin hadn't been there. He'd been absent from their lives since the day the two of them had stood in this very spot, nearly touching in the warm evening's breeze.

If Rowan hadn't come along...

She stopped her thoughts from going down that path. She focused instead on memories of Rowan, such a good friend to her David through the years. He had stayed in touch when they moved to Vermont, visited them every fall before David died. He hadn't left her side at the funeral, when she had so desperately needed his strength.

David's father had passed away when he was in middle school. There was no other family, and Rowan had asked his grandmother if his best friend might have a home with them. The way David told it, Dottie Mitchell never even considered saying no. Rowan and David's friendship had grown to include the younger Colin, and the three became close as family.

Until I came along.

She thought she had let go of the guilt, but sitting here with the man who had paid the biggest price for her transgression, she was acutely aware she had not.

She met his eyes, seeing myriad emotions reflected in their golden brown depths. "I'm sorry, Colin."

"What for?"

"Everything. That you and David weren't close in the years before his death."

He stared at her for some time without speaking, then

nodded. "That wasn't your fault. I did miss him though. I missed you both."

"It was David I came to talk to you about." She tucked a wayward curl behind her ear, words rushing to her mouth before she considered their import. "Why didn't you come to the funeral?" It wasn't what she'd planned to say. She had no intention of broaching the subject, but there it was, begging for her attention. "It hurt me, Colin. It hurt Rowan."

He stood up, shoving his hands in his pockets and turning away from her. He stared at the horizon for minutes without answering.

Gwen leaned back into her seat and let her eyes fall to the river. So many things hung between her and Colin. So many words unsaid, so many thoughts unspoken.

David, forgive me for coming here. She opened her eyes, shaking her head at her own ridiculous thoughts.

"Do you want a glass of wine?" he asked, ignoring her question.

She nodded and watched as he went inside. From the warm glow of the kitchen window, she watched him remove the cork with punishing movements, the muscles of his forearm standing out against his skin.

Mercy, that man is sexy.

He walked back outside and handed her a glass of something dark and spicy.

"I was at David's funeral."

She tilted her head and eyed him curiously.

"I was there, Gwen. He's buried in the garden at your home, with the little black gate around it."

She couldn't have been more shocked. "Why didn't I see you?"

"I hung back."

"Why?"

His mouth remained closed, his lips pursed, then relaxed. "I was there on official business."

A stillness overtook them both as they stared into each other's eyes.

"Then it's true. David was in witness protection."

The One Who Got Away

He nodded. "How did you find out?"

"I was told by a friend," she said, her tone implying he wasn't much of one for keeping it from her. "He was concerned that David's death might not have been accidental. I came here to find out what you know about David's past, if anyone might have wanted to hurt him."

"I've sworn an oath, Gwen. One that I take very seriously."

"I need the truth, Colin." She walked toward him, her eyes pleading. "You're the only one who can tell me what I need to know."

He cursed under his breath. "It's not that easy, Gwen."

"Don't make me beg." She stepped closer to him. "You're going to tell me. I can see it on your face, I can see it the way you're holding yourself," she said, her eyes roaming the length of him. She was angry that he was toying with her, keeping the information she so desperately wanted to know.

He grabbed her wrist and met her stare, his eyes mirroring her anger. "You can feel it, Gwen. Just say it. You know I'm going to tell you because you can feel it in your bones, just like you've been able to feel me since that day on the train."

In her mind she was in the train car, the seat swaying beneath her semi-sleeping form as she reveled in the fantasy of making love to this man. Embarrassment and lust mingled, flushing her cheeks with heat.

Not a fantasy at all.

"Stop," she whispered.

His stare dropped to her lips. "No," he said firmly. "Not this time, Gwen." He dropped his head and took her mouth in a kiss of determined pleasure. The intensity of it wiped rational thought from her brain, leaving only her animal self to respond to his lips on hers, his body pressed against her in a crushing embrace.

Chapter 5

"Stop it. Colin, please." He could hear the emotion in her voice, knew she was close to tears. He begrudgingly released her, cool air rushing in when she took a step back.

Damn, she is beautiful.

Dusk had settled in, her patrician features lit by the light spilling from the house. His body ached to rake her back into his arms, make her realize how good they could be together. He'd finally had a taste of her, and the thirst that had plagued him for years was now a raging need for the river that was Gwen.

She crossed her arms over her chest and turned away from him. His muscles itched to follow her, turn her back around, rewind time and get back to the moment when they first connected, the electric energy that went straight from her mouth to his very core.

Gwen walked back to the loveseat and picked up her wine. "Tell me, Colin. Tell me why he was in WITSEC."

She was asking too much, the only thing he couldn't reveal. It went against everything he believed in, everything that kept people safe.

David's already dead. You can't save him now.

"David's father was placed in the program when David was six."

"His father?"

Colin nodded. "He testified against his cronies in exchange for his freedom. The family was placed in Connecticut initially, but David's mother just couldn't keep herself from calling her mother to wish her a happy birthday."

"Oh, my God." Gwen covered her mouth with her hands.

"She was gunned down in a beauty shop outside of Hartford. The local cops did a phenomenal job of getting David and his father to safety quickly."

"How did they know?"

"We notify the local authorities when a witness is placed in their jurisdiction. A lot of these people are criminals, and a lot of criminals have a penchant for illegal activity. It helps to have the cops keeping an eye on things."

Gwen's bottom lip fell. "Is that what happened to his father, too? Was he killed?"

Colin sat down. "No. He went to prison."

She was confused. "He died in prison?"

"He didn't die at all."

"But, that's why David came to live with you and Rowan!"

"No. David came to live with us when his father went to jail. It was his idea to say his father was dead. He was ashamed. He wanted a fresh start with our family. He even went so far as to have my grandmother put a grave stone in the local cemetery."

"That's awful."

"Jerry ruined David's life once. David didn't want him to be able to do it again. He blamed his dad for his mother's death. She was unhappy."

"How did you find out he was in WITSEC?"

"He broke down and told Rowan the truth the first time he got drunk in Eddie Mangione's tree house."

She smiled. "I've heard a lot of stories about that tree house."

"David couldn't handle the lies. A lot of kids can't, it's just too much for them."

"I can only imagine."

"When David found out he was going to have to move again, the three of us hatched a plan to get him to stay. He told my grandmother the truth, and she couldn't bear to send him off to God-knows where."

"That was very kind of her."

He nodded. "Grams loved David."

"We all did."

"He's the reason I wanted to become a U.S. Marshal, you know. I wanted to help people like him."

"That's very noble of you."

He looked off to the side. "The idea was noble. The reality isn't quite so honorable. I spend my days getting health club memberships for people named Benny the Bull."

"And their families."

He nodded. "And their families."

The One Who Got Away

Gwen sipped her wine. "All these years, I thought my father-in-law was dead. I've never even met him. Do you know where he is now?"

"No. He was released from prison six weeks before David died, and never reentered the program."

"Six weeks!"

"Yes, why?"

Gwen put her drink down on the glass table with a clink. "I believe David may have been murdered."

Colin shook his head. "I investigated that possibility while I was in Vermont for the funeral. That was what I was sent there to do. I talked to the coroner, the sheriff. It was an accident, Gwen. The slopes were icy."

"That day on the mountain, just before he died, David saw someone he recognized from school."

Colin slammed his drink down. "What? Are you sure?"

"Yes. I was standing right next to him. He was a big man in a red ski parka and goggles. David called him Michael."

"Can you identify him?"

She shook her head. "Not with the goggles on. David saw his face, not me."

"Why didn't you say something sooner?"

"I thought I did mention it, actually. But I didn't know David was in WITSEC, Colin. I had no reason to think anything of it at the time."

"That's true. I'm sorry, I wasn't thinking." Colin ran his hand through his hair. "I screwed up. I should have talked to you myself."

"You were there?"

"I came as soon as I heard. But I let the local cops interview you. I didn't want you to know I was there."

"Sheriff McDonald?"

"Yes, why?"

Gwen looked down into her glass of wine, her brows drawn together. "I might be wrong about this, Colin, but I think I told McDonald about Michael."

"What?"

She nodded. "I think so." She shook her head. "But I was a

disaster. It's hard to be sure of anything."

~~~

Colin walked toward the trees in the light of the full moon, an hour after Gwen went to bed. He could hardly believe she was sleeping under his roof, having reappeared in his life so unexpectedly. He ducked under the boughs of the majestic old pines that separated his home from the train station and made his way to the river.

It was deeply troubling to consider the possibility that David was murdered. It had been Colin's investigation, his responsibility. He cursed himself as he made his way past the boulders at the Chapel Restoration, down the bank, and settled his body on a large rock. If he bungled that investigation, it was because of his feelings for Gwen, not wanting to interview her personally and see her pain.

He thought he could trust the sheriff to ask a few questions, never considering the other man might be part of a larger conspiracy. In fact, Colin had never really considered foul play. He admitted to himself that he had asked for the assignment only to attend services for his friend who had died and maybe to get a glimpse of Gwen. The investigation aspect was an afterthought, a procedural requirement, a bunch of paperwork he didn't take too seriously.

And David's murderer had walked away, because of his carelessness.

Colin lifted his head to the sky, taking in the twinkling stars above him. He didn't know if his friend could hear him, didn't know exactly what he believed about death. "I'm sorry, David," he said, his voice cracking. "I should have done better." A boat slipped past in the distance, its green and white lights glowing brightly. "I promise you, I'll find out who did this, make them pay for what they did. They won't get away from me again."

The One Who Got Away

Chapter 6

Restless dreams plagued Gwen as she slept. She imagined she snuggled closer to the heat of David's body, resting her head on his shoulder. She felt his arm lightly tracing a path from her lower back up to her shoulder blade and moaned in satisfaction.

"You awake?" he asked, and she nodded. He shifted to face her, running his hand up her hip to her arm and shoulder. "I had a dream about you," he said.

She opened her eyes to stare into his, a slight smile curling one side of her mouth.

My David.

Relief flooded her senses at the sight of him, a gratefulness filling her heart at his presence. Why was that? Had he been away on a trip and only now returned? Was he out when she went to bed, only sneaking under the covers after she had fallen asleep?

I can't remember.

"What was your dream about?" she asked.

"We were on a train." As he said the words, they seemed to fly through the air, landing, fully clothed, on a commuter train. It was nighttime, and though Gwen could not see beyond the interior of the car, she knew it rumbled alongside the Hudson River. David was turned away from her, staring past the reflected interior of the train car to the hidden landscape beyond, and she felt very far away from him.

When he spoke, it was so quiet she could barely make out the words. "I would let you go, if that's what you wanted."

"Never," she whispered, upset that he would suggest such a thing.

David turned toward her, his eyes wet with unshed tears. "I saw you with him."

Colin.

Shame filled her gut, clawing at her. "I never did

anything..." She shook her head.

"I saw you right here, on this train," he wept, "letting him touch you, letting him make love to you."

A loud feminine moan behind her made Gwen turn around. There, in the next seat over, was an image of herself astride Colin Mitchell's lap, wearing only a long set of golden beads, clothes hanging off her body. They were kissing passionately, their cheeks flushed, hands grabbing at each other as they rocked in an intimate dance. Gwen's stricken eyes met those of her twin, heavy-lidded with lust, as the image called out again, unashamed.

Gwen's throat worked, panic rising. "No, David, I didn't..."

"Do you love him, Gwen?"

Then she was the one with Colin, joined as lovers, so close to the edge she might explode, her eyes locked with the man beneath her. The feel of him was almost unbearable, the heat of his body and the slick stick of sweat between them indistinguishable from each other.

Colin fiercely pulled her body onto his, and she quivered. "Tell him, Gwen. Tell him you love me."

He moved beneath her and her eyes closed in surrender.

David's voice invaded her ears, whining, distracting her. "Do you love him?"

Her eyes flew open and she looked to him, the action returning her to his side, fully clothed. "I love you, David. Only you."

She was hot, her skin damp with sweat and her pulse pounding. Her body ached with sexual need.

David smiled. "I love you, too, honey." He kissed the top of her head and grasped her hand, turning back to his view of the darkness.

Gwen sat in stunned silence, afraid to see what might be beside her. Slowly, her head turned of its own accord.

A naked Colin stared at her with contempt. "You're a liar."

"I didn't lie," she said, somehow certain David could no longer hear her, even as she squeezed his hand. "I do love him, Colin. I'm sorry."

Colin stood, pulling on a pair of jeans with exacting

movements. "I know you love your husband. That was never the issue. But you told him you loved only him, Gwen, and that," he said, buckling his belt, "is a goddamn lie."

Gwen awoke to a cool breeze across her skin, one leg hanging out of the covers and draped back over the fluffy bedding. Taking in the unfamiliar room, her stomach dipped as she remembered where she was, glimpses of the kiss she had shared with Colin haunting her memory.

Not a dream after all.

She groaned, sitting up in bed as she flung back the covers.

She was getting sidetracked. She came back here to find out who had murdered her husband, not to get involved with Colin Mitchell.

Well, then maybe you should keep your lips to yourself, Gwen.

Brushing her thick golden hair in the mirror, she nodded. "I will definitely be keeping my lips to myself today." She gave herself a wink and headed downstairs to set the record straight with Colin.

~~~

"So, you're not going to be kissing me today?" asked Colin, a light smile on his lips. Gwen had come downstairs determined to make him understand that their amorous exchange yesterday was a mistake, pure and simple.

"No. I shouldn't have been kissing you yesterday, but I hadn't seen you in so long..."

"Oh, is that why?"

She cocked her head to the side. "Maybe. I don't know." She crossed her arms over her chest. "It does sound a little silly when I say it out loud."

"No. It doesn't sound silly at all. But if I were you, I would skip my high school reunion."

She pursed her lips and gave him a look before taking the bold red mug of coffee he offered. "Good heavens, this is delicious." Gwen inhaled the rich scent of the steaming coffee. "What kind of beans do you use?"

"I grow them myself in a hothouse in the backyard."

She stared at him, dumbfounded. "You're pulling my leg."

The One Who Got Away

He shook his head. "It's a lot of work, but it's worth it."

"I didn't even know that was possible. Where did you find a coffee plant here in the States?"

"Interesting story. Six years ago, I was in Columbia on a case for several months. I met a woman there. Paola. She was young. Beautiful."

Gwen watched as Colin's face was transformed by the memory, a twinge of jealousy curling in her stomach.

"Her family owned a coffee farm in the mountains." He turned away, slowly pouring himself a cup. "She took me there once." He paused, and Gwen wondered what he was keeping to himself. "They were the most exquisite blue-green beans you've ever seen in your life."

"You must have cared for her."

He rested his open palm across his heart and nodded. "When it came time for me to leave," he looked down into his cup, "she gave me a coffee plant. A single plant in a pottery jar she'd made for me on her pottery wheel."

"Oh, Colin, what a touching story. And you've nurtured and tended to that plant ever since, harvesting and roasting your own beans in a greenhouse here in New York." She was in awe. This was a side of him she'd never seen before.

"It's a lot of work, but the orphans help."

"Orphans?"

He nodded. "A few years ago, I got dressed for golf and I caught sight of myself in the mirror. I was wearing a nice new polo shirt, which cost about a hundred bucks. For a polo shirt. All of a sudden, it just hit me. I have to give something back. You know?"

Gwen settled onto a barstool, her eyes wide. "I do."

"So I started an orphanage. There used to be loads of them," he said, gesturing with his hands. "You know, like in Little Orphan Annie."

Gwen began to squint at him.

"But no one opens up any orphanages anymore. Where are all those orphans supposed to go? There was a need, you know, a real need, so I decided to fill it."

"Where is the orphanage?" she asked, taking another sip of

The One Who Got Away

the delicious brew.

"Underground."

Coffee sprayed out of her mouth, covering the floor in a fine mist.

He leaned across the counter, putting his sincere face close to hers. "Of course. I had to hide them from the Bald Eagles I raise on the lawn. They're known for snatching small children, those damn eagles."

She couldn't help the grin that was tugging at the corners of her mouth. "Colin, where'd you get the coffee beans?"

He opened a cupboard and threw a small white bag to her. The label read COFFEE BEANS, MEDIUM ROAST, $3.99/lb.

Gwen laughed in spite of herself. "I'd forgotten what an ass you can be."

"You mean you'd forgotten how damn cute I can be." He winked, and her breath caught in her chest.

Yes, she thought to herself. *I'd forgotten that, too.*

"But don't even think about kissing me," he said, holding his hand up between them. "These lips are strictly off-limits."

"Oh, I wouldn't dream of it," she said, her mind suddenly flashing to her dream from the night before. She instantly felt her cheeks color, and worked to keep an innocent look on her face. "What time is your train?"

Colin was headed to his office in the city to gather what information he could from David's WITSEC file. He checked his watch. "Twenty minutes. If all goes well, I should be back around lunchtime."

Gwen nodded, a strange and troubling apprehension weighing on her thoughts. "God speed," she said sincerely, then added, "Be careful, Colin.

Graham Walker leaned back in his large leather desk chair. "Do you know what you're asking me to do?"

Colin felt like a teenager being chastised by his father. When Colin first joined the Marshal's Office, he was green, out to prove himself. It was Walker who had taken him under his wing, worked with him, taught him when to be eager and when to pipe down. The older man showed him how to build a new life for a witness, how to pick a suitable environment and make a person disappear like a rabbit from a hat.

The Southern District of New York branch of the U.S. Marshal's Office was predominantly concerned with security for court trials and the safeguarding of witnesses. Colin was one of only a handful of deputies who worked for the WITSEC division, and he reported directly to Walker, as he had for the last eight years.

The two of them shared a bond, an understanding of sorts. Colin would trust Walker with his life, and suspected his boss would do likewise.

"I'm asking you to help me," said Colin.

Walker raised his voice. "You're asking for a hell of a lot more than that, Mitchell." He stabbed his finger at Colin. "You're asking me to sacrifice my integrity."

Colin shook his head quickly. He had known it would be hard to come here and ask Walker for help. The man walked the straight and narrow, following procedure to the letter and insisting that those under his command follow his example. In his tenure as head of the division, Walker had cleaned out the ranks, getting rid of deputies who failed to meet his high standards, either by firing them or having them shipped to other offices.

"No, sir, I'm not. I'm asking you to give me access to the information I need to make sure justice was carried out. You of all people know how important it is to get it right." Colin pointed his thumb at his breastbone. "I'm the one who handled the review of Beaumont's death. If my determination that his death was accidental is wrong, then that's the right thing to do in this case."

"You're personally involved."

"Exactly. No one cares about this like case I do."

Walker lowered his voice, his deep baritone like the hum of a motor. "No one could screw it up like you could. You're too close to this one, Mitchell. You have to know when to step back."

"That's not what you said back then, Graham. You hand-picked me to go to Vermont and investigate."

"That was a mistake on my part." Walker leaned forward

The One Who Got Away

over his desk, his eyes never leaving Colin's. "You were distraught, demanding to be included in the investigation. Do you remember?"

An image flashed in Colin's memory--a younger version of himself breaking down in this very office upon learning of David's death.

Walker shook his head. "I let my concern for you as a friend impact my judgment. I knew it then, and I allowed it anyway. I'm not going to make the same mistake again, especially if there's reason to believe an error was made."

Colin dropped his head a fraction, steepling his hands. "You and I go back a long way, Graham."

"Don't pull this garbage with me, Mitchell."

"If I had to pick out one person from WITSEC who I knew had my back, it would be you."

"I'm not doing it."

"Hear me out. I have a relationship with the widow. She trusts me, and she doesn't trust anybody right now. All we have to go on is what she remembers from that day."

Walker leaned back in his chair. "I thought you were estranged from the family."

"Not anymore. She's staying at my house right now."

"I see," said Walker, pursing his lips as he stood up and turned to face the cityscape beyond. He sighed heavily. "This view comes with great responsibility."

"Yes."

"I won't be looking at it forever."

Colin considered his words. Graham was sixty-five, and rumors had begun circulating about his retirement.

"Sometimes I think I've been sitting in this office for too long. That I've lost touch with the people we work to protect," said Graham, shrugging his shoulders and turning back to Colin. "Your friend's father was my placement. I worked with the family, arranged for their credentials. What do you know about him?"

"Only what David told me. He was an accountant for organized crime who turned on his buddies."

Walker scoffed. "He was no accountant. They called him the

The One Who Got Away

dispatcher. When something—or someone—needed to be taken care of, it was Jerry who sent the muscle to take care of it."

Colin's eyes grew wide. "Jerry Ahearn?"

Walker nodded.

Ahearn was infamous in WITSEC history. His testimony resulted in the conviction of four of the biggest names in the history of organized crime. While Ahearn himself was associated with more than twenty murders, he had never been present at a crime scene, never been the trigger man.

Colin's voice was barely more than a whisper. "Jerry Ahearn was David Beaumont's father."

"David *Ahearn* and his mother Adele went into WITSEC with Jerry in 1975. Adele didn't make it six months before making contact with her family, which resulted in her quick and certain demise."

"I knew about the mom."

Walker nodded. "I was there. Overkill. It was a bloodbath." He turned back around to face Colin. "Adele was beautiful and sweet, a striking woman, a loving mother. There is no greater tragedy." A sad smile graced his lips.

Colin had heard stories from David about the countless days the boy and his mother spent on the slopes, how she helped him collect rocks in the summertime and leaves in the fall. He knew just how much the woman had been missed.

Walker pinched the bridge of his nose. "Sometimes you know when a person's going to crack, when they can't handle the pressure and follow the rules. But I didn't see that one coming at all." Sadness was plain on his features, and he made a rough sound in his throat. "I would have bet my last dollar that Adele would follow the straight and narrow, that she'd keep herself and her family safe no matter what."

"But she didn't."

"No. She didn't. Damn shame, too. I pulled Jerry and his boy out of Connecticut and relocated them to Cold Spring. Ahearn kept his nose clean for a while, then got busted for drug trafficking, leaving his son a ward of the state. If your grandmother hadn't stepped forward, he would have gone into foster care at that point."

"What does this have to do with reopening the investigation into David's death?"

"Jerry Ahearn came to see me when he got out of jail. He'd been incarcerated in a WITSEC prison unit, so he didn't mix with the general population. He wanted a fresh start, a new identity. He felt he'd been compromised, and your grandmother had already put on a funeral for Jerry Beaumont, complete with a headstone. It left him with few options."

"Why did he think his identity had been compromised?"

"He felt the local authorities in Cold Spring were out to get him. He even accused an officer there of setting up the whole sting that got him arrested, claiming he was framed."

"What officer?"

Walker shook his head, his gaze unfocused. "It was a long time ago, I don't remember the name. It would be in my notes in the file."

"Was there any truth to Jerry's suspicions?"

"Not as far as I could ascertain. I looked at the evidence and I believe he was guilty. I refused to provide him with another placement. He had valid credentials; he could go anywhere he wanted except home to Cold Spring."

"Do you know where he is now?"

"Not exactly."

Colin looked at him quizzically.

"John Campbell testified against the same crime ring a few years ago. He insisted Ahearn's back in the fold." Walker shrugged. "We don't have any direct evidence that supports that claim."

Stranger things had been known to happen, though if it was true, it was a wonder he survived long enough to ingratiate himself back with his cronies.

"I need to see if David was murdered," said Colin.

Walker nodded in resignation. "I know you do. What do you need from me?"

The One Who Got Away

Chapter 7

Colin and Gwen were in Colin's dining room, the large rectangular table covered in stacks and piles of papers. "That's the last of the court transcripts," said Gwen, closing a binder and putting it aside.

"Find anything?"

"Three Michaels are mentioned. Michael Gallente was sentenced to three consecutive life terms based on Ahearn's testimony. Michael Hendrickson was one of the kills ordered by Ahearn in the year before he turned, and Michael Dobbs was one of the defense attorneys for Leveen."

Marc Leveen was the biggest fish Ahearn netted when he testified for the feds, and the second in command of the crime ring at the time. He was the enforcer, determining the punishments for infractions for the organization. Jerry Ahearn was Leveen's right-hand man, seeing that all of his boss's bidding went down smoothly.

"Doesn't sound like any of those could be our guy. Maybe a son with the same first name, but no direct link. I wish I knew where the hell Ahearn is. He's the one who could shed some light on who Michael might be."

"Your boss didn't know?"

He shrugged. "Walker heard Ahearn was back in Boston, up to his old tricks."

"I thought his old friends wanted him dead for testifying against their members."

"Things change. When Leveen went down there was a shift of power. Then Manning died of natural causes. Who knows who's in charge today, and how they feel about Jerry Ahearn?"

"That's true." She gestured to the papers in front of him. "Did you find anything?"

While Gwen had been going through court documents, Colin had been reading all the WITSEC files on Jerry Ahearn and his family. "One thing struck me as odd. Ahearn requested a placement in the southwest, not the northeast."

"He probably wanted to get as far away as possible."

The One Who Got Away

Colin nodded. "I'm sure. But we try to honor requests like that. It doesn't make a difference to us one way or another."

"That is strange."

"And the coroner's report on Adele Ahearn shows she was almost two months pregnant when she was killed."

Gwen cringed. "Oh, that's awful." She pushed back her chair and stood. "I'm getting a glass of wine. Would you like one?"

"Yes, please." Colin picked up his phone. "I still haven't heard back from Officer McDonald in Vermont."

She spoke from the kitchen. "When did you call him?"

"On my way back from the city." He scrolled through his messages, finding nothing from the sheriff. "Did you know him?"

"Sort of. He was in office the whole time I lived there, and it's a small town. We nodded to each other on the street, that sort of thing." She handed Colin his wine.

"Did David know him?"

Gwen thought about that. "Yes, I suppose he did. I wouldn't say they were friends, but I did see them talking a time or two." She shimmied her shoulders. "Something about McDonald always rubbed me the wrong way."

"Like, how?"

"Oh, nothing horrible, I don't believe. I just chalked it up to him being a politician." In her mind's eye, Gwen could remember the sheriff and the cool exchanges he sometimes shared with her husband. "Did McDonald know David was in WITSEC?"

"He shouldn't have. The Cold Spring authorities would have been notified because of Jerry, but by the time David moved to Vermont his father was long gone."

Colin spoke. "I need to talk to Jerry," he said, letting his pen drop to his yellow lined legal pad.

"Do you think we can find him?"

"I think we're going to have to try."

Gwen nodded. "We'll leave in the morning?"

"I don't see why not."

~~~

"Keep your eye on the ball. Watch it hit the bat."

The One Who Got Away

"I am."

"No, you swung and missed. Which is why I'm telling you this." Jason McDonald shook his head at his twelve year-old son, then wound up and pitched the ball up and away, just the way Garret liked them. Sure enough the boy went for it, the barrel of the bat hitting the ball with a metallic crack and propelling it deep into center field.

"Nice one." He looked at his son as he threw the next pitch, all long limbs and sharp corners. When had he gotten so big? More like a man than a boy, nearly as tall as his father already, and Garret was only twelve.

Jason found himself back in time, Garret a wobbly toddler, his wife Jeannie so young, with longer hair she used let fall around her shoulders. He could see himself on a podium at the town hall, the local news crew capturing footage of the picturesque family and the man who was running for town sheriff.

They'd been broke back then, he and Jeannie. She stopped teaching when Garret was born, unable to bear the thought of sending the baby to daycare. Jason wanted his wife to be able to stay home. He worked every overtime shift he could grab and tended bar at a friend's bar twice a week, while Jeannie looked after a coworker's son before and after school. Still, money was tight. They lived on hot dogs and rice mix, splurging only on a six-pack of beer to share Friday nights in front of the TV.

They were doing just that when a news teaser changed everything. "Local sheriff found dead of an apparent self-inflicted gunshot wound. Story at eleven."

"Holy...!" Jason turned wide eyes to his wife. "Bloom's dead?"

"He killed himself?"

"I just talked to him about the beat rotation schedule."

"Did something happen to him?"

"What do you mean?"

"I don't know." She uncurled her legs and walked to the refrigerator. "Divorce? Trouble at work?"

Jason ran his hand through his hair, grabbing a fistful of the dark curls. "Not that I know of."

"What's this going to mean for the department?"

He blew out air loudly. "Who knows."

"Who are the contenders for his job?"

"Gees, Jeannie, I don't know. The man just freakin' died."

"You could do it, Jason."

"Me?"

She nodded. "I've been thinking it for a while. You're popular on the force. You know what changes need to be made, changes that Bloom never seemed to get around to making."

He sank back on the couch. Him, be the sheriff? It would be more responsibility. He'd be able to see that the other officers' concerns were addressed. He'd make more money. Long before the eleven o'clock news aired, Jason had made up his mind. He would run for sheriff, and with Jeannie's help, he would win.

He couldn't have known Keith Patterson would run against him, a surname that he shared with the grocery store, the bank, and the biggest car dealership for a hundred miles. The Pattersons owned this town. They ran it. Jason may as well have been running against a Kennedy.

With every day that passed, Jason wanted the job more than the day before. Patterson had a bigger campaign, bolder, flashier, more expensive. Everywhere Jason turned he saw Keith Patterson's four-color signs mocking his own black and white ones, the other man's influence apparent at every turn. Jason's dream slipped further out of reach, and he began losing points in the polls.

You did what you had to do.

Sweat broke out along his neck.

It's a closed door.

At least he hoped it was closed. He imagined himself slamming a door in the face of a raging tiger, waiting for the cat's weight to hit the wood and see if it would hold.

Garret swung and missed, the third strike in a row. "This is freakin' stupid," said his son.

"Watch your mouth."

"Relax, Dad." He rolled his eyes. "I said 'freakin'', not 'fuckin'."

McDonald shook the ball in his fist at his son. "You will not speak that way to me. Do you understand? I won't have you using that sort of language."

"I was just saying freakin'!"

"That's unacceptable, and you know it." Jason's cell phone rang and he let it go.

"All the kids say it."

"You are not 'all the kids'."

"Oh right, I'm the son of the want-to-be-mayor."

Frustration mingled with anger and Jason fought to control his temper. The election was stressful enough without his son making it more difficult. He forced himself to take several deep breaths before allowing himself to speak. "Yes, I want to be mayor. We talked about this. Agreed, as a family, before I ever signed up to run." He took his glove off and stepped closer. "There's a spotlight on—"

"Spotlight on all of us, I know."

"That's right. It's not just me who's running for office."

Garret rolled his eyes. "It's the whole family."

"I know it's difficult for you." Jason's phone chirped, telling him he had a message. He checked it as they walked to the car.

The voice was familiar, adrenaline shooting into his belly. He had lost count of the nights he'd laid awake, fearing this moment. "Hi there, Jason. It's your old pal. Long time no see. I need you to do me another favor, Sheriff. Or should I call you Mayor McDonald?" The man chuckled. "I guess we'll see about that, won't we?"

Jason bent at the waist and threw up on his new sneakers. The neat world he had created for himself was about to come crashing down to the ground.

Chapter 8

Gwen sat upright in bed, her nose picking up the acrid scent of wood smoke. She flung the covers off her body and quickly got up, her pulse racing.

Twice before in her life she had awoken in such a fashion. The first time, she was eight years old and found her grandmother had fallen and broken her hip in the downstairs guest room. The second was when David was hurt in a car accident coming home from the airport.

For Gwen, smoke didn't always signal fire. But it signaled danger every time.

She flew down the darkened hallway toward Colin's room, clad in a simple satin sheath of vibrant pink. She opened his door and rushed to his beside, the light of the moon streaming in from an uncovered window. She touched the bare skin of his muscled arm, barely registering his nakedness.

"Colin, wake up."

He grunted in his sleep and moved to roll over.

She shook him. "Colin."

His eyes opened and he sat up. "What?"

"I had a dream, I smelled smoke. Something's wrong."

Colin inhaled deeply. "I don't smell anything."

"Trust me. Get up, you have to get up." She stood back and watched as his muscular form unfolded from the bed, clad only in a pair of black briefs. His body was beautiful, and she suddenly realized she should have gotten dressed. She crossed her arms over herself.

"What's wrong? There's no smoke..."

"I don't know. Go and check out the house. Quickly."

He rubbed his hands over his face, then grabbed a plaid bathrobe off a hook and headed downstairs, leaving the lights off and making his way through the moonlit house. He got two-thirds of the way down the stairs before he began to shout.

"Gwen! Get down here!" He turned and raced back to her, meeting her several steps down and grabbing her hand tightly as he reversed direction. "We have to get out of the house!"

Colin didn't stop running, pulling Gwen to match his steps, until he was more than a hundred feet from the building, finally releasing her hand and patting the pockets of his robe.

"What was that horrible smell?" asked Gwen.

"Propane. That's how the house is heated. Shit, my phone's inside." He put his hands on her upper arms. "Run to the neighbor's over there," he said, gesturing through a narrow band of trees. "Call 911. Tell them it's an emergency, that we have a propane leak." He took a step back toward the house.

"Where are you going?" she asked.

"I have to get my phone."

"No!" wailed Gwen, icy fear slicing through her consciousness.

"It will just take me a minute."

She was clutching at him now, digging in with her fingernails. "No you're not! I'm not going to lose you, too! Don't you go into that house, Colin Mitchell!"

He shrugged his shoulder, pulling his arm from her grasp. "Damn it, Gwen, go call 911."

"David! Stop this!"

Colin froze, his eyes staring into hers in the moonlit field. He ran his hands down her arms and spoke quietly. "I'm not David, Gwen."

Her mouth curled down and she stared at him, her chin quivering. "I know." She took a small breath. "Please don't go, Colin."

He lightly cupped her cheek. "Okay. We'll call 911 together."

She pulled him toward the tree line, and they began to jog, just as a fiery explosion lit the night sky. The force of the blast knocked them both to the ground.

~~~

Gwen walked into the Cigs-For-Less store in Beacon, New York wearing Colin's plaid bathrobe over her nightie. She held a hand to her temple, her eyes squinting against the light as she turned to the clerk.

He was young, with long brown hair stuck through the hole

in his brown baseball cap, and chuckled as he took in the sight of his latest customer.

Gwen's voice was a rasp. "Aspirin?"

He gestured to a small display of toiletries, watching as she grabbed a bottle of Advil and a six-pack of malt liquor, putting them both on the counter.

The clerk smiled, flashing a straight set of yellow teeth. "Rough night?"

She cast him a look steeped in camaraderie and trouble. "You have no idea. Pack of Marlboro reds, and I need to pick up a wire transfer."

He reached overhead for a form, which Gwen filled out.

"I.D.?" he asked.

She blew out a puff of air and rolled her eyes. "With my clothes and a guy named Teeter, if you can believe that."

"That, I can," he said with a laugh. "You got a keyword for me?"

"Hudson."

He typed the information into a computer, then counted out a neat stack of bills from the register. "You feel better, now sweetheart. Go get yourself some shoes for them pretty feet." He winked.

Gwen winked back, holding up the beer. "I'll be feeling just fine in a minute."

She stepped outside and into the waiting cab.

Colin raised an eyebrow. "Make a new friend?"

"Colin, dear," she said, her eyes roving over his bare chest, "you're sitting in a taxi cab in your underpants. You are not in a position to criticize my new beau."

He snorted.

"Colt 45?" she offered. "It works every time."

He seemed to consider her offer, a grin pulling at one corner of his mouth. "Not right now."

Gwen leaned forward, passing the Marlboros to the cab driver. "Here you are, Samuel." He was skinny and olive-skinned, with thick dark hair and a lined face. In the short ride from Cold Spring, he had endeared himself to Gwen by offering her a blanket from the trunk of his taxi and carefully avoiding the obvious question of why these two people were barely clothed and in desperate need of transportation.

The memory of the explosion made Gwen shudder. The sound had been deafening, her own shock from the being thrown to the ground overwhelming. Colin hadn't missed a beat, hauling her to her feet and running urgent fingers over her arms and legs.

"Are you hurt? Anything broken?"

She shook her head. "Colin, your home!"

"We can't worry about that now. We need to get out of here."

Gwen hadn't understood. "Why?"

"This isn't an accident, Gwen."

Time seemed to stand still as she stared at him, the light of the fire casting an orange glow over his skin and all-too serious eyes. "What do you mean?" she whispered.

"Someone tried to kill us. Which means they're probably going to try again as soon as they realize they didn't succeed." He took her by the arm and began pulling her toward a different bank of trees. Gwen could hear sirens in the distance, and was suddenly aware of her bare feet on the dewy grass beneath her toes. Colin's words were beginning to hit home, adrenaline rushing through her. David had been killed, murdered on a ski slope, and now someone had tried to kill them as well.

She jogged alongside him as he sped up. "Where are we going?"

"The train station. Sometimes you can find a cab there late at night."

And so it was that they had found Samuel, leaning against the side of his yellow cab, smoking his last Marlboro Red.

He turned grateful eyes to her in the mirror as he smacked the new pack against his palm. "Thanks, ma'am. Do you mind...?"

Colin opened his mouth to object, but Gwen put her hand on his knee. "Of course not." She placated Colin with her eyes. "You're driving us all the way to Boston. You can smoke if you like. And please, call me Gwen." They'd been exceptionally lucky Samuel had agreed to take them on the long drive. They were paying him a king's ransom, money from the wire transfer

The One Who Got Away

Rowan sent from Italy after they called him from Samuel's cell phone an hour ago. Yes, they'd been lucky to find Samuel indeed.

Gwen settled back against the seat, turning to Colin. "How long is the drive?"

"About three hours." He raised his voice. "There's a Wal-Mart up on Route 9, Samuel. I'd like you to go in and pick out some clothes for us to wear. Just jeans and t-shirts. And I'll need a cell phone of my own."

Samuel nodded. "Just tell me what size clothes."

Gwen watched the village pass by out her window, her eye drawn to a sign for The Dew Drop Inn. An image of Becky's cozy Craftsman appeared in her mind. The best friend of Gwen's niece Julie, Becky was dear to Gwen's heart, and the prospect of seeing her made her smile. *She always says I'm welcome anytime.*

She turned to Colin. "I know where we can stay in Boston."

Chapter 9

Becky flipped a purple pancake with a practiced flourish, the brightly colored batter spilling out the sides and onto the griddle with a pleasing hiss. A coffee maker gurgled behind her, its rich aroma mingling with the vanilla from the pancakes and making her moan out loud. "Damn that smells good," she said loudly.

"It really does," said Gwen from the doorway. "Pancakes?"

She nodded. "For you and your friend. I was dating this chef who taught me to make the most incredible pancakes."

Gwen's eyes widened. "Purple, I see."

Becky beamed. "That was my idea."

"Very nice touch. But I'm afraid Colin took the T to the city hours ago." Becky's house was just two blocks from the commuter train into downtown Boston.

Becky's face fell and she turned back to lift purple circles onto a plate. "Oh, when I didn't see him on the couch, I just figured he'd made his way upstairs during the night."

"We're not together."

A slow smile spread across Becky's face and she raised her eyebrows. "He looks at you like you're together."

"He does?"

"Hell, yeah."

"And how do I look at him?"

Becky nodded dramatically. "Like you got a little something for Christmas."

"Well," Gwen sighed, pouring herself a cup of coffee, "I'm afraid all I've received in that department is a big lump of coal."

"Have you been a good girl?"

"Of course."

"That's your problem." Becky brought the plate of pancakes to a large wooden table, along with a bottle of real maple syrup.

Gwen laughed. "It's good to see you, Becky."

Becky took a large bite of pancake, the purple fleshy insides showing between her teeth when she smiled. "You too."

"So tell me about the chef."

"What chef?"

"The one who gave you the pancake recipe."

"Oh," she said, waving her hand dismissively. "He wanted to play house."

"But you didn't."

Becky opened her arms, fingers splayed. "I already have a house."

"True."

"I just can't picture myself settling down with one man."

"Not ever?"

Becky grimaced, shaking her head. "It's not me, you know?"

Gwen nodded. "I do." She dragged a pancake through the thin river of syrup. "It's funny how we can see ourselves as singular, or as part of a duo. I've been single for eleven years, but I still catch myself thinking like a married woman."

"Do you still feel David..." she looked up to the ceiling, "...around?"

"I did. The first few years, especially. Sometimes he was so close, it was like he hadn't left at all. But gradually, it lessoned."

Becky took a sip of her coffee. It was dark and robust, with enough sugar and heavy cream to make it appeal to her childlike taste buds. "Do you still miss him?" she asked.

"I still wish things had turned out differently, but I suppose I've gotten used to living without him. It's been a long time." Gwen smiled softly. "Sometimes I feel like a very old woman."

Becky looked over Gwen's smooth, glowing skin, and took in the vibrant natural gold of her hair, her graceful posture, so like a dancer's. She said, "How old are you?"

"Thirty-six."

"No way."

Gwen nodded.

"My mom was forty-two when she had me."

"David and I wanted children."

"Do you still?"

Gwen shook her head. "Not by myself."

"Which brings us back to the beefcake you showed up with on my porch last night."

Gwen nearly spit out her food, and laughed. "I told you,

The One Who Got Away

there's nothing between Colin and me."

"Well, why the hell not? That man is hot. Smokin' hot, even."

"It's complicated."

Becky's eyes lit and she leaned forward. "Oh, I love complicated."

Gwen waved her away. "There's nothing, really."

"Spill it, Gwen." Becky stood, taking both their coffee cups to the counter for a refill. "I can be relentless. Want to see?" she asked, slamming the bright red mugs down too hard on the counter and flashing huge eyes just inches from Gwen's face.

Gwen sighed. "Oh, all right."

"Goody, goody!"

"Colin is the brother of David's best friend, Rowan."

"Okay."

"When David and I were dating, we went to a few parties at Rowan and Colin's house."

Becky flashed Gwen an excited smile as she covered her plate in syrup. "Go on."

"I found Colin attractive, of course, what woman wouldn't? But I wasn't interested in him that way."

"You were in love with David."

"Exactly. I was in love with David." She covered her face with her hand before taking a fortifying breath and continuing. "So one day, David and I were taking the train to another party at Rowan's house, and I was sort of dozing, but not really asleep. I was in that netherworld between the two."

Becky nodded. "Uh huh."

"And I was daydreaming about… Colin."

"Because he's hot. Smokin' hot. Hell, I was dreaming about him when I was cooking the pancakes."

"You have no idea," said Gwen, nodding. She took a slow sip of her coffee.

"And?" Becky asked.

"Oh, you won't believe it."

"You're killing me, Gwen."

A voice from the kitchen doorway turned both their heads around. "She got to the party, all gorgeous with her hair wound up atop her head, this wispy little dress clinging to her in the summer's breeze."

Gwen turned back around, covering her mouth with her hand.

"And?" asked Becky.

"And I called her on it." He was standing shock still, his brown eyes molten and fixed on the back of Gwen's head.

"Called her on what?"

"The dream."

Becky's mouth dropped open and she gasped dramatically. "You called her on the dream?"

Colin crossed the threshold and stepped into the kitchen, never looking at Becky as he continued, "I could feel her. Every touch. Every thought that ran through her mind on that train. We shared something." He knelt before Gwen's chair, and she turned back around, her cheeks highly colored and vibrant as she stared at him.

"Holy shit," Becky said loudly.

"I never even got to touch her," he said, reaching out and lightly stroking Gwen's face, making her chin come up. "But I paid the price as if I had."

Becky leaned forward in her chair. "Price? What price?"

"I lost her."

"I was never yours to lose," Gwen said quietly.

"And I lost David," he said.

Becky's voice sounded like she was trying not to cry. "I thought David was Rowan's friend."

Gwen leaned back away from Colin and rose, breaking their connection. "David lived with Rowan and Colin from the time he was twelve."

"Oh my God, so he was like a brother to you!" cried Becky, her hand to her chest.

Colin stood, continuing to watch Gwen as she busied herself with the breakfast dishes. "Yes," he answered.

"What happened next?"

Colin's mouth formed a hard line. It was Gwen who spoke. "Colin got drunk and nearly made a pass at me. Rowan had to ask him to leave."

"Oh my God." Becky was shaking her head.

Colin looked at Becky for the first time. "Rowan did ask me to go, but I didn't give a shit what Rowan wanted. I left when David asked me to go."

Gwen quickly turned to face him, a dishtowel in her hand. "David asked you to leave? My David?"

He nodded.

Gwen turned back to the counter and made a brief show of trying to wipe it down before throwing the towel into the sink. She brushed past Colin on her way out of the kitchen. "Damn it, Colin."

Becky listened to Gwen's retreating footsteps as she took in the measure of the man across the room. He stared at the dishtowel, his hands in the pockets of his khakis. She liked him instantly. "It's not going to be easy," she said.

He shook his head. "No. No, it's not."

"But she's worth it," Becky said.

He nodded. "I know."

Satisfied with that answer, Becky set about finishing the dishes Gwen had abandoned. "How do you feel about purple pancakes?"

~~~

Colin's meeting with Randy Barr had gone well. A fellow deputy U.S. Marshal and an old friend of Colin's, Barr didn't ask questions when Colin asked him to print out the paperwork and meet him in Quincy early this morning.

But Barr didn't have access to Jerry's entire file. Those papers had been turned into ashes by the flames that ripped through Colin's house, and he had no way to get them again without going through Walker.

He rubbed at the tension in his shoulder. Colin was doubting his mentor, and that fact had his conscience and plain good sense doing backflips inside his brain. Walker was the person Colin trusted above all others, yet the man was one of only a handful who could have been responsible for the explosion.

He cursed under his breath. He'd spent the better part of two hours skimming documents from the trials that Jerry Ahearn testified in, getting up to speed on the major players involved in

The One Who Got Away

each of the three cases. That, combined with what Barr had been able to tell him about the modern day Irish Mafia in Boston, gave him a good idea of where to begin his search for information.

"There's a bar called Flynn's in Southie," Barr said. "It was the epicenter of the organization, back in its day. Now it's a local-hangout-turned-tourist-trap, decorated with newspaper stories of crimes and stuff. I've been there a couple times with my boss for lunch. They have a whole spread devoted to Jerry Ahearn."

"What, with coverage of the trial?"

Barr nodded. "Other stuff, too. Pictures, a gun. There's this big map that shows everything he testified about. It's really cool."

Maybe he'd find something at Flynn's that he was not finding in this stack of governmental paper. Colin frowned, dropping his pen and rubbing his temple. He reached for the plate Becky had brought him, selecting a tall turkey sandwich from the miniature buffet of lunch choices. There were three pigs in a blanket, two California rolls, and a small glass bowl of what smelled like peanut noodles with chopsticks sticking out.

Chewing distractedly, he glanced at the door and wondered when Gwen would return. She'd left the house after storming out the kitchen. Colin didn't understand why she was so angry, though he was beginning to get used to being confused around Gwen. What difference did it make if Rowan told him to leave the party, or it was David?

As if on cue, the door opened and Gwen entered the room with Becky's little Pug on a leash. Lucy was dancing happily at Gwen's feet while she tried to unsnap the collar. "Oh, what a good girl. Did you enjoy your walk?"

Colin stared at Gwen, his pulse racing in anticipation of their exchange. *I could spend the rest of my life looking at this woman, even if she is mad as all hell.*

She met his eyes. "I'm sorry, Colin," she said, with a tone that implied she was not sorry at all.

"Thank you. Why were you so angry?"

She crossed her arms over her chest. "I loved David very much."

"Gwen, did I ever imply otherwise?"

"If he asked you to leave, then he was aware of your intentions."

Colin took a sip of his water, deliberately weighing his words. "They weren't just my intentions, Gwen." Her eyes darkened and realization dawned on Colin. "That's it, isn't it? You're upset because David knew there was something between us."

"There was nothing…"

He raised a hand to stop her protest. "But that's it, right? You're upset because David knew."

"Yes."

She looked like she was about to cry, and Colin felt a momentary concern. "You didn't do anything wrong, Gwen. You never cheated on your husband."

She shrugged. "I know. But if he asked you to leave…"

"I get it." Colin watched her win the fight for composure, gently rubbing her eye with her knuckle. Even under duress, she was lovely. How many years had he been missing this woman? Wishing for one more chance to find a way into her life?

No, not just into her life. I want it all. Everything.

His mouth had gone dry, and he felt his eyes glued to her face, waiting for her to glance his way like a dog waiting for a morsel to drop from the table above. When she did finally raise her lashes and meet his stare, she smiled prettily.

The words were out before he could think better of them. "Someday, Gwen, we're going to be together."

He watched as the remark affected her, eyes dilating and a soft pink glow moving into her cheeks. Her rounded bottom lip hung separate from its partner, teasing him with its invitation, even as her words belied her face. "No, Colin."

"Not now. I know you're not ready. But when you are, I'll be here."

Her gaze dropped to the paperwork on the table. "What are you doing?" she asked.

"Going through the papers Barr gave me."

"Were you able to get copies of everything you lost in the fire?"

The One Who Got Away

"Not even close. These are just the transcripts from the trials Jerry testified in."

"What have you learned?"

"I found this." He opened a binder.

She shook her head. "What am I looking at?"

"A document from discovery. It wasn't used in the trial, but just got stuck in the file with everything else, looks like. It gives an address for Jerry Ahearn's aunt Bernice. Apparently, he was living with her for a time before he turned himself in to the feds."

"I don't understand what this means."

"I'm just thinking, if Jerry felt safe enough to hide out there all those years ago, maybe he felt safe enough to return there. Especially if Walker was right and Jerry's back in the fold."

"What did your contact at the Marshal's office have to say?"

"He hasn't heard anything definitive, but he thinks it's possible. Jerry's testimony put away two of the top three guys, then the third one died a year later of natural causes. There's been a lot of upheaval. Nearly everyone he betrayed is no longer with the company, so to speak."

"But still, you think they'd trust him after he testified against their own people?"

Colin tilted his head to the side. "You have to remember, even within the organization there's a struggle for power. Jerry turned against some people, but not all. According to Deputy Barr, Jerry may have played his hand strategically. Everyone he testified against was old blood. He actually helped the new boss take over."

Gwen leaned forward and rested her chin on her hand. "You mean, he might even be considered a faithful servant to the organization."

"Maybe, yes."

"When are we going to the aunt's house?"

"What you mean 'we', Kemo Sabe?"

She dropped her chin and looked at him through her lashes. "I'm coming with you, Colin."

He began gathering the papers back into a neat pile. "No."

Gwen stood, pushing her chair into the table with uncharacteristic force. "Yes."

The One Who Got Away

A reply was quick to his tongue, but Colin met her fiery eyes and paused. She was the one who came to him, suspecting David's death was not an accident. She was the one whose quick thinking and acting had gotten them this far. Besides, he would call less attention to himself at the bar if he wasn't alone. "I want to stop at a bar my contact told me about first. And you can come, Gwen, but promise me this. If I believe it's too dangerous for you to do something, you'll listen to me and step back."

"Deal. Where are we going?"

"Flynn's. A bar in Southie."

"Fabulous." She checked her watch. "I could use a pint to wash down those purple pancakes, couldn't you?"

Chapter 10

Gwen felt Colin's hand on the small of her back, guiding her around a large buckle in the sidewalk. They parked Becky's car several blocks away, the nearest spot they could find in the tightly woven neighborhood of houses that existed solely with on-street parking. There were no front lawns here, with houses butting up against the sidewalk like storefronts on an old fashioned Main Street.

Gwen felt as though she was tromping directly through the family rooms of these people. She heard snippets of conversation, bits of television shows and the smell of something baking. "I wonder what it would be like to live here," she said.

"Crowded."

She clucked her tongue. "I think it's lovely. Quaint, with a modern vibe."

He looked around at the few people on the street. "We're at least ten years older than most of the people living here."

"Ah, but I am young at heart." She winked at him. "You would stand out like a sore thumb."

He glared at her, one side of his mouth hitched up into a grin.

She worked to keep pace with his long strides, the click of her high-heeled sandals tapping on the concrete. Walking next to him like this, she could almost believe no time had passed, that they were teenagers again with the world at their feet and the future at their door, as if David and Rowan were just a step behind.

Instead of a lifetime away.

Gwen found herself mentally searching the air for her husband's spirit, so longingly did she miss him in that moment. But there was no trace of him in her mind, only a memory that had grown tired of being remembered, and she sighed aloud.

Colin turned his head at the sound, opening his palm to her as they walked, and she placed her hand in his. It felt warm and solid, a strong hand to go with the strong man at her side.

They turned a corner, the change in direction blowing the

The One Who Got Away

scent of him right into her face. Was that cologne, or just the smell of him alone? It was both familiar and unnerving to smell a man so intimately.

"Are we almost there?" she asked.

"On the next corner."

The area was splattered with more businesses, storefronts clamoring for their attention. Chinese food. A diner. A dry cleaning shop. Up ahead she could see a neon orange sign that read "Flynn's" shining in the midday summer sun, and felt her stomach twirl with anxiety. She turned to Colin and found him watching her.

"Just follow my lead," he said, seeming to understand her reservation. They reached the bar and he pulled open the wooden door, holding it for her to enter first.

Gwen stopped short. "Do you want to sit at the bar?" she asked.

"Yes."

There were three people sitting there already, each seemingly alone, and Gwen smiled graciously at each one as she passed. "Hi, there. Hello. How are you?" she asked, finally reaching two black barstools at the end of the bar and sitting gracefully on one.

The bartender put coasters down in front of them. "What can I get for you?" he asked, raising an eyebrow.

"I'd like a black Russian, please," said Gwen.

"And I'll take a Glenlivet on the rocks."

"I was thinking about a nice Scotch too, but the black Russian seemed more cloak and dagger."

"Vodka martini. Now that's cloak and dagger."

"Bond," she said in a deep voice.

"James Bond," he finished. "I thought you wanted a pint?"

"Beer before liquor, never sicker."

"Oh. Well, now it all makes sense." Colin turned to the bartender. "So, this used to be a hangout for the Irish Mafia?"

"Sure was. This place controlled more of Boston than City Hall in the 70s."

Gwen turned to take in the room. Its walls were covered in photographs and framed newspaper stories. A small spotlight

The One Who Got Away

illuminated a handgun in an acrylic box. An enormous map took up the entire wall opposite the bar.

"Oh my goodness, is that a painting?" asked Gwen, rising to her feet.

"Sure is. The whole city of Boston."

She crossed to the map, climbing into a booth to get a closer view. The mural was large enough in scale to depict individual streets in the city, many labeled by name. But it was the detail that took her breath away. "Colin, come look at this!" she said.

He slid across the opposite seat. "Holy cow."

Drawn on the map were what seemed like hundreds of images—a truck overturned, a building on fire—along with descriptions of events in the history of the mafia. From notorious crimes to the men responsible for their commission, it was all detailed here in fine painting and the tiniest of brushstrokes.

Gwen's arm shot up to point. "Michael "The Boxer" Gallente kills Town Councilman Berger!"

"Gwen, look at this one." Colin pointed to a painted cameo next to a textbox in the middle of the ocean. "It's Jerry."

She scrambled out of the booth and moved to the next table over, reading, "Jerry Ahearn, trusted brother, cast out to sea after testifying against members of the organization." Her eyes rested on the image of the man, so like her David. The resemblance sent a shiver to her core. "Oh, my goodness."

"This is crazy," said Colin. "It's all here. Everything from the court documents."

"And a lot more, I'd say," said Gwen, sitting back on her haunches. Her eyes took in the enormity of the map as she sipped at her smooth drink.

Meet the in-laws.

The moment was surreal. David Beaumont was a good, decent man, but he was connected to this horror by blood and experience. It may have even killed him. The thought had cold awareness flooding her center. *One of these people may have killed my husband.*

Her eyes returned to the portrait of Jerry Ahearn. David's father. She felt in her heart that they would find him, that this man's introduction was in her future. Gwen realized with some

The One Who Got Away

surprise that her drink was empty. "I'm going to get another drink. Would you like one?"

Colin looked up from his examination of the map. "I'll get it for you."

She waved him off. "Not a problem. You go ahead." She gestured to the mural and went back to the bar, ordering herself a pint of Guinness.

A voice in her ear made her jump. "Gwen!" She turned and looked down the bar to see who called her. Three seats down, on an empty barstool, she imagined she could see her late husband. He raised his own pint glass to her and sipped, then pointed wildly over the head of an old man sitting next to him.

Gwen looked to Colin, who was still absorbed in the map, then turned back to David.

He was gone.

Her eyes narrowed. It certainly wasn't the first time she had imagined her husband's ghost, but it was the first time he had tried to communicate something to her. She observed the old man as he worked the coaster under his drink in a circle, spinning it absentmindedly as he watched the news on a muted television screen.

Gwen always enjoyed meeting someone new, and she saw no reason this introduction should be any different. She scooted onto the seat David had occupied and offered the man a big smile. "I'm Gwen," she said warmly, extending her hand.

"Martin." His eyes were watery and blue, their depths clearly expressing his joy at being joined by a beautiful woman. His fine white hair was neatly combed, his jacket identifying him as a member of the local freemason's union.

"You're a mason," she said, impressed. "I have a great appreciation for artistry. Walls and stone walkways, strong brick buildings and stately concrete constructions."

He smiled, revealing neatly polished teeth. "I been a mason for forty-two years." He gestured out the front door of the bar. "I laid the foundation for the Waller Building with my bare hands and a trowel."

"How interesting!" she said, picking up her pint and sipping the strong brew freely. "There is a barn on my property with a cobblestone foundation. The barn itself has been rebuilt twice that I know of, but that foundation's still going strong. They don't build them like they used to."

"Where's your property?"

She smiled generously. "In Vermont, about half an hour outside of Barre."

"You didn't sound like you was from around here."

She shook her head. "No, I'm not. But it's a beautiful town. I might stay a while."

"Your friend from Vermont, too?"

Gwen raised her eyebrows. No, he's from Cold Spring. Just north of New York City."

His eyes widened. "Cold Spring?"

She nodded. "Yes."

"Now, ain't that a coincidence."

"What?"

"I just ran into an old buddy of mine the other day, used to live in Cold Spring. I hadn't seen him in years."

"Oh, no?"

Martin shook his head. "He got himself in some trouble a while back. Did some time."

She turned completely and faced Martin, wondering if this kind-hearted old man had information that could help her. "I'm looking for my father-in-law. His name is Jerry. Do you know him, Martin?"

~~~

Graham Walker was double-parked, the corner of his Grand Marquis closer to the bumper of a Jeep Cherokee than most people could manage without swapping paint. He wore dress slacks and a button-down shirt, having long ago ceased to be comfortable in clothes of a more casual nature.

Walker had been sitting behind a desk for more years than he cared to count, and believed on any given day he was able to accomplish more there than he could out in the field. He was an administrator, through and through. He followed the rules. He documented everything. But he knew as he sat in his car outside of Flynn's that today's events would never be written down and filed away by him or anyone else.

The One Who Got Away

This one was personal.

Through the window of the bar, he could see Colin Mitchell looking at something on the wall, and Walker wondered if the widow had accompanied Colin to Boston. It would be easier if she had. He put his palm over his mouth and pressed in his cheeks.

Hell, it would be easier if Mitchell hadn't come at all.

A car honked its horn as it worked to maneuver around the Marquis. Walker twirled his wedding band on his hand, forcing it over the knuckle and back again, oblivious to the other driver's difficulty. He wanted a cigarette, despite having given them up eighteen years earlier, and he desperately wanted a drink.

The man's house blows up in the middle of the night, and he doesn't even call me.

Colin Mitchell was like a son to Walker. He even looked like Walker's son, when the boy had been alive. Tom Walker had been killed in a motorcycle accident when he was twenty-three, leaving his father to his job with the U.S. Marshal's Office and his mother to lose her mind. June had never been able to recover from Tommy's death, slowly slipping away to depression and alcoholism until she required constant care.

Mentoring Colin had filled a need in Walker's spirit that had gone unmet since Tommy passed away. Walker was meant to be a teacher, an instructor. A leader of leaders. Colin was meant to be the next in command, a designation that Walker conferred as much as recognized.

He cut himself loose like a kite in the wind.

What did it mean, that Colin hadn't called his trusted boss when someone tried to kill him as he slept in his bed?

He had no idea where to find Colin until Deputy Barr accessed the records on the Ahearn trials this morning. Walker had put that case to bed himself, tramped the dirt down overtop when Ahearn got out of prison. He sure as hell didn't want anyone digging around in that graveyard without his permission.

That's what burned him. Colin had permission.

He could have asked for the records again himself, and Walker would have given them. But Colin hadn't done that. Instead, he ran off to Boston and had Barr pull the transcripts.

The One Who Got Away

There could be only one reason for that, and the reality was chafing at Walker's collar.

He thinks I had something to do with it.

His thick fingers worked to twist his ring, popping it over the knuckle. A rap on his window had Walker turning his head. A uniformed police officer gestured for him to put the window down.

"You can't park here, sir. Move along."

Walker hesitated, the badge in his pocket heavy on his mind, his desire for anonymity winning out over expediency.

"Sorry, officer," he said, putting the car into drive and flashing a harmless grin. He drove once around the block and returned to the bar, finding both the police officer—and Colin Mitchell—gone.

Chapter 11

"Martin said he talked to Jerry for about fifteen minutes, but he has no idea how to find him," said Gwen.

Colin drove up the onramp to 93 South. "Did you believe him?"

"Not at all. I don't even think he wanted me to believe him."

"What do you mean?"

Gwen put her hand on the dashboard of the car, her heart suddenly pounding in her chest. "I don't want to go this way."

"But this is the way to Becky's."

"We'll have to find another way. Get off at the next exit, please." Her voice held an element of alarm.

"What's the matter, Gwen?"

"I don't know. I just know that as soon as you started driving on this road, I felt we were in danger. We need to get off of it, now."

Colin shook his head as he quickly moved to the right-hand lane. "You get feelings like this a lot?"

"Often enough that I know when to listen."

"Do you know what kind of…" he stopped speaking mid-sentence, his eyes wide on the rear-view mirror.

"What's wrong?"

"I think we're being followed." Gwen immediately moved to turn around, and Colin put his hand on her knee. "Don't look now."

"What do you see?"

"A big sedan. It got on with us, then cut over when I did and got off, too." He put on his turn signal and pulled into the parking lot of a convenience store. "What are you going to do now, mister?" he asked the other car. It continued past the entrance without slowing down. Colin pulled back onto the road, headed back toward the expressway.

"North please, not south," said Gwen.

"I want you to turn around in your seat and look out for that car."

They were at the very top of the on-ramp before she spoke.

The One Who Got Away

"I see it. They're just getting on the on-ramp."

"Damn it."

"Coming our way, quickly."

Colin pressed hard on the accelerator and slipped into the passing lane. The late afternoon traffic was oddly light, providing little cover.

Gwen had spent time in Boston before she and David were married, teaching art classes while he composed his first soundtrack. Her brain worked to remember the exits ahead. "Up over that hill, there's an exit with a rotary. A bunch of roads meet. If we can get there first, he won't know which way we went."

"Good idea."

Gwen watched as the needle on the speedometer crossed one hundred and continued to rise. She closed her eyes, saying a silent prayer for their own safe travels and those of the drivers around them on the road. A feeling of peace was punctuated by clear direction. "Take the first right on the rotary," she said to Colin.

"Where does it go?"

"I have no idea. Just take it."

"What the lady wants," he said under his breath as the car crested the hill. The exit ramp was visible five hundred feet down the road, and he hit the breaks quickly to take the turn. "Can he see us?"

"Not yet, not yet..." she said, watching the top of the hill behind them. They were nearly out of view when the other car popped over the horizon. "Yes!"

"Is he following?"

"Yes."

A sharp turn in the road forced Gwen against the car door.

"Sorry," said Colin.

"Quite all right."

The exit ramp circled down a full level beneath the highway, shielding the other car from view. Colin took the first right on the rotary at a speed that made her cringe. Gwen squinted through the trees, trying to make out the other vehicle. "He didn't see us," she said, the relief in her voice evident.

"Clearly, we got someone's attention at that bar."

"Not a good someone, either. I wonder if it was Martin," said Gwen.

"You said you didn't believe him."

She squinted her eyes. "Well, no. Not completely. He was endearing, but I just got the feeling he wasn't being completely truthful with me. Then he got talking about the riptide up at Sandwich Beach this time of year."

"Sandwich?"

"Yes. He said it's on the Cape."

"I know where it is." Colin shifted in his seat and sat up straighter. "Do you think he was trying to give you a clue?"

"I'm not sure. Maybe."

"That map was interesting, too."

"What did you find out?"

"It was like a complete history of the Irish Mafia in Boston, with key events, accomplishments, deaths and arrests. It even had information on politicians they controlled, and how many girlfriends they had. It was nuts."

"Was there anything else about Jerry?"

Colin nodded. "His face was painted on a pigeon's body next to Mickey Brady, the former leader who was brought down by Jerry's testimony, and on a rat's body next to Brady's right-hand man."

"People he testified against?"

"Yes. But he wasn't even mentioned next to two others, who he also testified against."

"That is strange."

"Our buddy, Mike Gallente, had his own entry. It said he was a beloved member of the organization who was tragically incarcerated."

"That would support the theory that Jerry helped to bring in a new regime."

"I thought of that myself. I think tomorrow we should go to the aunt's house and look for Jerry."

"Agreed. Perhaps we should check out Sandwich as well. We'll just find a hotel for the night, and I'll let Becky know we're not heading back to her place."

The One Who Got Away

"At all?"

Gwen sighed. "I feel like we would be bringing danger to her door. I don't want to do that."

"Agreed. I'm going to give Rowan a call and have him wire us more money. Let's put some distance between us and our friend, then we'll find a hotel for the night."

"Sounds like a plan," he said confidently, but he couldn't help but wonder who was chasing after them, and when they would meet again.

~~~

Colin hung up the phone and placed it on the hotel room desk. Rowan was sending more money. Colin rubbed his face. The fact that he had only the shirt on his back and a prepaid cell was upsetting to Colin, who never left home without his wallet and smartphone.

He and Gwen had stopped to buy more clothes when they passed a department store, using all but a hundred dollars of their cash-on-hand. They didn't have the money for a second hotel room, even if one had been available.

He heard the water come on and knew Gwen had gotten into the shower. The image of her naked body so near to him would normally have gotten his pulse racing, but as he sank onto the bed he was overwhelmed with guilt and self-loathing.

It was all his fault.

An image of David formed in his mind, as much as a brother as Rowan ever was. Their estrangement had been hell for Colin, even worse now that he was able to admit his responsibility. At the time, he insisted to himself that Gwen was as guilty as he, truly believing she had feelings for him instead of David. Now he knew he'd been wrong. Gwen may have been attracted to him, but she only ever loved her husband. Colin had been a young pompous ass who cared more about himself than he cared about his own family.

He had seen only what he wanted to believe, and it had cost him his relationship with David and hurt the woman he claimed to care for.

What would it have been like, to have been friends with them both? Visits to Vermont, skiing with his friend. Maybe he even would have been on the mountain next to David when his past came back to haunt him.

An image played in his mind like a movie, himself skiing off the lift beside David, at his side when he first recognized Michael and knew there might be trouble. He felt a physical pain in his abdomen at the possibilities lost, an opportunity to save the man he so cared for.

The past was in the past. There was nothing he could do to change it, but he could damn sure respect the memory of his friend and stay away from his wife—a woman who clearly still didn't want a relationship with Colin.

It was the least he could do. He would fix the mistakes in his past, make amends as best he could. He would find the person responsible for David's death, make them pay. And he would send Gwen on her way, free to make a new life with someone else. She was young, beautiful. She could marry again, become a mother if she wanted. Colin pictured her cradling a sleeping infant with rosy cheeks, a physical pain appearing in his gut at the knowledge that the baby would never be his.

Colin moved to the bed away from the window, leaving the one with a view for Gwen. He wouldn't bother her tonight, or ever again. Colin had to find a way to get her to safety and look for Jerry on his own. Now that he was seeing clearly, he understood that he had only allowed her to join him on this trip because he wanted the chance to be physically close to her, a mistake that could have gotten her killed.

I am an arrogant ass.

The water turned off and Colin braced himself for the evening ahead. Suddenly nervous, he didn't know what to do with Gwen if he wasn't actively pursuing her. He busied himself with the television, mindlessly flipping through channels as he waited for Gwen to come out of the bathroom.

~~~

Gwen ripped the tags off the pink brassiere and held it up to the light, its fine lace and shimmering ribbons mocking her serious expression. She had already slipped on the matching panties and stood in the steamy bathroom as she finally admitted the truth.

The One Who Got Away

She wanted Colin. She wanted Colin very much.

The lingerie set had caught her eye in the department store and she thought nothing of it, tucking the items under a dress and two shirts already in her hands. But more than an hour later as she dressed to confront Colin in the intimacy of the hotel room, she knew she had purchased the items in anticipation of something more.

Gwen closed her eyes and hugged the bra to her chest, both for fear of crossing the line she long ago drew in the sand and for her own eagerness to be done with pretenses. She and Colin had driven in silence after they lost their pursuer, a comfortable silence that reminded Gwen of everything she had once held in her hand and had long since learned to do without.

Friendship. Companionship. Physical love.

She loved the feel of him beside her in the car, the strength of his spirit and the scent of his skin. They drove along the country roads and Gwen knew she would make love to this man, to give in to the energy that connected them like electricity. It was not a fantasy this time, but a plan.

An overdue plan to give in to desire.

There would be no going back, though she would be the first to admit there were bound to be regrets. Gwen finished dressing by slipping a wide-necked jersey dress over her bra and panties, not knowing what tomorrow would bring for her and Colin, but knowing exactly what she wanted from today. She stepped into the hotel room as the last rays of the setting sun fell across the room.

Colin sat on one of the beds, legs stretched out before him, arms crossed behind his head as he watched her. The pose would have made her nervous just hours before, but now she welcomed the dance in her stomach. Gwen had never given half her love, and she was not about to start this evening.

"Good shower?" he asked.

"Mmm hmm. Your turn." Her eyes went to the TV.

"I'm not watching this. Go ahead and change it," he said as he stood.

"I don't want to watch TV," she said, her eyes telling him what she wanted instead.

The One Who Got Away

The energy hummed between them. He stared at her for several seconds before looking away, then stood and walked into the bathroom.

Gwen squinted against the orange rays of the sun and crossed her arms over her chest, feeling goose bumps along her arms as she did.

Be happy, Gwen.

The words were clear in her mind, though they were not spoken aloud. David's spirit was light, but undoubtedly present.

"Thank you," she whispered, a smile touching her lips as she closed her eyes and lingered in the moment. When she opened them, the sun had slipped beneath the horizon, coating the room in a softened dusk. The rush of water told her Colin had turned on the shower.

Be happy.

The cell phone rang and Gwen reached to answer it. "Hello?"

"Gwen, it's Rowan. How are you holding up?"

A flash of guilt went through her at the reminder of the hunt for David's killer, but she allowed it to recede as quickly as it had come. "Pretty well, all things considered."

"I'm flying into Logan. I just boarded the plane."

"You don't have to—"

"Sure I do, Gwen."

She considered for a moment how she would feel if she was an ocean away from these events, and understood that Rowan needed to join them. "Yes, of course you do. I'm sorry. When does your flight get in?" She wrote the information down and tucked the paper in her purse.

"Let me talk to Colin."

"He's in the shower."

There was a pause on the line. "All right. I'll see you in the morning. I don't know if my cell will work in the states or not."

"We'll be waiting for you, Rowan. Have a good flight."

A tension settled between Gwen's shoulder blades at the memory of Rowan's role all those years ago. She suspected her husband's best friend would not approve of her and Colin being together, and mentally decided to wait until morning to tell Colin

The One Who Got Away

that Rowan was on his way. She didn't want anything to come between her and Colin this evening—not David's memory or Rowan's hostility.

~~~

Colin dressed in the steamy bathroom, his damp skin sticking to the fresh cotton of his new t-shirt. It aggravated him as it pulled at him, the action seeming more difficult for the situation that awaited him outside the door.

He needed to apologize to her.

He needed to get her the hell out of harm's way.

He needed a football field between them and a cold shower.

He cursed under his breath as he tugged a pair of crisp blue jeans over his thighs. She wasn't going to go willingly, that much was for sure. Colin considered whether to discuss it with her at all, or simply tell her what was going to happen as he headed to Becky's house to drop her off.

He brushed his teeth and ran his fingers through his short hair before he opened the door, and his heart stopped beating. Gwen reclined against the pillows, wearing a sexy smile and a thoughtful look.

"Hi," she said softly.

Colin felt his blood stir and tramped down his desire. *Haven't you done enough to this woman? Do you need to keep pestering her for the smallest affection?*

"Hey." He turned to the desk and began digging through it. "You hungry?"

"I am. What do you have in mind?"

He could think of a few things, but none of them were on a menu. "I don't care. Pizza. Subs. Whatever you want."

Gwen walked to stand next to him, looking at the selection over his shoulder. She smelled like sweet soaps and something flowery, and she was standing too close. Reaching over him, she pointed. "Do you like Thai?"

"What, like seaweed and stuff?"

She chuckled and lightly hit his shoulder. "No. It's simple food, usually spicy. It has a light, balanced finish."

"Sounds like seaweed."

Gwen picked up the menu and began looking. "I want this.

You can have pizza."

Colin could still feel his skin tingling where she had touched him. "I'll try it. Just order me something that's not too scary." He watched as she picked up the cell phone and dialed, tossing her golden curls before putting the phone to her ear.

"About forty-five minutes," she said, coming to sit beside him. Gwen's hip was next to his on the bed, nearly touching, driving him crazy. He turned to her, his gaze questioning. Was it his imagination or was she flirting with him?

It would be so easy to kiss her. Just like that. Bend his head and do what he always wanted to do around her. Instead, he heard himself say the words that needed to be said. "I'm sorry, Gwen."

Her brows drew together. "What for?"

He stood and began to pace. "So many things. I don't even know where to start." How did you explain to someone that you held yourself responsible for everything that had ever gone wrong in her entire life?

"I'm listening."

"The party. When I made a pass at you, embarrassed you. I shouldn't have done that."

He watched her face soften, her full bottom lip curling up on one side. "Thank you."

"I hurt David, too." He shook his head. "He was as important to me as my own brother, and I didn't give a damn how he was feeling. I tried to steal the woman he loved. I would have done it in a heartbeat if you let me." He took a deep breath. "Now he's gone, and I can't ever fix that. Apologize. Make it right."

Gwen stood and took a step toward him. "He knows, Colin."

"Bullshit," he said under his breath.

She came closer, resting her hand on his shoulder. "He does."

Their eyes locked, absolution passing between them like consent. Colin slowly nodded. She seemed so sure of herself, he could almost believe it. "I hope you're right." He saw her stare drop to his own lips, an answering fire igniting in his belly. Hadn't he just apologized for this very thing? Not a minute later,

The One Who Got Away

he was already imagining kissing her. He took a step back and turned away. He had to make her understand everything. Once she did, she would never look at him like that again.

"David and I used to go skiing together all the time," he said.

"I know."

He spoke past the knot in his throat that worked to stop all communication. "Maybe I would have been there."

He heard her approach before she grabbed his shoulder and turned him around to face her. She looked angry. "Stop this, Colin. It is not your fault David died." Color flooded her cheeks as she shook her finger at him. "You are not the one who killed him, you are not responsible for his death. Do you understand me?"

"I should have been there. I should have been in his life. Who knows? I could have made a difference…"

Gwen stepped on her tiptoes and pressed her mouth to his, stopping the flow of words and shocking him into silence. She pulled back and met his surprised eyes. "He loved you, Colin, and he missed you, just as I did."

"You missed me?"

She nodded her head, wide-eyed. "But I was too ashamed to encourage David to contact you."

"Ashamed?" He held on to her when she would have stepped back.

"The attraction between you and me was never one-sided, Colin. With you gone, I didn't have to feel uncomfortable. I knew David missed you, and I just let it go because it was easier that way." She wiped at a tear that had fallen onto her cheek. "What kind of person does that make me? I never cheated on my husband, but I cheated him out of the family he loved."

Colin watched a second tear fall from her lashes, and bent his head to kiss it away. Every reason he had devised for keeping Gwen at arm's length vanished in that instant. She was here, of her own free will. She knew everything that haunted him and she forgave him.

She reached up and pulled him tighter to her, finding his lips with her own. Colin's heart swelled, knowing that she wanted

The One Who Got Away

him, that she cared for him, that she'd missed him. What had always been a physical attraction turned into something so much more, deeper, more meaningful. Colin was lost in her, lost in the moment, lost in their loving. Evening turned to nighttime and kisses to sweet passion, inching closer to the morning's light and what Colin knew he must do.

Protect this woman, as he had failed to protect her husband. He only hoped she would be able to forgive him when she awoke in the morning to find him gone.

Chapter 12

Dear Gwen,

I love you. Last night meant everything to me.

But I can't protect you if you're with me, and I can't bear the thought of anything happening to you. I called Becky—she's coming to pick you up. Don't go back to her house, just in case. Find somewhere safe. I'll see you as soon as I can.

Colin

~~~

Gwen let the paper fall from her hand and sat on the edge of the bed. She had awoken slowly, languid memories of her night with Colin stretching through her mind. Her fantasies hadn't done the man justice. When she wanted him again, she reached out for him with a cat-like purr, only to find his side of the bed cold and empty.

"Colin?" she called, sitting up. Her body felt funny, not used to lovemaking, and it made her feel good and alive.

She walked to the window and pulled back the curtain, light streaming in from the bright summer's day, making her flinch. It was then that she saw the note on the table.

Anger was slow to percolate, gradually taking over where shock had settled first. She was hurt, betrayed. Had he known that he would leave her, even as he became her lover? She had opened her heart and shown him the love that was growing inside, believing he was doing the same. But he was preparing to deceive her, to summarily lift her out of a situation that was vital to her wellbeing and drop her onto the sidelines like a spectator.

How dare he?

Gwen stood, just as a knock came at the door. She reached for a towel and covered herself before opening it. One look at Becky's sheepish expression told her all she needed to know. "Good morning, dear," said Gwen. "Just so you know, we are going after that damnable man, no matter what he wants. Are you on the side of righteousness?"

Becky's eyes lit. "Abso-freakin-lutely."

"Wonderful. Make yourself at home while I get dressed."

The One Who Got Away

~~~

The house was small and gray, its weathered shingles somewhat neglected. A cool breeze came in off the ocean, making a porch swing rock on its own and momentarily startling Colin. He walked up the wooden steps, which creaked beneath his feet, and rapped soundly on the door.

He could feel his sidearm in its holster, the weight of it adding both security and concern, his senses already on high-alert from knocking on what he believed was Jerry Ahearn's front door. Lace curtains moved to the side, revealing a boy with curling brown hair. "Can I help you?" he asked as he opened the door.

"I'm looking for someone."

The boy raised his eyebrows.

"An old friend. He used to live here." Colin's heart hammered in his chest. "His name's Jerry. Do you know him?"

The boy rolled his eyes. "Um, yeah. He's my dad. But he's not home."

Jerry was his father?

Colin's eyes searched his features for any similarity to David. Their coloring was completely different, the boy's warm skin tone suggesting his background was not completely Irish as David's had been.

David's brother.

Half-brother, he corrected. Adele died when David was six; this boy must have been born much later.

"How old are you?" asked Colin.

He eyed him wearily. "Who are you?"

He froze, unsure of what to say, just as a voice called from the door behind them. "Luke, who is at the door?" An attractive brunette appeared, wiping her hands on a towel. Her eyes met Colin's and recognition slammed into his consciousness, making him reel.

The woman's hands jerked and she dropped the towel, covering her mouth.

"Emma?" Colin gasped, his voice too loud as he stepped toward her, the boy all but forgotten. This wasn't really happening. It simply wasn't possible. He had looked for her for nearly a year, exhausted every possible avenue to find her.

The boy looked from Colin to the woman and back. "Mom, what's going on?"

"Mom?" said Colin, his eyes raking over the boy's face a second time, urgent now, easily noting her similarity to the brunette. "Oh, sweet Jesus..." He raised a shaking hand to the boy's cheek and he pulled away from him, just as his mother reached out and hauled the boy to her side.

Emma's voice shook when she spoke. "I can explain everything, Colin."

~~~

Rowan Mitchell stepped out of the terminal and into the bright sunshine of a New England summer's day. It had been too damn long since he set foot on American soil, the glamour of being an expat in Italy having long ago lost its appeal. He hadn't even seen his brother since his own wedding to Tamra three years earlier, an unconscious grimace crossing his face at the thought of his wife.

"Rowan!" Gwen was walking toward him in the sunshine, a bright smile lighting her face.

He held out his arms to her. "It's been too long," said Rowan. "You look fantastic."

"Thank you," she said, reaching up to pinch his cheeks. "And congratulations! I hear you are married. And a father! How wonderful."

He bobbed his head as words failed him, his recent wounds too fresh and overwhelming for conversation. "A lot has changed."

"She must be something, to have stolen your heart and taken you away to a foreign land," Gwen said with a wink.

Oh, she's something, all right. They began walking away from the terminal. "Where's Colin?"

Rowan had been waiting to get his hands on his younger brother since he realized Colin and Gwen were sharing a room at the hotel. *He's in the shower,* Gwen had said.

The thought had driven Rowan half crazy all the way across the Atlantic, imagining Colin doing all manner of inappropriate things to cajole the innocent widow into his bed. Why couldn't his damnable brother leave Gwen well enough alone? Why did he always have to push it, try for a relationship that was never meant to be? The thought that Colin would pursue Gwen now, with David dead, made Rowan extremely angry. It was like spitting on his best friend's grave.

"I'm not sure where Colin is. He was gone when I awoke this morning."

Rowan didn't miss the intimate phrasing, but decided to bite his tongue. More concerning right now was the fact that his brother had abandoned her. "He just left you alone?"

Gwen's chin came up. "He felt my tagging along was too dangerous, that he couldn't protect me. He went off on his own to find the elusive bad guys and see that justice is served."

Colin had a point. If David really had been killed and the two of them were walking around in harm's way, knocking on unknown doors, then maybe Gwen really wasn't safe with Colin. Rowan felt a begrudging respect for his brother, surprised Colin had the maturity to put Gwen's safety above his own lustful concerns. "That was probably a good idea, Gwen."

She stopped next to an orange Suzuki and opened the passenger side door. "And why is that a good idea, exactly?"

He squinted at the driver of the car, unable to see beyond the glare on the windshield. "We don't want you to get hurt."

"We?" she asked, raising an eyebrow. "I see. I am no more fragile than you are, Rowan Mitchell. I'm a better shot with a weapon and I am well versed in the martial arts."

He took in her graceful limbs and feminine frame, doubting her ability to fend off a sixth grader.

Gwen put a hand on her hip. "Don't let my girlish good looks fool you."

He chuckled in spite of himself and climbed into the backseat of the car, surprised to see masses of red curly hair on the woman behind the wheel. The car smelled like cinnamon and something spicy, and the redhead turned toward him.

"I'm Becky."

"Rowan. Pleasure to meet you," he said, extending his hand.

"Not so fast, slick," said Becky. "Gwen and I are in this, whether you like it or not. We're coming with you to find the bastard who killed Gwen's husband, and if you try to stop us I'm going to open a can of whoop-ass. You got that?"

Her eyes were incredible, a natural green that captivated him and drew him into their depths. Rowan was instantly aware of her, like he hadn't been aware of a woman in years. His eyes fell briefly to her lips, and returned to those eyes. "Whoop-ass?" he said, the lightest smile pulling at his mouth.

She raised her brows and moved her head from side to side. "Whoop-ass!"

"Got it."

"We do this together," said Becky.

Rowan nodded. "Whatever you say."

Gwen leaned her head back and peeked at Rowan. "Becky has a way with words."

"I can see that."

Becky held two cell phones in her hands, clearly copying a number from one to the other, then passed one to him. "You're calling Colin. It's ringing. Tell him you rented a car and find out where he is."

Rowan had the odd sense that he'd been kidnapped and was being held against his will. It rang several times before going to voicemail.

"It's Rowan. I just landed at Logan. Call me back at this number when you get this. My regular phone doesn't work in the States."

"Damn it," said Becky. "Where do we go now?"

"We go to Aunt Bernice's house. Six twenty-two Balina Place," said Gwen.

Becky backed out of the parking space. "Where'd you get that?"

"It was in the documents I was looking at with Colin yesterday morning."

"Good memory, girl."

"Actually, it's quite a coincidence. Six twenty-two is my anniversary—June twenty-second—and we went to Bali on our honeymoon."

Becky's slammed on the brake. "Are you kidding me?"

Gwen's eyes twinkled. "Don't you just love when things like that happen?"

Chapter 13

The disappearance of Emma Walker was newsworthy for a short period of time in the summer of 2001, wedged between the arrest of a serial arsonist and a scandal involving a small town sheriff's affection for child pornography.

Images of Emma's newly-rented apartment flooded the New York City suburban media for several days before the court of public opinion decreed she had likely left of her own volition. She was, after all, nearly twenty years old, and had recently broken up with her boyfriend. He was interviewed on channel six, telling the world that Emma longed for bigger and better things, and that he, for one, was unconcerned as to her whereabouts.

Colin had interviewed the boyfriend, though he had no legal authority to do so. The U.S. Marshal's Office had no interest in the disappearance of Graham Walker's daughter, but Colin certainly did. He clearly remembered the older man's devastation, a vacant look that haunted him as he sat at his desk and stared at nothing for what seemed like months. One minute Walker would be there, appearing to be engaged in his work—a meeting or paperwork—and the next he'd be gone, not to return for hours or even days on end.

The conversation with the boyfriend convinced Colin he knew nothing about Emma's disappearance, and despite Colin's best investigative efforts, the case soon disappeared off the radar of every legitimate agency.

That was when Walker really got bad. His clothes hung off his body, the collars of his shirts loose and awkward around his neck like so much knotted rope. His skin was ruddy and pale, his once-sharp eyes watery and bloodshot. Colin wondered if it was booze or sheer exhaustion, a lack of hope, that had gotten to the older man and destroyed his spirit.

Then came the day Colin stepped into Walker's office and was startled to see an older woman with short dark hair. "Where's Walker?" he asked.

She took off stylish reading glasses and eyed him frankly. "He's taken a leave of absence."

Walker lived for the job, had been good at it before his daughter vanished. He had run this department like his own personal kingdom, and it was unsettling to see anyone else sitting behind the big dark desk. Colin narrowed his eyes. "His request, or yours?"

"That's not for me to say."

"When's he coming back?"

"It's an indefinite leave. Perhaps you should contact him directly."

Colin tried. He called repeatedly, sent email messages like he was throwing rocks into a lake. He'd gone to Walker's house, only to find the old white colonial deserted. Colin stood in the driveway of his mentor's Connecticut home, taking in the peeling paint, the overgrown grass. Years earlier, Colin had stood in this exact same spot and thought what a lucky man Graham Walker was—the father of two beautiful children with a gorgeous house and a loving wife.

Now Walker's son was dead, crashing his motocycle into a tree with a blood alcohol level .21, Emma had vanished, and Walker's wife was living in an assisted care facility, though the reason she needed such help had never been offered. Perhaps the happy household was not what it seemed, or maybe it was simply a tragedy. Everything Walker cared about was gone.

Three months after Walker's sudden leave of absence, he returned just as unexpectedly.

"You're back," said Colin.

"Yes."

Colin took in Walker's straight posture, the clear eyes. "Anything on Emma?"

Walker didn't even blink. "She's not coming back."

"Is she…"

"She's fine, Mitchell," he bit out. "She has her own life now."

Colin nodded, understanding he would not be given an explanation. "I'm glad you're back, sir."

The One Who Got Away

Gwen stepped to the door of Jerry's aunt Bernice's house and rang the bell, taking in her surroundings as she waited. The neighborhood of small brick ranches was welcoming and quaint, with small square yards and mature shrubs and trees. An elderly woman at the house next door was watching her, and Gwen waved pleasantly, earning her a nod and a smile.

The door opened to a tall young man with warm brown skin.

"Hi there, my name's Gwen Trueblood. I'm hoping you can help me find someone."

The man was happy to help, but he had never heard of Jerry or his aunt, telling Gwen his parents had lived in the house for the past nine years.

Gwen slid back into the passenger seat of Becky's car and reached for the seat belt. "No luck." She shook her head. "I thought for sure we were going to find out where Jerry is." Gwen's intuition rarely steered her wrong, and she was nonplussed, unsure of what to do next.

"Wait for it," said Becky, pulling her sunglasses down and peering over Gwen's shoulder. The woman from next door walked gingerly toward them.

"Hello," said Gwen.

"Are you looking for Bernice?"

Gwen nodded. "I am! Her nephew, actually. He's my father-in-law."

"Oh dear, I'm so sorry," the woman's face fell. "You're looking for Jerry?"

"Yes."

"He passed away years ago, my dear."

Jerry was dead? Gwen didn't realize just how much she was looking forward to meeting David's father until the possibility disappeared. "Oh."

"I'm sorry to be the one to tell you." She sighed heavily. "Jerry got himself into a little trouble and he went into Witness Protection. It was a few years after that he passed away."

Gwen was confused. Was she referring to the dead Jerry of Cold spring, who was never really dead at all, or the true death of the man sometime later?

"Bernice," said the old woman, "moved out to Sandwich to

The One Who Got Away

live with her son and his wife, must be upwards of ten years now. She needed a little help to get along when she got the cancer."

"Sandwich?" asked Gwen, the hair rising on her arms as she remembered Martin's story.

Becky leaned close to Gwen, sticking her head close to the window. "Do you know where we can find her son?"

"Why, yes. A little place down the road from the boardwalk entrance. A gray house with white shutters. If you find the boardwalk, you can't miss it."

~~~

The boardwalk cut through marshlands and over inlets, the grasses providing no cover to someone who wanted to remain inconspicuous. James McDonald turned his collar up against the wind and tucked his chin inside the jacket.

He only had one chance to get this right.

His stomach hadn't stopped churning since that fateful phone call. He had packed a change of clothes and the unregistered Glock he'd been given years ago by his partner when the older man retired. You never know when you might need it, he had said. James had laughed, unable to imagine any such scenario.

Until now.

He walked along the wooden planks toward the beach, the sound of his footfalls like a ticking clock, marking the moments before he would pull the trigger. His fingers gingerly checked the safety on the weapon in the large pocket of his windbreaker, the shake of his hand alarming. Would he be steady enough to take the shot when he got there?

His feet stopped moving beneath him and he twisted around, eyeing the path that led back to his car. The wooden boards stretched out for what looked like miles, straight and still amid the blowing grasses. He could walk back to the car, leave this place behind forever.

He'd have to leave everything. His wife, his child. Go on the run. He could never be free that way, never be sure they were all right.

What looked like escape might really be the road to certain

death. He turned back around, the ocean now visible at the horizon. If he did what he came here to do, things could go back to the way they were. Yes, there might be another call. But there could also be another twelve-year reprieve. There had been so many good years, so much happiness between those two phone calls. His feet began to move again.

James wanted things back the way they were, before he ran for mayor, before he became sheriff, even. He wanted to be broke again, eating hot dogs and drinking beer with Jeannie in front of the TV in their little house by the river. Christ, when was the last time they'd even sat down next to each other on the couch, no less touched each other like they used to back then, all horny and wild?

Sand began to rain down like hail and he realized he was crying, the grains sticking to his face as he tried to wipe them away. He cried for what he was about to do, for the woman he loved and had married, for the son he might never see again, and the wretched hole in his soul that had allowed this horror to happen.

Chapter 14

Gwen didn't believe in worrying. It served only to magnify negative energy that would otherwise pass her by. So when she found herself concerned for Colin on the drive to Sandwich Beach, she gave the sensation due note and raised her head in silent prayer.

Be with him. Keep him safe.

Her heart was filled with such longing to have him by her side that the emotion gave her pause. Had she so easily become attached to the man that she was somehow incomplete without him, like a vacuum to be filled instead of a solid rock to stand on? Her brow furrowed as she watched homes slip by the speeding car, cruising toward Sandwich Beach.

Gwen hoped Becky was right, that the son living there was really Jerry. It was certainly possible Bernice found it easier to kill off her nephew than live in the shadow of his crimes, just as David himself had done. The thought of living in one's shadow brought her back to Colin, her conflicting emotions warring inside her.

Gwen deeply valued her independence, her own personality and strength of character. While she had given herself completely to her husband, her quick identification as Colin's lover was more troublesome. She was not a person who loved in degrees, yet this time she couldn't help but feel she would be losing something important, something she had never considered she was losing when she married David.

Herself.

In the years since her husband died, Gwen had become something more than she had been when he was by her side. She had become more fully herself, more comfortable alone than she could ever be with Colin. She tapped her fingers on the car door in a staccato rhythm.

Something else was bothering her, too. Colin had left her behind in consideration for her safety. While she wanted to understand that, what struck her most was that he did not see her as an equal, capable partner—an asset. His actions showed he thought her a liability, a responsibility, a problem to be handled.

Such was not love. At least, it was not love as Gwen experienced it.

The feminine in her spirit admitted it had hurt her to awaken to an empty room. She and Colin had shared something magical, the sort of connection that was reserved for the most special relationships in life.

But it couldn't be love. It made sense she should care for Colin. He'd been a player in an important part of her life, a time that she cherished and longed to revisit. Could she blame herself for falling so willingly into his arms? For enjoying the man and the sexual chemistry between them?

Colin had always mistaken what they shared for something deeper. He claimed an awareness of her while they'd been separated that she just didn't share. The truth was, Gwen had rarely thought of Colin in the years since she'd last seen him. She shifted in her seat, bristling at what she knew was an exaggeration. Yes, she had frequently thought of Colin, but had blocked the sensations out of lingering guilt over David. Maybe there'd been wisdom in that.

Rowan interrupted her thoughts. "Gwen, something's been bothering me, and I'm just going to ask, okay?" he said.

"Of course." She turned around in her seat to face him, pushing her sunglasses atop her head.

"Last night when I called Colin and you answered, you said he was in the shower."

She instantly saw where this was going. "Yes?"

"How did you know that?"

"I could hear the water running."

"Because you were sharing a room."

She faced forward. "And you don't approve."

Becky piped up. "What business is it of yours if they shared a room?"

"I was talking to Gwen."

"I don't care who you were talking to. You asked the question in front of me, so clearly you wanted me to hear it. And it just so happens I have an opinion about this matter that I'd like to share."

The One Who Got Away

"Oh, yeah? What's that?"

Becky yelled. "Mind your own goddamn business, Mitchell."

"It is my business."

Gwen couldn't believe his self-righteousness. He was treating her like a child, not unlike how his brother had treated her just this morning, and she was ticked. "How do you figure my sex life is any of your concern?"

"So, you admit you slept with him."

Becky shook her hand at the rearview mirror as she drove. "Someone needs to pound you in the face."

"Rowan, you are out of line," said Gwen.

"He's been after you since day one, back when you were with David, hitting on you all the time. It's not right."

Gwen could hear the pain in his voice, and suddenly realized the problem. Rowan's anger with Colin was a façade for a different emotion, one that she understood all too well. Grief took whatever shape it was allowed, often eking out when least expected. "David is gone."

"I know that, but how do you think he would feel about you and Colin..." he shrugged his shoulder, "being together?"

"He wants me to be happy." Gwen's eyes began to burn as she stared at her husband's oldest friend. "He wants you to be happy, too. He doesn't want you to hold on to this grief, this pain you feel from his death, and let it ruin your relationship with the brother who is very much alive."

She could see by his expression that her words had hit their mark.

"Colin makes you happy?"

Gwen faced forward and gazed out her window, considering her response.

Becky smacked her arm. "Answer the man!"

"Oh, I don't know. I'm still trying to figure that out for myself."

~~~

Rowan stretched out his long legs on the seat beside him. The backseat of Becky's car wasn't made for a man his size. He stared at her vibrant hair, knowing now that it matched an equally vibrant personality. She was a woman who could keep a man on his toes, and he found himself wondering about the lucky bastard who got to share her bed.

They must be lining up in droves.

She was too young for him, anyway. At forty-three, Rowan wasn't interested in dating a woman who must be at least fifteen years his junior. It occurred to him that not a lot of women wanted to date a married man, and he thought again of the divorce lawyer's business card in his pocket. It was long past time to make that phone call.

He put his hands behind his head and tried to stretch out. The flight was long and he hadn't slept well on the plane, too concerned about Colin and Gwen getting it on in a hotel room to close his eyes for more than an hour or two. He sighed. Gwen seemed to think he was upset with Colin because David was dead, not because Colin was interested in Gwen. The thought let an unpleasant taste in his mouth, though he could hear the lightest ring of truth in her words when she spoke them.

Rowan was still mourning his best friend, simple as that. He looked out the window and wondered if he would ever be able to accept Gwen and Colin being together. He doubted it, that was for sure.

The cell phone on his lap began to ring.

Rowan answered the phone. "Hello."

Colin's voice was harsh. "You're here?"

Rowan wasn't expecting a warm and fuzzy welcome, yet Colin's tone hurt nonetheless. Too many years had passed since he'd been close to his brother, too much foul water running under that bridge. "I couldn't let you do this by yourself. I flew in overnight, got a rental car."

"It's not your responsibility."

"He belonged to both of us, Colin."

A pause on the line had Rowan holding his breath. In that moment, he missed his brother desperately. Missed the relationship they used to have, long before the issue with Gwen had thrown a wedge between them. Rowan half expected his brother to tell him to get back on a plane and head for Italy.

Colin sighed heavily. "Okay. Thanks."

Rowan closed his eyes. "You got it. Now where the hell are you?"

Chapter 15

Colin walked along the boardwalk as gulls screeched overhead. There was a bench, right where he was told it would be, and he sat down to wait.

He could feel Gwen's spirit, worried for him, and reveled in their connection. She claimed she didn't feel it, but how could that be? Was it possible such a thing could ever be one-sided?

Memories of last night flashed through his mind. In the stress of the day and the hunt for Ahearn, Colin hadn't allowed himself the luxury of remembering his lovemaking with Gwen. Now he bathed in the images, subtle scents and sensations that swarmed him, wrapping around him like an all-consuming blanket.

It had been better than any fantasy, more intense than he could have imagined. Gwen Trueblood had touched him, body and soul, like no woman before her ever had. He could hardly wait to do it again.

She's going to be mad as all hell.

He reached up to rub at his neck. He knew the woman well enough to know there would be repercussions for his actions this morning, he didn't care as long as she was safe.

The sound of the surf seemed to intensify, one mother earth defending another. Colin's eyes were drawn to the horizon, the wind-whipped water reflecting the bright sunshine of a cloudless summer day. A heron appeared, tiny at first, gliding gracefully to the water and swooping low to catch a fish in the shallow water.

Colin turned his head toward a movement down the boardwalk. It was a man, head bent against the blowing sand, his gait a familiar stride that clawed at Colin's heartstrings. The recognition surprised him. This was Jerry Ahearn, David's father. Colin had been a young child the last time he saw Jerry, yet still he remembered.

Time dangled as the man approached, finally reaching the bench and sitting down so lightly that the seat barely moved beneath him. His posture was stooped, his jacket lightly pulling at his paunch. "It's been a long time, Mitchell."

The voice was familiar, too. More like David's than he remembered. Colin took in Jerry's wrinkled eyes, the gray and white hair atop his head, the pale fingers. Mentally he juxtaposed this old man with the beautiful Emma, her radiant youth only making Jerry seem older.

What had she seen in this man, that she would abandon her life and her family?

Jerry shook his head. "You're all grown up, Mitchell."

"I am. So you must be what, mid-sixties?"

He nodded.

"But your wife is only thirty."

"Emma said she explained."

"Maybe you can explain it better."

He cleared his throat. "The boy isn't mine, Mitchell. Emma was pregnant before I met her."

"Who's the father?"

He shrugged. "I never asked her. It didn't matter to me."

"You were in love and that's all that mattered? I'm not buying it, Jerry." He narrowed his eyes harshly. "Too much of a coincidence. I'm looking for the man who killed your son, and I run into my boss's long lost daughter, who just happens to be your wife. Don't you find that–"

Jerry grabbed his arm. "Killed my son?" His mouth worked. "David was murdered?"

Damn it. He'd forgotten that Jerry didn't know. "I believe so. I'm sorry, Jerry."

Jerry sank back on the bench, his jaw slack.

Colin wanted to feel sorry for this man, but all he could conjure was blame. Jerry could have sold cars, or worked construction, and David and his mother would be alive right now. Jerry was responsible for every tragedy that befell his family. He made a choice to engage in organized crime, he turned state's evidence, and he couldn't stay clean.

"They said it was a skiing accident."

"That's what we thought." Colin chastised himself again for not interviewing Gwen himself at the time. He knew now it was cowardice that had kept him away. "David recognized someone on the mountain that day. Someone from his childhood named

The One Who Got Away

Michael."

Jerry frowned. "Michael Gallente?"

"I was hoping you could tell me. David said it was someone he went to school with."

"They both went to Holy Cross. They were friends. That's the only Michael I remember."

"You testified against his father." Colin couldn't keep the accusation out of his voice. His own life's work was seeing that those who testified were kept safe, yet here and now, when it was his friend who had paid the ultimate price, he hated Jerry for what he had done.

"I thought we'd be safe, protected. Or I never would have done it."

"In WITSEC."

"Yes." He shook his head. "But we were betrayed."

Betrayed. Bullshit, they were betrayed. Colin had heard it before in his role as U.S. Marshal. It was a failure to take responsibility for your own actions, an inability to accept that you had created the very mess that worked to destroy you. "Adele was unhappy. She contacted her mother," said Colin.

Jerry's gaze was sharp. "What do you know about it?"

Reaching into his back pocket, Colin extracted his wallet and showed Jerry his badge. The other man met his eyes accusingly.

"Talk about your coincidences," said Jerry.

"What do you mean?"

"I go to prison, and the grandson of the woman who takes custody of my boy becomes a U.S. Marshal."

"I became a Marshal because I wanted to help people like David. He lived with us after you went back to prison. It wasn't a coincidence at all."

Jerry sighed. "You'll forgive me if I'm not impressed."

"I don't forgive you for shit, Ahearn. I don't forgive you for the crimes that put you in WITSEC, I don't forgive you for the death of your wife, and I don't forgive you for the death of my friend or the grief of his widow."

Jerry jabbed at him with his finger. "You ride in here on your high horse and think you know everything. Well, you don't know a goddamn thing, Mitchell. You've swallowed anything they put in front of you, hook, line and sinker."

A sudden cold breeze whipped off the water. "I don't have time for this crap," said Colin.

"Graham Walker killed my wife."

Colin opened his hands, flexed his fingers. His own lack of faith in Walker wouldn't allow him to defend the man, and he hated himself for it. "Your wife killed herself when she contacted her mother. You can't put that on Walker or anyone else, except maybe yourself. If you hadn't lived the life you led, forced her to leave her family behind, she wouldn't have been in that situation in the first place."

Jerry stood. "She didn't contact her mother. Walker made that up after he shot her."

"I don't believe that."

"Let me guess, he's a friend of yours." Jerry spit on the ground. "They were having an affair, Mitchell. From the time I first entered the program."

"How do you know?"

"My wife was pregnant, but she hadn't slept with me in almost a year."

Colin's heart stopped beating. Adele wasn't even two months along when she died. Jerry couldn't have known she was expecting unless she told him herself.

Or could he?

Had someone told Jerry about the coroner's report? Someone on the inside? Colin's thoughts reeled. He needed time to think, to sort out this new information.

An image formed in Colin's mind of Graham Walker and Adele Ahearn. Was it possible? The young deputy and the gangster's wife, caught in a love affair that could only end badly?

If Jerry was correct, Walker could have lost everything—his career, his wife. He might have been desperate, and desperate people did desperate things. Colin bit the inside of his cheek. "Go on."

"I went to see her at the beauty shop where she worked. We'd been fighting since she told me about the affair." He hung his head. "She wanted to leave me, take David with her and be with Walker. I was tired of it, defeated. I told her she could go to him if she wanted."

"Walker was going to leave June for her?" Colin pictured Mrs. Walker, beautiful and ever devoted to her husband. He couldn't imagine Walker ever choosing someone else over her.

Jerry shook his head slowly. "That was what she wanted, but he didn't want her. He said he never loved her, that he wouldn't leave his wife, and wanted Adele to get rid of the baby. He was coming to give her the money that day, but she didn't want to do it. She was hysterical, crying like a little kid." He wiped at his eye with the back of his hand.

"She begged me—begged me—to forgive her. She said we could keep the baby and no one would ever know it wasn't mine, that she'd be a good wife to me again." His face crumpled as he let out a sob. He shook his head quickly. "I told her no. No way. My pride was so hurt. I wasn't going to raise that bastard's child." Tears fell unchecked down his face.

"I didn't leave her a choice, don't you see? She needed me and I turned her away. She hustles me out the door, says he's coming. She's going to convince him they can make it work with the baby." Jerry pressed his lips together into a tight line. "Two hours later, I get a phone call from Walker. She's dead. He tells me she contacted her mother, someone walked into the shop and killed her, but I knew the truth."

Colin listened to Jerry's quiet sobbing as he watched as an orange car pull into a parking lot some hundred yards away. "Did you tell anyone what you're telling me now?"

"Hell no."

"Why not?"

Jerry crossed his feet and tucked them under the bench, his body huddled against the cold wind. "David."

The single word spoke volumes.

"It was just him and me, now. I was all he had..." his voice cracked and he cleared his throat. "Walker was my contact at WITSEC. If he suspected I knew about Adele, I'd be dead, either by his gun or with a simple slip of the tongue. I had to stay alive to take care of my son. I couldn't touch Walker."

The One Who Got Away

Colin wanted to say he was wrong, that there were enough checks and balances to keep any one man from having such power, yet he knew Jerry spoke the truth. To him, Walker was omnipotent, untouchable. But Jerry had managed to find Walker's Achilles heel, his singular weakness. "Until Emma."

Jerry nodded, taking a deep breath and exhaling slowly. "I didn't plan it."

A flock of seagulls landed on the beach, squawking. In the distance, a man walked toward them on the boardwalk. Colin thought of Walker, the man who represented authority and patriotism and integrity. He wanted to say Jerry was lying, but the story he told held a ring of truth that resonated deep in the pit of Colin's stomach.

"I came to see Walker when I got out of prison. I waited outside his office to talk to him and I could hear him fighting with Emma. He told her to get rid of it, and she was crying so hard..." His eyes met Colin's, their depths clear and bright. "Don't you see? It was my chance. My chance to make everything right."

"Your chance to get back at Walker."

"Yes. But I could take care of Emma, give her a safe place to have her baby." His chin quivered. "I could do for her what I didn't do for Adele."

Colin turned away, staring at the horizon. It was incredible. Two worlds had overlapped, usurping an entire person from one world and placing her in another. "She stayed with you all these years."

"We care about each other. We've raised a child together."

"Are you telling me you're in love?"

His smiled slightly. "As much as a beautiful young woman can ever be in love with an old man like me. I've done my best to be a good husband to her. The boy has been a joy." A shadow crossed Jerry's features. "Just like my David, even if Luke doesn't share my blood."

"One more question, Jerry."

"Yeah?"

"Why'd you go to Walker's office that day?"

The loud crack of a gunshot ripped across the beach. Blood

The One Who Got Away

appeared on Jerry's chest and Colin hit the ground like a dead man.

Chapter 16

Gwen watched in terror as Colin fell to the ground, the import of the loud bang only now registering on her consciousness. "Colin!" she screamed, the wrenching sound of her voice like a stranger's as she reached for the door handle and moved to get out.

"Stay in the car!" Becky grabbed Gwen's arm and yanked her back to the seat.

"I have to help him!"

Rowan was frantically unzipping his luggage. "I have a gun. I have a gun." He pulled it out and continued rifling through the bag. "Bullets. Bullets. Shit!" He found the box and loaded the weapon quickly.

Why did Rowan have a gun?

Gwen held out her hand. "Give it to me."

"No."

"I'm a better shot than you are!"

Rowan stared back at her, frozen with indecision. Another shot rang out along the beach.

"Give me the fucking gun!" Gwen yelled.

He slapped it into her hand and she was out the door, running toward the scene on the boardwalk, weapon drawn. The noise of the surf covered her footfalls as she quickly cut the distance in half and the shooter advanced on the bench, his back still to her.

Jerry was slumped at an unnatural angle, unmoving, but Colin was now behind the bench and Jerry's eerily still form. He must have moved there when she was getting the gun.

Close enough now to get off a shot, she stopped running and trained her weapon at the shooter just as he rounded the bench toward Colin and saw her.

Gwen pulled the trigger, her destiny hanging in the balance as the bullets made their way across the sand-covered boardwalk. The instant became a moment that stretched out and held, seagulls squawking in the distance, allowing her a glimpse at what might come to be.

The One Who Got Away

She could see herself and Colin, sitting on the porch swing at her house, love a living presence between them. She felt the warmth of sunshine on her arm as if she was really sitting there, and a contentedness in her heart like she'd never before experienced.

His brown eyes laughed into hers and she smiled. A breeze blew so sharply that she turned around, Colin disappearing in an instant. The sunshine still warmed her skin on a glorious summer day, but Gwen was alone on the swing, gently rocking. David stood before her on the porch.

"What do you want, Gwen?" he asked.

"I want Colin," she whispered, her heart singing with the admission. "I want to be a wife again. I want to be a mother."

David smiled at her, and she was filled with understanding. Her story would continue, and continue to be attached to and honor this man, even as she came to love another.

The warmth of the sunshine turned hotter and hotter, becoming a searing heat that burned her arm. Gwen looked down and saw blood, then raised her head to watch the shooter fall backwards to the ground. Then Becky was there, saying something, and Rowan ran to the bench to check on his brother's unmoving form.

~~~

The boy looked just like Walker's son Tommy had at ten. He was lean and tan, with tousled brown hair that fell in his face when he bent to weed the garden. Walker lifted his cell phone so the camera lens just peeked over the door of the car and took a picture, knowing that the distance would make it difficult for him to see the boy at all.

Ahearn had done this, taken his family away. Walker didn't even know his grandson's name. Blame was absolute and powerful, bitterness rising up in Walker's gut to eat away at any tenderness that once lived there.

An image of his Emma rose up in his memory, her body heavy with pregnancy as she screamed at him. He had thought her grotesque, disfigured, having never expected her to keep the child he was so eager to forget.

"Get away from me! I hate you!" she yelled.

The One Who Got Away

Walker had staked out Emma's best friend's house for weeks on end, knowing how hard it was to sever all ties to a former life. "It's time to come home and stop this foolishness, Emma. You've won. You get to keep your bastard."

"I'm never coming home." She held her chin high in the air.

"Where will you go? How will you support yourself?"

Her eyes gleamed as she delivered the blow. "I'm with Jerry Ahearn now, Dad."

Walker paled.

"He takes care of me. He loves this baby and he loves me."

Had that bastard touched his daughter? Dear God. Was that his baby? An image appeared in his mind and he forcibly pushed it back. "Ahearn's a monster. A murderer. You have to know that."

"Well, look at the pot calling the kettle black." She stepped toward him. "I know what you did, Daddy. You cheated on mom with Jerry's wife, then you killed Adele so she wouldn't have your baby."

He longed to cover her mouth with his hand, stop the filthy stream of words coming out. Secrets long buried rose up and danced, tormenting him. It occurred to him that Emma couldn't be trusted with his secret, that he had to stop her from leaving here, from ruining everything. There was only one way to do that, to keep himself safe. His fingers trembled.

Emma's face was snarled in disgust. "You killed your lover and your own child, like you tried to get me to kill mine." A single tear ran down her face and she swiped at it with the back of her hand. The movement was intimately familiar to him, something he had seen her do hundreds of times growing up. He stepped back, frightened by what he'd been considering. "What do you want from me?" he whispered.

"Stay away from us, or I'll tell everyone what you did."

"You can't do that."

"Why not, Daddy? Are you going to kill me, too?"

The fact that he had been considering that very thing filled him with a special horror.

I've lost everyone I have ever loved.

Adele was dead, June was tucked away in a nursing home

The One Who Got Away

with barely a memory of her own name, his daughter hated him and his son was dead. Mitchell had been a substitute for so many things in his life, and now he had turned on him too, left him alone to face his own demons by himself.

Walker watched as the boy raked up debris from the garden. There would be no relationship with him, no Christmas dinners or drawings made just for grandpa. Walker gripped his gun in his hand and for the first time considered using it on himself. The weight of the cold metal was an odd comfort, a choice that needed to be made. Colin was the final antagonist of Walker's life, Colin's defection the last chapter.

Walker released the safety, just as his phone began to ring, pulling him from his soliloquy.

"Hello?"

"It's Michael. Long time no see."

Chapter 17

Rowan stepped out of the hospital elevator and saw Becky at a vending machine, the curves of her body held tightly in a pair of equally curvy jeans. She bent to retrieve a bag of chips and he felt like a randy teenager.

He cleared his throat. "Hey."

A package of licorice fell from its perch. "Hey yourself."

"How's Gwen?"

She inserted a dollar bill and sipped at a Hawaiian Punch. "Good. The gunshot was purely superficial." A pair of cupcakes dropped. "She'll have a scar on her arm, but they didn't even admit her." She began feeding coins into the slot.

"Hungry?" he asked.

"Why, you want something?" A chocolate bar landed with a thud.

Did he ever. A certain redhead with the appetite of a horse. "No, I'm good." He shifted his weight. "Have you seen Colin yet?"

"He's still in post-op. They got the bullet."

"Good. Good. They say anything else?"

She took a swig of her drink. "Nope."

Rowan stared at her lips, full and unnaturally red from the punch.

"You sure you're not hungry?" she asked, putting one hand on her hip. "Because you're looking at me like you're starving."

Lust shot through him at her brazen words, her eyes challenging. "Sorry."

"Right." She took another sip, slowly turning and walking beside him, her arm lightly brushing his. "So, you live in Italy?"

"Yeah."

"How'd you end up over there?"

He cocked his head, seeing the brick wall that he was about to run into, but unable to slow down the vehicle. "I followed a woman."

"Ah, I see. How did that work out?"

"We got married."

"Married?"

He nodded, his face grim.

"Wait, you're married?"

He wanted to explain, but as he imagined the wretched story falling from his lips and her inevitable reaction, he changed his mind. "I am." *Crash.*

She raised her eyebrows but said nothing. Maybe it was just as well. He certainly couldn't get into a relationship right now with everything such a mess back at home. Rowan knew he had to deal with it, face facts and move on, but some things were easier said than done.

"Tell me something," Becky said.

"Shoot."

"What do you have against Colin and Gwen being together?"

"He was after her years ago, before she and David were even married."

"So?"

"So, he was totally out of line. He had no respect for Gwen or David, who was like a brother to both of us. It was messed up."

"Okay." She crossed her arms over her chest. "But that was years ago. He was a kid. Now David's dead and Colin and Gwen want to be together."

He bristled at her easy use of the word dead, as if he was an obstacle that was easily removed. "Really? Is that what Gwen wants?"

Becky's mouth moved to one side as she considered. "It's what she really wants, deep down."

"Says who, you?"

She rolled her eyes. "Fine. Let me rephrase that. If—" she stressed, "they want to be together, then who the hell are you to try and stop them?"

"I'm his brother."

"Well, duh."

"There are a million woman he can have. Why does he have to chase the one who got away, the only one in the whole wide world that it kills me to see him with?"

"We love who we love."

"He could find someone else."

"Oh, because we women are totally interchangeable, right?"

He sneered, getting flustered. "That's not what I said."

"Sure it is. But regardless, Colin wants Gwen. He doesn't want any of those other women." She let her eyes scan the length of him. "I know some men have eyes for lots of different girls, but men of character tend to pick one and stick with it."

Rowan knew damn well she was talking about him, and he didn't like it one bit. He was not about to explain himself to this woman who thought she knew everything. She had already put him inside a little box and scrawled "cheater" across the lid. He ran his hand through his hair. "I'm going to see if Colin can have visitors yet."

He wandered back to the nurse's station by the elevator. "Is Colin Mitchell out of post-op yet? I'd like to see him."

"And you are?"

"His brother."

She typed in a computer. "He's not awake yet, but you can go in. Room 318, just past the drinking fountain."

Rowan stepped into the room and saw his brother lying still on the bed. The seriousness of the situation hit him again, his agitation with his brother all but forgotten. Colin's arm was tightly wrapped and bound to his torso in type of sling, an IV in his other arm and several monitors working at his bedside.

Some things were more important than who Colin dated. Like whether or not he was alive. Rowan put his hands in his pockets and walked to the window. This day could have ended very differently, and he was filled with gratitude for their good fortune.

Footsteps behind him and he turned to see Gwen, looking uncharacteristically sporty in a pair of jeans and a Boston Red Sox t-shirt. Her eyes followed his down her outfit. "My clothes had blood on them."

Of course. She'd been injured, could have been killed, while he sat in the car and watched. Despite his wounded pride, he knew it had been the right decision. "I couldn't have made that shot," he said.

The One Who Got Away

"Yes, well..." her voice trailed off. "The shooter. Is he alive?"

He could hear the hope in her voice, and hated to be the one to crush it. "He died in surgery."

She nodded, staring at a spot on the wall. "I figured as much."

"You did what you had to do, Gwen."

"Did they find out who he was?"

"James McDonald."

"Why is that name familiar to me?"

"He's the sheriff of your town in Vermont. He was running for mayor."

"You've got to be kidding me." She sank down on the edge of Colin's bed and covered her hand with her mouth. "He was there the day David was killed, on the mountain. He interviewed me!"

"Maybe he killed David."

She shook her head. "I don't understand. David recognized someone named Michael that day, someone from his childhood. What are the chances of that happening, and someone else being the killer?"

"Maybe it's a coincidence."

"In my experience, the universe works very hard to provide us with the information we need. To call it a coincidence is to laugh in the face of the divine's most dramatic intervention."

"So who the hell is Michael?"

"I don't know, but I'm going to find out."

~~~

Colin could feel the weight of his arm, splinted across his chest, and remembered. He was on his knees on the sand-covered boardwalk, blood splattered on the ground. He couldn't get to his weapon, concealed on the same side of his body as his injured arm, and he flung himself behind the bench and Jerry's slumped form in search of cover from their attacker.

Gwen. The thought crossed his mind like a prayer. She had been there, running toward them, weapon drawn. Was Gwen okay?

Colin worked to open his eyes, the hospital room coming

into focus. She sat beside him, doing a crossword puzzle with a pen, and relief flooded his senses. "Hi." His voice was hoarse and didn't sound like his own.

Concern filled her eyes. "How are you feeling?" she asked, reaching for his hand.

"Like I went ten rounds with Mike Tyson."

Gwen smiled softly. "I'm so glad you're okay."

"What happened?"

She filled him in on the events at the beach and the identity of the shooter. The sheriff was dead, but Jerry was hanging in there.

"Thank God you're a good shot."

"We all have our gifts."

His mind worked to absorb everything she had told him. "McDonald must have been working for someone."

"Someone who knew who David really was."

Colin frowned. "Someone like Graham Walker." Betrayal seeped through him. Any doubt he had about Jerry's story vanished like so much smoke in the breeze. His mentor really was guilty, and Colin had to stop him before he was able to hurt any more people. "I need to get the hell out of this hospital room."

"What are we going to do?" asked Gwen.

His protective instincts reared up and he eyed her warily.

"Colin Mitchell, don't you dare try to leave me behind again. You underestimated my value once already and it nearly cost you your life. I am vital to your wellbeing, like vitamins or sunlight."

He gave an appreciative chuckle. She was more important that either of those things. "How did you find me?"

"Rowan. We picked him up at the airport."

"Where is he now?"

"With Becky in the cafeteria."

"I'm going to need his help. And yours, too."

"Are we going to find Walker?"

He shook his head. "I'm sure he's already here. We just need to tell him exactly where to find us."

Chapter 18

Rowan pulled under the portico of the hotel and put the car in park.

"Be right back," said Becky, as she and Gwen hopped out of the backseat and disappeared into the hotel lobby. Colin sat beside him, the tension between the brothers seeming to stretch on interminably.

As the oldest, Rowan was used to being in charge, used to being the authority, used to being right. It was hard for him to see when he was wrong, and even harder for him to apologize and make peace with Colin. He shifted uncomfortably in his seat. "How's your arm?"

"It hurts like a son-of-a-bitch. Why?"

"Could be worse. I'm glad you're not dead."

"I'm glad I'm not dead, too."

Rowan gripped the steering wheel. "Listen, about you and Gwen."

Colin sighed heavily. "Rowan, it's none of your business."

"I know."

"So then why the hell are we talking about it?"

"Because I'm sorry."

Colin narrowed his eyes. "Sorry for what?"

"For being upset about it earlier. For expecting you to act like she was still married to David even though he's gone."

"Thanks."

Rowan pointed his finger at Colin's chest. "It still wasn't okay, what you did back then."

"I know." Colin turned to stare after the women. "I'm sorry, too. It was selfish and wrong, and it cost me my relationship with David."

"How about we never talk about this again?"

"Deal."

Becky and Gwen climbed into the car.

"Pull around back and park by the blue door," said Gwen. "I got us a suite with a hot tub."

"I got a suite with a hot tub, too," said Becky.

The One Who Got Away

"What about me?" Rowan asked her.

"I got you a studio."

"Were they all out of hot tubs?"

"Nope."

Rowan shook his head. She wasn't one for subtlety, was she? He parked the car and tried not to picture Becky up to her armpits in a sea of shiny bubbles.

"Walker's meeting me at Flynn's at noon," said Colin. "I think you three should go in an hour earlier, play it like you're tourists, eat some lunch."

"We only have the one car," said Rowan.

"I can take the T. It's a block from here and just up the street from the bar."

Rowan raised his eyebrows. "The cops took my gun as evidence in the shooting."

"Damn it." Colin smacked his hand to his forehead. "Becky?"

"Me?" she looked around. "I'm a democrat. There's pepper spray in the glove box."

Rowan chuckled. "It's better than nothing."

"Okay, everybody get some sleep. I have a feeling we're going to need it. We'll meet back here tomorrow morning at ten."

~~~

The suite consisted of a kitchenette and living room, with a separate bedroom and bath. Oddly, the hot tub was in the bedroom, right next to the king-size bed. Gwen had been looking forward to exploring its depths, but now found herself feeling awkward and shy.

Colin must have seen her discomfiture. "You can close the bedroom door if you want privacy."

"I wish you could join me," she said honestly.

His eyes darkened. "The bandages…"

"I know. I just wish."

"Me too." He reached for the bedroom door, pulling it closed behind him. "Enjoy your bath. I'll be here when you get out."

She nodded, grateful for the opportunity to relax in the

water. She drew the bath piping hot, figured out how to turn on the jets, and added a tiny bottle of shampoo for bubbles before sinking into the tub. Her own wound was high on her arm, allowing her some freedom, and she rested her head along the back edge of the Jacuzzi like a cat stretching in the sun.

She loved that Colin was waiting for her, loved the lovemaking she was certain was coming. She loved the man himself, and the knowledge seeped into her bones like water seeping into the earth.

I love him.

Gwen was filled with the urge to create, to somehow describe with color and shape how this love lifted her up, made her whole where she had only been broken, made her sing where she had not had known the tune. Her mind went back to the painting of the storm, so meaningful now, the vibrant peacock green that was Colin Mitchell filling up her canvas as he now filled her mind.

The noise of the water jets became for her a roaring wind, an approaching thunder. They were indeed in the middle of a torrent, with evil very much alive and tormenting the new lovers. Tomorrow they would be in danger again, facing off the very forces that had conspired to take love from Gwen once before, whisking away her happiness like dried leaves in the breeze.

Would her love be safe this time, emerge victorious in the battle that had already claimed so many lives? Gwen's eyes closed tightly against her fears, her hands bouncing on the bubbles of air that forced their way to the surface. She wanted to believe she and Colin were ready to face the challenge ahead, prepared to pound evil into the ground and back to the very hell that had spawned it. But what if she was wrong? What if she would lose this man as well?

Sitting up in the bath, Gwen turned off the tap and the water jets. The room was suddenly quiet, the water still. Here in this moment, all was well with the world. Her love waited for her, time allowing them the gift of togetherness for another whole night. She would embrace it fully, disallowing the horror that lay outside these doors the opportunity to take love away from her again.

The One Who Got Away

She called out to Colin, inviting him in. She stood to help him undress and bathed him slowly with a washcloth, savoring the brush of her arms along his skin. Gwen told him what was in her heart, his words of love rushing to meet her own, and they sank onto the bed to make love, enough love to last them a lifetime.

~~~

Graham Walker motioned to the bartender. "Another scotch on the rocks." He checked his watch, pushing his wrist farther away so he could make out the numbers. Nearly noon. He'd been here since ten thirty, waiting for this meeting with Colin like a condemned man waits on death row.

He made no attempt to survey the patrons in the bar, figuring that Mitchell had at least one person in the vicinity. His precious protégé would no doubt be hunkered down for war. Wouldn't he be surprised when he found only a drunken, broken old man, ready to confess his sins?

The thought left a bitter taste in his mouth and he gulped at his drink to chase it away. He was a man with limited options, his actions now dictated by another. Walker had laced the string to himself years before, never imagining it could one day be used to control him.

The noise of the street grew louder, and Walker turned to see Colin step into the bar. The sling was unexpected, and Walker was immediately concerned, feeling responsible. "What happened to you?" he asked.

Colin's stare was cool, and Walker's heart sank a little lower in his chest. It was one thing to suspect the other man had lost faith in him. It was another to see it clearly etched into his features. Walker signaled the bartender. "Glenlivet—"

Colin raised his hand. "Just a Coke."

A line in the sand. The first of several, Walker was sure. His fingers shook slightly as he reached for his drink. May as well get right to it. "Why didn't you call me after the fire at your house?"

"Because I thought you did it."

There it was, so plainly said. "After everything we've been through together, you thought I would try to kill you?" His bloodshot eyes searched Colin's. "I tried to help you. I gave you the files you asked for."

"You knew Gwen was there. You know the paperwork was there. If we had been killed, the investigation into David's death might never be reopened."

Walker reached for his drink and realized it was empty.

Colin waved to the bartender. "Scotch on the rocks."

Gratitude welled up inside Walker as he watched the bartender pour the amber liquid. He couldn't have this conversation sober, couldn't give voice to the terrible things that needed to be said.

It occurred to him that this would be his last conversation with Colin, and he felt a profound sadness. Colin was his family. Walker had schooled him in righteousness and the law, only to be brought down by those very things he himself had admired. Again he checked his watch.

"Waiting for someone?"

"No."

"Tell me about Adele."

Walker's lips formed a hard line and he shook his head, the words locked inside like an unwilling confessor.

"I already know, but I need to hear it from you."

"Why, are you wearing a wire?"

"Nope." He leaned in close to Walker and whispered, "I looked up to you for damn near half my life, and you're a murderer and a fraud. I want to hear you say the words."

Walker could feel his lips pulling down hard at the corners, afraid he might disgrace himself and break down crying. He shot Colin a pleading look.

"Say it."

He opened his mouth to speak and felt his bottom lip shake wildly. "I killed her," he said quietly, tears welling in his eyes.

"Tell me why."

"I l-l-loved her," he choked out, the words costing him greatly. "She was pregnant, wouldn't get rid of the baby. She was going to tell June…" Walker reached for his drink and knocked it over, several people turning to stare. He brought his hand over his mouth to cover his crying.

"Why kill David? You'd gotten away with it. Everything was over."

"I panicked."

"Why?"

A fresh scotch appeared and he latched onto it. "Ahearn just got out of jail. His son hated him, but Jerry wanted to reconcile. David showed up in my office with a letter from his father, claiming his mother never contacted his grandmother."

"Did Ahearn say anything to David about you?"

Walker shook his head. "Not that I know of. But David didn't believe his dad. He thought Jerry had made Adele unhappy. He blamed his father for his mother's death. David came to see me because he wanted to know the truth. Of course, I told him she contacted her mother."

"So what's the problem?"

"He wanted proof. A piece of paper he could show his father that said he was a liar. But that paper didn't exist. That's when I realized my mistake."

Walker reflected on what he knew too well. In every crime, the perpetrator left behind clues. Some were subtle, some dramatic, and any one of them could bring him down. He sipped at his liquor without tasting it, awash in memories of the mistake that would be his undoing. "I told Jerry that Adele contacted her mother, but I never wrote it in the official file."

"You would have had to document it."

He nodded. "It was easier to write it up as a burglary. But now David was there, insisting, and I told him I couldn't give it to him. He was angry. Said he'd file a freedom of information request, go through the local police, whatever agency he had to petition, even go to the media if he had to." Walker remembered every word, every nuance in that conversation. "He said he'd throw so much light on my office it would be like sunshine in the middle of the night." He turned to Colin, his eyes beseeching. "Who knows what they would find if that happened?"

"So you killed him."

He shook his head. "I was too scared. I screwed up with Adele. This time I brought someone in."

"Who?"

The One Who Got Away

"He should have been a no one. An afterthought. He should have taken his money and disappeared." Walker's voice dripped with hatred. "But he turned into the devil himself."

Colin pulled the other man around to face him. "What's his name?"

"Michael Hinman."

"Emma's boyfriend." Colin's eyes were wide. "You hired Emma's boyfriend to kill David."

Chapter 19

"He wasn't her boyfriend then. They didn't even know each other until Michael showed up on my front doorstep looking for money, and June invited him to stay for dinner."

Colin raised his hand between them. "But David recognized someone named Michael on the mountain the day he was killed. David and Michael Hinman didn't know each other."

"Sure they did. They went to the same school right down the street from my house during the Ahearn's first placement."

"Of course. You placed the family in your town to be close to Adele. That's why Jerry's request to be moved to the Southwest wasn't honored."

Walker remembered filling in the form, spelling out Connecticut in careful capital letters. Adele had meant everything to him then. He would have moved the world to be close to her. If he could have foreseen how the affair would color and destroy so many lives, he may have allowed them to relocate to Arizona as Jerry had wanted.

"I'm not proud of what I've done, Mitchell. If I could, I would change it all, if only for Emma." He shook his head. "All through dinner that punk was hitting on her, taunting me. I forbade her to see him." He remembered the first pull of the string that turned him into a marionette, a toy. "Michael called me on the phone, says I'd better change my mind if I wanted him to keep my secret." He picked up his drink. "I should have killed him then."

"Then Emma got pregnant and Michael left. Jerry Ahearn took her in."

He nodded, looking shell-shocked and old. "I know. I found her. She hated me."

"Michael stayed away until last week. He shows up at my door again, saying how come I never told him Emma had his kid. Like I should have sent him a box of cigars or something." Walker checked his watch again, nausea washing through his stomach.

"Why do you keep looking at your watch?" asked Colin.

The One Who Got Away

Walker looked into his eyes like the dead, saying nothing.

Colin stood quickly. "Michael wants Luke." He looked quickly around the bar, his eyes landing on the man beside him. "Damn it, Walker! What do you know?"

"I had to do it." Walker shrugged his shoulders. "I didn't have any choice."

Colin's phone rang. "Mitchell."

"Colin, it's Emma," she was sobbing, hysterical. "Luke's gone!"

~~~

The Grand Marquis flew down the expressway like a sports car, Colin at the wheel with his one good arm and Gwen at his side. Walker was in the backseat, his hands bound in his lap with cuffs from the collection of memorabilia on the wall at Ray Flynn's. They worked well enough and had served in a pinch, but no one had a key. Rowan and Becky followed in Becky's car.

"Thank you for bringing me with you," said Walker. The alcohol and stress of his grandson's kidnapping had combined to make him weepy. "You could have left me there."

Colin felt a stab of pity for this man, even after all he had done. Walker's decision to destroy Adele had devastated his own life, a life that at one time had been good. Grief clawed at Colin as he mourned the good man he had believed Walker to be.

Somewhere out there, Luke was held hostage to a murderer. The fact that Michael was Luke's father gave Colin no comfort. Only a madman would hold his own flesh and blood for ransom. "There has to be a way to find him." Colin's eyes fixed on Walker in the mirror. "Do you have a cell phone number for Michael?"

"It showed up as unavailable," said Walker. "I looked for a cell phone listing in his name yesterday and didn't find anything."

"What did you do that for?" asked Colin.

"So I could find him and stop him once and for all."

"Why now, Graham?" asked Gwen.

He looked out the window. "I followed Colin to the house. I saw the boy, Luke. He looks like my Tommy. I wanted to protect him."

The One Who Got Away

Gwen turned to Colin. "Wait, you said Michael left a prepaid cell with the ransom note?"

"Yes."

"Maybe he bought two—one for Emma and one for him to call her. Is there any way to track where he bought them and get the other number?"

"It's worth a shot," said Colin. He tossed his own cell phone to Gwen. "Call Emma back and get the number for the prepaid phone. It's on the phone's menu somewhere."

When she was finished, he said, "Now give the phone to Walker." He met Walker's eyes in the mirror. "Call the best contact you've got at the FBI and have him run it, right now."

"We'll find him," Gwen said quietly, reaching to touch Colin's arm.

Colin's emotions were running high, every nerve in his body tingling. "I let this bastard get away from me once before, and I'm sure as hell not going to let him get away again."

"It's not your fault," she said.

How could she not see it? Michael was the one who got away, slipping right through Colin's careless fingers. "This is totally my fault, Gwen. If I'd stopped this guy after he killed David, he never would have had the chance to take Luke."

They were nearly at the hospital when Colin's phone rang.

After listening for a minute, Colin swerved to the right-hand lane and talked to Gwen, the phone still held to his ear. "The phones were bought yesterday at a Wal-Mart in Quincy. They've sold twelve of that model in the last two weeks, but only one at the same time as Emma's phone. It's showing up in Chinatown."

"Where in Chinatown?" he asked into the phone.

"Thanks." He hung up the phone. "It's between Kneeland and Tyler. They're setting up a stingray to track it."

~~~

The kid was a dead ringer for Michael's brother Rick at that age, even though Michael had a hard time seeing himself in Luke's features. Rick was a jerk who used to beat on his little brother with alarming regularity, the resemblance doing little to endear Michael to his long-lost son.

Luke hadn't touched the burger and fries Michael bought for

him. It cost $5.25, and he was pissed that he spent that much money for something the kid wouldn't even eat.

"Eat your burger," he said. The kid didn't move.

Michael rocked on the back two legs of a metal chair, bracing himself with the windowsill. The boy had a matching chair inside the small cell, though he was curled up in a ball in the corner of the room. He had to be ten years old, but he was acting like a baby.

Back when Michael used to work here, they stored a Bengal Tiger in the cage where Luke was locked up. They had some cool exotic animals in this place. It smelled like the animals never left, which is why the space was still vacant three years after the owner of the operation was deported. Michael lived here so long he didn't even notice the stench anymore, and certainly didn't find it as upsetting as the boy huddled in the corner.

"I said eat it!" he snapped, and was rewarded when the boy scurried to the center of the cell for the food. Luke took a large bite and chewed it slowly, his wide eyes trained on Michael's shoes.

So this is my kid.

Michael had never thought of himself as a father. He didn't use anything for birth control but he was still surprised when Emma got herself knocked up. She left town and Walker said it was taken care of, so Michael never gave it another thought until he saw Emma and the boy in the hospital cafeteria yesterday.

His parole officer set him up with the cafeteria job after he got released for grand theft auto, and since the animal shop was out of business he was stuck taking that shit job until he found something better. Then presto, in walks Emma, and he got an idea with lots of dollar signs in it.

She was there visiting some old guy, and all Michael had to do was look at the white board at the nurse's station to see who he was. Beaumont, Jerry. Same last name as the guy he'd been paid to kill by Walker. What were the odds of that?

He'd scribbled down the room number, smiling smugly. There was a reason those nurses weren't supposed to put names up there for just anybody to read.

Michael imagined money coming at him from all directions.

The One Who Got Away

From Emma, for sure, and from Walker to keep his mouth shut all over again. Michael wasn't sure how Jerry Beaumont played into all this, but he could only help with that financial plan.

So he'd snagged the boy.

It wasn't even hard. The trick was getting him to come voluntarily. Michael had donned a white doctor's coat and a swiped a stethoscope off a counter, then told the kid his mommy wanted him to give blood to help all the sick people in the hospital. He used Emma's name and smiled all sincere, and Luke had followed him to the basement like a puppy on the scent of a dog bone.

Luke had fought and screamed a little at the end when Michael picked him up and threw him into the van, but there wasn't anybody down there to notice.

The boy finished his burger and slunk back to the corner. "I have to go to the bathroom," he said quietly.

"Have at it, kid. I'll give you some privacy, okay?" He stood, pushing the metal chair into a metal table with a loud clang. "I ain't a pervert or nothing." He smiled, suddenly wanting the boy to know the truth. "I'm your real dad."

For the first time since Michael had kidnapped Luke, the boy put his head between his knees and cried.

~~~

Gwen looked up at a billboard for an accident lawyer as they drove, the phone number made almost entirely of threes. She didn't think much of it until she noticed the license plate on the car in front of them—333 TUH—then the sign for Route 93 and Route 3. Mentally she acknowledged the message.

Colin parked the car and put the windows down partway. "Bring the cell phone number with us in case we need it," he said to Gwen, "and grab Walker's gun from the floor."

Walker whined plaintively. "You're not leaving me here. I can help."

"I don't doubt that you could. I just don't know whose side you'd be on," said Colin, slamming the door.

He and Gwen headed for the street, the scents of cooking food and hot pavement mingling in a sickening way. "How big of an area are we looking at?" she asked.

The One Who Got Away

"Right now, about two blocks. Let me call and see if they set up the Stingray."

"What's that?"

"A device that acts like a cell phone tower, but isn't. It lets us track where he is much more accurately."

"How accurately?"

"In a city with this many towers, it can tell us the building." Colin pulled out his cell phone and dialed the FBI agent he spoke with earlier. "Is the Stingray in place?" He turned to look around him, finding a street sign and turning back around. Got it." He hung up and gestured to a six or seven-story building. "That one."

They began walking and his phone rang again. It was Emma. "Michael called," she said. "He wants me to put the cash in a garbage can at the corner of Dartmouth and Beacon Streets in thirty minutes."

"Are the agents going with you?"

"He said to come alone, but they're setting up nearby."

"Be safe."

Emma sound shaky. "Have you found Luke?"

"We're still looking. I'll let you know when I have something." He hung up. "We have to hurry. The cash drop's in thirty minutes, ten minutes from here. He's going to move soon."

The building was open, but appeared to be deserted.

"Start on the third floor," Gwen said.

"Why?"

"Call it a hunch."

They located the stairwell and climbed quickly, reaching the third floor landing and quietly opening the door. The horrible smell of animal waste hit their noses.

A man's voice yelled in the distance. "I said eat it!"

Colin turned to Gwen and whispered. "I think we found Michael."

Chapter 20

Luke Beaumont was almost eleven years old, but people usually said he acted much older. He was good at taking care of things, helping his mom with the garden and the projects she liked to do around the house. He especially liked the power tools his dad kept in the garage, the drills and different saws that could take something broken and fix it up, make it look nice. His mom said next summer he could help paint the house, even climb on scaffolding and go up the ladder.

He bit at his fingernail, staring at Michael walk from one side of the expansive room to the other. Luke had heard Michael talk to his mother, calling her names that made Luke want to hurt him. Michael wanted lots of money to bring Luke home, which felt really hopeless to him as he sat in a cage in the stink of his own urine. His mom and dad didn't have a lot of money, and Luke didn't see any way he was going to get to go home.

Michael said he was Luke's father, which felt almost as bad as when his dog got hit by the car and died last year. Jerry was his father. Jerry had always been his father, even if he was Irish and Luke looked like a Sicilian. No way was this guy telling the truth.

He tasted blood and pulled his hand from his mouth, raising his head just at the right moment to see a man peeking around the corner by the elevator. Luke's head snapped back to Michael, who continued to pace, unaware they had company.

Michael's watch began an electronic alarm, an annoying tune that would forever bring Luke back to this moment in time.

"It's show time, kid." Michael peered at his cell phone as if to check. "Your mom should be dropping the money as we speak. I need to go pick it up."

Luke's stomach flipped upside-down when Michael pulled out a gun and loaded it with bullets. "What's that for?"

"Just in case your mother gets smart."

Luke's mouth went dry. "Don't hurt her."

"If she follows the rules, I won't have to."

Luke was so scared for his mom in that moment. Wouldn't

The One Who Got Away

there be police there? Someone to help? The police might kill Michael, and then no one would be able to find him in here. He wondered who the man by elevator was. Surely it was someone to save him?

"You'll be fine," said Michael.

"What if you don't come back?"

He ran his hand through his hair. "Jesus, kid, you ask a lot of questions. I got to go." He walked toward the elevator and Luke held his breath.

"Freeze!" the man yelled.

A gunshot erupted, the noise overwhelming in the cavernous space, and the boy's whole body jumped. Several more shots followed, then the sound of someone running and Michael reappeared, gun pointed directly at Luke.

Michael was shaking, sweat visible on his forehead. He yelled out, "You come any closer and I kill the boy!"

~~~

Colin was crouched in the shadows between a stack of packing crates and a large pile of empty cardboard boxes. He held the gun in his bad hand, not trusting himself to fire a weapon with the opposite arm. Gwen stood across the walkway, shielded from view by a tall metal cabinet. She held Walker's gun at the ready, but Colin had the better line of sight to the elevator where Michael stood.

He could hear the boy asking questions, then footsteps before Michael rounded the corner. "Freeze!" Colin yelled, watching as Michael pulled a gun from his waistband. Colin aimed for Michael's femur and pulled the trigger decisively.

Pain ripped through Colin's shoulder as the gun recoiled, and he called out involuntarily. Michael didn't seem to be hit. He returned fire, debris flying into Colin's face and eyes as the bullet struck the concrete floor, sending rocks scattering.

Colin raised a shaking hand to train his weapon on Michael and failed, the wounds to his eye and shoulder preventing him from lining up the shot. He felt panicked for Gwen. Could she handle this by herself? Defend them all and take Michael down? Reproach overwhelmed him, but he couldn't help her now.

Michael took a step toward Colin at the same instant Gwen

fired, the bullet at once both hitting his shoulder and alerting him to her presence.

Colin could only make out Michael's silhouette against the wall of windows behind him, their brightness quickly dimming as his vision deteriorated. He could see Michael had been wounded from the hunch in his gait, and was proud that Gwen got a shot in. She fired again, but Michael had already turned, quickly running around the corner.

Colin knew what would come next. Luke was encaged over there. Michael Hinman got a hostage at the same moment that Colin's eyesight went completely dark.

~~~

Gwen crossed to Colin, the blood on his face making her fear for the worst. "Are you okay?"

"Go get him! He's going to get Luke!"

She stood, knowing she was already too late to stop such a thing, grateful that Colin seemed all right. Her mind raced as she stepped toward the corner.

Please help me save the boy.

Gwen often found in the most stressful situations that time was her greatest ally. She believed that time was flexible, more a construction of her own mind than any predetermined absolute. Her steps were quick and light, though in her perception the walk was interminable, stretching out as she considered what to do.

She had tools at her disposal—the weapon, her martial arts training. She had the heels of her sandals and the belt of her dress. Righteousness was on her side as well, and she wielded it like a sharply pointed sword.

Gwen took note of those who were present in spirit. David and Jerry, her own guardian angel. God himself. The boy's mother was here, as well as Rowan and Becky.

Tell me what to do.

She peered at the gun in her hand, suddenly certain she'd fare better without it, and rested it on the ground before taking the turn. She faced Michael with her empty hands raised, her blue eyes shining in the rays of the setting sun.

"You come any closer and I kill the boy!" he yelled.

Gwen could feel his stress, see the tremors that ran up his

arms. Her eyes went to Luke, a huddled mass of innocent fear, his head scrunched down to his knees.

"I'm not armed," she said.

Michael's face twitched. "Where's the gun?"

"I left it back there, on the floor."

"Why?"

"God told me to."

He blew out air. "Bullshit. You probably gave it to your friend, and he's going to come around here shooting."

"Hi might." She knew Colin would if he could, but she doubted he was able. "But I won't."

Michael's brow furrowed. "What do you want?"

"To trade places with the boy."

"No."

"Let me in there with him. He's scared."

Michael looked at Luke.

Gwen could see the resemblance between father and son, hoping some scrap of the paternal bond remained. "He looks like you," she said quietly.

"He's my kid."

She took a step closer, and Michael turned the gun on her, forcing her hands higher.

"You don't move unless I tell you to move."

"Please, Michael. Let me go in with Luke. I won't be able to hurt you in there."

Luke began to sob. He took in air like he'd been crying for some time, finally unable to do it quietly.

"Stop it," said Michael.

Luke instantly cried louder, the sound echoing through the empty space.

"Stop!"

Luke's wail became hysterical.

"Let me go to him," Gwen said loudly. "I can calm him down."

"Okay, okay." Michael took a key out of his pocket. "Stop fucking crying!" He unlocked the gate and Gwen stepped forward.

In Gwen's mind, she sauntered instead of walked, planning

her attack. Michael held the gate wide for her to enter, the distance between her foot and his face so perfectly measured as to be considered a gift. Gwen shifted her weight to one side and lifted her other leg, kicking Michael soundly in the throat with the pointed heel of her sandal.

He hit the concrete face first, the sound a sickening smack.

She made sure he was dead, then turned to the boy in the cell. "It's okay now, sweetheart. He can't hurt you anymore." She opened her arms and Luke ran to her, taller and older than she'd been expecting. "Come. We need to call for help."

The pair jogged back to the elevator where Colin sat on the floor, blood streaming from his face. "Gwen?"

"And Luke."

"Michael?"

"He's dead."

"Thank God you're okay." He took his cell phone out of his pocket and handed it to her. "You'll have to make the call. I can't see a damned thing."

~~~

There was a knock on the open door.

"Can we come in?"

Colin couldn't place the voice, the bandages over his eyes making him completely blind. With any luck, it was a temporary inconvenience and not a permanent disability.

"Of course," said Gwen. She touched his hand and said quietly, "It's Emma and Luke."

"How are you feeling, Colin?" asked Emma.

"Pretty good," he lied smoothly. "They think the vision will come back as everything heals up." There was some truth to that. The doctors were confident at least one of his eyes would see again.

Luke was beside Colin, closer than he realized. "Thank you for saving me."

"You're welcome, buddy, but it was Gwen who really saved you."

"Thank you too, Miss Gwen."

"You're most welcome, Luke."

"How's Jerry doing?" Colin asked.

The One Who Got Away

"He's great," said Emma. "Up and walking around already."

Luke shuffled his feet. "He told me I need a haircut."

"They might discharge him in the morning," said Emma. "He's going to need physical therapy for a while, but the doctor expects him to make a full recovery."

"Oh, what a relief," said Gwen. "I'll bet you want him home."

"Yes, I really do," said Emma.

Becky's overly loud voice joined the chorus. "Howdy kids."

Emma and Luke said their goodbyes, heading upstairs to visit with Jerry until his release, and Becky plopped down on the hospital bed at Colin's feet. "I got you something."

Something light landed on his lap and he picked it up, a stuffed animal of some sort.

"It's a bat."

He smiled at her sense of humor. "Blind as a bat. You shouldn't have."

"I really wanted a mole, because technically speaking, they're the only truly blind animal, according to Wikipedia. But no one sells stuffed moles. Apparently they're not cute or cuddly enough. And," she said with a flourish, "I brought you cake."

"What kind?" he asked.

"Carrot, cheese, chocolate and homemade rum spice made with real rum, thank you very much. I wasn't sure what you liked."

He chose some of each cake and made small talk with the people who cared about him. It was several hours later when Colin had to admit defeat. "I was trying to wait for Rowan, but I'm tired." His brother was headed back to Italy on a late flight this evening.

"It's been a long few days," Gwen said. "Get some rest. I'll wake you when he gets here."

Colin slept heavily, with strange dreams of a warehouse full of bats turning into seagulls on the beach. Quiet talking woke him slowly.

"I still miss him." It was Rowan, the sadness in his voice nearly palpable.

"As do I," said Gwen. "I've felt him around me more in the

past few days than I have in the past few years. It reminded me of how much I still love that man." She sighed heavily. "I'll be in love with David Beaumont until I'm an old woman, crossing over the River Styx and running into his waiting arms."

The emotion in Gwen's voice was so powerful, her love so profound. Colin's heart ached. Could there be room in Gwen's heart for any other man?

"Is that ridiculous?" she asked. "I've had that image in my head for so long. I can almost imagine it happening."

"You two were something special. That kind of love doesn't come around every day."

"And what about you?" she asked. "Your wife?"

"It's complicated, Gwen."

"Do you love her?"

He whistled between his teeth. "Don't know."

"Now that, I can relate to. It's not always easy to tell what love has in store for us, is it?"

"Definitely not."

Colin knew she was talking about him, and her ambivalence was like a slap to the face. He had known he wanted Gwen Trueblood since the moment he first met her, yet she was still uncertain. It seemed her indecision was a decision in itself.

"I wish you well, my friend," said Gwen. "Are you sure you don't want me to wake him so you can say goodbye?"

"Nah. I'll call him in a day or two once we're both home."

"I'll give him your love. Have a safe journey."

"I will. Bye, Gwen."

Chapter 21

Colin paced from the window of his hospital room to the hallway and back again. His left eye was bandaged but his right was revealed, allowing him to see despite the healing wounds around it. He had showered this morning and dressed in anticipation of being discharged, but the hour was getting later and no one had come with the paperwork.

"Good morning," said Gwen, carrying a tray of coffee and something wrapped in waxed paper. "You're up! How are your eyes?"

Good enough to take in the pretty picture she made, her hair whipped up off her shoulders, wearing a gauzy white tank top that ended at her hip in layers of generous ruffles. He stared at her, trying to memorize her face, the blue of her eyes, the curve of her jaw.

"The right one seems fine. The left, not so much."

"Did the doctor say anything?"

"Just that we have to wait and see. They're sending me home."

Gwen picked up a coffee and handed it to him. "I got bagels with lox from a delicatessen down the street. They're sinful, they're so good. Here, taste." She put the bagel to his lips, but he turned away.

"Gwen…"

"Yes?"

"I'm going home."

"That's good news."

He shook his head, rubbing his hand through his hair. "No, I mean, I'm going back to Cold Spring."

She dropped her hand. "What are you saying?"

She looked so vulnerable. He loved her completely, the knowledge only serving to make this more painful. He reached out and gently wiped her cheek with his fingertips. "I'm saying that I don't think we should see each other anymore."

Gwen stared back at him, her bottom lip falling into a cupid's bow. "I don't understand, Colin. What changed between

The One Who Got Away

us? I thought you loved me."

I thought you loved me.

She probably didn't even realize she'd said it. "I do love you, Gwen, and it's killing me to say this, but you don't have enough room in *your* heart to love two men at the same time."

She turned around, putting her hands on her hips. "David."

"Yes."

"He's been dead for twelve years, Colin. Twelve years! Are you really implying I haven't moved on with my life, that I can't love again?"

"That's exactly what I'm saying."

A nurse walked in, placing a stack of papers on the tray table. "Colin Mitchell?"

"Yes."

"I have your discharge paperwork. Have a seat, please, so we can go through it."

Two and a half hours he'd been waiting, and she comes at the worst possible moment. "Can you come back in a little while?"

Gwen raised her hand. "Not on my account. I was just leaving anyway."

"Gwen…"

She raised steely eyes to his. "It's fine, Colin." She pulled sunglasses out of her purse and put them on. "I trust you will have a safe trip home and a speedy recovery."

He wanted to stop her, to beg her to stay, but all he could say was, "Thank you."

"Goodbye, Colin."

Colin watched as the woman he loved for half his life turned on her heel and walked out of it.

~~~

Gwen knelt in the freshly cut grass, digging a hole with a small trowel. Her gardening gloves were heavily soiled, her work here near complete. Reaching for the plastic pot, she loosened the roots of a bright yellow chrysanthemum and set the bushy plant into the ground.

"I know you love marigolds, but they're not in season," she said to the plaque, now clearly visible in the tidy cemetery. It had taken her nearly a week to reclaim the overgrown space, the addition of flowers and some shrubbery making the area more beautiful and serene. "I think Lucy likes the color."

Gwen stood and brushed off her long legs, dirty circles still clinging to the skin of her knees. She put her hand over her eyes to shield them from the sun, and took in the expanse of her property.

She would miss it here.

Her work to ready the house for sale was complete. The porch swing had received a coat of red paint, sharply setting off the white house with its new green shutters. Gone were her more flamboyant art installations, leaving only a small sculpture of a young woman in the garden to watch over the rolling hillside in her stead.

The house didn't look like her own anymore. Funny how homes sell faster when they look like no one with any personality lives in them.

She walked to the shed and replaced the gardening tools, as a small red convertible pulled into the drive. A tiny woman with long black hair and very high black heels stepped out of the car. "It's open house day!" she shouted, coming close to Gwen for an airy hug. "Are you ready?"

"Oh, I'm ready all right. How are you, Beverly?"

"I'm good, thanks for asking. The porch swing looks fabulous. I love the red." She held out her hand, wiggling her fingers. "Did you pack up the…other things?"

The 'other things' consisted of everything Gwen owned that could not be bought at a superstore. Beverly called it "de-cluttering". It had taken a monumental effort, an enormous storage unit and the help of two high school kids Gwen hired from town.

"I did. I think you'll find everything very neutral."

Many of the things in the house had belonged to David, making Gwen realize how much letting go she still had to accomplish. It had taken her only a week to organize everything and donate it to various charities, but the emotional journey had taken her the balance of the summer and fall.

No wonder Colin had sent her away, insisting she was still

in love with her husband's ghost. In some ways, she had never let him go. Gwen had fooled herself into believing she was living her life fully, simply because she was no longer huddled in a corner, actively grieving her husband's death. But she had not opened herself up again to love and the wonders it could bring, somehow living in the small space between the two extremes.

"I'm just going to take a quick shower and be on my way," Gwen said, turning to walk into the house.

"Wonderful." Beverly flashed an overly white smile. "It's a beautiful home. It's going to go quickly, Gwen."

"Yes, I think it will." Gwen smiled and headed upstairs, her hands lovingly caressing the wooden banister. She had become a bride here, been a wife to her husband here, planned a family that had never been realized within these walls.

She was ready to leave it behind, like a winter coat in the spring. Excitement bubbled within her, anxious and alive. Gwen didn't know what the future held in store, but she couldn't wait to find out.

Colin had sailed all the way to Poughkeepsie, making the most of a perfect fall day. The sun shone brightly, not a cloud in the sky, with a dream wind that effortlessly pushed his eighteen-foot boat further than he had intended to travel. He made his way back slowly, in no hurry to dock and face another night alone at the quiet marina.

Construction of the house was going well, the foundation cured and the framing for the first floor nearly completed. The architect had worked from old pictures to recreate the lighthouse-like turret, though Colin had designed the rest of the house to suit himself, with larger open spaces and modern conveniences.

The project had consumed the bulk of his energy since returning from Boston, providing him with something to do outside of work and thinking about Gwen. Colin knew he did the right thing sending her away, but when he couldn't sleep for thinking of her, he cursed himself with every toss and turn. Was it really so important that she love him more than a dead man?

It was.

And so the days were long and nights were longer, the house

The One Who Got Away

he would occupy alone designed for the woman who would never set foot inside its walls, with an art studio no one would paint in and a nursery for a baby who would never exist.

~~~

Music flowed on the air, the sound of a string quartet. Gwen thought it was Mozart, but she couldn't be sure. Her feet followed the stone pavers as she listened, her sandals quietly clicking in time to the tune.

She thought of the last time was here, just a few months ago, so dreading her confrontation with Colin. Gwen knew now that she had been afraid, scared that he would awaken feelings that would require her to change.

The doors to the Chapel Restoration stood open in welcome, much as they had on her first visit to this magical place. Climbing the steps, Gwen let the sounds surround her, true happiness welling inside her soul. This was where she belonged, where she wanted to live for all time, with Colin by her side.

Would he have her?

She was grateful he had sent her away, refusing to accept only half of her heart. She had kept the memory of her husband held tightly in her clutches, which was not how David would have wanted her to live. To love again was to honor his memory, to carry on joyfully a testament to life itself.

But she wasn't doing this for David. Gwen's love for Colin was strong and true, completely separate from all that had come before. She hoped they would make a life, become a family in this little town on the banks of the Hudson River.

Gwen opened her eyes and stepped into the Chapel, the pews decorated with fall-colored chrysanthemums and yellow bows in preparation for a wedding. She smiled as she thought of Crystal, and hoped the flowers were for the young woman's much-anticipated celebration.

The music began to crescendo, making the hair on Gwen's arms stand up on end with its beauty. She stood in awe of the sounds, their majesty and tenor, frozen as she listened to the final chord and the silence that followed.

"Bravo!" she yelled out as she clapped. "Belissimo!"

A touch on her arm made her swiftly turn around. Colin

stood before her, a look of wonder taking over his suntanned features.

Gwen smiled widely, so surprised she nearly laughed out loud. How good it was to see his handsome face, to feel his warm brown eyes connect with hers so intimately. "Colin, what are you doing here?"

"I live here."

She giggled. "No, I mean in the Chapel. I was heading to your house next, but you surprised me."

"There isn't much of a house there anymore."

"I figured I'd ask around until I found you."

The violinist began to play a quick jaunty tune, and Colin touched her elbow, steering her to the door. "Let's go outside."

Her pulse raced at his ordinary touch, so excited was she to be near him again. They stepped onto the porch, a gentle breeze bringing the scents of fall leaves and flowers to her nose. "Where are you living, then?"

"On my boat." He gestured with his chin. "The marina's right over there. The house is being rebuilt. I was on my way over to check on their progress when I heard the music. Gwen, what are you doing here?"

"I love it here. I stopped by on the way to your house last time, too."

"No, not the Chapel. Why are you here in town?"

"To see you."

He stared at her, waiting for an explanation.

She opened her mouth to speak, tears instantly burning at the back of her eyes. "I missed you."

Colin turned to stare at the river.

"I was angry with you when you sent me away," she continued. "I didn't understand why. But then I got back to Vermont and I realized that I did understand. I understood completely."

He turned back to look at her.

"I had to let go of David before I could really love you."

"Yes."

She nodded, letting a single tear slip down her cheek. "I've been working on it." She laughed. "There was a lot to do, and it's

The One Who Got Away

taken some time. I hope you didn't give up on me."

He stepped closer. "Never."

"Good. Because I love you, Colin. And I want to be with you forever." Then his lips were on hers and joy burst into her heart, reunited with this man who meant everything and more.

His head came up so he peered into her eyes. "I didn't even dare to dream you might come back." He rocked with her, pressing his forehead to hers. "You've made me so happy. Do you know?"

"I'm staying, too. I hope it's a big boat."

He laughed. "We could go to your house."

"My Realtor just called. It sold for full asking price about an hour ago."

His head snapped up. "What? You sold your house?"

"I did." She beamed at him, happier than she could remember being in a very long while.

"You're serious. You're really going to stay."

"Oh yes, Colin. I'm really going to stay."

~~~

They were anchored off the shore near Storm King Mountain, the setting sun casting a pink glow upon the opposite shore. Colin held a chrysanthemum in one hand and Gwen in the other, spinning the flower by its stem as he gently rubbed the bare skin of her back.

"It was nice of Crystal to let us use her flowers," murmured Gwen.

He kissed the top of her head. He had proposed on the porch of the Chapel Restoration, seeing no reason to wait when everything he wanted was there for the asking. Crystal and her husband were their witnesses.

"Can I tell you something?" he asked.

"Hmm?"

"During the ceremony, when I turned to you to say my vows, I saw someone in the doorway at the back of the church."

She raised her head, a smile spreading across her lips. "I saw him too."

"He gave me a thumbs-up."

Gwen sat up and flung her leg over his torso. "He probably

The One Who Got Away

thinks you have excellent taste in women."

He reached up to touch her. "I love you, Gwen. I'm going to be a good husband to you. Make you happy."

She kissed his palm. "You already make me happy."

"I want to give you a baby."

She looked around the tiny cabin, laughing. "Where on earth would we put it?"

He thought of the blue prints, the nursery with the window overlooking the valley. "Oh, I think we can find someplace."

Artful Deception

For Sweet Cheeks,
Boo Girl and Ozzie

Chapter 1

They say marriage can change you.
Just not for the better.

The thought had sweat breaking out in the small of Rowan Mitchell's back as he strode down the gilded corridor of Boston's opulent Grand Hotel. The carpeting beneath his dress shoes muffled his footsteps, the hushed rhythm echoing over the pounding of his pulse in his ears.

He hitched his chin up a notch, angry words and accusations screaming in his mind, waiting to be launched in attack. Those words had been living in his head for so long, Rowan had become used to their voices like a man haunted by spirits, damned and cursed.

Hell, maybe I am damned.

At least it had always seemed that way. A vision appeared in his mind unbidden, his parents' minivan sliding silently across an icy intersection and into the path of an oncoming truck. Marlene and Jack Mitchell had been killed instantly, the lives of their children forever altered.

Rowan hadn't been there when it happened, but he had carried the image with him since childhood, so clear in its detail that he often wondered if it was something he had really seen on the news or a product of his then-young imagination.

He and his younger brother Colin had gone to live with their grandmother after that, and Dorothy Mitchell had done everything she could to give the boys a loving home. But there was a hole inside Rowan that refused to heal, a wound so deep that it lay forever at the edge of his consciousness.

It was his weak spot, his Achilles heel, the place where he would forever be the most vulnerable. For having learned what it was to lose his parents, he would never willingly allow a child of his to suffer a similar fate.

He reached up and wiped a thin film of sweat from his brow. His tuxedo was hot, his skin hotter. Rounding a corner, the hallway stretched out in two-point perspective, Tamra's suite at the end.

Artful Deception

Only the best for his wife.

They'd met in this hotel just a year and a half ago, at a reception for the Marquis de Brigit. The Marquis was loaning his extensive collection of paintings to The Museum of Fine Arts, an extremely valuable assemblage of masterpieces that warranted a great deal of fanfare.

Rowan had noticed Tamra immediately, her graceful form draped in a dress of liquid copper, dark curls artfully swept atop her head. She laughed, her head lifting to reveal the curve of her neck, and Rowan felt his blood begin to heat. Their eyes met across the room, each appraising, each liking what they saw. She raised her wine glass and dipped her chin ever so slightly. She was flirting with him, making him excited. He took a deliberate step forward and one side of her mouth slid into a smile.

A man intercepted his path to the beauty. "Mitchell. I didn't know if you'd make it."

Rowan turned begrudgingly to greet Enzo de Toffoli.

Business before pleasure.

He reached out to shake the ambassador's hand. "Wouldn't have missed it for the world. There are three Gauguins in this lot." That wasn't his real reason for coming, but the truth was none of the other man's business.

Rowan's eyes returned to where the brunette had been standing, but the beautiful woman who'd stoked the fire in his gut was nowhere to be found.

Enzo chuckled. "I'm here for the Agotsi."

The hair on Rowan's arms stood up and he met Enzo's eyes with a questioning look. The only Agotsi in the Marquis' collection had been stolen several months ago. The crime was the stuff of movies, with an extensive alarm system that miraculously failed to sound and security recordings showing no one. The art world was full of conjecture and theories about the perpetrators, with Rowan more interested than most. "The Agotsi?"

"But of course. Isn't that why we're all really here? To see if the ghost who stole the Agotsi will materialize out of thin air, perhaps tell us what he found beneath its aged canvas?"

The legend of Agotsi's works—that the artist supposedly hid valuable clues to untold treasures beneath their layers—was as old as the paintings themselves. A series of riddles implied that each of his famous works held something deeper. The verse that was most associated with Rowan's favorite Agotsi now rang through his mind.

The crown of the babe shall reveal its worth, in layers given to the earth. Greater riches shall be found beneath the ground than in her arms, the treasure bound.

It was believed to have been Agotsi's lover who circulated his riddles shortly after his death in Paris in 1781.

One by one Agotsi's pieces were disappearing, with four paintings stolen in the last three years alone. The remaining works were being scrupulously guarded by both Interpol and the FBI's Art Crimes Division, which was the real reason for Rowan's attendance at tonight's event.

"I suppose we are."

Enzo's dark eyes were amused. "Good boy."

Rowan narrowed his eyes. "Pardon me?"

The brunette appeared, taking a place beside the men as she brazenly met Rowan's hungry eyes. Her scent was light and clean with just a hint of the exotic, and Rowan longed to lean in and gobble her up.

"Ah, Tamra," said Enzo. "I wondered where you'd gotten to. Rowan Mitchell, this is my daughter, Tamra de Toffoli."

Oh, shit.

"A pleasure to meet you, Mr. Mitchell," she said in a cultured Italian accent, her eyes full of amusement.

"And you, Ms. de Toffoli."

"I've been anxious to speak with you."

"Really?"

She nodded. "I'm a curator for the Uffizi. I have a few things I was hoping you could help me with."

Rowan raised his brows. The Uffizi was a fine art museum in Florence, which meant Tamra de Toffoli was someone in her own right. "I don't know much about Italian art, I'm focused more on French."

"Ah, but some things in life are not specific to a particular country, no?" Her stare fell to his lips.

Enzo patted Rowan's back. "I'll leave you two to talk business. It was good to see you, old friend." He disappeared into the crowd.

"My father likes you."

"No, he doesn't."

She smiled. "I like you."

He stepped closer. "Now that, I can believe."

Rowan stopped moving in front of the presidential suite, his past and present colliding in his consciousness. He had made love to Tamra in this room that first night, spent hours the next day wrapped in her arms. The sex had been incredible.

Her finest performance to-date.

He rapped soundly on the door and waited, his mind continuing to flip through history. Tamra had gone back to Italy with a kiss and barely a glance over her shoulder. They had shared two days of mindless physical pleasure without promises of love or happily ever after, which suited him just fine. He never expected to see her again.

The door opened and his wife's patrician chin notched instantly higher. Tamra was as beautiful as she had been that first night he met her, but now all Rowan could see was ugliness.

He wasn't the same man he was when he married her. Anger had become a part of him, like a bone nestled deep inside his body, or a cancer, thick like syrup.

This was his wife. A woman who hated him, a woman he himself had grown to hate.

I'm pregnant, Rowan. You're going to be a father.

He thought they'd been careful.

Of course, now he knew that they had.

How could she do it? Play with another person's emotions like that? It was as if she had known his weakness, the fastest way to bring him to his knees. Make him believe he was a father, that Anthony was his son, and Rowan would do anything.

He could see the boy's chubby arms and legs, softer than he could have imagined, smell the baby's unique and oh-so-sweet scent, hear the playful giggle that filled Rowan's heart with happiness.

He married Tamra inside of a week, surprised at her easy agreement. He had tried to get to know her, learn what made her special, how to make her happy. But there was only so much you could do when someone rebuked your every effort at conversation. It quickly became clear Tamra didn't share Rowan's vision of wedded bliss.

Then Anthony was born and Rowan became a father. Any joy he had known up until that moment paled in comparison to this. Rowan made a deal with himself that day, that he would protect his family and work to bring Anthony and Tamra happiness all the rest of his days, no matter his true feelings for his wife.

And now you're going to tear that family apart.

The walls on either side of him tilted at an uncomfortable angle. There wasn't enough air, wasn't enough time, wasn't enough anything.

Tamra was dressed in a rose-colored evening gown that swept to her feet in a flourish. She crossed her arms over her chest. "Where have you been?"

"My room."

"You got your own room?"

"Yes." He stepped past her, his eyes taking in the expansive suite, the mess of luggage and toiletries, a small easel and a metal chest Rowan knew held an extensive selection of oil paints. There were toys, one of Anthony's blankets. "Where's the baby?"

"With Carmella." The nanny was a fixture in their household, a plump girl with pocked skin and uncertain eyes. "Why the hell did you get your own room?"

"I'm not coming back to Italy with you," he said. The words lingered between them, seeming to echo in his ears.

She walked by him and reached for a bracelet off the dresser. "Don't be ridiculous."

"I'm divorcing you."

Her lips opened into a cupid's bow. "Why?"

"Because I hate you almost as much as you hate me."

She sat down on a Victorian chair, her eyes staring away from him. "What about Anthony?"

"What about him?"

"How can you be so cold?"

"Cold? You cry pregnant and get me to marry you..."

She scoffed. "Cry pregnant..."

"I cut ties to my whole life in the States, then come to Florence and find out I get my very own room with a view, just as long as I don't try to touch you." He took a step toward her. "You let me raise another man's son as my own for eight months."

Tamra's eyes opened wide.

"Oh yes, I know about that, how you let me believe I'm a father when you were lying to me the entire time. I've had enough of your bullshit. I want to salvage some kind of life for myself, if that's even possible at this point."

She stared at him and Rowan felt his hand twitch, the tension in his muscles seeming to hum like a motor.

"I didn't mean to hurt you," she said quietly.

"Fuck you."

"You have a right to be angry."

"Angry? You think I'm angry?" He put his hands in his pockets. "Honey, angry doesn't even begin to describe what I'm feeling right now. Murderous. Let's go with murderous."

A knock at the door had Tamra out of her seat in an instant. "That's Daddy. Please don't tell him. Not tonight."

"You don't want him to know his little princess was sleeping around?"

"We just have to get through this thing at the Gardner, then you can tell him anything you want tomorrow, okay?"

Rowan had waited months to confront Tamra with what he knew, just so he could be here to deliver the *Madonna Fornirà* to the Gardner personally. This evening was important to him as well. His release from prison, the end of this horrible chapter in his life. Another knock sounded at the door.

"Please, Rowan."

"Fine."

Artful Deception

She stood and quickly opened the door. Enzo stood on the other side, his tuxedo immaculate. "What the hell's taking you two so long?"

"Nothing, Daddy." She smiled brilliantly, as if nothing were amiss. "We'll be right down."

"Are you ready for your speech, sweetie?"

"I am, but I have index cards just in case." Tamra picked up a stack from the table.

"Better to ad lib than read from a stack of cards."

She put them down. "All right, then."

He put out his elbow. "Time to go."

"Of course."

Chapter 2

Becky O'Connor leaped over a puddle of brown slushy water and onto the opposite curb, a taxicab speeding through the intersection in her wake. The evening streets were crowded and she moved quickly, the staccato sound of her heeled leather boots punctuated by the crush of salt on the winter sidewalk.

It was cold and blustery even by Boston standards, and she pulled the soft green yarn of her hand-knitted scarf tighter around her neck. Its childlike puffiness contrasted with her finely tailored dress coat and highlighted the red of her long, curly hair.

The hair was her nemesis. The bane of her existence in middle school, Becky had worked feverishly to straighten it, treating it with chemicals to make it more blond and less pumpkin pie, forcing it with mousse and spray to fall in careful waves like the more popular girls. In high school she took to fastening it in a series of unfortunate hair-holders, from pigtails and barrettes to giant bun holders and one that made her hair cascade down her skull like a horse's mane.

It was Julie who taught her to own her red hair. Becky's roommate at MIT and a fellow computer science major, Julie Trueblood had the ethereal beauty of the middle school girls that had made Becky sick with envy. When Julie suggested Becky let her hair down, literally, Becky figured she had nothing at all to lose.

That's when the men started to notice her.

Sometime between seventh grade and freshman year of college, Becky's gypsy features and wild mane had gone from unfortunate and awkward to exotic and tantalizing. It was like she'd been granted a magical power to attract men, an invisible wand she could wave at will and control the majority of the male population.

Becky liked men. She liked tall ones and short ones, the lanky and the thick, the handsome and the rugged. It seemed each one she met had qualities that had been lacking in his predecessors, something to make her laugh or entertain her easily bored spirit. Dating was to be enjoyed like a good mud wrestling match, not a means to an end or a search for one oh-so-special soul mate.

Becky didn't believe there was such a thing.

She vividly remembered as a child, her teacher asked the students to draw pictures of themselves in the future, all grown up. Still uncomfortable with her appearance, Becky had carefully sketched a woman more beautiful than she with neat auburn hair, standing proudly in front of a home of her own, birds flying freely in the sunny sky above.

"Where's your family?" her teacher had asked. Becky's eyes wandered awkwardly to the pages of her classmates. On every paper she saw people, lots of people. Some kids had drawn whole families with children and pets, others just a happy couple holding hands.

Everyone had someone except her.

It was the first time she realized she was different on the inside, not just on the outside. She had no desire for a family, no longing to be part of a couple.

Only one thing looked appealing about her friends' hopes for the future. "I forgot to draw a dog," she said, taking her picture back to her desk with a determined gait. She would name the dog Lucy, in honor of the most confident redhead Becky had ever seen.

Up ahead, a group of people walked slowly, effectively blocking the sidewalk. Becky checked her watch. *Damn it.* She was going to miss the opening face-off if she didn't bust a move.

"Excuse me!" she said cheerfully, breaking into a jog as the group parted to let her through. The rest of the way down Huntington she ran, grateful that the icy sidewalks from last night's storm had been reduced to wet concrete. Not many things could make Becky run, but the Boston Bruins and the promise of a frosty beer were high on the list of things that could. Heck, she might even get some chicken wings, her mouth beginning to water at the thought of deep fried goodness covered in hot pepper sauce and blue cheese dressing.

Her calf muscles began to balk at the strain of running in heels, just as the sign for the popular sports bar came into view. "C'mon, Beck. You got this," she said to herself, mimicking the deep voice of her trainer at the gym. Becky loved to lift weights almost as much as she hated the treadmill, her love for exercise as selective as her taste in general.

A hundred yards, maybe less. Justin would be there already, of course. Methodical and organized, there was no way her date would arrive at the last minute and sit somewhere in back, or worse yet let her stand through the whole first period. He was a gentleman, that one, and she enjoyed dating him, though she suspected they were nearing the end of their relationship.

Becky was no fool, and she'd seen the expression on his face last week at Legal's when he took her for a special "crabfest for one". Becky loved crab like nobody's business, with Red Lobster being her own personal nirvana, but Justin considered the restaurant sub-par. He'd actually used that word. *Sub-par.*

It was the handwriting on the wall.

So they'd sat at Legal's eating what must have been a hundred dollars worth of crab legs, as her date tried to find the words to tell her something she was pretty well sure she didn't want to hear.

She silently encouraged him to keep his mouth shut.

It was like trying to keep the victim in a horror movie from entering the bad guy's lair, or trying to fight gravity. There was only so long you could put these things off before they burst out on their own like water through a broken dam.

Becky opened the door of the bar, a cacophony of conversation spilling into the street as a smile spread wide across her face. She was a social person who lit up in social situations, more at home in a crowd than she could ever be in a more intimate setting.

The bar was enormous, with dozens of large TV screens in a huge half-circle. One movie-sized screen dominated the field, a shrine to the mecca that was sports television.

It was standing-room-only, a crush of bodies that smelled like men, cologne, beer, and food, and she took a breath deep into her lungs. Heads turned as she made her way through the crowd, the more brazen of the patrons exchanging friendly greetings as she passed. Becky made a beeline for the big screen, knowing the Bruins would command it, her ears searching the din for the familiar voice of Jack Edwards doing the play-by-play and grateful when she couldn't hear it. She'd made it on time.

Justin came into view, his handsome playboy face offset by his oh-so-smart-looking glasses. The man was hot, she had to give him that. With any luck, it would be too loud in this place to have any kind of real conversation, which meant he wouldn't be able to profess his undying love.

He caught her eye and stood up, bending to kiss her cheek. "I was wondering if you were going to show up."

She didn't miss the chastising tone. Yes, it was nearing the end with Justin. "You don't think I'd be late for the Bruins if I could help it, do you?" She stripped off layers of outerwear as she watched them prepare to drop the puck. Justin ordered her a cosmo from the waitress, and Becky turned to touch the woman's shoulder. "No cosmo," Becky yelled over the noise. "I want a beer. One of those tall ones," she said, gesturing with her arms, "the size of a small child."

"Foster's," said Justin, and the waitress nodded before leaving.

Becky shot him a look. "It didn't have to be Foster's."

"You like Foster's."

"I like beer."

He raised an eyebrow. "All beer?"

"Heck yeah. It's beer. Fermented grain. Each is unique and wonderful."

"Some of them suck, and you know it. How was work?"

She narrowed her eyes at him. "Fine."

Actually, work had been crappy, but she wasn't about to tell him that. As Vice President of Technology for Systex Corporation, Becky was in charge of the computers for the entire company. It was a job she'd worked hard to get and was proud to have, which challenged her eager mind and fed her inner nerd.

"Don't be angry." He smiled at her, his blue eyes twinkling. "I was trying to be nice." He raised his hands. "I won't order for you again today."

Oh, cupcake. You won't order for me ever again.

Artful Deception

"Thank you." She turned her attention to the TV as the game began, Boston getting control of the puck right away. "All right! Let's go, Bruins!"

Justin moved his chair closer to hers. "I've been thinking."

Becky's hope for a pleasant evening began to wane.

It's time. What was the sense in putting it off any longer?

She turned toward him with a sigh. "I've been thinking, too." The waitress brought their drinks, and Becky took a big sip from the comically tall glass.

"You have?"

"Yep."

"Do you want to go first or should I?" He smiled sheepishly.

She patted his leg twice. "Oh, I think I should go first."

Becky understood what it was to dump someone. She even knew what it was to be the one being dumped, though she had experienced that role far fewer times than the first. She liked to think of herself as a professional, a surgeon. Use a sharp enough scalpel to make a clean cut the first time. Separate what needs separating and get the hell out of there before anything starts to hemorrhage. Easy as pie, like killing a fly with a big ol' swatter.

Smack.

Justin was gone by the first intermission and Becky had the prime table all to herself. She took a sip of her second giant beer, though she ditched the Foster's this time around and suspected she had lost the taste for it forever. The waitress was seeing about some chicken wings and Becky leaned back in her chair, hands behind her head, in a pose her friend Julie affectionately referred to as the preying mantis.

"Is this seat taken?"

Snap.

"Nope." She smiled up at a man with skin the color of wheat and rich brown hair. "I'm Becky."

"Edward."

"Nice to meet you, Edward. Can I call you Eddie?"

He grinned. "You can call me anything you want, sweetheart."

Eddie was an engineer. He was also a hockey fan, thank goodness, and he insisted on ordering his own wings instead of sharing hers, a sign of good character in Becky's book. The Devils tied it up 2-2 by the end of the second period, when a special report banner appeared on the screen and the bar quieted down some to listen.

"Moments ago a woman and her eight-month old son were abducted from a private party at the Gardner Museum here in Boston. Authorities are asking for your help tonight as they search for the woman, Tamra de Toffoli, and her infant son, Anthony de Toffoli Mitchell."

That's right down the street!

They showed a picture of a beautiful brunette in a swimsuit, holding a chubby and angelic baby in orange swim trunks. Becky heard herself sigh as she stared at the infant, so perfect and fine. She let her eyes wander to the mother, who was stunning, and Becky frowned. She hoped that woman wasn't dead. *Oh God, I really hope that baby isn't dead.*

The screen switched to a reporter who appeared to be on-location. "You are Ms. de Toffoli's husband?"

The camera panned to include a man, and recognition slammed into Becky. She jerked upright, spilling her beer.

"Hey!" said Eddie.

Becky held out her hand and shushed him harshly, her eyes riveted on the screen. Rowan Mitchell stared back at her, his dark hair disheveled, his face sweating and pale, a haunted look in his eyes. It had been a long time since she'd seen him outside of her dreams, but his rugged features instantly affected her, making her pulse jump and her senses scream.

She'd been drawn to him, pulled as if by some outside force. They'd met when he flew over from Italy to help his brother Colin catch a killer, and Becky had gone with Gwen to pick him up at the airport.

From the moment Rowan climbed in the car, Becky knew there was something special about this man. And he had looked at her like he'd never seen a woman before in his whole entire life.

The chemistry between them sizzled right up until he told her he was married, and her respect for the man flew out the window

Artful Deception

in a heartbeat. Who the hell was he to look at her that way if he was married to someone else?

"Yes, I am." Rowan rubbed his hands over his face, his fingers shaking.

"Can you tell us what happened?"

"I don't know. I don't know what happened. They were here, then they were gone. I found a note…"

"What kind of note?"

"A ransom note, asking for money."

"What did it say? How much money are they asking for?"

Rowan stepped closer to the camera, staring into its lens. "Please, help me find my family." His eyes shone, watery and bloodshot. "If you know where they are, or you know anything at all, please call the police, the FBI." He covered his face with a shaking hand. "My wife is an Italian citizen, her father an ambassador. This could be politically motivated. Or the artwork. It could be anything."

The reporter came back onscreen but Becky was no longer listening. All she could see was Rowan's stricken face, his horrified expression, and the sweet little baby he might never again hold in his arms.

She couldn't stay here. Becky hurriedly wrapped her green scarf around her neck and grabbed her coat. "I have to go."

"What's wrong?"

"I know that guy." Her mind was racing ahead of her. She needed to call Gwen, Rowan's sister-in-law and her own dear friend, make sure she and Colin knew, right away. How long would it take them to get here from Vermont?

"You know that guy? On TV?"

She nodded, throwing a twenty-dollar bill on the table.

"Oh, my God. Hey wait, can I have your number…"

She didn't even slow down, already reaching for her cell phone as she pushed her way through the crowd and into the freezing night air. With a trembling hand she dialed Gwen's number, then held up a hand to flag down a cab.

The Gardner Museum was less than two miles from here, the horror of the evening close enough to have swept right next to her unconnected life.

Chapter 3

The taxi was hot, the defroster blasting warm air into the backseat and Becky's face.

"Can you turn that down?" she asked.

The driver reached forward and appeared to turn a knob, but the hot air assault continued unabated.

She unwound her scarf from her neck.

Rowan looked so scared on TV.

Gazing out her window, memories of the last time she saw Rowan played in her head. They were at the hospital, waiting for Colin to get out of surgery.

Becky was getting candy out of a vending machine when he came up behind her.

"Hey," he said.

A package of licorice fell from its perch, and she felt her heart rate pickup at his nearness. "Hey yourself."

"How's Gwen?"

Becky inserted a dollar bill and sipped at a Hawaiian Punch. She liked Colin's brother. Maybe too much, even. The guy was eye candy, for sure, but he was also sweet and stubborn, two of her favorite character traits. She'd seen the way he looked out for Gwen after her husband died, the way he stood up for what he thought was right with Colin.

"Good. The gunshot was purely superficial." A pair of cupcakes dropped. "She'll have a scar on her arm, but they didn't even admit her." She began feeding coins into the slot.

"Hungry?" he asked.

She heard the humor in his voice and added 'funny' to her list of things she liked about him. Her eyes dipped to his chest, then back to his eyes. "Why, you want something?" A chocolate bar landed with a thud.

He shook his head, his eyes never leaving hers. "No, I'm good. Have you seen Colin yet?"

"He's still in post-op. They got the bullet."

"Good. Good. They say anything else?"

Artful Deception

They said you should make mad passionate love to me. Doctor's orders.

She took a swig of her drink. "Nope."

He was staring at her lips and she couldn't help the direct words that flowed out of her mouth. "You sure you're not hungry?" she asked, putting one hand on her hip. "Because you're looking at me like you're starving."

His eyes widened. "Sorry."

"Right." She took another sip, slowly turning and walking beside him, her arm lightly brushing his and sending tingles through her whole body. "So, you live in Italy?"

"Yeah."

"How'd you end up over there?"

"I followed a woman."

"Ah, I see. How did that work out?"

He didn't answer for moment, the sound of their footsteps the only noise. "We got married."

She stopped walking. "Married?"

He nodded.

"Wait, you're married?" This had to be some kind of joke. Who the hell was this guy that he'd been hitting on her, flirting from the moment he met her, only to be married to some other woman?

"I am."

Loser.

The Gardener Museum came into view and the cab stopped at a red light. Somewhere inside was Rowan, and her pulse jumped at the knowledge.

Don't get too close, Becky.

She would stay aloof, distant. She would do her best to be a good friend until Colin and Gwen arrived, and that was all.

~~~

Rowan's eyes took in the grotesque arch of the dragon's back, its jaw wide with fangs exposed. A spike penetrated its mouth, the serpentine curve of the monster's neck allowing that same thorn to reemerge and pierce its own breast. St. George stood on horseback, golden sword extended for the kill, himself neither boy nor man, an unlikely hero for the princess on the distant hill.

Rowan knew the story of the painting before him, a Crivelli from the fifteenth century, and the irony did not escape him. As he sat in the Raphael Room of the Gardner Museum, Rowan knew he had entered into a battle with an evil so fine, it could reach into his life and steal an innocent babe and its mother right out of his own careful hands. Adrenaline flowed freely through his veins, making him sweat, and his fists long to hit something, but there wasn't a damn thing he could do.

A gruff voice interrupted his thoughts. "I got you some coffee."

"Thanks, Marco."

Marco Santori was about Rowan's age, with a thicker middle and shaved bald head. "The local FBI guy wants to ask you a few questions."

"Aren't you good enough?"

"You know how it is."

That, he did. He nodded and Marco left the room as a man with yellow hair entered.

"I'm Agent Ellington with the Boston FBI. I just need to ask you a few questions."

The agent settled into an antique chair and opened a small notebook. "When's the last time you saw your wife?"

"I already told Agent Santori." He knew Ellington had to ask, but it was just so damn stupid. This was how the FBI was going to spend their time, questioning and requestioning him while the kidnappers got farther away?

"Tell me."

Turning away, Rowan's eyes found an image of the Annunciation, the angel Gabriel telling Mary she was to bear a child. Tamra's face appeared in his memory, telling him he was going to be a father, her brown eyes oddly expressionless. She'd been lying to him, playing on his emotions.

Using up his life to fuel her own.

"I watched her give her speech, then she was showing off the baby to some people by the bar."

"Did you talk to her?"

"No."

"Mr. Mitchell, were you and your wife getting along?"

Rowan didn't speak for a beat. "Did someone suggest that we weren't?"

Ellington didn't answer.

Rowan laughed, a humorless sound. He stood. "No. We were not getting along."

"Why not?"

He settled for a half-truth. "Things have been difficult since Anthony was born. My wife has been struggling with post-partum depression." Or so she said. Rowan had often wondered if the vague generalities of PPD were simply an easier way of hiding her dissatisfaction with her marriage. Tamra never seemed depressed around the baby; quite the opposite. She was a loving and doting mother.

She was only depressed around her husband.

"Was she seeing anyone for the depression?"

"I don't know."

"How long have you and your wife been married?"

"It was a year in November."

He imagined the agent counting in his head, and Rowan's mind wandered back through time right with him. Had Tamra been planning, even then, to destroy him? Or had that plan only surfaced later?

"Was that unusual, for your wife to bring the baby to a function like this?"

"No."

"He's seven months old?"

"Eight on Tuesday." Rowan felt his jaw shake as he said the words, emotion suddenly overwhelming him. He had known he would not see Anthony again after today, and that was enough to bring him to his knees. *But kidnapped.* The baby had been *kidnapped.*

"Can you think of anyone who could have done this, Mr. Mitchell?"

"No."

Movement at the doorway caught Rowan's attention. A uniformed policeman walked into the room, his mouth opening, then closing again.

"What is it?" asked the agent.

"There's a woman here to see Mr. Mitchell. Becky O'Connor?"

The image of a sultry redhead who smelled like cinnamon and sugar flashed in Rowan's brain. He narrowed his eyes. "Redhead?"

The officer nodded.

"I know her."

What the hell was Becky doing here?

The officer stepped out of the room and Becky entered, her ivory cheeks flushed red from the cold. Rowan hadn't expected to see her again, and certainly not under these unlikely circumstances. At a barbeque, maybe, or a family get-together at Colin's house. Then he might have been prepared for the wildly inappropriate shot of lust that slammed into his gut as she approached.

"I saw on the news," she said, her big green eyes round with concern. "I was right down the street."

Right down the street?

"You live in Boston." This woman had invaded his memory several times since they met earlier this year, yet he had relegated her to some corner of his mind that was reserved for people who didn't really exist, like Superman or Cat Woman.

But she did exist. She lived here, in Boston. He could have walked right by her.

"Yeah." She threw her coat over a chair and opened her arms. Rowan realized she was going to hug him a moment before she did, time slowing as her body pressed against his. He slipped his arm around her shapely back, feeling the softness of her sweater against his palm. The lightest hint of alcohol surrounded her like perfume, making him wonder where she had been before this. On a date, with a man? Of course. She was young, beautiful, single. Why shouldn't she be on a date with a man?

"Thanks for coming." He reluctantly released his hold on her.

"Gwen and Colin are on their way, too. I called them."

Artful Deception

Relief came first, quickly followed by wariness. Rowan wasn't used to relying on his brother.

The two of them had been on shaky ground for too long, their recent reconciliation yet to be truly tested. It seemed like just yesterday they worked together to find what really happened to David, a close friend who died years earlier in what was thought to be a skiing accident. Colin went on to marry David's widow, Gwen, and the couple was expecting their first child this spring.

Rowan frowned when he thought of his sister-in-law. "Is Gwen up for the trip?" The last time he'd spoken with his brother, Colin said she was having a difficult pregnancy.

"I think she's fine. She wanted to come. You know Gwen."

He did, and he grinned. She was eccentric and good hearted, and he loved her a great deal. "Yeah."

Ellington stepped forward and introduced himself to Becky. "And you are?" he asked, taking notes when she explained their relationship. "Just one more thing, Mr. Mitchell," he said.

"Yes?"

"I'd like you to come back to the hotel. We're going to go through your wife's personal effects, see if we can find anything relevant. You can help."

"Sure."

Becky sat down with a great thud that belied her small frame. "So, what the hell happened?" she asked.

"We were here for a reception, celebrating the exchange of artwork between the Gardner Museum and the Uffizi." He sat down next to her. "It's an unprecedented event for the Gardner. Their collection is unchanging, but they decided to display one of the Uffizi's works for a limited engagement. The *Madonna Fornirà,* by Agotsi. It belongs here. It's part of the series that Isabella Gardner collected, the missing link. It's important for history's sake that the pieces be together, at least once. And it's excellent PR for the Italian government."

He shook his head. "I was so concerned about security for the painting. Everything was about the painting." Countless hours he had worked side-by-side with the Gardner's head of security. Rowan thought they had considered every possibility, every point of entry.

Becky's green eyes met his. "You said on the news there was a ransom note."

"Five million dollars for their safe return." A wave of nausea crested at the reminder. "The kidnappers said they'll be in touch within twenty-four hours." He looked at his watch.

"What the hell are you supposed to do until then?"

"I have no fucking clue."

A handsome man in a sharply tailored suit came to the doorway. "Rowan, we need you downstairs."

Rowan and Becky stood up, and the man's brows snapped down. "Who is this?" he asked.

"A friend. Becky O'Connor." He turned to her. "Gianni Amato. He's with Interpol."

"Something terrible has happened," said Amato.

The floor beneath Rowan seemed to drop several inches. "Did they find them?"

"No, but come. You must see this for yourself."

~~~

Becky picked up her coat and purse, then followed the men downstairs. On a tall easel stood a resplendent painting of Mary holding the baby Jesus, their pose instantly reminding her of the snapshot of Rowan's wife and son she saw on the news report. A small sign on the easel read, *Madonna Fornirà* by Giuseppe Agotsi.

Three years of French class had Becky loosely translating the Italian as Madonna provides.

Rowan stepped closer, his eyes darting around the painting, horror overtaking his features. "No," he whispered, his eyes raking over the canvas. "It's not possible. It's not possible!" He bent at the waist, muttered a curse, and came up with his hands on either side of his head.

"You see it, too," said Amato.

"Of course I see it! It's a goddamn forgery." He began to pace. "How is that fucking possible? I inspected the painting myself after the hall was set up for the reception. Then I was in the room, along with all of you," he gestured to them with his hands, "the entire evening." He turned to the Interpol agent. "When did this happen?"

"I noticed it after Ms. de Toffoli was taken."

"But how the hell…"

"I don't know. But somehow, someone has stolen your wife, your son and the *Madonna Fornirà* right out from under our noses."

~~~

Marco Santori was at the wheel and Ellington rode shotgun as the entourage made their way back to the hotel Rowan and Tamra stayed at the night before. Becky couldn't help but feel like an interloper, the piece that didn't fit, the one who didn't belong here.

She stared out the windshield, the image of a negligée laying on a hotel room floor popping into her mind unbidden, thrown there by Rowan as he stripped his wife in the heat of passion. She felt like an intruder as the car raced toward the hotel, slipping between husband and wife like an uninvited guest. She was crossing some line, breaking the rules again.

No, I'm helping a friend. That's all. As soon as Colin and Gwen get here, I'll be on my way.

Rowan spoke softly. "You didn't have to come. It wasn't necessary."

"Would you rather I go home?"

"No," he said, meeting her eyes in the darkness, and her belly flip-flopped. She could feel her body responding to his nearness, the scent of his skin affecting her like some primitive mating call.

Down, girl.

"Okay, then." Her stomach growled and she dug in her bag for a snack. Finding peanut butter cookies and a bag of pretzels, she held them up. "Hungry?"

"No."

Well I am.

She could picture herself saying the words as she yanked her sweater over her head and attacked him.

What the hell was the matter with her? This man was in the middle of an enormous crisis, his wife and infant son vanished into thin air, and she was fantasizing about him.

To be fair, I was fantasizing about him long before his wife disappeared.

She ripped open the cookies violently, the plastic rustling noisily in the silence, and popped one in her mouth. Chewing loudly, she watched the lights of downtown Boston go by as her body hummed with awareness and sexual need.

She had to calm down. She barely knew the man, yet her subconscious had featured him prominently in several dreams since he first made an appearance in her life. Rowan dreams were some of her personal favorites, second only to werewolves. Something about a shape-shifter—the full moon, the inherent danger—really got Becky's motor going.

She imagined Rowan as a werewolf now, baring his fangs, and sighed aloud as she bit into another cookie. The image was like Christmas morning and her birthday all rolled into one.

She must be a horrible person to be thinking sexy thoughts about a guy in this situation. Was it her fault she was drawn to the opposite sex like steel to a magnet, and this particular man like one of those high powered magnets they use to move cars? Deliberately she turned her thoughts back to the man she met in the bar. He was attractive, nice. He liked hockey. *What the hell was his name?*

"Why did you come tonight?" Rowan asked.

The question caught her off-guard, his voice strumming her insides like a musical instrument. She worked at an innocent look and met his eyes, remembering her visceral reaction to seeing him on TV. "I don't know."

"No?"

The blood rushed into her cheeks. *I've been dreaming about you, lusting after you in my sleep.* She shrugged. "I saw a friend on TV and thought maybe I could help."

He nodded slowly.

"I'm sorry. It's just…"

"What?"

"The last time we met, I think you got the wrong impression."

"And what impression was that?"

"You thought I was interested in you as a woman."

An embarrassed flush surged onto her cheeks as Agent Ellington turned full around to stare at her. "I wouldn't say that," she said.

"No? What would you say?"

She turned toward him. "I'd say you came on to me, Rowan."

"No. I told you I was married. That I had a family it Italy."

"Which is why it was totally out of line."

"This is ridiculous. I love my wife with my entire soul. I'm sorry if you somehow got the impression I did not."

She brought her chin up. "Okay, Rowan. Whatever you say." Shifting in her seat, her eyes locked with Ellington's. "You get all that?" she asked, her head bobbing, and he turned back around.

Rowan's voice was quiet. "I'm sorry, Becky."

"Whatever. I'll grab a cab from the hotel. I just want to go home."

Chapter 4

Becky sank into her deep sofa and pulled an ugly blanket over her lap. Crocheted from a rainbow of different yarns, each patch of color was completed in a different stitch, each color sewn together like a quilt. The blanket could have been done in complementary colors and an intricate design to great effect, but Becky's grandmother had never intended the blanket to be pretty. She had made it as a gift for her own mother-in-law, a woman who cared very much for beautiful things. It was a slap-in-the-face from one woman Becky loved to another, and Becky's most treasured family heirloom.

A small tan dog hopped up beside her and walked in two circles before settling into a curled ball.

"Me, too, Lucy," said Becky as she turned on the TV. Reaching for a big bowl of peanut butter ice cream, she wrapped its sides with the ugly blanket and sighed. Gwen and Colin had made it into town several hours ago, calling her to locate Rowan. She offered them her guest room and they accepted, though Becky had no idea what time they would make it back to her house. She wanted to wait up if she could.

Turning to the local cable news station, she mindlessly watched the weather as she ate. Her thoughts wouldn't let go of Rowan and the way he treated her in the car, as much as she wanted to forget about it.

How embarrassing!

Why had he felt the need to dress her down in front of that creepy FBI agent? It's not like she was making a pass at him or batting her I'm-available-even-if-you're-married-to-a-missing-woman eyelashes in his face. *Please.* She would never go after a married man. Not even Rowan.

Not even Rowan.

A big spoonful of ice cream sat at the top of her closed throat. Okay, so maybe she was attracted to him, and this was an inappropriate time in his life for her to feel that way. She forced herself to swallow. Or maybe he was right, and she totally needed him to get in her face and tell her to back off.

"Damn it," she muttered, spooning another heaping mound of peanut butter and cream. Her eyes went back to the TV and she froze as she read the words at the bottom of the screen. *Woman found bound and gagged at The Grand Hotel.* Becky turned up the volume, the remote now trembling in her hand.

"...a full recovery. A hotel employee confirms the room was registered to Tamra de Toffoli Mitchell, the woman who was reportedly abducted from a private event at the Gardner Museum this afternoon."

"Oh, my God," she whispered, her heart hammering as something cold passed through her like electricity.

They found Tamra...

Becky pictured the golden revolving doors of the historic hotel where she had stood and hailed a taxi not three hours before. And inside, while she walked away, Rowan walked in to find his wife tied up and hurt...

Where the hell was the baby?

"Oh, please!"

The newsroom cut to a uniformed police officer at a podium. "Carmella Bitetto, nanny to the infant who was abducted with his mother from the museum, was attacked and incapacitated by a man wearing a black ski mask."

A reporter from the press conference on TV called out, "What about the father? Was he involved?"

Becky scowled and leaned forward. Why had she left Rowan alone, when there were vultures like that woman out to get him? Suddenly, she seemed so far away from the action, too far away from the man who needed her help.

He didn't want you there, remember?

"Mr. Mitchell is cooperating with law enforcement and helping us find his wife and son. That's all for now."

The shot went back to an anchorwoman in the studio. "A painting valued at more than thirty million dollars was stolen from the museum at the same time as the kidnapping. Investigators refuse to speculate on whether the same person is responsible for both the kidnapping and the art theft."

Lucy stood up and began a low growl. Becky looked to the front door just as the bell rang and the dog bounded off the couch, barking furiously. Throwing aside the blanket, Becky went to the door and opened it to the blustery winter's night. Gwen stood on the threshold in a puffy pink coat stretched tight across her middle, a smile on her pretty face despite the news of the day.

"Becky, my dear!"

Becky threw her arms around Gwen like a child. Gwen was Julie's aunt, but Becky had long ago staked her claim on this particular member of her best friend's family. "Thank God you're here."

"Is that ice cream that I smell?"

Becky blinked. "Seriously?"

"Oh yes. This baby is quite serious indeed."

Becky took Gwen's coat, her eyes lingering over the other woman's curving breasts and swollen belly. Gwen had always been thin, with the grace of those who are naturally so. Now she was curvy—at least twenty pounds heavier—and even more beautiful, if that was possible. Her long blond hair fell in soft curls just past her shoulders.

"I'll get you a bowl."

"Don't be shy, now. Colin says I have the appetite of a linebacker."

"Where is Colin?"

"He's still at the hotel."

"I just heard about the nanny on the news."

"Awful. That poor girl."

"How's Rowan?"

"Upset. They told him they'd found a woman tied up in the hotel room, but no baby, and of course he thought it was Tamra but not Anthony. Moments of sheer hell." Gwen rested a hand on her belly and gently rubbed in a circle. "I hate to be rude, dear, but I want that ice cream now."

"Oh, of course." Becky moved toward the kitchen.

"I don't think the nanny would begrudge a pregnant woman her dinner, do you?"

Becky glanced at the clock. "Is this really your dinner?" She couldn't believe Colin would let his wife go so long without food.

Gwen dropped down on the couch. "I suppose it's my second or third dinner, but it feels like I haven't eaten in days. What a lovely blanket!"

"That's the ugly blanket."

"It has a wonderful feel to it."

"Soft."

"Yes, but that's not what I mean. It has love attached to it, strong womanly love. I like it."

Becky smiled out of the side of her mouth. Gwen was a special woman, whose special thoughts added something beautiful to the lives of everyone around her. "Thanks."

Gwen ate slowly, seeming to savor every bite. "I couldn't stay at that hotel any longer. There was nowhere to sit down and my feet and ankles have had it."

"What did I miss?"

"They found the poor nanny before we got there. Then they had to process the scene. Every now and then, they'd ask Rowan a question. Did Tamra bring this or that, did he know where she kept something."

The intimacies of marriage were not lost on Becky, and she felt a tug of guilt as she listened to Gwen talk. *Rowan and his wife have a life together, a real life as husband and wife.*

"That's when the concierge came over and talked to one of the policemen, telling him that Rowan had his own room, and all hell broke loose."

"What?"

Gwen nodded. "Apparently, they just assumed Tamra and Rowan were sharing a room because they're married. Some things were missing from her hotel room, so they didn't realize none of his belongings were there."

"And he didn't tell them?"

"No." She took another bite of ice cream. "I don't think anyone asked him directly. He just didn't correct their assumption to the contrary."

"Hmm."

"Hmm, what?"

"You don't find that strange?"

Gwen put down her spoon into her bowl with a clink. "I find several things about this strange."

"Shoot," said Becky.

"When Rowan flew to the States last year, he seemed unhappy."

"Yes, I agree."

Gwen seemed to consider her words. "Unhappy with his life, with the choices he's made."

"Did you talk to him about it?"

"Some, yes." Gwen draped the blanket across her protruding middle, fingering it's puffy stitches. "Becky, I need to ask you something."

A familiar heat began to creep into her cheeks. "Okay."

"You and Rowan..." she clucked her tongue, "seemed to have a connection when he was here."

"Nothing happened." Becky rubbed the back of her neck.

"That wasn't what I was going to ask." She smiled sweetly. "Did he mention Tamra to you at all, or the baby?"

Becky remembered every word of every conversation she and Rowan had. She especially remembered that the mention of a wife back home in Italy had come rather late. "He told me he had a wife, that he followed her to Italy and married her."

"When we spoke," said Gwen, "he told me their relationship was complicated. That he wasn't sure he loved her. Tonight, when the police found out about the separate hotel rooms, Rowan told them Anthony wakes a lot during the night so he got the second room so he could get some sleep."

Plenty of Becky's friends were settled down with husbands and children. She'd heard of similar sleeping arrangements. "Sounds reasonable enough."

"It does..." Gwen picked up her bowl and began stirring the ice cream into a creamy swirl. "But I was standing right there, and I didn't believe him. I love Rowan. He was a good friend to David, and a great help to me when David passed on. We may not have kept in touch through the years in between then and when I married Colin, but Rowan has forever been in my thoughts. I consider him to be part of my family."

"Well, he is, now."

Gwen nodded. "I'm afraid there's more going on here than Rowan has shared with us, or the FBI."

"I think so, too."

"They really started to question him after it came out about the separate rooms. They set up a makeshift interrogation room." Her eyes met Becky's. "I didn't see him again before I left tonight."

Becky didn't like the idea of Rowan lying, and she sure as hell wanted to know the real reason husband and wife were not sleeping together, but despite all of that she found it hard to believe Rowan could have done anything wrong. What were they imagining, that he had something to do with the disappearance of his own wife and son?

"He would never hurt them." Becky didn't know how she knew, but she did. She had never been more certain in her life.

"Oh, of course not, dear. I'm just worried for him. Worried that the police are barking up the wrong tree, and our Rowan will be stuck in the branches." She sighed as she leaned back and adjusted the blanket. "I think, if it's all right with you, I'll just lay right down here and close my eyes for a few minutes."

"You can go upstairs, I have your room all ready for you."

"Thank you, but I really just need a quick little power nap and I'll be fine...I'm sure..." Her eyes were already closed, the ugly blanket pulled up to her chin.

Becky must have fallen asleep too, because the next thing she knew, she woke up when Lucy began to growl. Her eyes met Gwen's, who was now awake and watching a movie. The clock said it was almost five o'clock, which Becky slowly realized must be a.m.

"Is Colin back already?" asked Becky.

"He was going to stay with Rowan, but you've been asleep for a few hours."

"It must be him." Becky shook off the last of her sleepy haze and shrugged. She opened the door to find both the Mitchell brothers on her front porch. "Come on in."

Colin walked over to Gwen and kissed her cheek. "I wasn't expecting to see you tonight," Gwen said.

Becky's eyes were stuck to Colin, his tired expression and his cold-red cheeks. She was avoiding Rowan's stare, though she could feel it down to her toes. It was surreal having this man in her home, standing just feet from her. Her knees felt wobbly and she remembered with horror that she wasn't wearing a bra, folding her arms in front of her chest as subtly as she could manage.

"We've had a change in plans." Colin looked to his brother. "Rowan's leaving town."

Becky's jaw fell open and she finally looked at Rowan. He was staring at her, just as she'd thought, his eyes dark and intense.

"Leaving town?" she asked.

Why would an innocent man leave town in the middle of the night when his wife and child have been kidnapped?

Because he's not innocent after all.

Rowan took two purposeful steps toward Becky, making her start. "And I need you to come with me."

Chapter 5

"What?" she snapped.

"I need your help, Becky. Your computer skills." His eyes were pleading with her, begging, and she was drawn into their depths.

Colin cleared his throat. "Why don't we sit down and explain."

"I think that's a good idea," said Gwen.

Rowan kept his coat on. "They're starting to think I had something to do with their disappearance."

Becky couldn't help herself. "Did you?"

"How can you ask me that?"

"Hey, I don't know you from Adam."

"I think you do."

"Careful, Rowan, or I might get the wrong impression." She glared at him, waiting for the comment to hit its mark.

He closed his eyes. When he spoke, his voice was eerily calm. "I'm sorry about that. I didn't have a choice. Ellington was starting to suspect you and I are lovers."

Heat rushed through her body at his words, and she knew she was blushing. She shrugged dramatically. "Why would he think that?"

"Why? Because you're beautiful, and you show up out of the blue right after they disappeared, and…" He shook his head. "I'm nervous around you. I can't be cool."

Time seemed to stand still.

He feels like I feel.

Gwen stood. "I'm going to get some more ice cream."

"Stay," said Colin, and she sank back down.

Becky had all but forgotten they were here, and she was flooded with embarrassment anew. For someone who was rarely embarrassed by anything, she was going into serious embarrassment overload.

Rowan was staring at her again. "I didn't want them to think we were together, so I had to get you to leave."

"Why are you here, now?" she asked.

"The painting, the forgery. Tamra's not just a curator for the Uffizi, she's also a forgery buff. Her father is huge in the art world. She grew up in that community, dinner conversations steeped in art thieves and forgers. It's a hobby of hers. She has countless images and exemplars from the best forgers in the world. If she weren't missing, she's the only person on Earth I would go to and ask who painted that picture."

Colin leaned forward. "Find the forger, find the thief."

Becky shook her head. "I don't understand. What can I do to help?"

"I need her computer files, but her computer's missing from the hotel. I need to get her files from her backup service, but I don't have the password."

"But you're sure she uses one?"

He nodded. "About six months ago she dropped her laptop on the sidewalk, cracked the motherboard. She bought a new one and had all her files restored from FileSafe."

Becky looked at Gwen accusingly. Julie was a Vice President at FileSafe, and Gwen damn well knew it.

Gwen pursed her lips. "I may have mentioned the relationship."

"So, have Julie do it. Or better yet, why not ask the police or the FBI?"

"To the police, I'm already guilty." He held up his palm and Becky could see the bits of ink left from where they must have fingerprinted him, and she gasped. *Mr. Mitchell is cooperating with law enforcement and helping us find his wife and son. That's all for now.* Until we arrest him for kidnapping and murder, that is.

Becky shook her head. "What about Julie?"

"I already spoke with her," said Gwen. "And she's willing to help by changing the limit on the login attempts so you don't trigger any alerts when you're trying different passwords. Beyond that, she felt you and Rowan would have a better chance of determining the correct combination."

She was right, of course. Cool-headed Julie was always right. But Becky didn't want to go anywhere with Rowan Mitchell, no matter the reason. "I don't understand why you need to leave town. We can do this right here."

"From a jail cell?"

"If it came to that, yes."

Rowan raked a hand through his hair and she noticed tiny beads of sweat on his brow. "The police aren't even looking for them, don't you understand? Neither is the FBI. They've spent more time interrogating me than they've spent looking at the surveillance tapes from the museum." His eyes bore into hers. "No one's out there trying to find my family, Becky. No one but me."

His words sank into her spirit. If that was true, it was a terrifying scenario. Where were Tamra and Anthony right now? Were they afraid and alone? *Or worse yet, not alone at all?* A horrible vision appeared in her brain, mother and child, dead, blood everywhere, the image overlapping with the snapshot of the beautiful woman in the bathing suit, holding the smiling little boy.

Colin spoke up. "I'm going to stay here. Use my connections with the U.S. Marshal's office to apply some pressure to the investigation. Get them exploring other leads."

That made sense. It all made sense in some crazy way.

Clarity settled over Becky, a calmness that was so unlike her she might have been frightened. Outside, a gust of icy winter wind pushed through the streets, up the wide stone steps of her Craftsman bungalow to the bright red door, blowing it open with a flourish. That door always needed a good pull for the latch to catch, and even though she knew it, Becky couldn't help the shivers that ran up her spine.

Rowan rushed to the door to close it again, and Becky followed him slowly, nearly there when he turned back around. "We may not be able to figure out the password," she said.

"I know."

His eyes were dark and ominous, the stress of the day showing in their shadows. Becky wondered what she was agreeing to, even as the words slipped past her lips. "But I will help you try."

~~~

"Whose house is this?" Becky asked as she made her way up the snow-covered steps, several inches of powder compacting beneath her feet with a crunch. She'd slept while Rowan drove her car out of Boston, the sunrise just beginning to crest when she awoke, which told her they couldn't be far from the city despite this seemingly remote location.

The house was small and stone, with a wooden porch and a detached garage. Becky's orange car was now parked inside it, protected from the flurries that continued to fall from the sky at a rapid pace. There were no other houses in sight.

"A friend's." The front door had a keypad instead of a lock, just as the garage had. Rowan entered several numbers and it opened.

He stepped back for her to go in first, and she took in her surroundings. Hardwood floors, a painted brick fireplace, and modest furniture that reminded Becky of her parents' house in Florida. "Where's your friend?"

"He doesn't live here. It's a vacation home." He walked over to the wall and adjusted the thermostat. "That's going to take a while to warm up. I'll make a fire." He left the room, and Becky heard a door open and close.

She began to explore. A tiny dining room led to the kitchen, an eclectic mix of old cabinets and modern appliances. She opened the refrigerator and was surprised to find it stocked full of groceries. The backdoor opened and Rowan entered, carrying an armful of wood. "Your friend come here in the winter?" she asked.

"Sometimes. He uses it as a hunting cabin."

She watched him disappear into the other room and withdrew a gallon of milk. She checked the expiration date, her brow furrowing. Kneeling down, she opened a crisper drawer full of fresh produce. "Maybe he's been hunting Sasquatch."

"What?"

"Sasquatch. Someone's been here. There are groceries."

Rowan appeared on the other side of the refrigerator. "Yeah. I asked him to go shopping for us."

That's weird.

"Fire's going."

She stood and looked into his face. "You need some sleep."

He shook his head. "Too much to do."

He was right, of course. They didn't have time for such luxuries at the moment, and she felt suddenly guilty. "I'm sorry I fell asleep in the car."

"No. Don't be. We didn't have Wi-Fi access there, anyway."

"You sure there is Wi-Fi here?"

"Yes."

She nodded. "Let me grab my computer and we'll get started."

Twenty minutes later, they were settled on the couch before a raging fire, Becky's coat over her lap like a blanket to ward off the last of the cold.

"Let's start with birthdays." She held a notebook and pen, her computer beside her on the couch.

"Seriously?"

"Yes, why?"

He shrugged. "I don't know. You're this big techie person. I thought you'd try something more sophisticated than birthdays."

"Movies have ruined cryptography forever. It's not that easy."

He looked at her like she was crazy. "My email account has been hacked into twice this year. How hard can it be?"

"That's totally different than FileSafe. Look, the only way I'm going to get into Tamra's account is to correctly guess her password. But I can use the computer to help me. It will auto-generate possible passwords based on the information I tell it to use, then work in the background while I'm trying my own passwords at the same time. The computer's more likely to hit on something than I am, but even still it's not terribly likely."

"You mean we might not get in at all?"

"I told you that, Rowan."

He looked at the ground. "What do you think? Are we going to get in, or is this just a waste of time?"

"I wouldn't put all of your eggs in this basket, if that's what you mean."

He nodded.

"So, give me birthdates."

One by one, she wrote down birthdays for Tamra, Rowan, and Anthony, along with the date of their wedding anniversary, mentally noting that Tamra must have already been pregnant when they married.

None of my business.

"Do you know their Social Security numbers?" she asked.

"They're Italian, they don't have Social Security numbers. They have Fiscal Codes, but they're not arbitrary like Social Security numbers. If you know enough information about someone, you can usually figure out their Fiscal Code." He pulled out his wallet, handing her a Post-It note. "There are our numbers. I can never remember them."

"I can see why." The numbers were long, consisting of sixteen alphanumeric symbols. She carefully copied them to her notebook and gave the paper back to Rowan. "What's your Social?"

He rattled off the numbers.

"Do you know any passwords that Tamra uses on other accounts? People tend to repeat them, or parts of them."

"Ninety-eight forty-four is our bank card PIN."

"Did she pick that, or did you?"

"She did. She had the account when I met her."

"Anything else?"

He stood and put his hands in his pockets, gazing into the fire.

"What's wrong?" she asked. He was quiet for so long, she thought he wouldn't answer.

"She could use the same damn password on everything, and I wouldn't know it."

His face was tormented, the glow from the fire the only warmth she could see. Becky wanted to ask more, wanted to understand this man and his relationship with his wife, but she didn't want to drag it out of him.

She wanted him to tell her because he wanted her to know.

"Becky, my wife didn't share her life with me." He slowly turned to face her. "Not her passwords, not her feelings, and not her bed."

She stared into his eyes, her mouth gone dry. It was none of her business. It was completely her business. She didn't know what to say. Moments ticked by before she let her eyes fall to his chest, breaking their connection.

He laughed without humor. "There you have it. Tamra and I were married in name only."

"What about Anthony?"

"I slept with her when we met." He turned back to the fire. "Then I went back to the States, never expecting to hear from her again. I think she felt the same."

"But she was pregnant."

"Yes."

"Whose idea was it to get married?"

"Mine."

Becky nodded, unsurprised. She, too, stared at the fire, thinking of this certain hell. Rowan may not love his wife, but he was married to her nonetheless. They shared a child together, and a tragedy in the making.

I'll love him forever.

The thought surprised her and she laughed quietly, a bitter sound. Becky, adored by men who could never matter to her, falling only for the one she could never have.

Her mind made a conscious effort to point out how little she really knew the man, but it was useless to argue with her emotions. A log popped, sparks flying into the room as she jumped, watching as he calmly stepped on a burning ember to extinguish the fire. "I'm so fucking tired," he said.

She knew he was talking about more than the lack of sleep. "Go take a rest. I'll get started while you're gone."

"No."

"Yes, Rowan."

He opened his mouth as if to argue, then closed it again and nodded. "Get me in two hours."

"I will."

~~~

Rowan stopped the use the upstairs bathroom. A large sticker was plastered on the mirror.

<u>Staying Safe at the Safe House</u>
- Stay indoors at all times
- Give all electronics to agent(s), including cell phones
- Stay hidden if anyone comes on the property
- Always do what the agent(s) tell(s) you to do

"Shit," he said under his breath, then began to peel the sticker off. The top layer separated from the sticky side, and Rowan wadded up the incriminating words and flushed them down the toilet. Whoever Marco asked to ready the safe house obviously forgot to check in here.

He then went to the bedroom, closed the door and pulled out his cell phone. His first call was to Enzo, though his father-in-law didn't answer. "Call me when you get this."

The second was to Marco Santini. "Thanks for getting the house set up for me."

"Sure thing."

"What's going on there?"

"Hang on." Rowan could hear Marco walking. "You're not going to believe this. Now the forgery's been stolen."

"What?"

"Yep. It's been gone for hours and nobody noticed. We just thought it got bagged and tagged. Somebody finally realized it never made it into evidence."

Rowan whistled. "It's got to be an inside job."

"Uh huh. And our good friend Gianni Amato about shit himself when he found out you were gone."

"Do you think he's involved?"

"I don't know, man, but somebody did it, and Gianni's all over me. Everybody's looking at everybody, trying to find the mole."

Rowan swallowed hard. "Anything on Tamra and the baby?"

"Nothing yet." Marco cursed under his breath. "How are you doing on the computer password?"

"She just started. Marco, we should have heard something from the kidnappers by now."

His friend was quiet. "Don't lose faith, Rowan. They'll be okay."

Artful Deception

Doubt mingled with fear, a sensation of true helplessness rearing up inside him. "Jesus. I hope you're right."

Chapter 6

Becky's laughter pealed above the crash of the surf and he chased her, red hair flying in the breeze. The scent of the ocean was everywhere, a gull squawked above them and the sun shone brighter than he'd ever seen before. A quick burst from his muscular thighs and he caught her, his arms wrapping tightly around the silky skin of her middle, so little and lithe.

"Let me go!" she screamed, pushing at him as she laughed, and he tickled her. She twisted in his hold and his hungry eyes landed on her nipple as it strained against the fabric of her bikini. It reminded him of his first glimpse of her at her house, braless and driving him crazy, only this time he could touch it. He could touch her, he could have her, he could possess her.

"Rowan…"

"Oh, yeah…"

"Rowan…"

"Becky…"

"Rowan, wake up!"

His eyes snapped open to find her sitting on the edge of the bed, and for a moment he stared at her with blatant lust, his breath coming quickly. Her eyes were wide and her lips fell open, her cheeks growing red and flushed.

"It's time to get up," she said quietly.

He sat up and braced his weight on one arm, his face close to hers, his eyes on her full lips that were waiting for his kisses. He leaned in closer and her eyes closed.

"You're not awake yet, Rowan," she whispered.

His lips touched hers and he was on fire. She was so soft, so willing and open. He leaned back in the bed, pulling her with him, their passion roaring to life in an explosive burst of heat and energy. He wrapped his arms around her waist and hauled her on top of him, her legs straddling his lap.

You're not awake yet, Rowan.

Her words mocked him and this moment, his desire for this woman fighting his memory of something else. Becky was here, in his bed, where he'd wanted her to be for such a long damn time. He'd dreamed of her, dreamed of this moment.

Then consciousness was there.

Tamra.

Tamra and Anthony are missing.

A cry escaped his throat and he sat up, awareness flooding his senses. Becky sat back and stared at him, unmoving, her face still. He was a wretch, a horrible man who couldn't bring himself to let her go, to push her away, to tell her to leave. It was the last thing on earth he wanted.

Gingerly, she brought her hand to his cheek and stroked the stubble there, then let her forehead rest softly against his. He was steeped in her scent, overwhelmed by her presence. He closed his eyes as her fingers ran through his hair, showing him with her simple touch that she knew his pain, would assuage it if she could.

His eyes burned and his arms closed around her waist, needing to feel her as close to him as she would allow. Becky's legs curled around his backside and he moaned, his lips again finding hers and loving her mouth with his own. It was wrong and he knew it, even as they moved together through the bedcovers as if they were making love. This woman could make it better. She could reach inside his very soul and heal everything that was wrong.

When she breathed out his name and arched her back, it was Rowan's undoing. He cried out and squeezed her hips to him, burying his face in her neck.

~~~

Enzo de Toffoli moved though the darkened room with the grace of a man half his age. His footsteps were light as a slippered child, sneaking for a glimpse of Santa Claus in the night, though Enzo himself had long since abandoned any romantic notions of good cheer and happiness. Life was business, and he was here to get his done.

In another lifetime he'd been a frequent guest in this house, welcomed and treated like family—a hearty prize for the boy who had none of his own. Cutting those ties had been like severing his own limb, and his mind was full of emotional memories as he worked.

He wore black from head to toe, as befitting a man who slips into the home of another, easily moving in on his target. Discovery would equal ruin, but Enzo had no intention of being discovered. He was comfortable in the knowledge that his old friend Leonardo was an exceptionally sound sleeper, who'd been the butt of practical jokes throughout their prep school days.

The large room was ornately furnished with a Persian rug and high-backed chairs, the scent of cut flowers perfuming the air. An enormous fireplace stood on the opposite wall, and Enzo moved toward it with anticipation. His prize waited to be collected, the ultimate win in a war that had been raging for decades.

Moonlight broke through the cloudy night sky, spilled its blue light onto the carpet.

"No…" he whispered, moving faster now, his eyes trained above the mantel. The frame was not befitting the *Madonna*, the wood simple and plain, the size too small, and Enzo felt rage rise up and fill his lungs. Shapes came into view, first lines, then the muted colors of grass and trees.

He stood before the illuminated canvas and forgot to breathe.

He would recognize Claudia's work anywhere, though he had never seen this particular piece. Sometimes in dreams he wandered through her paintings like he once reveled in her presence, her long brown hair gently curling around her porcelain face. He could almost see her reclining in the sun-spotted grass, a lazy smile gracing her deep pink mouth. Enzo stepped even closer to the hearth, longing to turn on a lamp as the greens and yellows came into focus, the sharp bits of dark tree trunk bolder now as he made out their shapes.

And just there, beyond the brightest sunlight, the form of lovers.

Reaching into his pocket, his hand grasped the knife and he exposed the blade, fingers clenched around its shaft. This was not why he came, but he could not let this picture alone. Not here, not in this house, not with this man. He brought his arm up

Artful Deception

above his head, intending to strike even as the muscles of he shoulder froze in utter stillness.

There is so little of her left, anywhere.

The world had gone on without Claudia de Toffoli as if she had never existed, never loved him, never died. Tears welled in his eyes as he stood there—her image in his eyes, her scent in his nostrils—until his arm, now weak from the strain, fell to his side.

Time passed and the moon was again shadowed before Enzo was able to move his feet.

Determined now, he resolutely checked every room, under beds and in the backs of closets, even the cellar where he played with Leonardo as a boy, and the shed where the gardener kept his tools. If the *Madonna Fornirà* was here, it was well hidden. But if not here, where?

He stepped into a wide kitchen and a small flash caught his eye, the blinking message light of a cell phone. Unlocking the screen with a swipe, he saw Anthony's familiar features, but failed to comprehend how one part of his life had just layered over another like a leaf fallen on a fire. Staring back at him was a picture of his very own grandson, with Claudia's eyes laughing back at him from the grave.

The sound of someone walking upstairs nearly made him jump, and Enzo pocketed the cell phone before slipping out the way he came, back into the cover of darkness.

~~~

Becky threw another log onto the fire and sat back down at her computer. She was getting bleary-eyed from trying to figure out Tamra's password for her computer files, feeling like a hack. What made her think she'd be able to crack someone else's password, just through trial and error?

She heard the water from the shower stop running and looked to the stairway. Rowan would be down soon, and she'd have to face him. A deep-seated self-loathing had settled in place of her lust, making her sorry she had agreed to come with him on this journey. What would the wife of this man use as her password, her secret passion, a little window into what was important to her?

Becky typed, "sorryisleptwithyourhuband"

INVALID PASSWORD
"eventhoughididn't*actually*sleepwithhim"
INVALID PASSWORD
"iknowitwasstillwrongandimsorry"
INVALID PASSWORD
"hopeyouandthelittleguyaredoingokay"
INVALID PASSWORD

Rowan started down the stairs and Becky felt her belly clench. "How's it going?" he asked.

A second after he walked in the room, the scent of soap and fresh clean man assaulted her. "Not so good," she said.

"No?"

"No." She met his eyes, his stare too personal, too close. "Why are you looking at me like that?"

"Like what?"

She scowled at him.

He put his hands up. "Sorry."

"Yeah. Well, keep your hands to yourself from now on, okay, mister man?"

"Whoa, wait a minute. I wasn't the only one in that bed."

Becky slammed her computer shut. "No, you weren't. And frankly I feel like absolute shit about it, okay? So can we please move on and not go there again?"

Rowan sat beside her. "Becky, don't feel bad about what happened between us."

"There's a perfectly good couch right over there," she said.

"We have to talk, and then I have to go."

"We don't have to talk. You can leave right now."

"Yes, we do." He ran his hands through his wet hair. "I didn't tell you everything about Tamra and me."

"Listen, Rowan. I really don't want to play marriage counselor between you and your missing wife."

"Well, I really need to tell you. I think it would help you to hear it." He shook his head. "I asked her for a divorce before we went to the museum yesterday."

The first ray of hope shined into her befuddled mind. "Why?"

"Because I don't love her, and Anthony's not my son. Tamra was already pregnant when I slept with her."

"Then why did you marry her?"

"Because I didn't find out he wasn't my son until about two months ago."

"How did you find out?"

"I just had a feeling. I ignored it for as long as I could." He smiled a sad smile. "I love him. It took me a long time to do what had to be done. I had my doctor run our DNA to find out for sure."

"Do you know who the father is?"

"No idea."

Becky shook her head. "You don't think the real father has anything to do with this, do you?"

He turned his head to stare at her. "I hadn't thought of that."

"I mean, if he knew Anthony was his child, maybe he wanted him back."

"That's possible. But the painting, the *Madonna Fornirà* has to be part of this, too." Rowan stood and began to pace. "Crap. Maybe I'm overthinking it and you've hit the nail on the head. I'll call Marco from the car and let him know."

"Who's Marco and where are you going?"

"Marco Santini. The FBI agent."

She wasn't good with names, but it seemed odd that Rowan and Santini were on a first-name basis. "Okay."

He smiled. "I have a cousin named Marco."

"I was wondering how you remembered his name." She opened the cupboard. "And where are you going?"

"I have to check on a few things."

She closed the cupboard and raised an eyebrow. "You have to check on a few things?"

"Yeah."

"So… you're not going to tell me where you're going."

He sighed heavily. "I'm going to see about Anthony's DNA."

"What do you mean, see about it?"

He faced her. "I'm going to get Anthony's DNA results from my doctor and see if Marco can run them through the FBI's computers."

"What are we, on *Dragnet*? That's a little far-fetched, don't you think?"

"Anthony's grandfather's an ambassador and there are stories of art thieves in the family tree. It never hurts to look. Besides, they can check for relatives now, too, not just parents. Maybe it will give us something to go on."

There's something funny going on here.

She wasn't sure exactly what it was, but something just wasn't quite right. She bristled at her suspicion that Rowan wasn't being honest with her, but saw no benefit in challenging him at the moment.

Gwen's words echoed in her mind. *I was standing right next to him, and I didn't believe him.*

Amen, sister.

"Ask him if I'm related to the Pope while you're there."

He grinned. "I'll do that."

"Are you going to be back in time for dinner?"

"Probably. Give me a few hours." Rowan peered at his smartphone, seeming to check his messages.

Becky opened a cupboard. "Whoever did the grocery shopping did a great job."

He looked up. "Huh?"

"I said whoever did the grocery shopping did a great job."

"Oh, yeah."

She knew she should let it go, even as she heard herself ask the question. "Who did the grocery shopping?"

He looked up, wide-eyed. "My friend. Bill."

"The hunter?"

He nodded.

"What does he hunt?"

"Moose."

She raised her eyebrows dramatically. "Moose?"

"Yeah. See anything for dinner?"

Becky scowled at him. Her dad was a hunter, and she knew damn well no one was hunting for moose in these woods. He was lying to her, an offense she took very seriously. "Maybe there's some moose in the freezer."

"You know, don't even worry about cooking. I'll pick something up on my way back. We need to come up with that password."

"What about 'Bullwinkle'. That might be the password."

He looked at her.

"Or bullshit." She smiled. "Or 'you can suck it if you think I'm going to believe a damn thing out of your mouth after this.' That might be the password."

He put his phone on the counter with a thud. "Deer?"

"Yes?"

He shook his head. "I meant to say deer, not moose."

She stepped close to him, her hand on her hip. "Don't know when to cut your losses and come clean, do you, cowboy?"

"This is ridiculous. What difference does it make what he hunts?"

"What's your friend's name again?"

"Bill!"

"It makes a difference because you lied to me. People who lie to me don't get the chance to do it again. If you're lying to me about moose, what else are you lying about? Huh? Maybe that wife of yours isn't such a bad person after all. Maybe you're not really going where you say you're going. Maybe you're just trying to get me into bed, you dirty slimebag cheater man." She stormed out of the kitchen and dropped onto the couch, then opened her laptop. "As soon as we figure out this damn password, you are on your own, mister. I am so outta here."

"Becky, you can't seriously think I would lie..."

"We're done talking about that." She held her hands frozen over her keyboard, then clenched her hands in frustration. "We need the name of the baby's father. Someone she cared about. Something besides Fiscal Codes and birthdays."

He picked up the keys off the counter. "I'll see what I can do."

Chapter 7

Becky was quiet for a long time after he left, the tapping of her fingers on the keyboard the only noise in the cabin. He was right that she needed to be working on the password, but frankly she was running out of ideas.

She stood and went back to the kitchen. She found real crystal glasses and poured herself a glass of red wine. The alcohol hit her empty stomach with an acidic splash, and she took another sip before turning to stare into the well-stock refrigerator.

Who was this woman who was married to Rowan? Was she sentimental, the type of person who would use the name of an important person or event? Or was she analytical, choosing passwords strictly for their unlikely combinations? If it was the latter, they were well and thoroughly screwed.

Becky opened what she thought was a pantry, which turned out to be the door to the basement. Her eye caught on a small sign.

<u>Staying Safe at the Safe House</u>
- Stay indoors at all times
- Give all electronics to agent(s), including cell phones
- Stay hidden if anyone comes on the property
- Always do what the agent(s) tell(s) you to do

Confusion crystalized into a strange kind of clarity. She squinted to read the small print at the end of the list. "Copyright 1982 by the Federal Bureau of Investigation."

She closed the door, walked to the table and sat down.

A safe house, like on TV.

What did it mean? Could this little house really be a place to hide people? Maybe that sign was nothing more than a joke, a silly sign that Bill or Bullwinkle or whoever actually owned this place saw one day at a flea market and just had to have.

Or maybe it was real.

Artful Deception

It rankled that he was lying to her, no matter the reason. Becky had a zero tolerance policy for liars, and the fact that she was still here, still trying to help this man, was a source of sheer frustration to her own good sense.

By the time Rowan returned nearly three hours later, she had worked herself up into a full-fledged snit. She heard his fingers on the keypad.

Keypad. Who has a keypad on their front door? Why, the FBI, of course!

"Hey," he said, stepping into the house and shrugging out of his coat.

"How did it go?"

"He's going to try, but he told me not to get my hopes up." He rubbed his eyes with a sigh.

"How long until we hear?"

"A couple hours. You have any luck here?"

"Not a bit. Oh, and I changed my mind, I'm not cooking. There's some moose jerky in the pantry you can gnaw on."

"We're back to that again?"

She slammed her laptop shut. "Open the basement door."

"Huh?"

"Open it!" She stook up and followed on his heels into the kitchen.

He opened the door and looked at the sign.

"Should I give you all of my electronic devices, Agent Mitchell?"

He closed the door. "I've got some fried chicken in the car."

"What?"

"I wasn't sure if you were cooking or not, and I didn't want to go hungry, but I didn't want to piss you off, so I left it in the car. But since you're already angry, I figured we could have dinner."

"Is that all you have to say for yourself?"

He opened the front door. "No. But it's all I'm going to say right now."

~~~

Rowan lifted the axe high above his head and brought it down swiftly, splitting the log in two. In his mind the noise was like a loudly ticking clock, counting down the moments until something horrible would happen to his son.

Not my son, really. But forever the son of my heart.

He wondered where Anthony and Tamra were right now, and immediately stomped on the thought. He would not wonder. He would not imagine. He would pray they were safe and unharmed and he would work his hardest to find them.

The axe came down again, sticking in the wood, and he yanked it back out, aware of the stinging in his eyes that threatened to destroy this façade of composure. He had to keep it together, or he'd never find his family.

He thought of Becky, her wild fire-kissed hair and glorious body rocking on his own, and longed to touch her again. She was troubled by what they had done. Hell, maybe he should be, too, but he couldn't be sorry, no matter how much he tried to conjure the emotion. He wanted Tamra to be safe, but he was not betraying anyone by loving the woman he'd wanted since the moment he met her.

Crack, and the wood cleaved again, his breath forming clouds in the icy evening air. It wasn't just Becky's body. He wanted her mind, her sweet conscience, her in-your-face attitude. This was a woman who could keep him on his toes.

Or on his knees.

Of course, she hated him now for the lies he must tell. There was no more pretending he was being truthful. Lying never came naturally to Rowan, though he had learned to do it and do it well.

But not with Becky.

It occurred to him that maybe he had slipped with her, revealed too much, because he didn't want to lie to her in the first place. A dangerous situation for an undercover agent to be in.

The ringing of his cell phone brought him out of his reverie, Marco's familiar number on the display. "What do you got?"

"Okay. You ready for this?"

Becky stepped onto the porch, her arms crossed over her chest against the cold night air, and Rowan held up one finger.

"We got two hits, paternal and kinship, and you won't believe either one of them. Anthony's real father is none other than our very own Interpol Agent Gianni Amato."

"*What?*"

"It gets better. Anthony's a kinship match to Leonardo Depaoli."

"The art thief?"

"That's the one."

"Holy…" Rowan swallowed hard. What did it mean? Gianni was there at the time of the kidnapping. That couldn't be a coincidence. Did he know Anthony was his son?

Was it possible he was the one responsible for their disappearance?

"Where's Gianni now?"

"He just went to the coffee shop across the street to get some bagels. Figured I should call you when I had the chance."

"Has he been at the hotel the whole time?"

"Far as I noticed, but he says he has to go soon to take care of some personal business. You think he's in on this?"

"I don't know. Shit, how could he not be?" He let the axe fall into the chopping block, the blade sticking in the wood. "Thanks for letting me know."

"You got it."

Rowan clicked off his phone and met Becky's curious eyes. "Anthony's biological father is an Interpol agent who was at the museum at the time of the kidnapping."

"The stuck-up guy with the gray suit?"

"That's the one. And Anthony's somehow related to the Depaoli family, who're best known for their great love of art, both legitimately acquired and stolen."

"That's one hell of a coincidence."

"I don't know what it means." He ran his hand through his hair. "Maybe Tamra's mother was a Depaoli."

"This is one doozey of a tangled web, Rowan."

"You've got that right."

She rubbed her hands up and down on her arms. "What's the name of the Interpol agent again, so I can try it in the computer?"

"Gianni Amato."

"Am I related to the Pope?"

"Half-cousin, once-removed."

"Sweet." She turned and walked inside, then reappeared a moment later. "Rowan?"

"Yeah?"

"Just now, you asked if that guy if Amato was still at the hotel. Weren't you just there?"

His features turned to stone.

She shook her head. "That's what I thought. You're lying to me again. Damn it, Rowan!" She stomped her foot. "Where were you today?"

The two of them faced off under the stars, long moments passing without a word. Becky was the first to move, turning on her heel and heading inside.

She wasn't gone five minutes when he heard her holler, "We're in!"

Chapter 8

"You didn't have to come with me," said Rowan as he drove in the darkness. The car picked up speed as he merged onto the expressway.

"That's true. I could have kept the homefires burning back at the cabin, so you could tell me all sorts of tall tales when you got back."

"Ha, ha."

"Who's joking? You lie to me more often than you tell the truth."

"That's not true."

"Whatever." She looked out her window. "So where are we going?"

"Leonardo Depaoli's house."

"The art thief."

"Yes. He's an old man who's somehow related to Anthony. Depaoli did a few really big jobs in the 70s and 80s, served some time with the feds after he was implicated in the theft of some Paul Klee paintings from the Guggenheim. He's kept a low profile since his release, but word on the street is that he's still very much involved in the black market sale of stolen goods."

"Word on the street."

He sighed.

She turned in her seat to face him. "Who are you?"

"I'm an avid art fan. When I owned my own publishing company in California, I did a lot of work in the fine art genre, including a coffee table book on art heists. They interest me. Always have." He handed her his phone. "Google it."

Becky ignored him and turned back around.

"It's true."

"Oh, I'm sure it absolutely is."

Rowan exited the expressway and they drove down a two-lane road in silence. The houses got bigger the farther they drove, with the occasional tennis court or horse farm visible in the distance. He rounded a wide bend and turned off the headlights.

"I don't think that's a good idea."

Ignoring her, he let the car drift to a stop as he pulled to the shoulder and engaged the emergency brake. They had a good view of the property, the wide house with its brightly lit grand entrance and rolling fields. Lights blazed from the lowest windows, squat and close to the ground.

"Someone's in the basement," he said.

"Maybe they're doing laundry."

"There aren't any other lights on in the house."

"Maybe they left them on for the dog." She met his glare. "I'm just saying, there might be a perfectly rational explanation for that."

"Maybe. Or maybe that's where he's holding Tamra and Anthony."

Her brows snapped down. "How did you get from A to Z and skip the whole rest of the alphabet?"

"Look, Leonardo's related to Anthony somehow, right?"

"Right."

"And Leonardo's a bad guy who's been known to do bad things, right?"

She rocked her head from side to side. "Right…"

"So, who's to say he doesn't know about this relationship to the boy and decide he wants to keep him for himself?"

"LMNOP."

"Exactly."

"I wasn't agreeing with you. So what now, Rambo? You going to go over there with your machine gun and shootout the place?"

Rowan leaned across her lap and opened the glove box, retrieving a small handgun.

"Whoa!" she yelled, her eyes wide. "Where the hell did that come from?"

"It's mine. You stay here. I'm going to go see what's in that basement."

"You put a gun in my car?"

Artful Deception

"Yes."

"My car is totally non-violent."

He looked at her, his lip quirked. "You have a peaceful, passive resistance, hippie chick kind of vehicle?"

"Yes, I do."

"I'll keep that in mind the next time I need to store firearms." He got out and disappeared into the darkness.

Becky stared at the big house. Was it really possible that Tamra and Anthony were in there? Had Leonardo moved from stealing works of art to stealing people instead? The thought was disturbing, the elegant estate taking on a sinister appearance in the moonlight. Minutes ticked by and Becky wondered where Rowan was now.

A car was coming up behind her and she sank lower in the seat. It passed, then slowed and turned into the driveway of Leonardo's house.

"Oh, crap. Oh, crap. Oh, crap..." she chanted.

The car pulled up to the closed garage door, and there, silhouetted between Becky and the house, stood Rowan. She breathed a sigh of relief, then watched in panic as he began to walk away from her and back toward the house.

"Oh, come on, Rowan!" Why couldn't he call the police, like anyone else? Did he really have to sneak up on the bad guys all by himself?

Another ten minutes passed before he returned, each moment seeming longer than the last. He opened the door and slid across the seat. "You were right."

"I was?"

"There's a big laundry room, and some storage."

She released the tension in her shoulders she hadn't realized she was holding.

He turned toward her. "And a baby's crib."

"But no baby?"

"No. That was Leonardo who just pulled in. He had a big pizza box. How many single old men do you know who order big pizzas for themselves?"

"Maybe he likes leftovers."

"Maybe. Or maybe he's feeding my wife and son."

Becky bristled at him calling them that, then immediately chastised herself. If there was anything wrong with the relationships here, it was with hers and Rowan's, not his with his family.

They drove back to the cabin, each of them thoughtful and quiet. There was simply too much to take in, too much to understand. Once inside the kitchen, they stripped off their coats, neither meeting the other's eyes.

"I'm going to take a bath," said Becky.

"Okay."

He looked so upset and vulnerable, she longed to reach out and draw him into her arms, but instead she turned away.

"Becky."

"Hmm?"

"Thank you."

"For what?"

"For coming with me tonight. For accepting that there are some questions I can't answer."

She nodded. There was more to say, she could see it on his face, knew that the scene would change dramatically if she simply took a step toward him. "You're welcome." She walked up the stairs and closed the bathroom door.

Safe in the small room, she let herself imagine she had taken that step, had crossed that line. Turning on the hot water, she slowly stripped off her clothes, pretending she was undressing before her lover.

She slipped into the huge tub, letting the water cover her legs and backside. The tub filled as she sank deeper. She longed to be home in her own bathtub, surrounded by her things, far away from Rowan and the frightening way he made her feel. She had all but slept with a married man, and knew she might do it again if she couldn't get away from temptation.

She loved him.

She couldn't explain why she felt that way, knew it didn't make any sense. Curling her legs up to her chest, she let her head fall back, wetting the top of her head, then rolled onto her side.

The sound of running water was loud and comforting beneath the surface.

She imagined he knocked at the door.

Come in, she would say.

He would see her naked body, the welcoming look in her eye, and take her here, right now. The thought made her arch her back, a light moan escaping her lips.

There was a knock at the door.

She sat up quickly with a whoosh of water. "What!" she shouted.

"Save some hot water for the rest of us."

She reached out and turned off the faucet. She didn't want to save him any water. She wanted him to be uncomfortable, to be unhappy, just like she was.

"Thanks," he said, and she heard him continue down the hall.

"Hey, Rowan!" she yelled.

"Yeah?"

Invite him in. There's plenty of room for two. She clenched her fists. "I'm going to bed after this. I'll see you in the morning."

He didn't answer.

"You hear me?"

"I thought we were gonna go over stuff."

"There's nothing to go over until the hard drive gets here in the morning. Right?" FileSafe was sending a copy of all of Tamra's files overnight priority delivery, with delivery by eight AM.

"Yeah, I guess."

"Then goodnight."

She listened to his steps retreat down the hall. It was better this way. In the morning, she'd help him load the files onto his computer and be on her merry way. There had to be a bus station around here somewhere. She leaned back, resisting the urge to fantasize about him. Fantasies only got you so far in life, and this one was going to get her in a hell of a lot of trouble.

The next thing she knew, she awoke to knocking on the door. "Are you alive in there?"

"I fell asleep. Sorry, I'll be right out." She flipped the drain and dried herself off, wrapping her body in a big brown towel. The hallway was dark, and when she turned out the bathroom light she saw him beside her, making her start. Her heart hammered in her chest. "Hi," she said.

He took two big steps toward her, surprising her, and kissed her passionately.

Was he waiting for me?

His arms came up and pinned hers to the wall, and she felt her towel begin to slip.

He pulled back just enough to speak before kissing her again. "I need you, Becky. Please don't send me away."

It was better than a fantasy, and her pulse pounded in her heated veins as he pressed his weight against her. His voice was a breathless plea. "I need you so bad." He reached around to her backside and squeezed her against him, making her knees weak. She'd never wanted a man this intensely, had never felt passion roar to life so quickly or with such force. She was wild, her arms snaking up his body to wrap around his neck as she let herself be carried away by this sharp wave of lust.

He's married, her conscience screamed.

But he doesn't even like her! She lied to him. She won't even sleep with him. She made him think the baby was his.

"Come to bed with me," he whispered, his breath coming in pants as his hands slipped beneath the hem of her towel to pull her tighter against his body.

If he's telling you the truth.

A sudden stillness settled over her.

He lied to you about this cabin. He lied to you about more than that, you know he did.

You can feel it in your gut. He's not being truthful.

Rowan leaned in to catch her lips and she raised her chin away from him.

"No, no, please..." he whispered.

She wanted to cry. She wanted to smack him across the face for tormenting her. "Let me go."

Slowly he dropped his hands. She reached up to grab her towel and secure it. "I'm not sleeping with you," she said forcefully, thankful for the darkness that hid her flushed cheeks and face. She was pushing away the one person she wanted more than anything, and she couldn't be trusted to do it in the light. "Leave me alone, Rowan. What happened earlier was a mistake. I shouldn't have done that and I'm sorry."

He moved toward her so slowly she was afraid he might try to kiss her again, but he only whispered in her ear, "Is this really what you want?"

"Yes." She closed her eyes to shut him out, listening as he leaned away from her and finally walked downstairs.

Chapter 9

The room was dark and musty, with block concrete walls and a bare concrete floor. Tamra assumed it was a basement, though her memory of getting to this place was jumbled and hectic.

Slowly she rocked, the baby's warm weight cuddled to her chest as she swayed. Anthony was asleep, but she wasn't ready to put him in the cold crib that had been prepared for him. Her lips grazed the top of his head and she inhaled his unique scent.

She would know her baby anywhere, just by the smell of him.

Finally she loosened her embrace and lowered the him to the mattress. He lay on his back, arms stretched over his head as if he had fallen asleep mid-yawn, and Tamra smiled lightly—the first happiness she could remember since this nightmare began.

Thank God Anthony was with her. She longed for safety and the comforts of home, but as long as she had her son, she knew she would be okay.

Heavy footsteps cascaded down the stairs and she stepped quickly to the door, slipping into the brighter room at the same time as her visitor. A sick dread boiled up within her at the rage she saw etched in his features.

"You haven't finished!" He was tall and wide, the dark curly hair on his head nearly grazing the ceiling.

"Leonardo only brought it to me a few hours ago, and I had to get the baby down to sleep."

The man dragged a wooden chair loudly across the floor, stopping in front of an easel.

"Get to work. We have only a few hours."

She swallowed against the dryness in her throat while she walked past him and took her place before the painting. A print of the real *Madonna Fornirà* hung on the wall behind it, and she considered where to begin. The lighting on the corona was the most obvious defect, and she picked up her palette and began mixing several hues of gold and brown.

He was standing so close behind her, she could feel his body heat on her shoulder. "I don't get it," he said. "How could she get some of it so perfect, then screw up the rest so bad?"

Tamra imagined her mother sitting before this same canvas some thirty years earlier. The mistakes were too glaring to have been accidental, Claudia too good an artist to have made them. "Maybe she did it on purpose."

"How long will it take you to fix it?"

"I'll have it done in time."

The man grunted and stepped away. She dropped her shoulders and took a deep breath before touching her paint-laden brush to the canvas. The scent of oil paints perfumed the air as she corrected the *Madonna*'s corona, memories of painting side-by-side with her mother drifting over her like the wind.

Look at the strokes, at the depth of the color variation. If you're going to copy someone's work, you have to take on their mannerisms, their tics. You have to be willing to trust their judgment as your own.

Tamra lost all track of time long before she finished.

Surveying her work, she stood and straightened her aching back, the light scrape of her chair on the concrete announcing her movement. The man came to stand at her elbow.

"It's good," he said.

"Yes, I think so."

He turned toward her, an unpleasant grin spreading across his face. "We have some time before he gets back." He ran his hand down her arm and she recoiled.

Tamra felt sick as his meaning registered. "No."

"Come on, baby." He chuckled, a thick sound that disgusted her as he stepped even closer and reached for her.

Tamra thought of running, the stairway looming in her peripheral vision, a possible means of escape, then thought of Anthony sleeping in the next room. She could never leave her son. "Get your hands off me!"

He leaned even closer, his body touching hers. "Oh, you're a feisty one…"

"Stop it!" She backed away and he caught her, his grip unyielding, real fear biting into her consciousness and she screamed.

Then his hand was on her mouth and she couldn't breathe. He worked to unfasten his pants and she tried to knee him in the groin, but missed. He stood upright and slapped her. "You bitch!"

In one horrifying moment, a gunshot ripped through the basement and into the man's head. Tamra yelled in staccato bursts, covering her mouth with her hand. Leonardo stood at the bottom of the stairs, gun still in his outstretched hand.

Tamra looked back and forth between the big man on the floor and the blood splatter covering the freshly touched-up *Madonna Fornirà*. Anthony cried from the next room, but Tamra made no move to get him.

"Are you okay?" asked Leonardo.

She nodded.

"That stupid bastard. I knew we shouldn't have brought him in, no matter his connections. The painting is ruined, and he scared you to death."

Tamra thought she might be sick.

"At least there's still the real one," he said.

Tamra stared at him, wide-mouthed, then turned and went to get the screaming baby.

~~~

The *Madonna Fornirà*'s soulful eyes seemed to bore into Tamra's conscience.

This is your fault.

"No, it's not," Tamra whispered to herself, dipping a swab into the heady solvent, rinsing it in a chemical neutralizer before bringing it back to the *Madonna*'s face.

The blood separated from the paint, one layer dissolving as the other remained intact. It was nasty work to wash away pieces of a human being, and her fingers trembled with the sheer force of will it took to remain focused on the task.

Leonardo walked up behind her, placing a cup of tea on the table. "Let me help you," he said.

"No. I've got it." She turned to look at him. "May I ask you something?"

"Of course."

"The painting over your fireplace. It's my mother's work. She had its mate in her sitting room." Her mouth twisted and she sniffed. "I used to stare at that painting for hours. So beautiful! Of course, I always thought the man in it must be my father. But it wasn't, was it?"

He suddenly looked quite old, the corners of his mouth pulling down. "No. I never knew she made two." He stared into the past. "We were in Florence on holiday. She insisted we have dinner in the woods, bread and cheese, a bottle of wine. We dined on a bed sheet from the hotel."

"Was she married to my father?"

He shook his head. "No. I thought she would be married to me."

"You loved her."

He frowned, his eyes gleaming. "Oh, yes. But I was a fool. A selfish, stupid fool who cared more for money than for love." He gestured with his hand, palm open, to the blood-stained painting spread before them. "I cared more for this than for your mother."

"The painting?"

"All of them. She could paint all of them, each so well. Carvaggio and Rembrandt, Renoir and Lautrec. I wanted the money she could earn selling her forgeries. I thought together we could be unstoppable."

Her mother would never agree. Claudia de Toffoli was a woman of great character with a sound moral compass. If she loved a man who wanted her to do wrong, she would sooner be without him than oblige. "She left you."

He nodded. "And married your father instead."

The pain on his face was evident, and Tamra reached out and covered his hand with her own. "She kept the painting close to her through all her days."

"As I have, mine." He smirked. "Sometimes I talk to that painting, imagining she can hear me."

A door closed in the distance and he raised both hands with a smile. "At last, my son has arrived." He turned back to Tamra.

"I hope you will treasure your love more than I treasured mine, my dear. For it only presents itself but once in a lifetime."

Chapter 10

Rowan dreamed of serpents, their thick muscular necks skewered with giant shards of wood, hissing and breathing fire. He didn't see Anthony anywhere, but knew his son was here among the beasts, the baby's cries piercing even over the roars and the violent thrashing of the serpents.

He had to find Tamra. She and the baby. A snake larger than all the other serpents stopped him in his tracks, rearing up as if to strike.

I have no weapon.
How can I defeat this monster?

The baby cried again and he heard himself cry out, "Tamra! Where are you, Tamra!"

"What's the matter, can't find your wife?"

Becky appeared like an apparition, her body barely covered by thin strips of fabric. She was voluptuous and strutted around like a streetwalker, her red hair blowing up and around her. Reaching up, she beckoned to their leader, the enormous snake lowering itself for her to climb on.

The baby cried out again and Rowan knew he should go in search of Anthony, but his feet stayed still of their own accord. There was evil standing between him and the boy, and he was rooted to this spot, spellbound by Becky as she rode the monster's serpentine back like a lover.

She's a distraction, sent here to keep me from finding them. It's a trick. You must go!

The thought forced him to look away from the spectacle before him, Anthony's cries seeming to come from all directions. Then Becky was beside him, the sharp nails of her fingers digging into the flesh of his arms as she purred, "Stay with me, Rowan."

"I have to find my family." He looked into her eyes and was mesmerized, all other thoughts vanishing as if spellbound.

Then he was kissing her wildly, all reminders of his purpose forgotten. There was only this woman who burst into his life like an explosion, leaving cinders and searing heat in her wake.

Never before had he felt so alive, so free and so desired. Passion pounded through his veins, no room for regret or excuses, and he clutched her body to his own.

A movement caught his eye and he raised his head, his eyes suddenly locking with those of his wife.

She stood just feet away, surrounded by hellish flames, holding baby Anthony. "Help me," she whispered, the words reverberating through his consciousness. The fire leapt up around her, and she vanished.

"Tamra!" he yelled, the word ripped from his throat like a piece of flesh. "Come back!"

~~~

Becky had woken with the dawn, which was certainly not her norm. She was high-strung, anxious to finish what she came here for and to get the hell out of Dodge. She made coffee and began working on breakfast.

This place was a palace of food choices. She dug out a muffin tin she'd spied yesterday and got to work filling each compartment with a different food, cheese and grapes, olives and crackers. She had just sat down to eat when the sound of an approaching vehicle brought her to the window.

It was a Fedex truck. The hard drive with Tamra's computer files would be on it, along with the new computer and Firewire Becky ordered yesterday after Rowan went to bed. It would be hard for her to leave if her personal computer had Tamra's files on it, and she had every intention of hitting the road as soon as she was able.

The delivery truck was like the cavalry, if only slightly less welcome.

She was looking forward to going home, she really was. She had enough of being Rowan's stress-reliever, his sexual distraction for everything that was going on in his life. Her feelings for him weren't enough to bridge the gap between their lives, and she was growing weary of wanting the only person on the planet she couldn't really have.

Opening the door to the chilly winter air, she said good morning to the driver and signed for the packages.

Artful Deception

There was no reason to wake Rowan until the files were installed on the new computer and accessible, so she let him sleep while she set up the machine, began the file transfer and ate her breakfast.

That was the plan, anyway. Before she heard *the yelling.*

It was guttural, like he was in pain. Becky stood outside his door and debated what to do. Clearly he was having an upsetting dream, but it seemed like an invasion of his privacy to just walk in. Besides, what if he slept naked?

Would that really be so awful?

She raised her eyebrows and turned the knob.

Rowan was stretched out on his back, moaning loudly, a thin blanket covering him from the waist down. It was instantly obvious that she shouldn't have opened the door, but she didn't move as she watched him thrash and heard his breath come in ragged, excited bursts.

The skin along the back of her neck grew hot and tingly. She lifted one foot to get closer to the bed, some half-formed, ill-advised plan taking shape as she moved.

You shouldn't do this. Turn around right now and get out of this room!

Her cheeks were flushed and hot, her steps unsure.

See? This is why I need to leave this cabin. I can't stay here. I can't be trusted to keep my hands off this man.

Reaching out, she hooked her fingers on the blanket, sliding the covers down so she could slip in next to him, the side of his naked torso peaking out to tease her.

"Tamra!" he yelled out.

Becky dropped the blanket like it was on fire. She backed away from the bed, her ego shriveling like a cut flower.

She stumbled to her room, a horrible feeling of worthlessness clinging to her skin. Tears bit at her eyes as she grabbed the few belongings she'd brought on the trip and shoved them into her duffel bag. The file transfer was nearly complete, her obligation to this friend of a friend now fulfilled. There was nothing to keep her here, and every reason to leave.

She picked up the box with the address of this house, then used her cell phone to dial information.

Good thing I didn't give it to my agent.
"I need the name of a cab company that services this area."

~~~

Rowan threw the muffin tin into the porcelain sink with a loud crash. "Damn it!" he yelled, covering his eyes with the heels of his hands. Becky was gone, long gone, and there wasn't a freakin' thing he could do to get her back.

The computer on the table was open to a FileSafe restore window that claimed to be 98% done. How long ago did she leave, and why the hell did she sneak away like some kind of criminal?

He remembered the incident in the hallway, his hands groping her naked bottom beneath the towel.

You just couldn't keep your hands to yourself, could you? She told you she wasn't interested, asshole. Now she's gone.

He smacked his open palm hard on the table. "Damn it to hell!"

He didn't have time to go find her. He had to focus on Tamra and the baby. A flash from his dream tormented him, Becky as a distraction that was keeping him from finding his family. "Bullshit," he said out loud to the empty kitchen. "Bull. Shit. She was helping me."

He wandered to the window, fresh tire tracks visible in the snow. She must have called a cab to pick her up, the keys to her own car safely tucked in his pants' pocket.

What did you think, she was going to stay forever?

Rowan bristled at the direction his thoughts had taken. As much as he cared about Becky, it wasn't until that moment that he really considered their future. For the past year he had planned ahead only until the evening at the Gardner. Secure the painting in the museum. Extricate himself from this sham of a marriage. The future beyond this adventure never even entered into his mind.

But if he was going to have a real relationship with Becky, it had to enter his mind. He had to want her there, had to plan for her to be with him, had to make her understand. No wonder she ran away. He was living for the moment with a forever kind of girl.

An electronic chime brought his attention back to the computer screen.

Complete.

He clicked off the FileSafe program and found himself staring at an exact replica of Tamra's computer. Somewhere in all these files were clues that would lead him to his family. He just had to find them.

Rowan's chin touched his chest. He couldn't remember the last time he had prayed, but he couldn't remember ever having so much to lose.

Please help me find what I need to see.

Doubt covered him like darkness. Uncertain there was a God, uncertain there were answers, and unsure he could do any of this without Becky by his side.

Chapter 11

"Just pull over here," said Becky. "I'll walk the rest of the way."

The cabbie met her eyes in the rearview. "I come with you."

She rolled her eyes and huffed. "Look, I don't want him to see you. You'll get your money."

"So they always say, but I do not always get it. I come with you."

How could I be so dumb?

She got all the way to the bus terminal forty minutes from here before she realized she left her wallet in the bedroom and couldn't pay for the cab ride, no less a bus ticket out of this godforsaken town. "Suit yourself."

She glanced at the clock. Surely Rowan was awake by now, and she felt her stomach knot even tighter. She felt like a wayward teenager being returned home from the big city by the small town sheriff. Which was totally stupid, because she hadn't done anything wrong.

"Leave your things in the car," said the driver.

"Oh, don't worry, I will. I'm sure as hell not staying here."

She got out and took the front steps two at a time. Rowan opened the door when she reached for it, and her stomach fell when her eyes met his.

"Where've you been?" he asked. "I've been worried sick. I thought you left."

She pushed past him. "I did."

"You did?"

"Yep." She made a beeline for the stairs. "Just forgot my wallet." She retrieved it from the nightstand and turned to head back down, but Rowan blocked her bedroom door.

"What the hell, Becky?"

He looked mad, and her palms began to sweat. "What the hell, yourself. I wanted to leave, so I left. I'm a big girl. I'm allowed to do that. You got your computer."

He nodded. "You're leaving because of what happened last night."

"What?"

"Is that why you left?" He narrowed his eyes. "Because of what happened in the hallway?"

She scrunched up her face. *The man was obtuse.* "No."

He took a step toward her. "Then why?"

"It doesn't matter." She moved to step around him. "I've got a cab waiting outside."

"Then tell him to leave."

"No."

"Why?"

She was panicking. She didn't want to stay here in this house with him. Didn't trust herself if she did. *This house...*

"Whose house is this, Rowan?" She advanced on him.

"I told you. It belongs to a friend."

"That's a lie. Tell me the truth." She gestured to the cab outside. "Or I'm hopping in that cab and leaving right now."

He swallowed and stared at her intently.

"See you later."

He grabbed her arm when she tried to turn away. "I can't tell you, Becky. Please don't ask me."

She was suddenly furious. She'd had enough of these games, enough of the lies. "What does that mean, you can't? What the hell's the matter with you that you find a simple answer so incredibly complex? Is it an FBI safe house? Are you an FBI agent?"

"I would tell you if I could." He put his hands in his pockets. "I should have stuck to the freakin' moose story."

"I wasn't buying it."

"Now here we are."

They stared at each other, sizing one another up. It was Rowan who moved first, stepping close to her and closing the distance between them. "Trust me, Becky. I know that's a lot to ask, but I need you to trust me. I'm the good guy here."

I'm the good guy here.

Her gut told her it was true, but suddenly it was all too much. He was married, but if you listened to him, *he wasn't really married.* He was totally lying about this house and who it belonged to and who did the grocery shopping and hunting freakin' moose and about Marco and about God knows what else, but don't worry, *he's not really lying.*

Trust me.

"I don't want to trust you. I want a straight answer."

"I can't do that." He reached up and threaded his fingers through her hair, his short nails on her scalp giving her goose bumps, and she leaned into his hand.

Why am I letting him touch me?

Because it feels so good...

She could feel herself falling in, like a diver on a board falls into the water. Wasn't there some reason she didn't want to do this?

He's been lying.

The thought failed to get a reaction from her as Rowan's lips grazed hers, his teeth nibbling on her bottom lip.

Her mind went into overdrive, trying to focus on her reasons for turning tail just hours before.

Tamra! The scent of him thick in the room, the blanket slung low on his hips.

The cab driver honked his horn and Becky pulled back. She screamed toward the street, "Just a minute!" then turned back to Rowan and shook her finger. "If I stay here, we need to be able to drive a truck between the two of us. Do you understand? No touching, no kissing, no stares across the room."

He licked his lip. "Okay."

"You'd agree to anything right now."

"Maybe."

She nodded and took a deep breath. "I'll stay."

~~~

Becky expertly sliced two green peppers into thin long strips and added them to the bowl full of onions. Rowan was shifting through Tamra's computer files and there wasn't much Becky could do to help, so she figured she'd make herself useful.

She tried to remember the last time she made a meal for another human being. Christmas? Maybe Easter. Surely it was a holiday and she was related to everyone at the table. Now that Julie had moved away, Becky didn't have anyone in her life she was close enough to sauté for. The thought made her sad, and she dropped the knife to search for a big frying pan.

My life is full. I have a career. I date. I have fun.

Her defenses echoed in her head without finding purchase. She put the pan on the stove and turned the heat on high, a quieter voice now responding. It had always been enough, the life she had deliberately chosen, eyes wide open. But she now knew it would never be the same.

I want a family. A husband. I want a baby.

"Whoa, big fella," she whispered to herself, shaking her head. Where the hell did that come from? She was a woman of black and white with little tolerance for the variances in between. Two days ago she'd been completely content with her life, and now she was utterly unhappy with it. All because of *him*.

She stole a glance at Rowan in the next room. He was totally focused on his work, unaware of her stare, and she took the opportunity to observe him unnoticed. Was it any wonder she had a hard time keeping her hands off him? He was like a giant piece of man candy with a big red bow that said, "FOR BECKY".

Walking back to the stove, she added a small amount of oil and watched as it spread in a wavy circle. She threw in the vegetables, which hissed and popped.

Maybe once all this was over, she and Rowan could start from square one. Go to dinner and a movie without worrying about his missing wife, son, and marriage in general. What would it be like to be with Rowan, unencumbered? Would he still be interested in her months down the line? More important, if he lied to her now, would he continue to lie to her once their lives returned to normal?

She scraped the bottom of the pan with the spatula to unstick the onions, pungent steam rising into her face as a frown turned down one corner of her mouth. No matter how much time passed, she would still be interested in Rowan. Of that she was sure. Hell, he could probably stay married to Tamra for ten or twelve years, have a few more kids who really were his, then show up unannounced and she'd be all over him.

I'm such a loser.

Grabbing a red potholder, she opened the oven and withdrew a cookie sheet full of sizzling chicken nuggets and tater tots. Maybe she'd find someone else, and fall head-over-heals gaga for him, forgetting all about Rowan in the process. She tried to imagine what this new man would look like, but all she could see what Rowan's handsome face, mocking her imagination.

The food was ready and she should call him in, but she found she had lost the desire to share. *Let him go hungry for a while, then his wife can make him a sandwich.*

She was halfway through her fajita when Rowan walked in the kitchen and she looked up, cheeks full like a chipmunk.

"I found a strange email."

She spoke with her mouth full. "I thought you were looking at forgers."

"I did. I can't find anything similar anywhere. So I started going through her personal files." He got out a plate and began helping himself to the food, her eyes following him. "She wrote someone two weeks ago to confirm a meeting in Manchester, Vermont for tomorrow afternoon."

"So?"

"So, she was supposed to go back to Italy with me yesterday."

Becky stopped chewing. Rowan continued, "Unless she totally got her dates messed up. I mean, Manchester's not that far from Boston."

She forced herself to swallow, her mind well ahead of her voice. "But what if she didn't mess up the date?"

He turned to look at her.

"What if she had every intention of making that meeting, and no intention of going back to Italy with you." She could see the moment her meaning hit home.

"Anthony's father."

She nodded.

"You think she might be meeting Gianni, and leaving me."

"It's possible."

He sat down across from her, his features slack. "If you're right, you know what this means."

"Tamra wasn't kidnapped."

He checked his watch. "I need to call Enzo."

Chapter 12

Rowan sat in the car outside the historic inn and allowed his mind to absorb the impact of all that had happened. All through the three-hour drive to Vermont he'd avoided the doubts and recriminations that screamed at his subconscious, determined to get here before he allowed himself the luxury of exploring all the horrible possibilities.

Scenarios and conspiracy theories now clamored for his attention, a dull ache throbbing in his temple with every beat of his heart. It wasn't hard to imagine Tamra capable of such duplicity. It was far more difficult to believe she would steal the *Madonna* after her father had worked so hard to see its safe return. Enzo had worked for months on the touchy negotiations between the Uffizi and the Gardner.

Wasn't that what he'd been waiting for, as well? The relocation of the *Madonna Fornirà* to the Gardner? Rowan's objective all along, the reason he had stayed with Tamra as long as he did. Was it possible she was working to foil his attempt even as she smiled by his side?

Becky emerged from the building and headed for the car, and he felt the weight of his own troubles as he worked to put a less dour expression on his face. Soon he would be in his own hotel room, the privacy he craved at his disposal.

"All set," she said, sliding into the seat. "Pull around back, second door."

He pulled up in front of it, but left the car running. "I saw a liquor store back there. You want anything?"

"No, I'm good." She handed him a small envelope. "You're in 211, I'm in 209."

"Thanks."

~~~

The room was large, with a king-size cherry poster bed and matching armoire and dresser. Rowan threw his bag on the floor and stripped off his clothes, not bothering to close the drapes despite the darkness outside the window. He noticed the door to

Artful Deception

the adjoining room and was grateful it was locked. Becky could only complicate his already disjointed thoughts.

He stepped into a steaming hot shower and pulled the curtain closed with one yank. The temperature was punishing, just shy of injurious, and he reveled in the feel of it rushing down his skin. He bent his head and let the water pulsate on his skull, fighting his headache for the upper hand. When he couldn't stand the heat anymore, he stepped back, lathering his body with spicy soap and stretching out the muscles of his neck and back.

Back in the bedroom he tugged on clean briefs and poured several fingers of scotch. He turned off the lights and walked to the wide window overlooking a quaint village with a golf course and ski slope in the distance. The latter reminded him of his friend David's death and his first meeting with Becky, neither of which improved his mood.

He took a swig of his drink, allowing it to linger and burn, then took an even bigger breath. He didn't know what Tamra was up to, didn't know if she was responsible for this mess, didn't know if she was safe or in danger. He didn't even know if he cared.

But Anthony. Rowan's face contorted and a small cry escaped him.

Where was his boy?

Suddenly, every fear he had refused to dwell on, every horror he had tried not to imagine came to life in vivid color. His baby was lost and afraid. He was cold and hungry. He'd been abandoned and was utterly alone. Rowan rested his head on the cold windowpane and sobbed, scotch spilling to the floor, emotions overwhelming his spirit as great shakes racked his body. Anthony mattered more to him than any other human being in the world, no matter who shared his DNA, and the little boy was gone.

Rowan stood like that for a long time.

Becky stood in the shadows, her heart constricting with sympathy. Somehow she knew why he wept, could feel the emotions that crested over him as if they could drown all happiness in the world.

She hadn't intended to come in here—that wasn't part of her plan. She had meant what she said when she told Rowan she wanted to be able to drive a truck between them, yet she was utterly compelled to keep crossing that road.

It's not him. It's me.
I'm the one who wants this.

So she'd showered, taking her time with the soap and shampoo, preparing herself to love him. She bent at the waist and dried her thick hair, allowing her mind to explore the possibilities that awaited her.

She hadn't expected to find him like this, shattered and broken. It made her realize how hard he must work to appear in control, and she loved him even more than she had before.

When at last he turned around, he shook his head and frowned. "How long have you been there?"

"A long time."

"Great."

"It's okay."

"Whatever."

She walked to him and embraced his stiff body. "It's going to be okay."

"You should get outta here."

"No."

"Yes." He moved away and gestured toward the door, then walked to the desk and poured himself another drink, taking a long sip before turning back to her. "Becky, I mean it. Get out."

There was anger beneath his words, but she wasn't afraid. He needed her now. She could feel it, and she wasn't going to leave him in his darkest hour. "I'll take a scotch."

"Don't you freakin' listen?" he yelled, rounding on her. "I don't want company. I'm a goddamned wreck."

She felt his eyes travel down her body, suddenly aware of her stretchy t-shirt, the pants that hugged her shapely thighs. He stared at her sex before finally raising his eyes.

"Don't you get it?" He raised his hands in the air, his muscles clenched. "All I want to do is fuck you, forget all my problems and fuck you until I can't remember my own goddamn name. Do you understand?"

Becky's heart pounded like she was about to dive off a cliff, jagged rocks clearly visible beneath the sharp blue of the sea. She hoped the water was deep enough to catch her when she fell. This man was everything, her feelings for him all that mattered. She forged ahead on the thinnest ice of faith, her wobbly knees threatening to give out as she walked to the desk. "Guess I have to get my own drink, then."

"Get the hell out!"

She sipped at the fiery scotch, eager to wet the dryness that had suddenly invaded her throat. "No."

They faced off in the darkness. Becky took another sip, bolder now. Rowan didn't even twitch. "Don't you pity me, Becky. Don't you do it."

"Pity you?"

He moved toward her. "Don't make love to me out of some, 'Oh, poor broken Rowan' bullshit. If you come to me, you do it because you want me. Not because you feel bad for me."

"I do want you, Rowan." She put her drink down. "I've wanted you since the first moment I met you." It was only now she was able to separate the man from the circumstance, make it okay in her mind to follow her heart. Crossing her arms in front of her chest, she grabbed the hem of her t-shirt and pulled it over her head. "And pretty much every moment since."

His eyes were fixed on her breasts as she unhooked her bra and let it drop to the floor.

She pointed to the adjoining room door. "I was sitting on the other side of that door and all I could think about was you on this side of it. It wasn't even locked. How pissed would you be if I were an axe murderer or something?"

He didn't answer her, just stood there, staring at her nakedness. She resisted the sudden urge to cover her breasts as the moment stretched between them. Would he come to her, or would he send her away after all?

His voice was a throaty whisper, sending tingles down her spine. "Take off your pants." She hooked her fingers on the waistband and took them slowly to the floor.

"Panties, too."

He reached down and slipped off his briefs, her eyes drawn to him there.

He came to her, his arms snaking around her body as his mouth laid claim to hers. Never before had a touch felt so good, her skin sensitized and alive. He tasted like liquor and mint, the manly scent of him intoxicating her like the scotch spilling into her own bloodstream.

His hand trailed along her ribcage and her body moved against him, breath coming quickly.

"Please, Rowan…"

"You're ready for me already, aren't you?" he whispered.

She whimpered, her skin on fire. "Yes."

They came together quickly, as if every moment leading up to this one was part of their lover's dance, foreplay at its finest. The only touch they needed was the ultimate connection. She felt herself losing control, in awe of the sensations running through her. The emotional current electrified her, a new and powerful rhythm.

I love you.

The words stuck between her mind and her mouth, no way out and no way back in. There was only Rowan, the meeting of their bodies, and the sweet awakening of her heart.

~~~

The sky outside went from black to purple as Becky watched, the minutes streaming together into hours. She had slept after the second time they made love, and been awake since the third, enjoying the beating of Rowan's heart beneath her ear and the whoosh of his breathing in the darkness.

This might be their only night together.

She was a realist, first and foremost. There was no telling what tomorrow would bring, and the way she figured, it was more likely to end without Rowan by her side than with him there.

But I will have the memory of this night forever.

Gently she stroked her hand along his arm, his springy hair tickling the pads of her fingers. The last thing she wanted to do was sleep, needing to remember as much of this night as possible, for like Cinderella at the ball, she knew in her heart it could be only temporary.

The hotel phone began to ring, and Rowan jerked awake, breaking the spell that had settled over the quiet room while he slept. Becky moved off his shoulder so he could answer it.

"Hello?"

He met her eyes and mouthed the word *Enzo*.

She nodded and went to take a shower while he talked. She emerged ten minutes later in a cloud of steam, wrapped in a towel that barely covered her and disappointed to find Rowan out of bed and digging through his bag.

"Enzo wants me to meet him in half an hour."

"He's here?"

"He came into town after I called him yesterday."

She didn't like the idea of Tamra's father being so close to the bed she'd shared with Rowan. "Why does he want to meet?"

"I don't know." He walked to the computer and turned it on. "I need a map."

She knew better than to ask if she should join them. *Hey, Enzo, this is the-woman-I-boffed-all-night-long. Woman-I-boffed-all-night-long, this is my father-in-law.* She flopped on the bed and stared at the ceiling.

I refuse to be sorry.

"I'm going to hop in the shower," said Rowan.

"Okay."

"You all right?"

She smiled. "Yeah."

He leaned over her, bracing himself on the bed and kissing her soundly on the lips. "I forgot to say good morning."

"Morning."

"I'm sorry I've got to run..."

"It's fine, go ahead."

He nodded and stepped into the bathroom. Chilly now, Becky curled on her side and stared at the computer, a screensaver of famous works of art catching her eye. Several images in, she saw the *Madonna Fornirà*.

What was it about that painting that captivated so many people?

She threw back the covers, pulled the top one off the bed and wrapped herself in it, then sat down at the desk and hit the cursor back button until she once again stared at the painting.

Tamra must have lots of famous works on her computer; she was the curator of an art museum, for goodness' sake, but it seemed this particular painting was there every time Becky turned around.

The bathroom door opened and she called to him, "Look at this."

"It's the *Madonna Fornirà*," he said, coming closer.

"It just popped up on Tamra's screensaver."

"Well, it was part of the Uffizi's collection…" He leaned over her shoulder to get a better look. "Holy shit."

"What?"

"That's not the original. That's the forgery!"

Becky turned back to the screen. "How can you tell?"

"The light on her corona, for one. It's unidirectional. In the real painting its bidirectional."

"You're sure this is the forgery?"

"Positive." They looked at each other. "Which means Tamra had access to it before the reception at the Gardner." He shook his head and slammed his fist on the desk. "She wasn't kidnapped at all. Maybe she even painted the forgery herself!"

"She could do that?"

"I don't know. She's good. Maybe not that good." He hung his head. "Oh, Tamra. What the hell have you done?"

Chapter 13

Becky dressed and twisted her hair into a fat bun of wet curls, then sat on the bed with the room service menu. If she was going to be left behind, she was at least going to dine like a queen.

There was a knock on the door, which wasn't surprising to her in the slightest. As a rule, she never remembered to put out the "do not disturb" sign.

"No, thank you," she yelled.

A second knock, and she hopped up to answer it. The hotel must have thick doors, which was probably a good thing after the amount of noise she and Rowan made last night. The thought brought a smile to her face, but instead of housekeeping, there stood a silver-haired man in a jacket and tie.

"Yes?" she asked.

"I am Ambassador Enzo de Toffoli. I have come to speak with you about Rowan Mitchell."

There must have been some miscommunication. "Rowan just left to meet you, he's not here."

"I came to speak with you, miss. May I come in?"

Me?

Why the hell did he want to talk to *her*?

She thought of the bed, messy from her lovemaking with Rowan, her clothes mixed with his on the floor. "Uhm…"

"Please." His lips formed a hard line. "I have something you must see."

Becky stepped back and let him enter the room.

"You are…" He seemed to struggle to choose the right word. "Friends with my son-in-law."

"Yes." She looked at the picture on the wall.

"What is your name?"

"Becky O'Connor."

"Becky." He opened a brown briefcase she hadn't noticed he was carrying. A sick feeling a dread settled deep in her stomach. "Rowan is not who he seems."

Well hell's bells, I know that already.

"You have fallen for his lies, just like my daughter, and now she is missing, possibly worse." He closed his eyes. "Rowan is a criminal. He is a murderer. I suspect he is responsible for their disappearance."

She stood up quickly. "That's bullshit. He's trying to find them."

"Is he? Tell me, what has he done?"

Becky thought of the time they spent at the cabin, working to find the password, but she said nothing.

Enzo stood. "He ran away. He hid in the woods."

"How do you know about that?"

"I've been watching him."

A sense of violation wafted through her like nausea. What exactly did that mean? Had he been watching them when they thought they were alone?

"I'd like you to leave," she said.

"I have evidence." He opened his briefcase. "If I can save another woman, then maybe my Tamra's disappearance will not have been in vain. You know her kidnapper was an art thief."

"Yes."

He threw an envelope on the desk and gestured for her to open it. "Rowan Mitchell is an art thief."

Hundreds of pictures were inside, the group like stills from a video camera. They showed Rowan dressed in black, in what looked like an art museum. "What are these?" she asked.

Enzo picked up the pile and held them out to her, then fanned through them quickly. Just like an old movie projector, the images before her become one animated film. Rowan took a painting off the wall, then a guard emerged, brandishing a weapon. The guard fell to the ground and Rowan knelt beside him. A blonde man who was also wearing black emerged from off-camera and gave Rowan a high-five.

Becky couldn't breathe. "I don't understand. What is this?"

"The robbery of the Uffizi, a year and a half ago."

Enzo put the stack of photographs down and picked up an envelope. He pulled out a newspaper article. "This is the man who was killed during the robbery."

Artful Deception

Her eyes glazed over as words jumped from the page. *Father of three. Devoted husband. Burglary gone wrong.*

"Another guard was bound and gagged. He managed to free himself and reactivated the security cameras that Rowan and his partner had disabled."

"How did you get these pictures?"

"The theft took place at the museum where Tamra works as a curator. The chief of security shared them with her after he met Rowan at the company Christmas party."

She narrowed her eyes. "Why didn't the security guy go to police, if he thought he'd figured out who did it?"

"He did. They referred him to Agent Marco Santini at the FBI."

I have a cousin named Marco.

Becky's head dropped into her hands. "Oh, my God..."

~~~

Rowan snapped his harness to the cable and deftly descended into the rotunda, his soft shoes landing on the polished marble floor with barely a sound. The motion sensors and surveillance cameras had been disabled through the computer control system with a password given to him in an email. Rowan didn't know where it came from, but he didn't really need to know, either.

All that mattered was access. Access was ninety-nine percent of the fight. Getting inside and actually lifting the precious paintings from their gilded nests was simple compared to creating the opportunity to do so. He gestured to his partner and waited as the other man dropped like a spider into the great hall. Ruud was his name, a Dutchman, more than that Rowan didn't know. They'd been introduced only three days prior at a clandestine meeting in the Italian countryside.

It was the first time Rowan met the man who would become his father-in-law. Enzo had stood tall in a plaid button-down shirt that seemed somehow too casual for his regal bearing. "We move on Thursday," he said.

"We need to study the layout, the security systems, that's not enough time," said Rowan. Thursday was only two days from now.

"It has to be Thursday, that's when our man is working. You will learn what you need to know quickly. You will disable the interior security systems before you go in. Only the perimeter alarm and the door and window sensors will remain for you to deal with."

"What about guards?" asked Rowan.

"Two. One circles between the rotunda, the fountains and the long gallery, the other handles the mezzanine and the first floor. I've been assured the upstairs guard will not be coming downstairs, so you have only to handle the downstairs guard. He is armed, of course, as you both will be."

"If we fire a weapon in there, it will trip the alarm," said Rowan.

The Dutchman addressed him for the first time with a smile. "So don't fire your weapon." He laughed.

Enzo lit a long thin cigar and took several quick puffs. "The downstairs guard must log in at the security station between midnight and twelve-o-five. You will slip into the rotunda when he is gone, and wait for him in the shadows. Tie him up. Take his radio and weapon."

The instructions played in Rowan's mind as the nylon rope in his hands caught the security light. He wound the rope around the guard's wrists as the guard grunted in pain, whether real or fake, Rowan couldn't tell. Ruud held the guard in an effective choke hold, his wiry arm keeping the other man quiet. Rowan taped the guard's mouth, wrapping the roll completely around the other man's head before tearing off the end and moving to bind his feet.

Once the guard was secure, they moved into the long gallery and zeroed in on their target. There were several pieces they hoped to acquire this evening, but *The Lady in the Long Blue Dress* was number one on their list. Valued at more than seventy million dollars, it was easily one of the most valuable paintings in the museum. Rowan stepped over the rope that separated it from the visitor's area and spread his arms wide to lift the heavy gilt frame.

He felt it slip from its hook and exhaled the breath he hadn't realized he'd been holding. Despite his knowledge of the security systems in place, he half-expected some loud alarm to go off when the painting was taken down from its perch.

They worked quickly to strip the canvas from its frame, then rolled it and secured it in a long tube from Ruud's duffle bag before moving on to the next painting, a small portrait of a girl by Renoir valued at more than twenty million. They worked in silence, deftly packaging the masterpieces and moving to the next until they had exhausted their list.

"Upstairs," said Ruud with a wide smile and a challenging nod.

"We got what we came for."

"I want the Degas."

Rowan didn't need to ask which one. It was one of the master's most famous works, and a personal favorite of Rowan's. It was dangerous to deviate from the plan and he knew it, even as the adrenaline in his body said he was up for anything. He felt an answering smile touch his lips. "Okay, but it's the last one."

~~~

An expressway loomed in the distance, its on and off-ramps seeming to tangle together like worms in a can. Rowan was standing in the parking lot of what had once been Pat's Family Diner, the pavement beneath his feet now cracked and buckled, dotted with piles of melting snow, watching the traffic and wondering what the hell happened to his father-in-law.

Enzo was late, more than forty minutes, and he wasn't answering his cell phone. Rowan might have been concerned, but his mind kept returning to memories of with night with Becky—the eagerness of her body, the soothing calmness of her soul. It was as if with one night she had tempered the bitterness that had haunted him and brought back a piece of happiness he thought was lost forever.

He remembered her face, all flushed, her lips falling open.

Why I am in an empty parking lot, while she's alone in our hotel room?

"Screw this." He climbed in the car and started the ignition, already imagining what he would do to her when he got there.

Artful Deception

A silver sedan pulled into the parking lot, stopping some thirty yards away, and Rowan cursed out loud. Enzo got out of the sedan and began walking, his trench coat flying behind him in the warming wind like a cape.

Rowan stepped out of his car. "What happened to you?"

"I was tying up some loose ends." He withdrew a long, narrow box from his breast pocket and peeled off a layer of cellophane. "Sorry to keep you waiting, Agent Mitchell."

A stillness took over the scene. The noise from the expressway now seemed muted in comparison to the sudden chaos in Rowan's mind. He had trained for this moment. Prepared for it as much as anyone ever could.

Discovery.

A death.

The death of a character, the mask of whom he had worn for so long it felt like his own skin. Deep cover was unlike any other assignment. You became the mobster, the biker, the art thief, the murderer. You sympathized with the world around you, came to love the people within your life, good and bad alike. You saw yourself as you projected yourself to be, becoming the manifestation of your own design.

He flashed back to the wedding, remembering the white latticework covered in flowering vines, Tamra stunning in form-fitting off-white. He'd been hopeful then that they could make a life together with their child, believing he could make love appear through hard work and determination. Tamra and their guests didn't know it, but Rowan had been grieving, that day. Mourning for the life he would never return to.

A life he could now have, with Becky. One filled with laughter and sunshine, here in the States, where he didn't need to worry about covering his tracks, contradicting himself about a made-up past, and hating the man in the mirror. He could be happy with her. Hell, he was already happy with Becky, way more than happy.

I'm in love with her.

What a hell of a time to realize it.

He was about to fight for his life.

Enzo blew out a cloud of smoke, the breeze spreading it over Rowan like unwanted incense. "Since when did the Art Crimes Division of the FBI start stealing paintings?"

Rowan's mind raced. Enzo had his facts straight, and there were a limited number of people on this earth who could have given him that information. "We call it relationship building."

"Relationship building." A gust of wind whipped between them with physical force. "And the dead guard?"

Rowan nodded almost imperceptibly. "A mistake."

Enzo chuckled. "Mistakes seem to surround you, Agent Mitchell. First the guard, then my daughter disappears along with the *Madonna*, now Santini, who I now realize must be a friend of yours…"

Who I now realize must be a friend of yours…

The words reverberated in Rowan's mind, their meaning too horrific for quick comprehension. *Marco.* Rowan's stomach sank. "Santini?"

"Aw, you haven't heard." He flicked imaginary ashes off the end of his cigar as he shook his head. "They found him in his car this morning. Two bullets to the back of the head."

The grin on Enzo's face belied his sympathy, and Rowan struggled to keep his face impassive. Marco was a friend, and a good one. A father of a newborn boy, a husband.

Rowan's mind raced ahead of him. Surely Enzo didn't intend for Rowan to leave this place alive, but his father-in-law was no match for him physically. Rowan began to scan the horizon.

Enzo blew smoke out of his nose like a bull. "There's only one thing I don't understand. Why is the *Madonna Fornirà* so important to you?"

Rowan blinked. "Who says it's important?"

"Don't condescend me. I can see what motivates you, like a clock with its gears exposed."

He laughed. "Really."

"I know that you're partial to redheads."

Rowan froze. "What?"

"Fiery, outspoken redheads with bodies made for sin."

The distance between them was gone in three steps, the muscles of Rowan's arms flexing in preparation for battle. "You stay away from her."

Enzo clucked his tongue. "I'm afraid she doesn't want to see you. I brought her up to date on your checkered past, including the guard you murdered in cold blood. That's why I was late for our little tête-à-tête."

I was tying up loose ends.

Rowan grabbed a fistful of Enzo's shirt and tie. "Where is she?"

"Let go, or you'll never see her again."

Rowan's fingers snapped open, and Enzo righted his skewed tie. "I want the *Madonna Fornirà*."

Rowan needed to calm Enzo down, to get some control of the situation. He worked to regulate his breathing. In the blink of an eye, everything had changed.

Becky.

The irony wasn't lost on him. Just days ago, he believed Tamra and Anthony had been kidnapped. Now Becky truly had been taken.

"Why do you want it? You were willing to put it in the Gardner. What's changed?"

"I was never going to *leave it there*, you fool! I was going to swap it out for the forgery. I have an inside man at the museum."

"The forgery's not good enough to pass for the real thing."

"These things can be fixed. Ninety-eight percent of it is spot-on. But Tamra was foolish and selfish, and now the forgery is sitting in a police warehouse somewhere."

Except it wasn't.

Marco said someone took the forgery. Either it wasn't Enzo, or he was lying. Rowan narrowed his eyes. "Did Tamra know about your plan to switch it out for the forgery?"

"She knew the legend, of course. It's a matter of history. She wanted to see what was behind that painting as much as I did."

"You want to destroy the painting, this piece of history, just to see if there is an even greater treasure hidden beneath it."

"Yes. And you will get it for me, or the redhead dies, just like Marco. You'll have to work quickly. They have a meeting with their black market contact in two hours."

"Who?"

"Tamra and Gianni, of course!"

"How do you know that?"

Enzo chuckled and held up Leonardo's smartphone. "People put their whole lives on these stupid things."

Chapter 14

Rowan sat slouched in his car, a baseball cap pulled low over his brow. Enzo had given him the address of the meeting, but it was his own idea to look for the nearest park. Tamra was a creature of habit, always taking the baby to swing after lunch when the weather allowed, and his certainty in her appearance increased as the sun broke through the clouds.

She has to come here. She has to. Or else I don't know what I will do.

His eyes scanned the playground for Tamra's familiar form. Here they would have a chance to talk. He could reason with her. A shady meeting with a stolen art broker was destined to end badly, with someone getting hurt, or maybe worse. He turned to the clock. Less than an hour remained.

Damn it, Gianni. Why'd you have to do this shit?

Rowan closed his eyes and rubbed his temples. If Tamra and Gianni wanted to run off together, why not just do it? Why did they have to fake her kidnapping and steal the one painting on earth he'd been assigned to protect?

He raised his head and saw them, Tamra in a long red coat carrying little Anthony in her arms. She wore big black sunglasses and a knit hat that was too warm for the weather. The woman and boy headed straight for the swings, Anthony's joy evident as he smiled and clapped his hands.

Rowan smiled broadly and fought a wave of emotion as he watched Anthony play. Relief and love poured through Rowan, constricting his throat.

Anthony is okay.
Tamra is okay.

Now he just needed Becky to be okay, too. That was all that mattered. The painting, the theft, the kidnapping—all of it paled in comparison to the wellbeing of these people.

He swiped at his eyes and opened his door, slipping on a pair of aviator sunglasses and crossing into the park. Only when he stood directly behind her did he remove them. "Tamra."

She jumped. "Oh, my God…"

"It's all right. I'm not going to hurt you."

"Da!"

He smiled at Anthony, genuine love radiating from his smile. "You want to come up?"

The baby gurgled with delight and held out his hands to Rowan.

Tamra looked like she was going to be sick.

He settled the baby against his hip, aware of just how lucky he was to be doing so. He turned to Tamra. "You faked your own kidnapping. Do you know how worried I've been? The hell you put me through?"

"I had no choice."

"Bullshit. You had every choice, right from the beginning. You could have told the truth when you got pregnant. You could have married Gianni instead of lying to me."

"How did you know?"

"It doesn't matter. You convinced me I had a son, and then you snatched him away. Do you know what that did to me, Tamra? Do you even care?"

She frowned severely. "I wanted to marry Gianni, more than anything, but Enzo refused to allow it."

"Tamra, you're a grown woman! Why do you bow to him like that?"

A sob escaped and she covered her mouth, the anguish on her face more real than any emotion Rowan had ever seen there. "Because he was blackmailing Gianni."

"What does he have to hide?" Rowan had never cared much for the man personally, but Gianni was an Interpol agent. Professionally he was a saint.

"I can't…"

"Tell me." Just then, Anthony reached up and put one hand on each of Rowan's cheeks, and smiled at him. The boy was so beautiful, such an incredible kid, and Rowan was completely moved. He wanted Anthony to grow up with a mother and a father. He wanted the boy to be happy, even if it was not with him.

"Tell me, Tamra, or I can't help you."

"Help me?"

He nodded. "If I can."

She took a shuddering breath. "Gianni used his position with Interpol to sell stolen goods for Leonardo Depaoli."

Rowan jerked his head back. "Why would he do that?"

"Gianni's mother was Leonardo's housekeeper. She died when Gianni was young, and Leonardo never had any children of his own so he raised Gianni himself. He and Leonardo are family now." She smiled through her tears.

"And your father hates Leonardo because they're rivals in the stolen art trade."

"No," she whispered, "Enzo hates Leonardo because my mother loved him first."

Baby Anthony opened his arms and leaned toward his mother, who took him back from Rowan. She moved from side to side, swaying. "My mother was a painter. She was very good, especially at copying things. Even as a teenager should could produce forgeries of outstanding caliber. Leonardo wanted her to use her talents for profit."

"To steal the real ones."

She nodded. "But my mother wouldn't do it. That's what split them apart. My father was waiting in the wings. He and Leonardo were schoolmates."

"You're kidding."

"As close as brothers, once. They always loved the same things, my mother and stealing paintings. But only one of them could have both."

"Enzo couldn't let you be with Gianni, because Leonardo would win."

"Exactly."

The pieces were falling into place. All except one. "Why me?"

"Because Enzo could control you. He set you up, got you to steal *The Lady in the Long Blue Dress*, even murder a security guard, and he got it on tape. What better son-in-law could he ask for?"

"Tamra, I work for the FBI. Enzo can't control me."

Her eyes widened with fear. "What I said about Gianni…"

He raised his hands. "It's okay. I'm not after him."

Tamra leaned forward and covered her mouth with her hand. For the first time, he was able to see her not as some manipulator, but as a victim of her father's determination to control her life. A plan began to form in his mind.

"Is Gianni good to you?"

She nodded. "Yes."

"And to the baby?"

"Oh yes, the few times they've seen each other. He can't wait to be a real father to Anthony." She touched his sleeve. "Rowan, you can't know how sorry I am for everything I have done to you."

He nodded. For that moment he did know, did understand. They weren't that different, he and Tamra, each of them in love and willing to do whatever was necessary to protect the other person. "I need your help, Tamra."

"Anything."

He took a breath and exhaled it, meeting her eyes head-on. "Give me the *Madonna Fornirà*."

Her eyes widened. "But we need the money to start a new life."

"Do you trust me?"

She stared at him for long moments, then checked her watch. "I don't have it with me, it's in a storage facility in Boston."

"I thought you were selling it today?"

"Just a negotiation meeting. Gianni thought we shouldn't have it with us, just in case." She sighed heavily. "But I'll give it to you, Rowan."

~~~

Becky's traitorous stomach growled loudly, and she wrapped her arm around her midsection.

Cosmo laughed, making his belly shake. "You should eat your breakfast."

She didn't answer.

He was tall and muscular, with dark hair and comically heavy eyebrows. He had stood in stark contrast to Enzo when the older man introduced them, Enzo in a suit and tie, Cosmo in jeans and a polo shirt. "He's my bodyguard." Enzo had said. "I'll feel better if he stays with you."

She'd reluctantly agreed, more shell-shocked from Enzo's revelations about Rowan than anything. But now that she and Cosmo had spent some quality time together, Becky was wishing she had opted to go it alone.

Better yet, she wished she was home.

"Do you have a car?" she asked.

He picked up his bagel and lox with wide, dirty fingers and took a bite. "Nope," he said with his mouth full, and Becky silently swore to improve her own table manners.

"Then I'll call a cab."

"Where are you going?"

"To the train station, or bus station or something. Home."

He took a big sip from a large take-out cup, rocking back in his chair. "Mr. de Toffoli wanted you to wait for him."

"I know, but that's stupid. I just want to get out of here." She dug in a side table and found a phone book, flipping to the yellow pages and searching for a taxi.

The front legs of Cosmo's chair hit the ground. "I'm afraid you can't do that."

"Sure I can." She pointed to the open phone book. "There's one right here."

"You're not understanding me. You need to stay with here until Enzo comes back."

She looked left, then right. "Or…?"

He walked toward her, picked up the hotel phone and yanked the cord from the wall. "There's no 'or.' You stay with me. Give me your cell phone."

"What, you're like, holding me hostage?"

"Either give me your cell phone, or I will find it." He raised one heavy brow.

Becky swallowed, reached into her pocket and handed him her phone. "When is Enzo coming back?" she asked.

"Don't know. You should make yourself comfortable. We could play cards."

"Seriously? You're holding me here against my will, and you want to play Crazy Eights?"

He shrugged. "Suit yourself."

She walked to the window, remembering how Rowan had stood here just hours before, nearly naked and drinking scotch. Last night had been her ultimate high, the happiest she had ever been. Today was like it's polar opposite.

Rowan killed a man.

She took a deep breath, letting her eyes wander over the picturesque village. If she hadn't seen it with her own eyes—Rowan firing the gun, the uniformed security guard clutching his chest as he fell to the ground in a heap—she never would have believed him capable.

Just goes to show how well you know the man.

Being a burglar was a poor career choice. But a murderer? She couldn't love a murderer, wouldn't allow a man like that to stay in her life, even if that life felt totally empty without him.

That's what it's going to be like from now on, isn't it?

Her life would forever be broken into two pieces, before and after, whole and incomplete, the happy-go-lucky single girl and the miserable old spinster. She couldn't imagine going back to the way she used to live her life, date after date, man after man. She had no desire to do that again.

So then, what? Buy a creepy house on a hill and start adopting stray animals?

There was only one thing she knew for sure, and that was Rowan Mitchell was the first and last man she would ever love, if only because she would never allow anyone else this close again. Only people who were allowed this close could do this kind of damage.

Rowan.

An image of his handsome face appeared in her mind, and she allowed herself the luxury of examining it. The slightest cleft in his strong chin, the warm honey brown of his skin. She wanted to cry when she realized her heart was singing with love, no matter that her head kept screaming at it to stop.

This is what I'm going to be thinking about, up on that hill with all those damn cats.

A dull ache settled at the base of her skull. Cosmo belched, and her eyes found him in the image reflected in the window.

Artful Deception

What would happen if she just walked past him to the door? Didn't she at least have to try?

The ringing of Cosmo's cell phone interrupted her thoughts. He answered it, saying little, then hung up and smiled at her. "Time to go, carrot top."

She scowled at him. "Where?"

He raised his eyebrows and smiled like a child. "Skiing."

Chapter 15

Rowan was beginning to panic.

He needed backup, but he'd been in deep cover for nearly three years. If you masquerade as an art thief long enough, you become an art thief for all intents and purposes. Which is good, unless you suddenly need to prove you are not, in fact, an art thief.

Marco.

Rowan felt a stab of sadness at the death of his good friend. The Art Crimes Division of the FBI was small, and the two of them had been together since Rowan joined up four years ago. They each came to the FBI later in life, Marco after a brief career in the Navy and Rowan after selling his small publishing house in California, where he'd focused his work on art theft and the black market for stolen goods. They were partners in crime, quite literally, though Rowan was the only one undercover.

Marco could have set the record straight about Rowan's identity in a heartbeat, but with him gone, there was no quick and obvious way to do it without being buried under an administrative tidal wave.

Rowan left another voicemail for his boss and checked the time. Enzo should be arriving with Becky momentarily, if he wasn't already here. Rowan grabbed a long cardboard tube and got out of his car, walking past tens of skiers in colorful jackets and pants.

The ski resort was the most crowded place in the entire town, and Rowan knew that was why Enzo had picked it. It had nothing to do with what had happened to David on a slope just like this one, less than two hours from here, but that was where Rowan's thoughts immediately went, anyway.

The gun in his pocket weighed against his abdomen and his mind, but Rowan was more likely to jump from the top of the building than fire anywhere near this mass of people, and he cursed under his breath.

He made his way into the crowded lodge, a large fireplace centered on one tall wall. Someone touched his arm, once, twice, before he realized they were trying to get his attention and he turned around.

Enzo stood before him. "This is Cosmo," he said, gesturing to a big man in a New England Patriots sweatshirt. "Give me the painting."

"I want to see Becky."

"After I see if this is authentic." He turned back into the crowd, and Rowan moved to follow him.

Cosmo easily blocked his path. "You wait here, and we don't have any trouble."

He was powerless, like a bug in a jar. He should have backup and assistance from local law enforcement. Truth was, he'd been afraid to ask, afraid they would mess up his one chance to get Becky back safely. Now he feared he had sealed that fate himself by coming here alone.

Was Becky even here? *God, have they hurt her?*

Then through the crowd he saw her, red hair flowing as she walked. Relief was instantaneous.

"Looks like her, doesn't she?" said Cosmo, chuckling. "But it ain't her."

Sure enough, as the woman got closer and closer, the resemblance faded with every step.

Son of a bitch.

"Told you so."

Rowan turned around. "Where is she?"

Cosmo shrugged, and Rowan imagined pulling out his gun, brandishing it in the other man's face, forcing him to comply. But imagining was the most he could do. He closed the distance between them. "If you hurt her, so help me God…"

"I'm here."

Rowan whipped around at the sound of her voice. Becky stood not two feet away from him. "Oh, thank God." He turned back to Cosmo, surprised to see him retreating into the sea of people, and moved to follow him.

"Rowan!" she yelled. "Let's just get out of here, please."

And in that moment, it didn't matter that Enzo had the painting, or that Rowan hadn't gotten to beat the bad guys down into the dirt. All the mattered was that Becky was all right, that she was standing in front of him, safe and sound, apparently unharmed.

"Okay. Let's go."

She'd been quiet when she first got in Rowan's car, not even knowing where to begin. He'd hugged her and held her tight, and she reveled in the feel of his arms, the scent of his skin, even while she didn't hug him back. When he reached for her hand while he was driving, she pulled it away and stared out her window.

There was no more reason to stay, and many reasons to leave, yet still she clung to his presence and this car speeding down the freeway like a drowning person hanging onto a life preserver. She had to let go, no matter the icy ocean that surrounded her. There would be life after Rowan. There just had to be.

"Just take me to the train station. Please." She closed her eyes and exhaled every breath in her lungs. All she wanted to do was curl up on the couch with Lucy and the ugly blanket for a week. Maybe two. The very last thing she wanted to deal with was a confrontation with Rowan, but that was apparently the only way to get from point A to point B. When she saw the sign for the train station, she had finally found her voice.

Rowan stole a sideways glance at her. "Why the hell would I do that?"

"So I can go home, where I belong."

"You belong with me."

"No, I don't."

"Yes, you do. I love you, Becky." He reached for her hand again, leaving his extended on the seat when she did nothing.

Her heart squeezed tight and she covered her face. How long had she waited to hear those words, believing they would never come?

I thought I would be alone forever, and it would be okay. Now I'll be alone forever, and it just might kill me.

"I know the truth. You murdered someone. You're a thief, a burglar, and a liar. Enzo showed me the pictures when you shot that man. Are you going to tell me they're not real? That there's some explanation?"

Rowan pulled over to the side of the road and stared straight ahead, jaw clenched. "They're real. But there is an explanation. Becky, I'm an undercover FBI agent with the Art Crimes Division. I burglarized that museum because I was doing my job."

She stared at him hard. When they were at the cabin, she might have believed that. But now? Now she didn't know what to believe.

Enzo's voice was in her head, telling her not to trust Rowan.

"Becky, I'm telling you the truth."

Her head whipped around to face him. "Oh, yeah? Well how the hell am I supposed to believe you when you've been lying to me since day one?"

"I had to lie! I can't go around telling everyone I meet that I'm an undercover agent."

"But I'm not 'just anyone' to you, Rowan." She leaned back against the seat. "Or am I?"

He furrowed his brow. "What does that mean?"

"It means maybe our relationship is just another one of your lies."

"How can you say that?"

She shrugged her shoulders. "No harm, no foul, I suppose. It's not like you and me could survive in real world, anyway." It was what she was most afraid of, and she said it to lash out at him, a slap in his smug, lying face.

"You don't mean that."

"Tell me, was the murder staged just for the cameras?"

He lowered his eyes. "No. That one was real. I did kill that man, Becky."

"But you said you were one of the good guys."

"I made a mistake. A horrible mistake that I have to live with for the rest of my life."

Becky shook her head. "I don't know what you want from me here. I don't know who you are. Maybe I never did. Take me to the train station, or I'll get out right here and walk the rest of the way. I want to go home, Rowan."

Artful Deception

He pulled back and hit a button on the dash, a handsfree cellphone image coming up on the display. "Call Colin."

It was on speakerphone. Colin answered on the second ring. "Becky's here. Tell her what I do for a living."

"You own a publishing house."

"No, tell her the truth."

"You're an undercover FBI agent with the Art Crimes Division."

She took a deep breath in, a ragged one out. He really was one of the good guys. Relief swept through her in an exhausted wave. When had she ever been this tired?

"Thanks, bro. How's Gwen?"

"She's good. How are you guys making out?"

"Better now. But listen, I think you and Gwen should leave Becky's house. Maybe get a hotel. There's a chance somebody's looking for her and I want to make sure you're safe."

"You got it."

Rowan hung up, put the car in gear and pulled back into traffic. "If you want to go, Becky, I won't stop you. But I wish to hell you'd stay."

Within a minute she was sobbing loudly.

"Here's the exit for the train station. Want me to drop you off?"

She cried harder.

"'Cause, I'm a big believer. If you love something, set it free…"

She hit him in the arm. "Asshole."

He reached for her hand and she took it. "I'm an asshole who loves you very much."

I love you, too.

The words rose up inside her, but her throat couldn't let them by. For all the men she'd dated in her life, Becky had never fallen for a single one, never uttered the words she now longed to say.

She settled for an easier truth. "I'm sorry I doubted you."

Rowan frowned, taking his hand back to signal and change lanes. "I didn't mean to kill that man, but I did kill him."

"What happened?"

"It was my first job working for Enzo. He sent this Dutch guy in with me, Ruud. Guy was an idiot. He wanted to take a painting from the second floor, where we knew we had a guard on patrol. It was my own fault, I agreed to it when I should have told him no way. I didn't want to seem like I was scared, but it was my first heist as an agent. I wanted to come off like a badass."

"Next thing I know, I'm staring down the barrel of my gun to this kid, this young security guard. Couldn't have been more than twenty-six or twenty-seven. He reaches for his own gun, and I want him to stop, I want him to turn around and run like hell, so I can just leave him alone. But he doesn't stop. He draws his gun on me, and just like that, I shot him."

"I hit him in the shoulder. I just wanted to take him down, make him stop advancing. But Ruud had bought the ammo. Hollow tips. Shoot-to-kill. They break apart into little pieces and travel through the body, doing as much damage as they possibly can."

Becky covered her hand with her mouth, not sure if she was more distraught for the young security guard or for Rowan himself.

"One piece traveled into his chest cavity, killing him instantly. The alarm went off, all hell broke lose, and Ruud gives me a fucking high five. And I let him. *I just let him.*"

"You didn't mean to kill him."

"I shouldn't have gone up there." He smacked his palm on the steering wheel. "I shouldn't have shot at him, for Christ's sake. It's all my fault."

"You didn't mean to kill him."

"He was just a kid…" He looked to her, his eyes desperate.

She unbuckled her seatbelt and moved to his side, wrapping his body into her embrace. Her voice was a whisper as he began to shake. "You didn't mean to kill him."

Artful Deception

Chapter 16

Enzo had waited a lifetime for this moment.

The *Madonna Fornirà* was spread out on the table before him, decadent in its palette and providence. He found it erotic to be in its company, stripped of its frame and support like a woman stripped of her clothing and artifice.

Greed and curiosity warred with his desire to prolong this moment, the anticipation a sharp sword that threatened to destroy him. He began cutting in a horizontal line at the top of the baby Jesus' corona and extended to the right edge of the painting, hundreds of years of history destroyed with a single slice. He was physically excited like a teenage boy alone with a worldly woman, and he reveled in the sensation as he made a second cut perpendicular to the first.

He picked up the smaller rectangle he had cut out of the canvas and held the newly formed vertex under the light. Donning his glasses, he worked with gloved hands and a scalpel to separate the centuries-old paint from its backing.

Agotsi was a madman, a genius living before his time. A writer of riddles, a keeper of clues that would torment men through the ages.

The crown of the babe shall reveal its worth, in layers given to the earth. Greater riches shall be found beneath the ground than in her arms, the treasure bound.

Enzo tried to slip the scalpel on top of the canvas, the thick blade slicing through his glove and sinking into his fingertip. "Ah!" he screamed, blood already dripping onto the painting. Quickly he grabbed a tissue and wrapped the injury, covering it with another glove to hold it in place.

"Merda!" he yelled upon seeing the drops, the freshly cut edge of the painting bright red. Frustration emanated from him like heat from a burning coal, and he forced himself to put down the knife until he regained his composure.

He had waited too long, had risked too much, to foil this opportunity.

When he once again picked up the section of painting and bought it to the light, he could see the bloodied canvas had separated from the hardened paint. He smiled, again working to slip the scalpel between them, and this time doing so easily.

"I knew it," he whispered. "I knew you were telling us the truth." Rumors had circulated for centuries, claiming Agotsi had perfected a way to keep the paint from settling into the fiber of the canvas, resting instead on an intermediate layer that could be mechanically separated. While easily done today, the process was unheard of in the artist's time, the message that had been hidden for hundreds of years now about to be revealed.

Enzo barely breathed as he peeled back the layer of paint. A shape came into view, then an entire letter. A word, now two.

Goodbye Daddy.

"No!" he screamed, his arms reaching out to hurl everything he could reach onto the floor. The bulb in the desk lamp shattered with a pop, throwing Enzo and all he had hoped for into darkness.

~~~

Rowan threw the car keys onto the hotel room dresser. "You want first shower?"

"Hell, yeah."

"Have at it. I'm going to call Colin and see where he and Gwen ended up."

Colin's phone went right to voicemail and Rowan left a message. "We're back in Boston. Call me when you get this."

He opened the bottle of soda he bought at the vending machine and kicked back on the bed. There was only one and he liked knowing they would share it together, making love in the night and sharing their sleep when they were through.

He could hear Becky singing quietly, but not well enough to place the tune. He imagined the water cascading over her luscious body, her long hair hanging wet down her back, and he longed to sink his hands into her soapy curls.

He felt luckier in this moment than any man had a right to be. He was free of his joke of a marriage. Little Anthony was safe and sound, in the arms of his true parents. Enzo was getting his due at that very moment, and the woman he loved was in the shower, readying herself for his bed.

The scent of fruity shampoo reached his nostrils and he closed his eyes, inhaling deeply, before capping his soda and standing to strip. He walked to the bathroom door and smiled. *Stairway to Heaven.* He knocked.

"Yes?"

"Can I shower with you?"

"Abso-freakin'-lutely."

The room was filled with steam and the scent of her. He pulled back the curtain and stepped inside, the reality of Becky in the shower far surpassing his fantasy.

She cocked an eyebrow. "Hey, handsome. Want me to wash your back?"

"Do I." He turned around and braced himself on the wall, the feel of her hands on his tense muscles instantly making him moan in satisfaction. "That feels incredible."

"That's the idea. At my house I have a steam shower with twenty-four jets that could knock your socks off."

He lifted his head, stretching each side of his neck in turn. In his imagination, he could feel those jets all over his body. He chuckled. "Can I move in with you?"

Her hands stopped moving.

"I was only kidding. That shower sounds fantastic."

She turned her back to him, putting her face in the water and rubbing her eyes.

"Becky, what's the matter?"

"Nothing's the matter."

Rowan could feel the tension settling back in his shoulders. He watched as she slowly turned her body in the spray, her eyes closed against him. "Something's bothering you. Why don't you tell me what it is?"

"Let's not, and say we did."

"You got all freaked out when I said I wanted to move in. I was kidding, but frankly I don't see why it would have bother you, even if I were serious."

Her eyes opened. "You don't see why that would bother me."

"No."

She shook her head, holding up a hand between them. "Let's not talk about this. Let's have a nice night together. Just let it go, Rowan."

"I love you."

She met his eyes.

"I've said it to you several times now, but you haven't said it back. Why is that?" He frowned. "Do you really not feel it too?"

"I told you we shouldn't have this conversation." She pulled back the edge of the curtain and moved to get out.

"Whoa, hold on. You don't love me?"

"It's not that simple."

"What's fucking complicated? You love me, or you don't."

"You lied to me."

He rolled his eyes. "Oh, come on."

"More than once."

"I explained that already."

"Did you? Did you really, or did you just tell me a little tiny piece of the truth so I would back off?"

"I told you the truth."

The heat in the bathroom was suddenly too much, the steam overwhelming. She needed to get out of there. "But I don't believe you." She pulled back her half of the curtain. "I can't believe you." She stepped out of the shower. "I told you, you should have just left it well enough alone."

~~~

Light snow fell on the grand stone steps, and Enzo climbed them carefully. He pressed the glowing button, his finger clad in fine black leather, and he was struck by the differences time had made in his life. Though he'd snuck into this house just two nights earlier, it had been more than forty years since he stood in this spot and openly rang this bell.

In his mind's eye he was there again, a young man just home from his studies, anxious to see his friend and enjoy a meal at his family's table. His cloth gloves worn and in need of darning, his pulse jumping as he waited to see if Claudia would be here, too.

Enzo had a tremendous crush on Leonardo's girlfriend for the last year and a half, since the Christmas party when she wore the long green dress that flattered her young, womanly body.

Before that, Enzo had thought her a child, a nuisance, but afterwards he spent his days comparing every woman he met to the ethereal Claudia, every one of them coming up short in the balance.

It was that evening, after dinner and too many drinks, that Leonardo broke down and confided in his friend. Claudia had broken their engagement.

Enzo wasted no time. He plotted his courtship while he listened to his friend's grief.

The tall door opened and the men stood face-to-face for the first time in more than a quarter century. "Have they found Tamra and the baby?" Leonardo asked.

"No. May I come in?"

Leonardo stepped back for him to enter, closing the door and saying quietly, "No one deserves to have the one they love stolen from him. I, of all people, know that."

Enzo rounded on the other man in an instant fury. "I stole *nothing* from you. You chased Claudia away with your greed and your arrogance."

"Perhaps." Leonardo led the way into the large sitting room where Claudia's painting above the mantel. "But if that is true, then I have spent the years between then and now working to change that which reviled her, while you have become the very essence of what she hated."

Enzo's eyes scrupulously avoided the mantel, falling instead on a velvet patterned sofa. A small stuffed bear peeked out from behind a pillow. "I received an update from Interpol on the status of the kidnapping investigation," he said. "Gianni Amato didn't show up for work this morning."

"Perhaps he's unwell."

"Perhaps not." Enzo picked up the bear. "I bought this for Anthony when he was born."

"How nice of you to buy something for my grandson."

"Wishing Gianni was your boy does not make it so. He will always be a servant, never a lord."

"You were once lower than a servant. *A bastard.* But I welcomed you in my family home, shared all I had with you."

"You were a fool."

"And look at you now! An abomination. Gianni is strong and righteous. I very much wish he were my child."

"But alas, you have no children."

"Ah, old friend. You are mistaken. I have a daughter, dark-haired and as beautiful as her mother." A sly smile slipped across his features, transforming him. Anthony is my grandson because Tamra is my daughter."

"Liar!"

"Claudia told me herself before she died. She asked that I not reveal it to you, but I no longer feel bound by my promise. You have tortured my daughter long enough, and now she will escape your rath."

"Where are they?"

"Gone."

Gone.

Yes, everything was gone. Claudia, the traitorous wife. Tamra, her daughter from an unholy union. Anthony, the grandson of his enemy. The *Madonna Fornirà*, the prize he'd been pursuing for more than half his life. Suddenly, he felt old and tired, nearly defeated. Then he realized.

Leonardo was to blame for it all.

In one easy movement, Enzo withdrew his pistol from his jacket pocket and held it just inches from the other man's head. He took off the safety and clenched his teeth as he moved to pull the trigger.

Then he was a boy, the happy memories of his years in this house with Leonardo mocking his current intent. Time ceased to move forward as Enzo stood suspended between what could have been and the horrors he had brought upon himself. He could see himself as a young man sitting at the Depaoli table, enjoying the warmth that radiated from Leonardo's family like light from the sun.

He could see Claudia, unbearably young and beautiful, laughing with Leonardo and him, the three of them unaware of the divergent path their futures would take. Enzo watched as young Leonardo exchanged a glance with Claudia, the color rising in her cheeks, and Enzo felt jealousy flare to life in his breast like a wild beast.

Artful Deception

The warm metal trigger was again solid against his finger, and he began to squeeze.

A baby's scream pierced the silence, and Enzo turned toward the sound. He would know Anthony's cries anywhere.

They were here!

It had never occurred to him they might still be in town, might be under this very roof.

"Run! He has a gun!" Leonardo screamed, and Enzo brought its barrel down hard on the other man's temple, an audible crack before Leonardo fell to the ground.

Pivoting on his heel, Enzo ran deeper into the house, gun at the ready. He rounded a corner into the arboretum, following the baby's wails. Gianni emerged from the foliage and began to raise his own weapon.

Anthony's cries seemed to escalate as Enzo fired quickly, shooting Gianni in the belly. Enzo advanced toward him, ready to shoot him again.

"Daddy! No!" Tamra was there, standing between them, hands raised to her face while baby Anthony wailed in the distance. "Please! I'll give you the painting!"

Chapter 17

Rowan opened one eye, the other pressed into his pillow. *Was someone kicking the door?*

He sat up in bed, taking in the single beam of sunlight that shone through the crack in the mostly closed drapes.

Where was Becky?

Two more sounds, like a knock, but they were definitely kicks. He threw back the covers and went to the door, spying Becky through the peephole. He opened it, standing behind it so he wouldn't flash the hotel hallway with his naked body.

"Breakfast!" She was carrying two trays of food, each laden with several plates and glasses. "There's a free buffet. Everything looked so good!"

He smelled bacon and something sweet, maybe pancakes, and his stomach roared to life. "Awesome. Coffee?"

She put the trays down on the dresser and reached for a mug. "Coffee."

He walked to the window and opened the curtains, standing naked before them.

Becky made sure to swallow what was in her mouth before she spoke. "You're an exhibitionist."

"No one can see me."

"You mean no one's looking, but if they were, of course they could see you, and you like it."

He shrugged.

"You ever have sex in public?"

"What, like outdoors? Sure."

"Not just outdoors. Someplace you might get caught."

He thought about that and she laughed, gesturing below his waist. "I think he likes that idea."

"Huh. I guess he does."

"Another time. When does the FBI open?"

They had come to Boston to return the real *Madonna Fornirà* to the Gardner Museum, but to do it, Rowan had to be recognized as an FBI agent instead of some guy off the street. A quick stop at the local FBI office in Center Plaza should take care of that. "Eight fifteen, but the Gardner doesn't open until eleven." He kneeled on the bed and began crawling toward her. "So we've got time."

The ringing of his cell phone stopped him, and Becky handed him the phone.

He glanced at the caller ID. "It's Tamra!"

~~~

The first time Becky laid eyes on Rowan's wife, her shirt and hands were covered in blood. Even then she was beautiful, her movements at once efficient and graceful, and Becky felt a stab of adolescent envy.

The man she loves is in a heap on the floor, and I'm back in junior high school.

"I can't get the bleeding to stop," Tamra said, pressing hard on a towel over the gaping wound in an unconscious Gianni's belly.

Rowan knelt down to explore Gianni's wound. "He needs to get to a hospital, Tamra. Now."

"It's a gunshot wound! They'll have to report it, and then they'll find us and put Gianni in jail." She turned around and noticed Becky. "Who is she?"

"A friend. At least in a hospital he'll be alive, Tamra, which he's not going to be for much longer if he stays here."

Tamra stared at Rowan for a beat, then nodded her head.

"I'll call 911," said Leonardo. He'd been hovering near the doorway, rocking baby Anthony, who was half asleep in his arms.

"Tell me what happened," said Rowan.

"Enzo fought with Leonardo. We were nearby, listening. We were supposed to leave this morning, but the baby was sick with a fever and I didn't want to put him in the car, or we would have been gone." She shook her head, as if she couldn't believe it had happened. "He pulled the gun on Leonardo just as Anthony woke up and started screaming. Then everything happened so quickly."

"Do you know where Enzo went?"

She nodded, her eyes wide. "I told him about the storage unit we rented."

Rowan got to his feet. "When did he leave?"

"Right before I called you. But you can't go. Just let him have it. Who cares? It's not worth your life…"

"I have to." He turned to Becky. "Stay with them. I'll meet you at the hospital."

"Okay." Becky understood why he needed to go. It was his job to protect the *Madonna Fornirà* and she trusted him. "Be careful."

Tamra scooted in closer to Gianni, resting his arm on her abdomen as she tried her best to staunch the bleeding.

"Can I help you?" asked Becky. "I could take a turn."

Tamra eyed her wearily, then nodded, showing her where to press, and Becky did as she was told. The smell of blood was thick and sweet and she wanted to gag, so she spoke instead. "I'm Becky."

"Hi."

"I'm really glad you and the baby are okay."

Tamra frowned and rested her head on Gianni's, effectively ending the conversation.

~~~

Becky and Tamra rode to the hospital in the back of the ambulance that carried Gianni, the paramedics working to stabilize him as they flew down the rural road. Leonardo had stayed home with the baby. It was frightening to watch them work, the monitors beeping frantically.

"Is he going to be okay?" asked Tamra.

"He's lost a lot of blood, ma'am. But he's young and healthy. Let's hope for the best."

Tamra nodded, tears slipping down her cheeks.

It seemed they'd been driving forever, but still the landscape was anything but metropolitan. Gianni seemed to be stable, and the paramedics had calmed considerably.

Becky desperately wanted to make small talk, but they only thing they had in common was Rowan, and she figured that would get awkward pretty quickly.

It was Tamra who finally spoke. "I never meant to hurt Rowan."

It didn't seem like the proper time to call the other woman a stinking liar, so Becky didn't say anything at all. How the hell did you decide to convince some man he was the father of your baby so he would marry you, and not intend to hurt him?

"My father forced me to do it."

Keeping quiet didn't come naturally to Becky, and there were only so many times she could bite her tongue before the words came flying out of her mouth. "Your daddy made you?"

"It's more complicated than it seems."

"So explain it to me."

Tamra glared at her. "You wouldn't understand."

"Try me."

"Rowan got stuck in the middle. I guess I should have been stronger. Fought harder for what was right, but I didn't. I'll have to live with that for the rest of my life."

Becky heard the regret in the other woman's voice and believed it was genuine. Still, it was difficult for her to empathize with someone who took so little control of her own life. "I hope you find happiness. I really do," said Becky.

"I wish the same for you." She smiled lightly. "Rowan's a good man. He always deserved better than I could give him."

Chapter 18

Rowan flew down the expressway, passing cars as if they were standing still.

"911 what's your emergency?"

"I'm an FBI agent with the Art Crimes Division, on my way to intercept a robbery in progress at the South Street Public Storage facility. The suspect is armed and dangerous. I need backup, quickly."

A pickup truck in the left-hand lane was barely moving faster than the car he was working to pass. Rowan got up on his bumper and flashed his headlights. "Come on, come on, come on!" The truck sped up slightly and got out of the way, the driver gesturing obscenely as Rowan drove by.

"Sir, how do you know there's a robbery?"

He disconnected the call and shot over two lanes of traffic, his exit looming around the next curve. A light at the end of the exit ramp had just turned red and he slowed to a roll, then ran the light as he crossed the intersection.

The storage facility was up a few blocks on the right.

He was sweating, possible scenarios zipping through his brain. The building was closed, which meant Enzo would have to break in—not a difficult task for a man who had broken into some of the most secure buildings in the world.

From what Tamra told him in the park, Rowan knew there was an exterior gate with a keypad and another keypad to access the indoor units. The *Madonna* was in a climate controlled unit on the third floor.

Enzo had a head start, but he didn't have the access codes or the key to the unit. The facility would have security cameras, but it was highly unlikely anyone was watching the feeds in real time. The only thing that might slow down the old man was if the keypads were wired to an alarm system, but even that was well within Enzo's capabilities.

Rowan cursed under his breath as the storage facility came into view, and parked on the street beside the building. He retrieved his gun from the glove compartment of the car, checking to make sure it was loaded before heading toward the building at a jog.

Becky wouldn't be happy if she knew he still had his gun in her car.

A six-foot black gate surrounded the property. Rowan's code wouldn't work after business hours, so he used the keypad as a foothold instead and quickly scaled the fence, a task made simple by the adrenaline pumping through his veins.

He moved to the front entrance, the second keypad mounted on the brick wall just to the right of the door. There were several small lights on its face that he knew should be lit, their darkness a confirmation that Enzo was already inside. Rowan pulled on the door and it opened easily, the hinge squeaking loudly and making him cringe.

Inside were a small lobby and an elevator, with a long hallway of storage units in either direction. Reaching inside his jacket, Rowan touched the metal of his handgun and froze.

He was back in the museum, Ruud at his side, egging him on to go upstairs.

I want the Degas.

The thunderous crack of his gun firing, the recoil. He smelled gunpowder, heard the sound of the guard's body landing in a heap of bones and muscle on the marble floor a split second before the alarm began to screech.

It was as real as if he were there, the moment resurrected from his memory in living color, taunting his present intent. He had to go upstairs, find Enzo and the *Madonna*, but his feet were glued to the floor, heart racing.

I can't do this.

A mechanical *whoosh* came from the elevator, forcing him to act, his wild eyes searching for a place to hide.

There was nowhere.

The elevator chimed, signaling its arrival. Memories dissipated, leaving a simple choice to live or die. Rowan grabbed the butt of his gun and trained it on the elevator doors, his fingers steady, his aim true.

He rested the pad of his finger lightly on the trigger, sweat appearing on his forehead. The doors opened with a loud rattle.

The elevator appeared empty. He took two steps closer to be sure no one was hiding in the corners, and was kicked hard in the back from behind.

He was thrown to the floor of the elevator, hands sprawled in front of him.

How could I be so stupid? How long had he stood in the lobby, memories overwhelming him as he considered what to do next? It had seemed like mere moments, but it had been long enough for Enzo to see him. Scrambling to his feet, Rowan turned and saw the doors closing behind him, the big man from the ski lodge smiling broadly in the lobby beyond.

Rowan's hand shot out, the doors squeezing his fingers before reversing their course. The other man took off running for the front door, and Rowan moved to follow him, then stopped short as understanding registered in his brain.

The big man was a distraction, an attempt to clear a path for Enzo's escape. He wouldn't be traveling in Enzo's wake. No. Enzo was here, and so was the *Madonna Fornirà*.

Enzo's still in the building.

Rowan opened the stairwell door and raced up the steps two at once. He got to the third floor in record time, carefully checking the hallway before slipping into it, gun at the ready. Halfway down the hall, a single orange garage-type door was rolled up a foot off the ground and Rowan inched toward it.

Flattening himself against the wall, he hooked his shoe on the edge of the door and pushed it up hard with one motion. Gun drawn, he turned to look into the small, empty space.

Sirens wailed in the distance as Rowan doubled back to the stairwell. He again heard the sound of the elevator as it rushed past his floor on its way up higher.

The roof.

It was as accessible to a cat burglar as the front door.

Again he raced up the steps, losing track of what floor he was on. A final half-flight of stairs ended abruptly at a dark metal door, a thick chain hanging from the horizontal crossbar and swaying slightly. He pushed the door open with one hand and stepped outside, leading with his weapon.

Artful Deception

Enzo stood before him with his arms held high, pointing his own gun at the sky, a large tube resting on the ground at his feet. A single siren wailed loudly in the cold night air. "I just want to talk," Enzo said calmly.

"Put the gun down, slowly."

"We can be partners."

"I said put it down."

Enzo didn't move. "Together we'd be unstoppable. First the *Madonna Fornirà*, then anything we desire. With your connections…"

Rowan stepped closer, closing the distance between them. "No."

"Afraid they'll find out?" he gestured to the police cars below. "All I have to do is throw this tube onto that roof over there. You tell them you saw Cosmo take it and we're free."

"You're not going to be free for a very long time."

The older man's face fell. "I'm sorry to hear you say that, Rowan. I always liked you."

"I always thought you were an asshole."

The moonlight caught the sheen of metal as Enzo twisted the gun and pointed it at the younger man. Rowan could see the guard from the museum in his memory, two separate moments merging into one fateful scene. Rowan fired once, right on target and without hesitation, directly into Enzo's shoulder muscle, exactly as he had shot the museum guard.

Enzo dropped to the ground, screaming in pain. Rowan kept his gun trained on him as he neared the edge and yelled to police on the street, "We're on the roof!" A flashlight beam turned toward him and he knew he had been heard.

"I have diplomatic immunity," said Enzo. "You can't touch me."

"We'll see about that."

The door behind them burst open, officers racing onto the rooftop and taking over. Rowan gave his gun to a CSI and slowly backed toward the stairs.

It's over.

Artful Deception

Enzo was in custody, the painting was safe, Tamra and Anthony had been found. Rowan made his way slowly down the stairwell, the rhythm of his footsteps calming his frenzied nerves.

An hour later, as he sat in a warm police car parked outside the storage building, Rowan was finally handed the tube that contained the painting.

The *Madonna Fornirà*.

The Madonna will provide.

It was a promise, a comfort, a message. Emotion sang deep in Rowan's belly and he longed to see the painting with his very own eyes, hold its skin in his hands just this one time. He spoke to the officer in the front seat. "Yo, you got a pair of gloves?"

Then he was pulling the canvas out of the tube, gingerly unrolling the top of the painting like a father holding his newborn son. In the flashing lights of the emergency vehicles, he unfurled the portrait just enough to get a close-up view of the face he had worked so hard to protect.

Recognition was a shock.

The image in his hands looked just like Becky.

With her elaborate robes and gilded aura still rolled up and out of view, the resemblance was incredible.

The funny little grin on her full lips, the graceful curve of her feminine neck, the shape of her nose. This was the woman he loved, the woman he would always love. The corners of his own mouth turned down harshly and he let the canvas curl up on itself once more, his gloved hand covering his mouth.

Is this what the Madonna was giving to him? A gift from the heavens, a love like no other, true and proud and more than he had ever hoped to receive. His eyes gazed out the window at the lamp-lit street, a sliver of the night sky visible just above the storage facility.

Thank you.

Emotion sang within him, his eyes stinging as he shook his head and laughed, quietly at first, then louder.

At the darkest hour in his life, Rowan Mitchell had been given the world.

Chapter 19

Becky found a vending machine on the fourth floor of the hospital, filled with sandwiches and tiny containers of yogurt. She cursed under her breath and flagged down a passing doctor.

"Excuse me, isn't there any junk food in this place?"

He smiled, his eyes dipping lower in an appreciative appraisal. "What, like candy?"

"Yes." She smiled. "Chocolaty, peanut buttery goodness, maybe some potato chips and giant bottles of Mountain Dew?"

"Not in the vending machines." He stepped closer and raised one eyebrow. "But I have a secret stash in my office I'd be willing to share."

He's hitting on me.

Wow, she hadn't seen that one coming. His nametag said Dr. Magrite and his empty ring finger screamed available, but he wasn't on her radar. More precisely, *her radar wasn't even on.* "Oh, I…"

He smiled, perfectly aligned pearly whites twinkling under the fluorescents.

"I'm with someone," she stammered.

"Lucky guy." He winked. "The gift shop carries some contraband. They open at nine."

"Thanks."

It was a little after four in the morning, so Becky wandered the halls after that with no certain destination. She wasn't ready to return to Gianni's bedside and the uncomfortable vigil she'd been keeping with Tamra. He was doing fine now that he had the proper care, and the police interviewed him shortly after their arrival. Tamra hadn't shared the outcome of that meeting with Becky, and Becky sure as hell wasn't about to inquire.

Was Tamra always so cold? She wondered what Rowan had ever seen in the woman. Then it hit her.

Duh.

Tamra was beautiful in a way Becky could only dream of being. *A man would have to be dead not to want to sleep with that.*

Becky walked through the lobby all the way past the cafeteria, then up a flight of stairs and back again. She thought about the doctor who should have seemed sexy and hadn't, she thought about pretty girls with curls, and she thought about her newfound desire to settle down with one man and have a child of her own.

No, not one man. With Rowan.

Becky headed back toward Gianni's room, one of many that came out from the nurse's station in a spoke-like pattern. She came up short when she looked through the doorway and saw Rowan and Tamra standing together in a loose embrace, talking quietly.

Intimately, even.

Becky took a step backward, right into the path of a nurse carrying a tray of metal instruments that went flying across the floor. "I'm sorry," Becky said, crouching to help the other woman collect the scattered pieces. She was keenly aware of the open doorway and her own visibility, her cheeks heating in embarrassment.

Rowan's voice was amused. "There you are." He crouched down beside her and helped to gather the tools. "Where've you been?"

"Oh, I don't know. Around."

"Around?"

"I was looking for a snack, but the cafeteria's closed and all the vending machines are stocked with health food."

He stood and offered his hand, which she accepted. "Walk with me?" he asked.

She considered telling him she'd been walking for the better part of two hours, but she didn't. "Okay."

"Enzo's going to be all right. They took him over to Mass General but he's stable and expected to make a full recovery."

"That's good."

"How's Tamra been?"

"Worried. She's afraid they're going to put Gianni in jail."

"Not if I can help it."

"Did he really help Leonardo steal paintings?"

"He helped him sell them, yes."

"Then how..."
"He was working with me."
She squinted. "But I thought..."
Rowan stopped walking and met her eyes. "He was working with me. I forgot to notify my supervisor that I needed Gianni's help on a few things."
"Ah." She smiled. This was a good man she was in love with. A very good man.
He nodded. "I have to go to Washington for my debriefing."
"When?"
"Now." He rubbed his hands through his hair. "I have to get some sleep first, but they want me there as soon as possible."
"To explain about Gianni?"
"And other things, yes."
"How long are you going to be there?"
"I'm not sure. Just a few days, I hope."
"Can I do anything for you?"
He threaded his fingers with hers. "Come back to the hotel with me. Sleep next to me before I have to go."
She nodded, a knot forming in her throat. "I'd like that."

~~~

Becky and Rowan made frenzied love in the night without conversation, each afraid that words might separate them, and desperate to be together.

Nothing she could say would fix what was wrong between them, nothing he might answer could assuage her deeply set doubts. Still, she clung to him like the mast of a sinking ship, bracing herself for whatever might lie ahead.

The blazing morning sunlight slipped between the curtains and fell across her face, demanding that she face reality.

Ugh.

Rowan snuggled close to her side and she shriveled from his touch. "Don't." She sat up in bed, the darkened hotel room coming into focus around her.

"You okay?"

"Yeah." It was a lie, and she knew it. A lie she'd been telling herself for days now so she could justify what was happening between them.

Artful Deception

He rolled over and stood up.

"Rowan?"

"Yeah?"

"I'm not okay."

He sat back down on the bed. "What's wrong?"

"When we were at the cabin, you were having a bad dream. I walked in, and you called out Tamra's name."

"Honey, the only dream I remember having at the cabin was about you."

"That may be. But I heard you."

"So, what are you saying?"

"Rowan, are you still in love with Tamra?"

He touched her arm, turning her around to face him. "I was never in love with Tamra. Not ever. Do you understand?"

"You were holding her in the hospital."

He sighed and rolled his eyes. "She was apologizing for all the crap she pulled. For nearly ruining my life."

"You didn't seem too upset with her."

"Well, I'm not, okay?" He stood and pulled on his pants. "Now that I know about Gianni and everything Enzo did, I think she was as much a victim as I was."

"Really?" Rowan had lied to her so many times, she just couldn't be sure he was being honest now, and that just about killed her. No matter his marriage, or his job, or their current situation, it was her simple lack of faith in him that was destined to tear them apart, and Becky was beginning to think it could never be restored.

"Yes, really." He sat next to her. "I want to see them settle down together with the baby. To have a chance to be a family. I want that for them, and I want it for Anthony." He lifted her chin and she pulled away.

He dug the heels of his hands into his eye sockets. "I have to get in the shower. My flight's in two hours."

"Have a good trip."

He took a step, then turned back. "Aren't you going to be here when I get out?" he asked.

She shook her head, careful to keep her voice even. "I'm going to head home. It's been a long couple of days."

"I see. Well, have a good trip."
"Yep. You, too."

The drive home only took Becky twenty minutes, which seemed ridiculous. Like she'd been ripped out of Kansas by a twister, followed the yellow brick road for days, and got back to her own bed in seconds, with the mere click of her heels.

Snow fell heavily from the sky as she pulled into the driveway of her old Craftsman bungalow. She was surprised to see Colin's Jeep parked in her regular spot, having figured he and Gwen would be long gone by now. Her plan for the day went from "sit in a dark room and cry" to "entertain company," and she sighed heavily as she threw the car into park and turned the key in the ignition.

She would not tell them what had happened. It was between her and Rowan, not his brother and Gwen. Becky was a grown-up, and it wouldn't be right to share her own heartache, no matter how much she wanted to unburden herself.

Gwen sat at the kitchen table, her feet propped up on a second chair. "You're home!" She put down the sandwich in her hand and stood, wrapping Becky in a tight squeeze and kissing her hair.

Becky clung to her. Gwen smelled like cookies and peanut butter, like safety and love. Tears bit at Becky's eyes.

"What is it? What's wrong?"

The floodgates opened and Becky began to sob openly.

"Is Rowan okay? Anthony?"

Becky nodded. "They're fine."

"Oh, thank God. Tamra?"

"She's okay, too."

Becky pulled back and wiped at her eyes with the back of her hands. "I'm sorry. I wasn't going to do this."

"Do what, dear?"

"Lose my shit in front of you."

"Come. Sit down." Gwen put her arm around Becky's shoulder and ushered her to a chair at the table. "Tell me what happened."

Becky took in the mountains of food on Gwen's plate, but realized she wasn't even hungry. She let her head drop to her chest. "I'm an idiot."

Gwen handed her a tissue. "Go on."

"You're supposed to say, 'I'm sure you're not an idiot.'"

"That remains to be seen. Is this about Rowan?"

Becky nodded as she frowned.

"Do you love him?"

"Yes. But I think he still has feelings for her."

"For whom?"

"Tamra, his wife."

Gwen put her feet back up on the chair. "And why do you think that?"

Becky told her about Rowan's dream at the cabin. "He called out her name."

Gwen picked up her egg salad sandwich and took a leisurely bite. "Do you have any green olives? I didn't see any in the refrigerator."

"Olives?"

"Green ones. I only found black. Frankly, I don't like the black ones. They taste like motor oil smells."

"I don't like the green ones." Becky watched Gwen take another bite. "Did you hear what I said?"

"About Rowan calling Tamra's name during a dream? Yes. I heard."

"And?"

"You know, since I've been pregnant, my dreams have been outrageous. Last week I was the captain on a containership bound for Newfoundland. Just this morning, I was making love to Colin in the middle of a shopping mall, only it didn't look like Colin, but I know it was him."

"Who did it look like?"

Gwen leaned forward. "A black bear. I was afraid he'd tear me to shreds when he was through with me!" She chuckled.

"This was different."

"How so?"

"You don't dream about a woman you supposedly hate, who you used to have sex with."

"Oh, no? You've never dreamed of an old lover?"

Becky rolled her eyes. "Yeah, okay. I guess."

"Then how is this any different? I realize it hurt your feelings, but you should know better than to believe it means anything at all about their relationship. Do you have any more pickles?"

It couldn't be that simple. She'd been wrecked. Devastated. "There's a whole jar in the door of the fridge."

"I finished those yesterday."

"Oh." Becky furrowed her brow as she stood and opened the pantry. Was it possible Gwen was right, and she was completely upset over something that didn't mean anything at all? She found the jar and placed it in front of her friend.

"Thank you, dear."

"I saw them hugging."

"Rowan and Tamra?"

Becky nodded.

"When?"

"In the hospital."

"Were they fully clothed?"

Becky scowled. "Yes."

"Was there any passionate necking?"

"Stop it."

"Heavy petting?"

"Gwen!"

"Did you ask Rowan about it?"

She nodded. "He said she was apologizing for everything."

Gwen piled pickle slices onto her egg salad. "That sounds completely implausible. Clearly the man is screwing his soon-to-be ex-wife behind your back."

"Stop!" Becky could see what Gwen was doing, and she didn't appreciate the other woman trivializing her feelings.

"No. I will not allow some jackass, untrustworthy loser to hurt one of my dearest friends in the world."

Colin walked into the room and opened the refrigerator. "What did my brother do now?"

Becky covered her eyes with her hand. "Nothing. Forget it."

Gwen picked up her now comically tall sandwich. "Apparently, he fell in love with our dear Becky and then had a dream about another woman."

"I think he fell in love with me after the dream."

"Well," said Gwen through her egg salad, "that's even worse!" She turned back to Colin. "He had a dream about another woman and then fell in love with poor sweet Becky. You can see why she's upset."

Colin looked at the Diet Pepsi in his hand and turned back to the fridge, grabbing a beer instead. "I'm going to watch the game. You feeling any better?" he asked Gwen, bending to kiss her head.

"I am. I think I was just hungry."

"Good." Colin walked out of the kitchen.

Becky raised concerned eyes to her smart-ass friend. "Were you sick?"

"A bit." She winked. "Just for the past few months or so."

"Seriously, are you okay?"

"I'm fine. I didn't think my body was up for the car trip home today, especially with this weather. Now are you okay?"

Becky thought about that for a moment. Here, in her kitchen, far away from Rowan, everything seemed clearer than it had been just hours before. "Yeah. I'm feeling pretty stupid, though."

"Idiot."

"What?"

"You were waiting for my determination on whether or not you are an idiot. I'd have to give a resounding affirmative."

Becky chuckled. "Thanks, Gwen."

"Anytime, my dear. Anytime."

Artful Deception

Chapter 20

Rowan stepped out of the conference room and turned on his cell phone. His first official debriefing had taken just over five hours, though he suspected there would be further questions about Gianni's involvement when the time came.

Most important, they'd gotten the official word from the Italian government: Enzo's diplomatic immunity was being waved. He would have to stand trial for his crimes in the United States.

Eleven missed calls.

He scowled, scrolling to see the numbers.

Most of them were from Becky.

His heart picked up in his chest. Her early morning departure had hurt him more than he thought possible. He took a deep breath as he returned her call.

"Rowan?"

"Hey…"

"Where the hell have you been?"

"My debriefing."

"I left you messages…"

"My phone was turned off."

"Can you come?"

He broke out in a smile. "Really?"

There was a pause on the line. "You didn't check your voicemail."

"No…"

"Gwen had a seizure this morning. She's been having headaches, and she's all swollen. She has eclampsia, Rowan. They tried controlling the seizures with medication, but it didn't work. They just took her in for an emergency C-section."

He began to run. "Oh my God. How far along is she?"

"Thirty-three weeks."

"I'm on my way."

"Please hurry, Rowan. I'm scared for her."

~~~

421

The flight was just over an hour, but it felt a hell of a lot longer than that. When Rowan got to the airport in Washington, he'd pulled out his badge and done his damnedest to convince the manager at the ticket counter that securing a seat on this plane was a matter of national security.

The lie didn't even scathe his normally strict conscience. Everyone he loved was held in the balance, and he would do whatever he could to tip the scales in their favor.

The thick dark clouds that had stuck to the windows of the airplane as they cruised now disappeared, revealing a whirling mass of snow and rain. His mind wandered to the baby, his tiny niece or nephew. Anthony had weighed almost eight pounds when he was born, and Rowan thought that was incredibly small. He could only imagine the size of a thirty-three week preemie.

Poor Colin and Gwen. They didn't deserve this. Rowan didn't know what he'd do if it was his kid, if it was Becky having the baby. The thought made his spirit roar up protectively, the idea of her carrying his child at once overwhelming and erotic.

He shifted in his seat.

He loved her, that much he knew. And he certainly wanted children now that he knew what it was like to be a father. He and Becky could get married and have the life he thought was impossible for him just months before. A life filled with love and real emotion, ups and downs and a true companion with whom he could weather the storm.

If she would give him the chance.

He'd just have to convince her.

A smile tugged at his lips as he imagined life with Becky, her flaming red hair swinging around her as they argued.

It certainly wouldn't be boring.

Hell, it would be awesome, and he knew it.

He imagined waking up next to her every morning, falling asleep by her side, sharing the moments and the memories in between. They could be happy together.

But she was keeping an emotional distance from him he needed to break through, and he wasn't even sure of its source.

Artful Deception

He frowned. An eligible bachelor, he was not. Some women might have a problem with that. His mind snapped back to Becky's earlier accusations that he had real feelings for his soon-to-be ex-wife. Nothing was further from the truth, but what could he do to convince the woman he really loved?

The cab pulled up outside Brigham and Women's Hospital and Rowan stepped out, already dialing Mass General and ringing Enzo's room. A genuine smile lit his face, having just completed another call with FBI headquarters.

Enzo's voice was as crisp and authoritative as always. "Yes?"

"It's Rowan."

"Ah, I was wondering if we'd have a chance to say goodbye before I headed back to Rome."

His smug tone only forced Rowan's smile wider. "About that. You're not going back to Rome."

"Of course I am. I have diplomatic immunity, Mitchell. There's not a damn thing you can do to stop me."

"Unless your own government sold you out and waived your privileges."

"They would never."

"Hang on a second." Rowan stopped at the information desk. "Gwen Mitchell?"

The young woman typed into her computer. "Room 317. Take the green elevator to the third floor."

"Thanks so much." He put his phone back to his ear. "Cosmo turned himself into police this morning."

Enzo didn't respond.

"Turns out, he knew a few things that really shed some light on the rash of art thefts on the East Coast over the last couple of years. I'd say his information was downright compelling."

"Really."

"Sure was. Compelling enough to convince the Italian government to revoke your immunity and allow formal charges to be filed."

"I don't believe that for a second."

Rowan stepped into an elevator. "I know for a fact, there are two armed police officers parked outside your door who are going to arrest you any minute."

Enzo's voice was a low growl. "I thank my lucky stars you're not really Anthony's father."

"That's funny, because I thank mine you're not really his grandfather."

He hung up the phone with a satisfying click.

~~~

"Knock, knock," said Rowan as he nudged open the hospital room door.

"Come in," said Gwen.

She was sitting up in bed, a tiny bundle nestled in the crook of her arm and a radiant smile on her tired face.

"Oh my gosh, she's here with you." He put a bouquet of yellow flowers on the table. "She must be doing well."

"She is."

He hugged Gwen over the baby's head. "I'm so glad. What's her name?"

"Joan Dorothy, after my mother and your grandmother. We'll call her Joanie."

His grandmother had practically raised him and Colin, and the namesake moved him deeply. "That's awesome."

"Do you want to hold her?"

"I'd love to." Before Anthony was born, Rowan had been terrified of infants. Gingerly, he took Joanie in his arms. "She's so tiny."

"Four pounds two ounces, but healthy as a horse."

The baby's eyes were closed, her tiny face perfectly formed. "She looks like you, Gwen."

Colin's voice chimed in behind him. "She's got my chin."

"And your nose," said Gwen, smiling.

"Congratulations," said Rowan, opening his free arm to embrace his brother. "She's beautiful."

Colin bent and ran his finger along the baby's cheek. "She's already got my heart on a string."

Gwen sighed. "You and me, both."

"How are you feeling?" Rowan asked her.

"Pretty good. Tired."

"I heard you had a seizure." He handed the baby back to her mother.

"Yes, I heard that, too. I don't remember it, though. I remember the ambulance, then the operating room, then she was here."

The door opened and Becky walked in carrying a cafeteria tray covered with food. "Okay. I got your ice cream, your eggplant Parmesan and a double side of bacon. Colin, are you sure you didn't want…" her voice trailed off as she looked up and saw Rowan. "Hi."

"Hi."

"How was D.C.?"

He nodded. "Good. They got Cosmo to turn on Enzo for Marco's murder and the thefts. The Italian government waived Enzo's immunity, so he's going to stand trial for all of it."

"What about shooting Gianni?"

"Enzo will be charged, but I suspect Gianni and Tamra will be gone before it comes to that."

Becky scrunched up her face. "Too bad they couldn't help put him away first."

"It's okay," he said, moving to take her hand. "He's going down anyway, and they need to get on with their lives. We all do."

"What about Leonardo?"

"Tamra was thrilled to learn he's really her father, and Anthony's grandfather. They're working on finding a new normal, I think."

"Walk with me?" she asked.

He nodded. "We'll be back."

They wandered past the empty nursery, down a long stretch of maternity rooms, each bustling with activity. "I don't like the way we left things." Becky looked at the floor, gathering her courage. "I shouldn't have made such a big deal about you lying, and the dream, and I'm sorry."

"If you called out some guy's name, I'd be pissed, too. But those kinds of dreams don't really matter. All that matters are the dreams we make together, about our future, about what we want. Those are the real dreams."

"I don't know if I can trust you."

He stopped walking and turned to her. "How can you say that?"

"You've told so many lies…"

"For work. I've told so many lies for work. I never lied to you about who I am, or how I feel about you, about what really matters. Think about it."

Her mind backpedaled over her memories, every lie he'd ever told coming under scrutiny. The owner of the cabin in the woods. Working for Enzo, and the theft of *The Lady in the Blue Dress*. Each time he was untruthful, he was protecting his identity as an undercover agent.

"You know I'm right," he said. "You can trust me, Becky. Today, tomorrow, and every day after. I love you."

He had said it so many times, but it was the first time she let herself really believe it. She swallowed it up, the knowledge making her glow from within. Her voice was a whisper. "Me, too."

The words were out, and her heart sang with joy. Rowan would be hers to love after all. He kissed her gently, with a tenderness that nearly brought tears to her eyes.

Pulling back, he smiled and said, "You are the love of my life. I couldn't ask for more than what we have together."

She rolled her eyes and giggled. "That's so corny."

"It's true. And you'd better get used to corny, because I'm going to be laying it on you full force for the rest of my days."

Her brows snapped down. "The rest of your days?"

"Yep."

"Is that supposed to mean…"

"Marry me, Becky."

Her jaw dropped open. "You're already married."

"A technicality. Will you wait for me?"

He's serious.

With the knowledge came an answering certainty. She wanted to marry Rowan more than she had ever wanted anything in her life. Her eyes stung, threatening. "How long are we talking?"

He squinted one eye. "I'll be honest with you. It could be a while."

"Can we live in sin in the meantime?"

"Of course."

She threw her arms around his neck and squeezed. "Then yes, I'll marry you." He lifted her off the floor in a tight embrace and kissed her soundly on the lips.

"When do I get to meet your family?" he asked.

"Ooh, yikes!"

"What's wrong?"

She clenched her teeth and bared them. "I've never brought anyone home before."

"Never?"

"I never liked anybody enough."

"Well then I'll be the first."

She scrunched up her nose. "Just don't mention your wife, or my father might have a heart attack."

"That's probably a good idea. Do you have any brothers or sisters?"

"One older sister, Meghan. She's married with a daughter. She caused enough family drama when she ran away from home at sixteen. I don't think my parents can handle a married fiancé, too."

"How long was she gone?"

"Fifteen years. She was pregnant when she left town with her boyfriend Liam, who was wanted for arson. But that's another story all together."

"Did he really do it?"

"Come home with me. Meet the crazies, and I'll tell you all about it."

Chapter 21

Becky's hair was elaborately braided on the sides, masses of red curls cascading down her back. She stared into the mirror, fiddling with its riotous bulk in an attempt to tame the beast.

Her old friend Julie stilled Becky's hand with her own. "Stop it. You look ravishing."

"Says Mrs. Perfect Pants." Julie's purple bridesmaid dress had a boat-neck that looked both classy and elegant. "I feel like the ugly stepsister next to you."

Julie held her arms out to her sides. "You picked out this dress!"

"I have good taste." She looked in the mirror and cursed like a biker. "Can you help me with my hair, please? I just want it a little less poofy."

"Oh, give me that." Julie lifted Becky's hair and ran the brush through the curls on the very bottom, making the top fall perfectly.

"How do you do that? You're like Jesus calming the storm."

"Thank you very much." Julie put the brush back on the vanity. "Stand up. I want to see."

Becky did, her massive skirts rustling, and she smiled widely. For all of her bravado and modern fashion sense, when it came to picking a wedding gown, she had gone completely traditional. The white satin bodice was rich with elaborate beading, fine lace covering her arms, her shapely shoulders bare.

"You look incredible. Are you ready for this?"

"As long as I don't throw up on my shoes when it's time for my vows, I should be golden."

"Did you write your own?"

Becky nodded. "Rowan's idea. He's a total sap."

"I think it's sweet."

"That's because you're a total sap, too."

The door opened and Gwen yelled in, "Knock, knock! It's me and Fiona!"

"Come on in," said Becky.

Joanie was sleeping on Gwen's shoulder. "Becky, my dear! You look stunning. The minister says he's ready to begin when you are."

No turning back now. Not that she would want to. "Is Rowan here?"

"He is. Colin says he's a nervous wreck!" She smiled gleefully.

"Good." Becky took one last look in the mirror and picked up her bouquet of yellow and purple roses. "You ready to get this show on the road, Fiona?"

"I sure am!" Becky's niece looked just like Becky had at her age.

How could I have thought I was ugly? So much had transpired since those early years, but even as she thought it, she knew the real change had come with Rowan's love. She bit back the sentiment. "I am not going to cry. Let's go get hitched!"

Becky turned around just as her father stepped in the room, and a wave of emotion nearly knocked her to the floor. She pointed her index finger accusingly at the only other man she had ever loved. "Don't say anything nice to me, or I'm going to lose it."

He smiled, a gleam lighting his eye as he stared at his youngest daughter. "You really wearing white?"

Becky burst out laughing and walked to her father, locking her arm with his. "Thanks, Daddy."

~~~

Rowan stood before the people who mattered in his life and turned to the woman he loved.

"I promise to honor you, to love you and respect you, to go to the store for you when you want ice cream, to make you laugh and to fix the furnace, to believe in you when you stop believing in yourself, and to always remember that you are the most important person in my life. I look forward to spending my days steeped in your company, my nights holding you in my arms, to every fight and every making up. I love you, Becky O'Connor, and I will do my very best to make you happy every day for the rest of our lives."

Becky couldn't keep the tears from falling, couldn't contain this emotional high. She threw her head back and screamed, making the congregation laugh. "Okay. Here goes. Rowan, I love you. I never thought I'd find anyone to love me, not like you do. You are my sunshine when it's cloudy, my rain when everything's too dry. You've made me so happy. I promise to love you, to honor you, and to keep you, all the days of my life. Oh, and I promise not to make you sorry we did this."

The congregation laughed again, and Becky leaned forward to kiss Rowan soundly on the lips.

The minister cleared his throat. "We didn't get to that part yet."

"Whoops! Sorry," she said.

Rowan was smiling. "Get to the 'I now pronounce you' part."

"By the power vested in me by the Commonwealth of Massachusetts, I now pronounce you husband and wife."

Rowan and Becky threw themselves at each other, to the delight of their family and friends.

The minister shrugged his shoulders. "You may now kiss the bride!"

~~~

The reception was in full swing.

The cake had been cut, and thrown and mashed into Rowan's ear, Becky had danced with her father and shared her first dance with Rowan as husband and wife. Music and laughter permeated the air, candlelight twinkled from every table and glasses clinked in merriment.

Becky danced to "Cotton-Eye Joe" with her brother-in-law Liam, laughing herself silly, then went in search of her beau. She found him just as he stepped up to the bar and she slipped her arms around him from behind.

"Well, hello there, Mrs. Mitchell."

"Hey, baby. What do you say we blow this taco stand?"

His brows drew together. "It's early. You really want to go already?"

She smiled devilishly. "We won't be gone long. You know that balcony off our hotel room? I thought we could see how well it's bolted to the wall."

His eyes widened. "You serious?"

"Heck yeah, sailor!" She took him by the hand and started to walk backwards.

"It faces the Drake. Someone might see us."

"Yep." She raised her eyebrows. "They sure might."

He picked up his pace and spun her around, his hand at her waist. "Have I told you how much I love you?"

"You have, but you can say it again when I get out of this dress." They reached the elevator and she pressed the button, her eyes slowly taking in the length of his body, perfect in his tuxedo.

"I can't wait to make love to you," he whispered.

"Wait 'till you see my 'something blue'."

The doors opened and they stepped inside.

"You're driving me crazy."

"Oh, sweetheart." She smiled as he took him in his arms. "I haven't even gotten started yet."

~~~

Meghan's Wish

For Deyon,
who wanted to read the next one.

Meghan's Wish

1997

Meghan O'Connor had been in love with Liam Wheaton since as long as she could remember.

Her parents had done what they could to stop it, carefully erasing his name from the birthday party invitation list and failing to pass on phone messages when they intercepted his calls. But Largo was a small town, with only one class at each grade level, and ten months out of the year Liam and Meghan spent six hours a day together.

There was talk of sending Meghan to boarding school at Saint Catherine's, but in the end Tom O'Connor couldn't justify the additional expense, just to get his daughter away from Chip Wheaton's son.

Chip was a drunk, and a mean one at that, who could be found at The Well any night of the week. He worked at the quarry, or doing construction, in-between layoffs and being fired time and again. His wife Lindsay cleaned houses and cared for the couple's five children, who always seemed a shade dirtier and a tad more disruptive than the other children of Largo.

Liam was the oldest. He got a job as a stock boy at the Super Duper when he was fourteen, and the townspeople could often be heard commenting on how clean and polite he was *for a Wheaton*.

Meghan didn't care that Liam was a Wheaton. All that mattered to her was that he was gentle and kind, going out of his way to make sure she was happy, and flashing his devil-may-care smile to cheer her up when she was not.

He had the darkest brown hair and strong, handsome features, marred by a razor-thin scar that ran from his left ear to his chin. His father had crashed the family sedan into a maple tree when Liam was five, propelling the unrestrained boy face-first through the windshield.

Meghan thought the scar made him look like a warrior.

For the most part Liam was quiet, keeping his smart wit and quick temper hidden from those who didn't like a fast tongue on those they look down upon. He excelled in school, but with the

434

Meghan's Wish

future before him like so much blank paper, Liam knew only that he wanted to spend it with Meghan.

He only got in serious trouble once, when Ricky Powell asked Meghan to go with him to a dance and she said no. Ricky touched her face and called her a bitch who'd rather go slumming with trash. Liam broke Ricky's nose in two places.

The pair signed up for track and field instead of soccer so Liam didn't have to buy cleats and a ball, and when Meghan tried out for a part in the school play, Liam volunteered as a stage hand. It was after a performance of My Fair Lady, in the heavily draped wings of the stage, that they shared true love's first kiss.

Patty O'Connor didn't miss the high flush on her daughter's ivory cheeks, nor the newfound spring in Meghan's step. Patty was in the crowd when Liam broke the school record for the hundred meter dash, and saw Meghan embrace Liam like only a woman holds a man.

A shocked Patty could feel the eyes of the other parents upon her, shame covering her like fire, wishing the bleachers would give way beneath her just to draw attention away from that filthy embrace.

Meghan was taken out of track and field, and the theater troupe, and her father sat her down to explain exactly what kind of people the Wheatons really were.

Meghan seemed to take his words to heart.

Over the next several weeks, she went out of her way to make it up to her mother, watching her younger sister, cleaning the house and doing the shopping. Patty was just beginning to think things were back to normal when Bonnie Harrison called to say she saw Meghan and Liam making out behind the Super Duper, "like a couple of horny teenagers."

Saint Catherine's was called, only to find that the nuns were in the process of shutting down the school due to poor enrollment.

Patty marched a mortified Meghan into the principal's office at school, and Meghan shriveled as she listened to her mother reprimand the administrator for allowing Liam Wheaton to get his *grubby paws* on her innocent daughter. Well aware on which side his bread was buttered, the principal gave Liam his own

Meghan's Wish

private lunch table, away from his classmates, and Liam's desk was moved to the opposite side of the classroom.

It was a full year before her mother sent Meghan back to the Super Duper.

"I need eggs for the casserole, and I can't walk away from these," she said, gesturing to several pots bubbling on the stove. Patty exhaled loudly, staring at her daughter. "Go to the store. And no funny business, young lady. Do you hear me? If that Wheaton boy is there, you ignore him. Not a word."

Meghan's bike flew down Main Street as fast as her feet could pedal, her dark hair blowing behind her in the breeze. All the way there her heart pounded in her chest, her hands gripping the handlebars too tightly as her emotions raced in anticipation.

They hadn't even spoken since the fateful track meet, the adults keeping a close watch on them at every turn. Meghan pulled her bike up on the curb, hastily snapping the lock and running inside. She scanned the aisles one by one until she found him, his long body reaching onto a high shelf.

She bit her lip as she started toward him. "Liam," she called out lightly, and his head snapped up.

His eyes held hers, devouring her, setting her belly to tingling. "Meggie."

"My momma let me come buy some eggs." What a stupid thing to say, but it didn't matter, because they were together again, face-to-face.

"I've missed you," he said, his eyes falling to her lips.

Meghan felt herself flush, loving the sound of his words after so much silence. "Meet me," she said quietly.

"Where?"

"I don't know."

He took a purposeful step toward her. "The old powder mill, by the river."

She had heard stories about what went on there. Dirty stories about men and women and what they could do to each other. She felt dizzy, even as she nodded her consent. Anything to be close to Liam. "When?"

"I get off at six."

Her parents were going to a concert, and Becky had a sleepover at a friend's house. "I'll be there."

And so it was that Meghan O'Connor and Liam Wheaton made love at the old powder mill, the summer they turned sixteen. When Meghan slipped from Liam's arms and raced to beat her parents home, she had no idea that two great changes were about to take place, that would alter her life forever.

A new life was forming in her belly, and the old powder mill was about to go up in flames.

Meghan's Wish

2012

"I'm home," Meghan called from the doorway of the apartment, her arms wrestling with a seven-foot spruce. Warm, humid air and the smell of something baking greeted her, making her mouth water. "Fiona?" She pushed the top of the tree over the threshold, a branch whipping back to scratch her face. "Damn it," she muttered. "I could use some help here, please!"

Footsteps padded to the other side of the doorway, Fiona's heart-shaped face and green eyes just visible over the foliage. "You got a tree!"

"I think the tree got me, actually. I'm bleeding, and I'm stuck. Help me get this in there."

"What do you want me to do?"

"Crawl under there and pull the trunk in first. What are you baking?"

Fiona knelt down under the boughs, her red hair just visible beneath the full branches.

She looks more like Becky every day.

"Rhea's making a spice cake," said Fiona.

"It smells fantastic."

"It has rum in it. She's been hitting the sauce ever since."

A sing-song voice came from deeper in the apartment. "I hear you, Fiona dear."

"You're hallucinating, Rhea. I left an hour ago," she yelled back.

"This isn't working," said Meghan. "Grab the top of this thing and pull."

"Here?"

"No, here," she said, pushing the largest branch toward her daughter. The tree snapped free of the door frame and into the living room, falling onto its side.

"Nice one," said Fiona, her gaze meeting her mother's eye-to-eye, a light smile at her lips. She wore a plaid button-down shirt and leggings that hung off her body like borrowed clothes. Her skin glowed more pale than ivory, a new and unflattering change.

Meghan's Wish

Meghan forced a smile onto her face. "How was your day?

"Good. I take it we're decorating a Christmas tree tonight?"

"Unless you have other plans."

"Rhonda and Kathy asked me to catch a movie. But that's okay, I'd rather decorate."

A petite, fifty-something woman with short brown hair walked in the room. "Can I help too?"

"You'd better. We're not doing all the work ourselves."

The phone rang and Fiona ran off to answer it.

"How was work?" asked Rhea.

"Good, good." Meghan nodded, then stopped abruptly. "Bad. It was awful, actually. I spent the whole day redoing all the artwork for the Gazelle account that I just did on Friday."

"I thought that nightmare was finished!"

"Yeah, me too..." Meghan trailed off as Fiona came near with the phone.

"It's for you," she said, her eyes wide. "It's Dr. Haring."

Meghan's brows drew together. She took the phone and walked into the kitchen, turning to be sure Fiona hadn't followed her. "This is Meghan."

"Ms. O'Connor, it's Dr. Haring. I know I said I wouldn't have anything for you until Monday, but I just got the lab results and I wanted to let you know ASAP."

Every muscle in Meghan's body clenched in anticipation.

"I'm afraid it's not good news," he said. "Three out of six alleles, which is quite common for a parent."

Meghan slid down the cupboard and sat on the vinyl floor.

The doctor cleared his throat. "I told you it was extremely unlikely you would be a match, Ms. O'Connor..."

"One in two hundred." Tears began to collect in her eyes.

My baby. My poor, sweet baby.

She wanted to get off the phone, but didn't trust herself to speak.

"Forgive me, Ms. O'Connor, but I need to ask again. Does Fiona have any other family?"

"No." The word hung in the air, and Meghan waited to see if he would challenge her with a basic knowledge of biology.

Meghan's Wish

"Well then, you may want to organize a donor drive. But the chances of finding a match from an unrelated donor, not already on the registry, are formidable."

~~~

Rhea Goldstein sipped her mug of tea as she cleaned up the last of the spice cake dishes. She was more at home in Meghan's kitchen than her own, having cooked the balance of her meals over the last eight years in this space. The mirror image of her own apartment, the kitchen had a breakfast bar that overlooked the living room, and she could see Meghan sitting on the floor in the glow of the Christmas tree lights. Fiona had gone upstairs to take a bath.

Rhea pulled out a bottle of fragrant red wine, poured two glasses.

She drank one down and refilled it, taking a moment to prepare for battle before joining Meghan by the tree, handing her a glass and sitting herself down rigidly in a side chair. "I think it's time you told me the truth," she said.

Meghan looked confused. "What?"

"The truth, the whole truth, and nothing but the truth so help you, God." Rhea felt her voice shake, knew that her grasp on her wine glass was tight enough to snap the stem if she wasn't careful.

Rhea sipped her wine, remembering the first time she saw Meghan and little Fiona with her Santa hat, unpacking everything they owned, two days before Christmas. Peeking though her front curtains, Rhea knew right then they were running away from something. She'd been drawn to the woman and the girl from that first look, imagining she might find a way to befriend them, or prove herself useful.

Rhea had been alone for a long time.

She introduced herself and offered to help, which they politely refused, then Rhea came back to her apartment. The squalor that greeted her was a surprise.

When did I let it get so bad?

Dirty dishes that had been sitting in the same place for weeks, stacks of papers and heaps of clothing--whether clean or dirty, she didn't know. She opened the windows to the icy

Meghan's Wish

December air and cleaned her apartment for the first time in months, then showered and blew dry her hair.

She drove to the discount store and bought chocolate milk for Fiona, *such a beautiful name*, imagining the girl might come over for a visit. On a whim, she filled her cart with Christmas ornaments, then she drove to where the boy scout troop was selling real Christmas trees, and bought a beauty for Meghan's apartment.

Like a child who finds someone else's puppy, she selfishly ignored whatever had brought them to her. Meghan and Fiona gave her the first sunshine, the first taste of love, since her Bill passed away.

But she would give it all up in an instant, if it meant Fiona could be well again.

"What are you talking about?" asked Meghan.

"I'm talking about the two of you. You and your daughter. Where you came from, what happened that brought you here."

Meghan stared at her hands as she fiddled with something small. "Why are you asking me now, Rhea?"

"Because it's time. Where is that baby's father?"

Meghan gazed at the tree. "I don't know. We left him in Connecticut."

"Did he hurt you?"

"No, but I was afraid of him." She uncrossed her legs, stretching them out before her on the soft rug. "He was burning down buildings—the grocery where he used to work, his parents' house. The building where we first made love."

Rhea shook her head, shocked by what she was hearing.

"The first fire was before we left Largo. Liam was implicated, but I thought he was being set up by someone else." She scoffed. "Turns out, that was just what I wanted to believe."

"They say love is blind."

"And foolish. I walked away from my family to start a life with a boy who was lying to me and running from the law."

"You must have loved him very much."

The corner of Meghan's lip turned down. "I did."

"I wondered why you sometimes seem so sad," said Rhea quietly. "Is it because of him?"

Meghan's Wish

Meghan nodded as she wiped at the tears on her cheeks. "And I miss my family."

"Why didn't you go home when you left him?"

"Honestly? I told myself it was because he'd be able to find us there. But I think that was only part of the reason." She took a shaky breath in, exhaling loudly. "I don't think my family can forgive me."

Rhea knew a thing or two about forgiveness, and knew it would be difficult for anyone to turn these lovely women away. "I think it's time you find out."

Meghan shook her head, looking at Rhea like she was crazy. "I'm not going back there."

"You have to. Fiona can stay with me."

"They hate me."

"I doubt that very much, but regardless, you have no choice."

"I'm going to hold a donor drive. I'll contact the radio and TV stations, and the newspaper. The community will support her. We'll get people tested."

Rhea leaned forward. "You're looking for a needle in a haystack, instead of going to the sewing store. Does Liam have brothers and sisters?"

"His family doesn't even know Fiona exists!"

"So you'll need to tell them. How many brothers and sisters?"

Meghan stood, taking Rhea's empty glass into the kitchen. "Three brothers and a sister."

Rhea closed her eyes and sighed. "That's someplace to start. They might even have kids by now, too, which would mean cousins who could be tested for Fiona."

"The odds still aren't good. You know that." Meghan cursed under her breath. "I don't want to go to those people. What if they tell Liam?"

"Then you will deal with him face-to-face. It's time to stop running from the past, Meghan. That baby needs her family more than she needs you right now."

~~~

Meghan's Wish

Liam bent at the waist, driving his shovel beneath eighteen inches of heavy, wet snow. He was sweating and hot despite the frigid weather, the hard work compensating for his lightweight jacket.

He'd been at it for more than an hour, his muscles aching from the punishing task. It was the numbness in his mind that Liam was after, a trance-like calm that he couldn't get from the snow blower parked in the garage.

God knows he needed to be numb right now.

It was just after dark, his breath making little clouds in the triangle of light that shined on his driveway. Up and down the street, neighbors' Christmas lights heralded a season that Liam found difficult to tolerate.

Eight years they've been gone, almost to the day.

In that time, he had learned to breathe in and out, despite having no desire to do so. He had been beaten down, paid a debt to society that he never even owed. Created a life for himself that included a thriving business and a beautiful home, neither of which meant a damn thing without them.

Liam couldn't look at a tree or a candy cane without feeling the crush of longing and regret. They were gone, his wife and his little girl, and they were not coming back. His shovel scraped the pavement, the rhythm of the sound marching forward like time itself.

He was worse today than usual, having dreamed about Meghan last night. His unconscious mind held no grudges against his traitorous wife, remembering only the tangle of their bodies, the fevered pitch of their lovemaking, the touch of her soul against his own.

The dream had left him aching, desperate and angry, knowing full well that no other woman could satisfy this desire. He stopped shoveling and straightened his back, allowing his tightened muscles to stretch. A full moon graced the night sky, illuminating the world below.

"Damn you, Meghan O'Connor. Damn you straight to hell."

~~~

Meghan stopped for gas just outside of Stockbridge, the snow-covered ground reflecting the bright winter sun. She was

Meghan's Wish

close enough to Largo that the landscape reminded her of home, the Berkshires rising up from all sides like great, wholly arms. She followed the sign for gas from the interstate, up a meandering hill that was oddly familiar. It wasn't until she pulled in front of The Galaxy Diner and Gas Station that her mind snapped to attention.

She and Liam had stopped here the night they left Largo.

Suddenly, she missed him so acutely that she moaned aloud, her lips curling into a frown. Her heart was prone to forgetting that she didn't love her husband anymore.

She shook her head and sat up straighter in her seat, turning the wheel to pull up to the pump. She opened her door just as a man in a heavy winter coat bent his head to her window.

"What can I get for ya?" he asked.

"Fill it up with regular, please."

Meghan's gaze fixed at a point in the distance, the memory of her last day in Largo coming to life before her eyes.

It was glorious and sunny, the summer air humid and still. Becky had lied for Meghan, telling their parents they were going to the park, when really the girls met Liam at Hunter's Point—a wide, grassy field where the creek ran shallow over a rocky bed.

Liam taught Becky how to catch crayfish in the cold water, while Meghan lounged on a boulder, soaking up the sun. When Becky climbed a tree across the creek, Liam joined Meghan.

"How was work?" she asked him.

He skipped a rock into the rushing creek. "Not so good." He picked up another handful of rocks. "I got fired."

She sat up, shading her eyes from the sun. "Why?"

"The police found my pocketknife at the old mill," said Liam. "Officer Spaulding must have mentioned it to his wife, because she remembered I used it to open a crate of pears for her right at the end of my shift that day. They can prove I was there, Meghan."

"Lots of people go to the old mill. That doesn't mean anything."

Liam nodded, throwing more rocks. "After Grimley fired me, I walked out to the parking lot and Spaulding was waiting for me. He took me to the stationhouse for questioning."

Meghan's Wish

"All because of a pocketknife?"

"No." He stopped throwing rocks and turned to look at her. "Ricky Powell told Spaulding he saw me that night, walking down Main Street with a gas can."

Fear seeped into Meghan's brain, knowing that an accusation like that could mean serious trouble for Liam. "But that's a lie. Why would he say that?"

Even as she said the words, she knew.

Ricky had been asking Meghan out for years, but recently he'd grown more insistent, calling on the phone, walking too close to her in the hallway. He even left a letter in her school bag, telling her she was beautiful.

Liam threw the last of his rocks and put his hands in the pockets of his shorts. "He wants you to himself, Meghan. He was standing right there when I showed up for work and Grimley fired me, like he wanted me to know he had something to do with it."

"I'll tell Sheriff Spaulding you were with me."

He shook his head. "That will just ruin your reputation. I was still there when you left, remember?"

She reached out and laid her hand on his arm. "Then I'll lie."

He smiled a humorless smile. "It's not going to come to that."

"What do you mean?"

"If they arrest me, ain't nobody in this town going to give a Wheaton a fair trial."

She wanted to tell him he was wrong. She wanted to hold him forever, keep him safe from the people who couldn't see what she saw every time she looked into his eyes.

"I'm leaving town, Meghan."

Her face fell. "No!"

"Yes. Tomorrow," he swallowed, turning to look into her eyes. "Don't you see? I don't have another choice. I lost my job, Ricky's out to get me, and the sheriff's just biding his time before he arrests me. I need a fresh start. Someplace I can just be me, not Chip Wheaton's son."

"Then I'm coming with you."

"No," he said, shaking his head, and she thought she could see an extra shine in his eyes. "Your family and your life are here. I'm not going to let you give that up for me."

She reached out and touched his face. "You are my family and my life now, Liam. I'm pregnant."

His shocked expression held something else—a spark of wonder, a touch of joy. *"What?"*

"Pregnant," she said softly.

He pulled her against him in a fierce embrace.

"So now you have to take me with you," she whispered.

He pulled back to look at her. "You're not just saying that so I'll take you?"

She shook her head. "I found out on Tuesday, I just didn't know how to tell you."

"A baby..." he said, tears now clearly visible along his lashes. "I love you, Meghan O'Connor."

"I love you, too, Liam."

A sharp rap at her window made her jump, and Meghan fumbled for her purse. "Ancient history," she said to herself. That was fifteen years earlier. She didn't even recognize the naïve girl she had been. She drove down the hill and got back on the interstate toward Largo, less than an hour away from her parents' house.

~~~

Becky O'Connor went all-out at Christmastime.

Her 1920s bungalow was covered in fat colored lights, their strands wound around the posts of her chunky front porch like gumdrops on a gingerbread house. The living room window showcased a glorious evergreen, the lawn graced with miniature Christmas trees that followed the meandering path of the walkway.

Inside, the smell of spicy chili permeated the air, along with the tang of wood smoke from a fire in the hearth. The table was set with fancy dishes and cloth napkins in preparation for the meal to come.

Becky opened a bottle of wine as she sang along to "Rockin' Around the Christmas Tree". Her long red hair hung in two thick plaits on either side of her head, like a child. She wore a T-shirt that said "In your dreams" and a pair of jeans that hugged her feminine curves. Her feet were bare, her toenails painted bright pink.

Her parents' flight should have gotten in almost an hour ago. Tom and Patty O'Connor bought a place in Florida when they retired, and they lived there most of the year. They returned to Massachusetts for the holidays and the high summer months, but didn't bother to open their house for the shorter of the two trips. Becky's home was the new home base for Christmas, and she loved every minute of it.

She'd just gotten back in town the day before, having spent several days in New York City for her best friend Julie's wedding. Julie married Hank Jared, who she met last Christmas when he was a Navy officer investigating Julie's father's murder—or so it had seemed at the time. The wedding had been spectacular—a holiday themed wedding that included the entire bridal party ice skating in Central Park.

Wandering into the front room, Becky danced and twirled, her braids swinging from side to side as she remembered the DJ playing this same song at the wedding. She had danced with a handsome groomsman named Pete, one of two she flirted with throughout the reception.

Meghan stood on the other side of Becky's front window in an icy wind, tiny shards of freezing rain pelting her as she watched her baby sister, all grown up and beautiful, dancing.

It had taken Meghan forty-five minutes to get the courage to step out of her car, just as Becky appeared in the large picture window and stopped Meghan in her tracks.

Little sobs mixed with laughter as she watched Becky dance, making Meghan's nose run and sniff. Her gut ached for every time she had missed Becky, the price of her exile never before so plain.

She might have stayed there on the sidewalk all night, but a car turned down the residential street, it's headlights prodding her toward the door. She reached up and knocked before she could think better of it.

Meghan's Wish

The high-pitched barking of a little dog cold be heard before the door opened and Becky appeared, her prominent green eyes widening at the apparition before her.

"Hi, Monkey." Meghan said softly. She knew she was a mess, her eyes red and teary. She hadn't meant to use the old endearment, but the word wanted to be said more than she cared to keep it inside.

Becky slapped her hand over her mouth. "Meghan!" she screeched, opening her arms and pulling her sister to her. Then they were both crying, clutching each other.

"It's freezing out here!" said Becky, flashing Meghan a brilliant smile. "Come in, come in." The women hugged for long moments before finally stepping back.

"I tried Mom and Dad's house first, but no one was home," Meghan said. "Do they still live on Becker?"

"Well..."

A knock sounded at the door.

"Oh, my God, that's perfect," said Becky with a smile. "Open the door, Meggie."

Meghan was confused, but she did as Becky asked. There on the porch stood her mom and dad.

There was screaming and grabbing, holding and hugging as the world before Meghan blurred into a swirl of emotion. She heard her own sobbing as she rested her head on her mother's shoulder, Patty's scent exactly the same as Meghan remembered from countless hugs and kisses growing up.

Her father stepped back, catching his breath and wiping at his face. "I've been praying for this day for fifteen years."

"I'm sorry," wailed Meghan, sounding to herself like a younger version of the woman she'd become. "I wanted to come home for so long."

"Where have you been?" asked Patty. "I was worried sick."

Becky handed Meghan a glass of red wine, and she took a sip, its rich smoky flavor mixing with her nervous stomach to make her nauseated. Suddenly, she was so scared, she wished she could disappear in a puff of smoke like a magic trick.

Sorry, just kidding. I'm not really back after all.

Meghan's Wish

Could her family understand the fears of a sixteen year-old child and forgive her for running off with Liam? Could they love their granddaughter, who was Chip Wheaton's granddaughter, too?

Her father spoke, his voice deeper now than she remembered. "Don't you know, there's nothing you can ever do that will make us stop loving you?"

A mother now herself, Meghan knew her father spoke the truth. She took a deep breath. "I left with Liam. I was pregnant, and he was about to be arrested for setting the fire at the old mill."

Her mother nodded, her eyes shining and bright. "And the baby?"

She's not even surprised!

Remorse was bitter on Meghan's tongue. "Fiona is fifteen."

"Is she here with you?" Patty's hopeful eyes darted to the living room doorway, and the look of longing on her face was more than Meghan could bear.

"No. She's staying with a friend."

Patty's eyes were bright. "I'd like to meet her."

Meghan nodded, staring at her mother, wishing for forgiveness but too afraid to ask. "Fiona's the reason I came back here today." She couldn't stop the tears, didn't try to. "She has leukemia, mom," she said, the words stumbling over the knot in her throat. "She needs a bone marrow transplant."

Patty held her hand to her heart. "Does Liam know?"

That surprised her. "No. I haven't talked to Liam in eight years. I don't even know where he is."

Her family exchanged knowing glances.

"What?" asked Meghan.

"He's in Largo," said Becky.

"What?"

"He came back my freshman year, so that was..." Becky looked at the ceiling, "...eight years ago."

Meghan was flabbergasted. Of all the places in the world, she never imagined Liam would come back to Largo. "He's been here the whole time?" she asked. "But the sheriff was going to arrest him for the fire at the old mill."

Meghan's Wish

Becky nodded. "He *was* arrested. And convicted."

"Convicted?"

Patty nodded. "He served three and a half years in prison, Meggie. He's been living in Largo since his release."

2004

Liam and Meghan lived in a two-bedroom apartment on the second floor of a complex, with an outdoor landing Meghan had covered in Christmas lights. The building was dated, but the grounds were well maintained and the living space generous.

Liam stepped into the kitchen and kissed his wife on the cheek. "Have a great day, Meggie. I love you."

He smelled like aftershave and soap, and she licked her lips. "You too, baby," she answered him, as she buttered Fiona's toast. "Good luck with Flanders."

"Luck's got nothing to do with it," he said with a wink. He was an outstanding salesman, and she was proud of him.

He picked up little Fiona from her coloring at the table and hugged her tightly, her red curls peeking out from beneath a big red Santa hat. "Goodbye, little mouse."

"Can you stay and make Christmas cookies with us, Daddy?"

"I can't, sweetheart. Daddy has to go to work." He rubbed his nose against hers. "I'm going to be late tonight."

"Again?" Meghan asked, handing Fiona her breakfast. Several nights in the last few weeks, he'd gotten home after she'd gone to bed.

Liam shrugged. "It just so happens, I'm working on a very special Christmas gift."

"Oh, really?" she asked, digging in the cupboard, trying to remember what she'd been looking for. "How hard is it to find a jewelry store?"

"Oh, no, no, no. Not for my wife. I'm getting her something from the heart."

"Cheapskate," she said, laughing.

"Materialistic Scrooge." He poked her with his finger. "I'm getting you the greatest gift you've ever gotten in your whole entire life."

"Wow, that's a lot of hype. What if I don't like it?"

"Sorry, all items are sold as-is, no refunds or exchanges."

She smiled at him. "I love you."

Meghan's Wish

"I love you, too." He checked his watch. "I've got to run. Have a great day!"

Meghan watched the door close behind him, thinking she was the luckiest woman on earth. Christmas was the hardest time of year for her, and Liam was always trying to make it better.

No matter how hard she tried to stop it, she could feel herself retreating into her shell, so sad over missing her family during the holidays. Every year it was a little more difficult, lasting longer into the new year before she was able to find some relief.

She didn't regret choosing Liam when she had to make the choice, but the price that she paid only compounded over time, increasing the burden on her conscience and her wellbeing. For the last two weeks, she couldn't seem to stop crying.

She bustled around the kitchen, grabbing her own breakfast dishes and putting them in the dishwasher, keeping her face averted from her daughter to hide her tears. She didn't want Fiona's memories of Christmas to be affected by her own depression.

The doorbell rang.

"I'll get it!" Fiona yelled, bouncing out of her seat. Meghan followed her, taking time to wipe her face and eyes. She walked into the living room just as Fiona opened the door—to Ricky Powell, standing on the threshold.

"No!" Meghan yelled, running to pull the girl back as if from the edge of a cliff. She put herself between Fiona and Ricky.

He held up his hands. "I just want to talk to you."

Adrenaline surging, she snapped at him. "No. You get the hell away from me, Ricky. You stay away from my home." Her arm flung the wooden door with all of her strength, only to watch Ricky easily stop it with his hand.

"It's important, Meghan. Look, I'll stand right here. I won't even come in."

She looked down at her daughter, who clung to her waist.

"I won't hurt you," he said.

Despite her anxiety, she believed that was true. Ricky had never threatened her.

Meghan's Wish

Meghan pried the girl's arms from around her waist and talked in a calm voice. "Fiona, I need to talk to this man."

The girl shook her head.

"It's okay, he's an old friend of mine. I was just surprised to see him. Can you please go to your room and play for a little while?"

Fiona glared at her mother, then at the stranger, shaking her head no.

"Yes. Go to your room, please."

"I want Mommy."

"It's okay, Fiona. Go now."

The girl begrudgingly left the room, and Meghan crossed her arms over her chest, facing Ricky. "How did you find us?"

"I followed Liam here from Largo yesterday."

Liam would sooner drive through hell. "That's a lie." She reached for the door.

"Call his work," said Ricky. "They'll tell you he wasn't there. He was stopped next to me at the intersection of Washington and Church. He didn't see me, but I got a good look at him. It seemed fishy that he'd be back in town just two days after someone tried to burn down the Super Duper, so I followed him."

"Someone tried to burn down the grocery store?"

He nodded. "Fortunately, they had a sprinkler system. But the damages are in the tens of thousands."

"I don't see what that has to do with us."

He reached in his pocket, pulling out a cell phone with a large display and tapping buttons while he spoke.

"Let's see if you understand after you watch this." He held up the screen to face her, a black and white video beginning to roll. "This is the surveillance tape from the parking lot of the Super Duper. I just got it late last night."

She crossed her arms over her chest, suddenly nervous. The grainy image was difficult to see, particularly on the tiny screen. A figure emerged from the shadows with what appeared to be a gas can, and began dousing the walls and foundation of the building.

Meghan's Wish

"Ricky, I don't know what you're hoping to prove..." her voice trailed off as the figure came close to the camera, his baseball hat and 49ers jacket clearly visible in the frame.

"Liam's a 49ers fan, isn't he, Meghan?"

She couldn't move, couldn't breathe. She was watching the figure on the screen, with a coat and hat just like her husband's, move in a hauntingly familiar way.

"Is that his jacket? His hat?"

She should know. She had bought the matching set for his birthday last fall. She was constantly kidding him that they would be threadbare in no time if he wore them as often as he did.

Ricky was watching her. "That fire was on Friday. There was another one yesterday."

Oh, God. "Where?" She felt sick.

"Liam's parents' house. It was burned to the ground."

"Oh my, God. Was anyone hurt?"

He shook his head. "No, thank goodness. Chip and Lindsay weren't home."

"What about the kids?"

He smiled without humor. "The kids are all grown up now, Meghan. You've been gone a long time." He stared at her. "And I've missed you."

"Don't." She held up her hand. "There was never anything between us, Ricky."

He looked down at the phone in his hands. "I know you think I set Liam up, but I didn't."

"You lied about seeing him on Main Street with a gas can."

"You're right. I did. He wasn't walking down Main Street with it, he was at the old mill with it."

"Oh, bullshit, Ricky."

He was quiet for a moment, just staring at her. "I followed you to the old mill that night."

A wave of violation rolled through her abdomen. "You bastard."

"I hid in the woods by the water. You were wearing a white shirt and a long pink skirt. Not what you'd worn to school that day."

454

Meghan's Wish

"How dare you?"

"I tried for years to get your attention, Meghan, but you only had eyes for Wheaton. It burned me up inside, to see you with him, to know what you were doing in there."

He said it like it was dirty, and Meghan could feel her cheeks flaming hot. Her arms itched to scratch his face, hit him with her fists for invading her cherished memories. "You had no right."

"After you left, I just sat there in the woods. I was devastated." He swallowed, shaking his head. "Then Liam comes out of the mill, and I thought about hurting him. I remember I hated him for putting his hands on you. I hated him so much."

Ricky took a deep breath. "He walked to his car and opened the trunk. He took out a red and gold gas can."

The world tilted on its axis. Liam kept a red and gold gas can in the trunk of his truck to this day, a leftover from that first car with the broken gas gauge.

"And he goes back to the mill and starts pouring the gas all around it. I knew I should stop him, but I was scared of what he was doing, scared of what he would do to me if he knew I had seen him. So I ran," he continued. "I ran as fast as I could back home. I didn't even make it out of the park before I smelled the smoke."

Meghan felt her faith in her husband wavering like a leaf on a tree, caught up in a storm she hadn't even seen coming.

Liam started those fires.

"The next morning, I told Sheriff McDonald I had seen Liam with the gas can." He met her eyes. "But I didn't want to tell him about the old mill, or that you were there, too."

2012

Liam was in a bad mood.

He climbed out of the cab of his pickup truck and into the snow-filled air, slamming the door behind him. He should be halfway to Boston right now to bid on a job, but his father had phoned and told him to come over right away.

It was important, he said.

Important to Chip Wheaton could mean he had another run-in with the sheriff, and it had come to blows like last time. Or it could mean he was sitting in a corner of his bedroom, terrified that if he walked out into the kitchen where his keys were, he'd climb in the car and go buy a beer or three bottles of whiskey.

Liam strode up the walkway of the tired old duplex, wondering what level of hell awaited him beyond the front door. Chip had been sober for almost three years, but Liam was weary from trying to keep it that way. Most days, Liam worked harder at keeping Chip sober than Chip did.

When Liam got out of jail, the townspeople who once found him so pleasant at the Super Duper were now afraid to have him stand next to them in line. No one would hire him in sales, despite his experience, but he had strong hands and an able body that no one could take away.

His mother died from pancreatic cancer just two weeks before his release from prison. A grieving Liam used his share of her meager life insurance policy to start his own landscaping business, caring for the lawns of Largo's most prestigious citizens while they locked their doors and huddled inside.

He stepped up to the right-hand unit and rapped soundly on the door, before letting himself in.

Meghan was sitting on the couch.

Holy shit.

Liam strode toward her purposefully and she stood, raising her hands defensively. Anger warred with grief and longing as he stared at her.

Here was the woman who had ruled his thoughts, stolen away his heart, his love, and his child. His nostrils flared as his breathing came in quick pants and his eyes scanned the apartment for Fiona.

Meghan looked panicked.

She should be scared. I'm going to kill her.

Blood surged into his loins, his body remembering this love, even as his mind fought the sensations. "Where's Fiona?" he said, barely recognizing his voice for the emotion it held.

She raised her chin. "She's not here."

He turned and threw his fist into the wall beside him, seeing Meghan jump as he released the energy that was surging through his body, breaking through the drywall. "Where is she?" he yelled.

"Someplace safe."

He rounded on her, coming to stand just inches from her body, his own responding with a desperate plea that he pushed away with his mind. "How dare you imply she's not safe with me? I'm her father, damn it. You know I would never hurt her."

"You're also a convicted felon."

He smiled, a dark light in his eye. "Well hell, that must mean I'm guilty." He walked several feet away, then back toward her like a lion. "I want to see my daughter, Meghan. You can't keep her from me."

"I know," she said quietly.

She was so close he could smell her familiar scent, and it was doing things to him he didn't want done. His very soul thrilled at her presence even as he hated her more than he had ever hated another human being.

His hand reached up to her face of its own accord, touching her cheek and raising her chin until her eyes found his own. "How could you do it, Meghan? Huh? How could you take her away from me like that?" He felt her chin quiver beneath his fingers. "Didn't you know what it would *do to me*?"

She pulled away from him. "You lied to me. Coming here instead of working, *setting fires*, Liam." Her eyes pulled at him. "I was afraid of you. I was afraid for Fiona."

He stepped too close to her, pushing the limit of what she would allow. His muscled chest brushed against her breasts, his breath grazed her lips. "Are you afraid of me now, Meghan?"

Meghan's Wish

Her eyes were dilated, her lids just a touch too heavy. He knew that look, had seen it hundreds of times on his wife's face, and it sure as hell wasn't fear.

"I was scared of who you had become," she whispered.

He stepped away from her.

If she really had been afraid of him, he was glad he hadn't been around to see it. Liam had seen fear on many faces in his years, first as a good-for-nothing Wheaton, unworthy of simply courtesy or love, then as an arsonist, a convict, a criminal.

But he had never seen that look on his Meghan's face, the only person who ever mattered, the woman who had seen his inside his very soul and found him worthy.

"If you're so scared of me, why the hell are you here?"

She looked at the doorway to the kitchen. "I came to talk to your parents."

He shrugged. "Mom's dead. But I get it—you didn't come to see me." He saw her cringe at his careless words. He cracked his knuckles to keep from putting another hole in the wall, took a deep breath. "Why did you want to see my parents?"

She swallowed, her eyes anguished and her chin puckered. "Fiona's sick, Liam."

He scowled, concern rising up within him. "What's wrong with her?"

"She has Leukemia. She needs a bone marrow transplant. I came back to Largo to find her a donor."

~~~

Meghan walked to the front window, looking at the overcast winter's day from Chip Wheaton's dark living room. She had underestimated Liam's pain. She didn't consider herself to be a cruel person, but seeing him like this, she understood the hatred she felt emanating from him like heat from the sun.

She was a coward, keeping her back to him now. She didn't want to share in his grief, didn't want to feel responsible for it.

"I'll give her my marrow," he said, his voice wavering.

"There's only a one in two hundred chance that you'll be a match. I already tried."

"Before you came back here, of course."

"Yes."

"My God. You weren't even going to tell me, were you?" He closed the distance between them, grabbing her by the shoulder and turning her around. "If you'd been a match, you wouldn't have come back here at all."

She shook her head, her pulse racing from his nearness. She looked at his tortured face and wanted to cry, too.

No, Meghan, don't feel bad. He's the one who lied to you. He's the one who broke the law, who snuck away to destroy other people's property, who sought vengeance on those who had belittled him.

A chill ran up her spine, remembering the fear that had made her pack up their little girl and run away. The Liam she loved was just one side of his personality, a figment of her imagination.

If that Wheaton boy is there, you ignore him. Not a word.

She should have listened to her mother.

"Your family has as similar chance of matching Fiona as you do. Your sister and brothers, cousins. It's still not likely."

"Who would be a good match, then?"

She couldn't meet his eyes. "A full sibling would be her best chance. A one-in-four possibility of a full match." She felt her cheeks heat at the suggestion, and was grateful when he ignored it.

"What about your family?" he asked, his lips forming a tight line as he realized. "Of course. You tried them already, and they didn't match."

She nodded, taking a step back from him. "You have a bigger family, and we both have Irish roots. There might be someone."

"We'll try. I'll ask everyone in my family to be tested. On one condition."

She'd been expecting it, waiting for it. It was the price of poker, and Meghan had come to play.

"You let me see Fiona."

She nodded.

"And not just for a minute. You bring her here, and you let me be a part of her life again, Meghan. Forever."

Meghan's Wish

If he was going to be part of Fiona's life forever, then he would be part of hers, as well. She shook her head. "We live far away, Liam, it's not feasible..."

He closed the distance between them, speaking with an eerie calmness. "I could have you arrested for kidnapping, Meghan. I can take her away from you in a heartbeat."

She raised her chin. "You're a felon."

"What do you think kidnapping is? A misdemeanor?"

An eye for an eye.

Meghan was frozen in place, her eyes screaming into his. Could he really take Fiona? Legally? She had come back here to save her daughter's life, but it could cost her the very daughter she was trying to save.

When she spoke, her voice was small and plaintive. "Liam, please..." she begged, leaning toward him as tears suddenly threatened. She saw the slightest softening in his eyes, a kindness, a caring she hadn't seen there since he walked through the door. His hand touched her face again, feather-light, and he leaned toward her.

Her body remembered him, and her back arched in anticipation of his kiss, his lips finding hers and taking her swiftly. She wanted it. She wanted it so badly.

She had been so alone.

Not one single date in the eight years without him, no desire for a man besides this one. His arm snaked around her waist, pulling her to him, and she reveled in the feel of his body pressed to hers. She knew his touch and his desire better than her own, moaning in his arms, his name escaping her lips on a rush of air.

He pulled away from her, abruptly letting her go and taking a step back. He swiped the back of his hands across his lips as if trying to clean her off his lips.

"Go get my daughter, Meghan. Once I see her, you can test anyone you like." He turned on his heel and walked out the door, getting into his truck and driving away.

~~~

"Pass me the garlic," said Becky, holding her hand open for the bulb that Meghan handed her.

Meghan's Wish

The women were making their grandmother's lasagna, a recipe they had each been taught some ten years apart. It was a family tradition, though the old Irish woman's cuisine could hardly be called authentic Italian.

"Do you remember how Grandma used to fall asleep halfway through a sentence?" asked Meghan. "You'd turn around, and she'd be snoring with her head on her chest. That used to creep me out."

Becky elbowed her in the arm. "Remember how she used to fart and blame it on the dog?"

"That was her?"

"Oh, hell yes, that was her."

Meghan laughed so hard she snorted, which got Becky laughing, too.

The women took turns layering the meat, cheese and pasta in a baking dish. "Your hands look just like mine," said Becky.

"Except for the purple nail polish," said Meghan.

Becky felt tears begin to well in her eyes. "Do you have any idea how much I missed you, Meggie? You were my best friend, then you were gone."

"I know."

"No, you don't know."

Meghan picked up a towel and wiped her hands. "Why don't you tell me."

Becky swallowed, looking at the ceiling. "Everything changed when you left. Mom was destroyed. I don't think she even saw me anymore. I kept trying to get her attention, but it was no use. For a while, Dad was crying all the time, then he just shut down. Neither of them mentioned your name at all anymore."

"I'm so sorry, Becky."

"But you know what the worst part was? *I missed you.* I missed you every moment of every day for years and years." She looked down at her hands, twisting a silver ring. "I was closer to you than I was to anybody, and you just left me behind like I didn't even matter to you."

"Oh, no, no," said Meghan, reaching out and embracing her sister. "You mattered to me, Becky, more than you know." She

Meghan's Wish

pulled back to look into her sister's eyes. "I used to pretend I was your real mother, do you know that?"

"So how could you just leave?"

"Because I became an actual mother, to Fiona. I had to take care of her before I took care of anyone else. And that meant staying with Liam."

Becky wiped at her eyes. "I guess I knew that."

"It doesn't make it any easier."

"No. But I'm glad you're here, now."

"Me, too."

Becky reached into the ricotta with her finger, popping a dollop into her mouth.

Meghan glared at her. "Eeew."

"What? My hands are clean."

A devilish grin spread across Meghan's face. "Do you remember the time Grandma caught you sneaking whipped cream from the top of the chocolate cream pie?"

"Of course I do. She threw a whole glob of it right in my face." Realization dawned, and her eyes went wide. "Don't you dare!"

Meghan smiled devilishly as she scooped out a handful and whipped it at her sister.

"Ah!" screamed Becky, reaching for the container of tomato sauce.

"Whoa, whoa, whoa," said Meghan, raising her hands in front of her. "Enough," she said firmly.

"Enough, my ass." Becky laughed, dumping the sauce on her sister's chest.

"You little punk!"

"Bring it on, sister!"

In just moments, the ingredients that had covered the counter were splattered all over the women's faces, clothes and hair, the two of them laughing hysterically.

Becky sighed contentedly. "Looks like pizza for dinner."

"Oh, well. Grandma's lasagna sucked, anyway."

Becky doubled over, laughing uncontrollably. "I'm going to pee my pants! I hate her lasagna, too!"

Meghan's Wish

"It's so good to be home, Monkey," Meghan said, kissing her sister's cheese-covered hair. "So good to be home."

~~~

A light snow fell from the sky, making Meghan wonder if she should have checked the weather report before heading out to Rhea's. Red lights flashed in her rearview mirror and she cursed, wondering what she had done to get pulled over. She stopped under a banner that read "Merry Christmas from the Largo Chamber of Commerce".

"Do you know how fast you were going?" asked the officer.

Meghan turned to stare at him, seeing only a helmet and reflective glasses.

"About thirty-two?" said Meghan.

"Thirty-five. The speed limit is thirty."

Are you kidding me?

She turned her head and rolled her eyes. She didn't have time for a small town police officer on a power trip.

"It was really the plates that got you pulled over, Meghan O'Connor," he laughed. "We don't like out-of-towners speeding down Main Street. If I'd known it was you, I'd have looked the other way."

He took off his glasses, revealing twinkling blue eyes that went with his handsome smile, the slight bend in his nose marring an otherwise perfect face.

"Ricky Powell," she said, taking in his badge and uniform. "You're the sheriff?"

He nodded. "You back for good?"

"Looks like." She was surprised to find that time had softened her reaction to Ricky. He wasn't a bad guy. He had only tried to help her, after all.

"Where's that pretty little girl of yours, Fiona?"

Someone had been paying attention.

"Connecticut. I'm on my way to get her."

"Listen," he said, bracing his weight on the car door and leaning closer, "would you like to grab a bite to eat when you get back? See a movie or something?"

Liam's kiss flashed in her mind, followed by his look of disgust.

Meghan's Wish

He hates me.

"Sure. Why not."

Ricky raised his eyebrows and gave her a hundred watt smile. "Great. Give me a call at the station when you get back in town."

"I will."

What did I just do?

She had no interest in dating Ricky Powell, she was just reeling from her run-in with Liam. When she got back into town, she would have to set Ricky straight.

He patted the side of her car, and she put it in drive. "Bye," she said.

"See you soon, Meghan O'Connor." he said with a wink.

~~~

Liam was pacing back and forth in his expansive kitchen, his father perched on a barstool, watching him.

"Relax. You'll be fine," said Chip. At sixty, he had pale skin and ruddy cheeks from years of heavy drinking. His hair was white and thin on top, his belly fuller now that he nourished his body with food instead of liquor.

"The last time I saw her, she was seven," said Liam. "She's going to be sixteen in March." He stopped pacing and braced his arms on the granite counter across from his dad. "I used to tickle her until she was screaming like crazy. I don't think that's going to work anymore."

"I don't think so." Chip dragged a carrot through a tub of veggie dip. "She's probably into boys and makeup. Loud music. That sort of thing." He shrugged. "Think of what you were like at that age."

Liam flashed to himself at sixteen, an image of naked Meghan appearing in his memory. He wanted to stuff his father's mouth full of carrots to keep him from saying anything else.

"Thanks for that, Dad."

"You're welcome," he said with a smirk.

Liam resumed his pacing, trying to see his home through his daughter's eyes. Would Fiona like it? The three story colonial was virtually falling down when he bought it. He had renovated it himself, bringing the old home back to its former glory and adding modern touches.

Looking around it now, he admitted he had done all of it with Fiona and Meghan in mind, from the purple bedroom at the top of the stairs to the sunroom off the master suite.

Son of a bitch.

The ring of the doorbell made his hands break out in a sweat.

"I'm going to stay here so you two can get reacquainted," said Chip, gesturing with a stalk of celery.

"Thanks, Dad."

Liam was a wreck of excitement and jangled emotions. He had lost a little girl, and she was being returned to him a young woman, a changeling. What would he say to her? Could he give her a hug? He opened the door with a trembling hand.

Fiona stood alone, Meghan nowhere in sight.

"Daddy?"

She was up to his shoulder, with beautiful red hair like her aunt Becky, her mother's green eyes, and his very own smile. She used it now to light up his world.

He felt his eyes begin to burn as his arms reached out to pull her in for a tight hug. "Oh God, Fiona. I missed you so much."

She was shaking in his arms, her laughter mixing with sobs as she clutched at him.

Liam lifted his head to the heavens in gratitude, opening his eyes into the sun. His smile hadn't stretched this wide since the day his daughter disappeared from his life.

His gaze dropped to the car in the driveway, Meghan sitting behind the wheel.

Meghan.

Giving them time.

He waved to her, begrudgingly signaling her to come inside. He relaxed his grip on Fiona, letting his arm fall naturally around her shoulder. "Your grandfather's in the kitchen. He can't wait to see you."

Fiona bit her lip. "I don't remember him."

"You've never met him, sweetie. His name's Chip."

"Can I call him grandpa if I want to?"

"I bet he'd love that."

"Hi, Meghan," he said as she stepped onto the porch. He held out his hand. "Truce?"

The look of relief on her face was obvious. "Truce."

He held the door for her. "Let's go inside."

~~~

"Lindsay was upset. To be honest with you, I didn't care too much about anyone back then, so long as I had a drink in my hand," said Chip. He was sitting with Meghan in the kitchen, while Liam and Fiona looked at photo albums on the dining room table.

Meghan was surprised Chip brought up his drinking. "You seem better now."

"As better as an alcoholic can ever be. If Liam hadn't picked me up and dried me out at rehab, I'd be shit-faced someplace right now, instead of eating veggies and dip with a beautiful young woman." He winked at her, and Meghan was surprised to find him charming.

"It is some pretty good broccoli."

"Sweetheart, you should try the peppers," he laughed.

"So, Liam did that? Got you into rehab?"

Chip nodded. "Though, you have to wonder why he came back here at all, with the sheriff looking for him and all."

"I've wondered that myself."

He picked up a piece of broccoli, breaking tiny florets off the larger piece and dropping them on his paper plate like a little forest. "Liam doesn't give up, Meghan. He's thickheaded. He didn't give up on me, and I don't think he ever gave up on you."

"Are you kidding? He hates my guts," she said, talking quietly so Liam wouldn't hear her now.

"Let's just say, he doesn't hate you as much as I'd hate you, if you'd done to me what you did to him."

Liam walked into the kitchen, a smile on his lips and Fiona on his heels. "Who wants to go out for pizza?" he asked.

"Sounds good to me," said Chip.

Meghan looked at her watch. "We can't. I have plans," she said, watching as Liam and Fiona's smiles fell in unison. On an impulse, she added, "You know what? You guys go without me."

"Are you sure?" asked Liam.

She nodded. "I'm sure. Just have her back at Becky's by ten."

"I can do that." He looked at his daughter. "Do you still like veggie supreme?"

Her eyes widened. "Heck, yeah!"

He turned back to Meghan. "We're going to Little Joe's. Let me give you my cell number."

She was enjoying the two of them, the love they so easily shared. "Have fun, you three."

~~~

The waitress was young and busty, with a white button-down shirt and black pants that were painted onto her thighs. "Can I get you guys another round?" she asked, batting her eyes at Ricky.

"Oh, I think I'm all set," said Meghan, giving the waitress her best check please look. The restaurant Ricky had chosen was more of a bar than anything, and it smelled like stale beer and cigarettes. She had tried to cancel her date when she got back in town, but Ricky wasn't taking no for an answer.

"I'll have another draft, there, darlin'," he said, handing the girl his glass. He was oblivious to Meghan's desire to leave, but he'd been oblivious to her in general all evening.

"So there I was, the best sharpshooter in the whole academy, trading lead with this instructor who just went completely ape shit, off his rocker, crazy." He sniffed like a coke addict. "The papers were all over it for weeks, interviewing me for the TV news and all."

"Wow," she said, deadpan. "That's awesome." She looked down at her watch, resting against her green cashmere sweater. It was just after ten o'clock. This was quickly turning into one of the longest nights of her life.

Meghan had just decided to make her excuses when she saw Liam walk through the front door of the restaurant, his eyes scanning the crowd.

Uh, oh.

Meghan's Wish

His eyes connected with hers and he started toward the table. She could tell the instant he recognized her dinner date, and she cringed inwardly at what could only end in a confrontation.

"This was your plan for the evening?" he asked when he reached their table.

"Yes," said Meghan. "I ran into Ricky the other day. Well, actually, he pulled me over. Ricky, you remember Liam."

Ricky looked up from his beer, a smirk on his face. "Of course. His parole officer and I go way back."

Meghan's head snapped toward Ricky. "That was rude."

"It's also the truth," he said, sipping his drink. "Next time you check in with Raymond, you tell him Ricky says hi, okay, sport?"

"Ricky likes to pull women over to get dates." He turned to Meghan. "I've got ten bucks says you weren't even speeding. Am I right?"

She pursed her lips. "It doesn't matter. What do you want, Liam?"

"I wanted to talk to you about our daughter, but I guess you're otherwise engaged." He turned to leave.

"That's not fair."

"Do you really want to talk to me about fairness, Meghan?"

Ricky pushed his chair back and stood. "I think you should leave, Wheaton. Ain't nobody wants you here, anyway."

"Is he right, Meghan? Do you want me to go and leave you alone with this asshole?"

"Who you callin' asshole, you white trash punk?" Ricky puffed out his chest, posturing for Liam, who didn't move. Meghan recognized the look on his face and knew it was about to get ugly in here.

"Tell you what," she said. "I've had about enough of both of you at the moment, and I'm going to go. Ricky, thank you for dinner."

At that, she grabbed her purse and headed for the door. She made it to the parking lot before Liam caught up to her.

"Wait, Meghan, I'm sorry."

She stopped and turned around.

"You can spend time with whoever you want. I was just surprised you picked that particular idiot, is all."

"Why did you come here tonight, Liam?"

He ran his hands through his hair. "Honestly? I was on such a high from talking to Fiona. Spending time with her. She's an incredible person, Meghan." He shrugged his shoulders. "I wanted to talk to the *other* person in this world who thinks Fiona is as incredible as I do."

All annoyance dissipated. "She is pretty special, isn't she?"

He stepped closer. "Oh, she's awesome. Funny, and so smart. Beautiful, like her mother."

Meghan was suddenly shy, uncomfortable. "She has your dimples," she said, which was true. They were one of his greatest features, and her eyes dropped to them as she spoke.

His expression changed, and she felt an answering excitement in her abdomen.

"My truck's over there. Walk with me," said Liam.

She nodded, letting him lead the way.

"My dad and my brothers and sisters and I went to get HLA tested this morning."

She stopped walking. "You did?"

"There was never any question I would do it, Meghan." He reached out and took her hand, walking once again. "The technician said it will be a day or so before we get the results."

"Thank you."

"You're welcome."

Liam was parked in the far corner of the lot, away from the bustle and the lights of the restaurant. Meghan's pulse hammered in her veins as he stopped next to a white truck and slipped his arms around her like he had every right. He turned her around, pinning her between his body and the hard metal, and took her mouth in a not-so-gentle kiss.

She welcomed his lips on hers, loving the way he pushed his body against her. From his first touch she was a puddle of need, aching to be touched, savored, loved by her lover once again.

Her nagging voice in her mind told her to push him away, having worked for so long to keep her love for this man at a distance.

He's already a part of Fiona's life. Why can't I have him, too?

It felt so good to admit to herself how much she wanted him, how much she missed him. It was thrilling to be molded to his body, his skilled hands leaving her skin tingling in their wake.

Meghan let herself go, kissing Liam back with all her might.

He was lost in her, the scent of her skin, the taste of her mouth. She was responding to him just like he remembered, and he was on fire. "Come home with me," he said between kisses, his mouth trailing a path down the side of her neck, his mind filled with images of the two of them making love.

She was twisting against him, making him crazy with need. "Yes." She pulled back, seeing his beautiful face covered in shadows. "I have my car. I'll follow you."

"Drive fast," he said, hanging on to her hand until she was too far away to reach.

Her car was an icebox, the defroster blowing cold air onto her heated skin. Meghan trembled with anticipation. It had been so long since she'd been with any man, she felt as nervous as she had been the first time, riding her bike to the old mill for their rendezvous.

They got to his house and he opened her car door, pulling her body to his and staring into her eyes. He led her in through the garage, and she froze at the sight of the old red and gold gas can sitting by the snow blower.

She had to know the truth. "Liam, did you start those fires?" She couldn't imagine it, but the evidence was there. He'd been convicted for the crime by a jury of his peers.

"No," he said, looking deep into her eyes. "How on earth could you believe I would do such a thing, Meggie?"

"Ricky came to see me at the apartment, the day Fiona and I left," she said, not wanting to break the mood but needing to talk at the same time.

"Ricky was in our home?"

She nodded. "He said he followed you there from Largo. He told me about the fires, and he showed me a videotape of..." she hesitated, "...a man wearing your 49ers jacket and hat, setting

Meghan's Wish

fire to the Super Duper. If you weren't in Largo, how did he find us?"

He shook his head. "I was in Largo, Meghan." He ran his hand through his hair. "And I got pulled over by none other than Sheriff Ricky Powell, who got a good look at my 49ers attire. It's freezing out here. Come inside."

They stood next to the kitchen island, Liam dropping his keys on the stone countertop and holding her hands in his. "You were so sad. Do you remember that?"

She nodded, biting her lip.

"I could hear you crying when you thought I was asleep. It tore me up inside every Christmas, but that last year was the worst. And it was all my fault. You couldn't go home because of me. You gave up everyone who mattered to you."

"Not everyone. I had you and Fiona."

"But you lost your parents and sister." He rubbed his forehead with his palm. "I was trying to fix it."

"How?"

"I knew who set the fires. I just had to find a way to prove it so we could go home again."

Meghan's eyes were wide. "Who set the fires?"

"Your hot date from this evening."

"*Ricky set the fires?*" she was incredulous. "How do you know?"

"My father saw him. Ricky actually had a conversation with him while he was pouring gasoline on the porch of my parents' home."

"*What?* I thought no one was home at the time of the fire!"

"Oh, he was home all right. He had third degree burns over both his legs. Ask him, and he'll show you the scars from the skin grafts."

"Why didn't Chip say something?"

"He did. He told everyone who would listen, which wasn't a whole lot of people. And none of them believed him, anyway. He and Ricky still go at it a couple of times a year, throwing punches and accusations. Only now, since Ricky's the sheriff, Dad ends up getting arrested."

"I can't believe it."

Meghan's Wish

Liam hooked a lock of her hair behind her ear. "I just wanted you to be happy again."

"You made me happy, Liam."

"No, I made you leave your family. It was all my fault."

She put her hands on either side of his face, staring into his eyes so he might hear her. "None of it was your fault." She kissed his lips. "None of it at all." She kissed him again, then rested her forehead against his. "Why did you come back to Largo, Liam? You had to know what might happen."

He grabbed her wrists and brought their joined hands between them. "When I realized you were gone, I was a wreck. I didn't understand why you'd left me, taken Fiona with you."

Meghan's heart squeezed with remorse.

"I stayed there for a year, hoping you would come back. I filed missing persons reports on you and Fiona. I got fired from my job. I couldn't function. Then the next Christmas, I remembered the gift I'd been trying to get for you. I wanted Ricky to go down for the fires, so you would be free to go home to Largo. I figured I could still give you that."

Tears ran unchecked down her face. "But instead, you went to jail."

"Yes."

"I'm so sorry, Liam."

"I'm not. I still want Ricky to pay for what he did, but you're free now, Meghan. You've got your family back. That's all I ever wanted."

"For me? You did that for me?"

He nodded. "Merry Christmas."

"That's the greatest gift anyone could ever give me."

"I did it because I love you. I still love you, after everything, Meggie."

Liam had sacrificed himself so that she might find happiness again. Meghan was overwhelmed with this man, and the lengths that he'd gone to for her. What had she done in return? Abandoned him, lost faith in him. "How can you ever forgive me for what I did to you?"

"I already have, Meghan O'Connor. You came back to me. That's all that matters now."

Meghan's Wish

She bowed her head in gratitude for this love. She had her husband, she had her family, she had her home. Now she just needed her daughter to be well again.

~~~

It was after two in the morning when Meghan got back to Becky's house and let herself in the side door, walking up several steps to the kitchen. She'd come home from Liam's so Fiona wouldn't realize where she'd been.

She needn't have bothered.

Fiona sat at the kitchen table in Becky's zebra stripe bathrobe. "Where were you?" she asked.

Meghan felt her cheeks heat, moving to the counter to put down her purse. "I was with your father," she said, as if they'd been shopping for groceries. "What are you doing up?"

"I don't feel good."

Meghan flipped on the overhead light and knelt before Fiona, her anxiety slipping into overdrive. Fiona's skin was waxy and pale, her eyes glassy and unfocused. Meghan held her hand to Fiona's forehead and felt the fever inside.

"How's your belly?" she asked, lightly prodding the girl's abdomen.

Fiona flinched. "Full and yucky."

"You should have woken Aunt Becky."

"I was going to, if you weren't home by two thirty."

"How long have you been sitting here?"

"Since midnight."

Guilt sucked at Meghan. "Come on. Get dressed. We're going to the hospital."

"Mom?"

"What?"

"Can we call Dad, too?"

She nodded, reaching for the phone. "I'll call and have him meet us there."

~~~

They'd been at the hospital for five hours.

Patty O'Connor sat with her back to window, morning sunlight streaming in around her. The waiting room was painted an unfortunate yellow, with rust-colored furniture and black plastic tables.

At least we had some privacy here, compared to the downstairs waiting room, with its huddled masses of humanity.

Liam paced the length of the space in front of her, periodically stopping to talk with Meghan or refill his coffee. Patty bristled at his presence, though the reason for her discomfort no longer had anything to do with class or status, and everything to do with regret.

For every kindness he displayed toward her daughter, and every soft word he spoke to Fiona, Patty O'Connor knew she had made a terrible mistake.

Not with trying to keep Meghan and Liam apart. They truly were too young for that type of relationship. But in the years since then, when she could have stepped forward to make Liam's life better, she had not.

She'd been too bitter, too angry, too sad. Her daughter was gone, had up and walked away without a word fifteen years earlier, and all because of him. Liam's arrival back in Largo infuriated Patty, because he hadn't brought her beloved girl back home with him.

She uncrossed her legs and crossed them again, watching her ankle bob up and down with the swing of her hip. Perhaps it was a kindness that Liam hadn't told her she was a grandmother. Certainly, it would seem that way now.

A nurse walked into the waiting room, catching Meghan's eye. "She's asking for you."

Becky and Tom had gone to the cafeteria, which left Liam and Patty alone. Liam sat at the opposite end of the room, leaning forward over his knees, his hands covering his face.

God, I will tell Liam the truth if you help Fiona get better.

Her foot stopped its bouncing, and her eyes began to burn. Her own selfish prayer was her undoing.

He was a good man, after all, a husband to her daughter, a father to her granddaughter. With every ounce of courage she possessed, Patty crossed to the coffee maker and took a Styrofoam cup, her hand shaking as she poured the hot liquid.

"Liam, I have something I need to tell you."

Meghan's Wish

"What are you doing here?" Meghan asked. She was standing in the hospital corridor outside Fiona's room.

Ricky held his sheriff's hat in his hand, and he fingered the brim. "I was looking for you. I stopped by Becky's twice today, and no one was there. I called her cell, and she said you were here."

"Fiona wasn't feeling well."

"Is she okay?"

"She has leukemia. We're not sure yet what's making her feel so bad today."

Ricky's face fell. "Oh, my God. I'm so sorry."

"Thank you." She crossed her arms over her chest. "Why were you looking for me?"

He shrugged his shoulders. "I had a nice time with you last night. I just wanted to say hello, see if maybe we can do it again sometime."

Meghan stepped back. "Listen, Ricky, I think you should know that Liam and I are back together."

"Oh." He shrugged. "Just like that?"

She nodded. "I'm sorry."

"So, you leave dinner with me at, what..." he looked at the ceiling, "...like eight o'clock, and you end up in bed with your ex-husband on the same night?"

She jerked her head back. "That's none of your business."

"Sure it is, Meghan. I'm the sheriff in this town. I'm the good guy. But for some unknown reason, you just keep going back to that loser, ever since we were kids. Why? Answer me that. Do you get turned on by scum bags with rap sheets or something?"

"Stop it."

"Or maybe you just like a guy who destroys the things you care about." He stepped closer to her, into her personal space. "Because I can do that too, Meghan."

She saw Liam a second before Ricky did, his hands already yanking Ricky backward and away from her, spinning him around to connect his fist with Ricky's face. It was his

Meghan's Wish

cheekbone that made the sickening crack, though two of his teeth were also knocked loose by the blow.

"Don't you touch my wife, asshole."

Ricky staggered to his feet, his cap on the floor, his hand on his bleeding mouth. "You just assaulted an officer, and you're still on parole. You're going back in, Wheaton."

"The only person who's going to jail is you, Ricky," said Liam.

A uniformed state police officer approached from the end of the hall. "Ricky Powell, you have the right to remain silent."

Patty followed behind the officer, her eyes weary as she approached a confused Meghan. "The night of the fire at the old mill, your father and I were coming home from a concert. I saw Ricky riding his bike a block from the river, with a gas can tied to the book rack. Then we saw the flames shooting up from the old mill."

Meghan's jaw dropped. "Why didn't you say anything?"

She watched as her mother worked to get the words out. "I thought it was odd. But the Powells were friends of ours. I thought there must be an explanation."

"What kind of explanation, Mom? Boys will be boys, burning down buildings and such?"

Patty hugged herself tightly, her eyes glassy and red. "I thought it was just some kids playing around. I knew Ricky might have been involved, but…"

"*But he was one of us*," said Meghan. She stepped closer to her mother, baring her teeth. "And when Liam took the blame, you figured that was okay, too."

Patty held up her hands. "Loraine Spaulding said she saw him with that pocketknife earlier in the day. So he must have been at the old mill that day."

"He was there, mom." She walked over to Liam and held his hand in her own. "He was there with me."

Tears fell down Patty's cheeks as she nodded. "When you two ran away, you took my whole world with you. I could barely be a mother to Becky, barely function. Then Liam came back alone. He wouldn't tell me anything. I hated him. I had so much

Meghan's Wish

anger. He wouldn't help me find my baby girl." She was openly sobbing now.

Liam stepped forward, placing his hand on Patty's shoulder. "I didn't know where she was, Patty."

Patty cried harder. "I know, I know. Can you ever forgive me?"

"That depends." He looked at her with kindness in his eyes. "Will you be a good grandma to Fiona?"

"I will."

"Let her date whoever she wants."

"I will."

To Meghan's astonishment, he nodded.

"You did what you thought was right at the time," said Liam. "That's not so hard to forgive."

The doctor appeared in the hallway. "Mr. and Mrs. Wheaton, can I have a word with you, please?"

Meghan tensed at his serious tone.

"It's okay," he said, smiling widely. "I have good news."

Meghan's Wish

2013

The Christmas tree glowed with tiny colored lights, enchanting the living room with its fresh pine scent. The family was gathered in the large formal dining room, every leaf in the table to accommodate the crowd.

"Hush up now, and let the old Jewish woman say grace," yelled Rhea, chuckled erupting around the table. She held out her hands, Fiona on one side of her, Chip Wheaton on the other.

"I love it when you say grace," murmured Fiona with a smile, nudging Rhea with her shoulder.

Rhea cleared her throat and closed her eyes. "Dear Lord, thank you for the food that we are about to eat, for the turkey and the stuffing, the cranberry sauce and the sweet potato casserole with the mini rainbow marshmallows. Thank you for the glorious wine, and for the blanket of fluffy white snow outside our window. Thank you for my family, for this new home we share, for your good grace that brought us together and filled my heart with love. Thank you for Fiona's good health, for baby Oscar's blue eyes, for his mama's sweet smile and the love that she shares with her generous husband. A year ago, Lord, you sent us a storm." She shimmied her shoulders. "But you gave us your guidance to get through it, pulling together with those we love, who we had somehow managed to lose along the way. We thank you for your blessings, Lord. Amen."

"Merry Christmas, Rhea," said Meghan, who was holding baby Oscar in one arm at the table. He'd been born just a week earlier. "Everyone, Liam and I have some news we'd like to share."

"Already? Oscar's not even a month old." said Chip, earning him another round of laughter.

"No, no." Meghan smiled, meeting Liam's eyes over the table. "Oscar had a doctor's appointment today, and they gave us the result of his HLA typing."

Everyone froze. Fiona had been doing exceptionally well on the new medication, which had succeeded in putting her back into remission. But there was still a chance she would need a bone marrow transplant one day.

Tears began to fall down Meghan's face, and reached for Liam's hand. "He's a perfect match to you, sweetie. Six out of six alleles." A cheer went up around the table, and Fiona's eyes glowed with joy.

"It's a Christmas miracle," said Patty.

"Just another reason to love my baby brother," said Fiona. "That has got to be the greatest gift I could ever receive."

Meghan felt tears slip down her cheeks.

The greatest gift of all is love, and each of us is blessed with it in abundance.

She turned to her husband, his knowing eyes glistening with tears. "I love you, Liam."

"And I you, Meghan O'Connor."